Virginia Autumn

OTHER NOVELS BY SARA MITCHELL

❧✦❧

SINCLAIR LEGACY SERIES

Shenandoah Home

SHADOWCATCHERS SERIES

Trial of the Innocent
In the Midst of Lions
Ransomed Heart

Montclair

SARA MITCHELL

Virginia Autumn

WaterBrook
PRESS

VIRGINIA AUTUMN
PUBLISHED BY WATERBROOK PRESS
2375 Telstar Drive, Suite 160
Colorado Springs, Colorado 80920
A division of Random House, Inc.

Scripture quotations are taken from the *King James Version.*

ISBN 1-57856-485-9

Printed in the United States of America
2002—First Edition

10 9 8 7 6 5 4 3 2 1

For my husband—a noble man
who makes noble plans
and stands by them.

For over thirty-three years
he's been my hero and my love.

Acknowledgments

Many thanks to Thomas Dixon, President of C&O Historical Society, and Margaret, the C&O staff archivist, whose patience is inexhaustible and whose help was invaluable.

As always, any historical inaccuracies (unintentional or deliberate!) are the fault of the author.

Part I

Leah

Prologue

Sinclair Run
Shenandoah Valley, Virginia, April 1895

*T*wilight stole over Great North Mountain like an elderly woman slipping a soft gray shawl over her shoulders. Jacob Sinclair paused from working the foot lathe, thinking with an inward laugh that it was a sorry day indeed when he caught himself imagining elderly women and their shawls. 'Twas not the sort of musings a healthy man of any age should be entertaining, particularly one so blessed by his Maker.

Why, had not his granda danced a Highland reel his eighty-first year? And his father was past seventy-five when he fashioned a highboy with naught but handsaw and joining plane. At only a few years past the half-century mark, Jacob himself was in the prime of his life.

So. He straightened his shoulders, drew in a good draught of pure mountain air—and eased onto the old settle outside his workshop door. Just for a short spell, he promised himself. Long enough to bask in the spring evening. No place on earth was more beautiful than the Shenandoah Valley at twilight.

Mary had loved this time of day.

Jacob leaned his head against the settle's warped high back and closed his eyes. The memory yet possessed a wistful sting. A man shouldn't have to put his young wife in a grave and live out the rest of his years in solitude.

Solitude, Jacob?

Smiling, he opened his eyes and quirked a brow toward heaven. *Aye, Lord, it was no' that kind of solitude I was thinking of, and well You know it.* But Jacob accepted the wry rebuke, feeling as always the mix of humbleness and awe, that the Lord of all life would, at the most unexpected times, spare a divine second to converse with a simple Scottish cabinetmaker. Though his Mary had been taken in the springtime of her life, God had blessed Jacob through their three daughters, and through two of those daughters' families. *Think on it, Lord. I'm a grandfather.* Life…always the joy and the pain inextricably twined, generation upon generation.

His thoughts drifted over the past five years. His two older lasses, Garnet and Meredith, were both mothers now, though Leah, the youngest, had forsworn marriage to become a teacher. Jacob shook his head. For most of his life he had struggled to understand his youngest daughter.

At least through the offspring of his two older daughters there was the promise of continuity. Leah, now…och, but would his scholarly youngest child ever know the joys and sorrows of marriage, of family? Wasn't she ever lonely, with only her studies and her students? None of those could warm a cold bed at night or offer comfort when loneliness gnawed at one's vitals.

After Mary's death, Jacob's loneliness had been bearable only because he'd had his girls. Though to be sure, a widower with three young daughters faced hurdles other men could never fathom. He smiled, remembering one of those hurdles in particular, a score of years ago—no, 'twas back in '79, sixteen years. Jacob's smile grew as misty as that long-ago day. A mid-October Sunday morning it had been. Draped in thick white mist, with a bite to the air and the odor of wood smoke and damp leaves filling his senses as he hurried across the yard.

He'd gone out to hitch the horses so they could go to church, leaving the girls to finish dressing in their Sunday frocks…

❧✦❧

The moment he reentered the house, chaos reigned.

"Papa, I can't find my shoes. Can I wear Garnet's?" Meredith, of course, was already wearing them. She pirouetted prettily, her lissome twelve-year-old form tightening Jacob's throat. "See how much better my dress looks with ribboned shoes?"

"Those are *my* shoes!" Garnet wailed, racing the rest of the way down the stairs, her red hair flying about her scowling freckled face. "Papa, Meredith stole my church shoes. Make her give them back!"

"Meredith, return your sister's shoes. If you can't find your own, wear your boots. We bought those for you just last spring. Nobody pays attention to your feet at any rate."

Jacob suppressed the urge to scuttle for the haven of his workshop instead of the church's sanctuary. He could work on the corner cupboard he was making for a man in Winchester, or even the second heartwood chest—the one for Garnet—he'd begun last winter. At least pieces of furniture and wood tools couldn't talk back, much less concern themselves with fashion. When had these two shrieking harpies replaced his sweet-faced lasses? "Stop scowling at each other," he ordered. "You'll warp the floorboards."

"Papa, do I have to go to church? Reverend Elephant talks too much."

"Garnet, how many times have I asked you—*all* of you, not to call him that? The minister's name is Reverend Oliphant, and—" He stopped, studying his middle daughter in consternation. "Why isn't your shirtwaist fastened? It's almost time to—"

"Papa, doesn't it take us almost three-quarters of an hour to reach the church?" Leah had followed Garnet down the stairs. Her own dress and over-apron hung neatly, with only two pressed-in wrinkles showing; wispy brown hair had been arranged in a single slender braid.

Aye, now, Jacob thought with an inward smile, even at the tender age of nine his youngest possessed a mother's air of sweet efficiency. Mary had lavished love upon all her wee daughters, but she'd been no more efficient than a playful spring wind, God rest her blessed soul.

Leah tugged his sleeve, then glanced at the regulator wall clock hanging in the hall. "We need to leave, Papa, so we're not late like we were last week."

"That skirt's too short, Garnet," Meredith announced as she tugged off the shoes and thrust them toward her sister. "You should wear boots, not me. Everybody's going to see your ankles. I bet Rufus will—"

"That's enough, Meredith." Jacob began buttoning Garnet's

shirtwaist for her, but gratefully relinquished the task to a far more nimble-fingered Leah. "I'll not have a spiteful attitude in this house, do you understand? Apologize, and go find your shoes, or your boots, I care not which. We'll wait for you in the buggy."

"Please don't look sad, Garnet," Leah consoled her suddenly silent sister. "Meredith's just jealous. You're taller than she is, even if you're a year younger. *I* think your skirt is just fine." She gave Garnet a hug. "Besides," Jacob heard her whisper as he reached for his black felt hat and frock coat, "if we go to the buggy now, me and you sit beside Papa, not Meredith."

Two hours later, in an effort to keep from dozing off in the middle of one of Jonathan Oliphant's long-winded sermons, Jacob's attention wandered back over the morning. *Aye, Lord,* he thought with deep gratitude, *'twas a bitter draught You allotted me, taking my wife home so prematurely, but You have blessed me with three fine daughters, each of them a—*

"Papa?" Leah breathed his name as her small head burrowed beneath his elbow.

Jacob glanced down into serious brown eyes, the same rich shade as walnut. He decided then and there that when he made Leah's heirloom chest, it would be from walnut. "What is it?" he whispered, enfolding her hand in his own and leaning down. She looked so innocent, uncorrupted by life's bitterness, even the petty squabbling of her two older sisters. Childlike yet self-possessed was his Leah.

"Reverend Oliphant doesn't know what he's talking about, Papa."

The barely audible declaration rang in Jacob's ears like the sound of a rusty saw biting into green wood. "Ah...um..."

She snuggled closer, her glance darting about as though to ensure nobody was listening. That conscientious, was his baby. "First he says nobody's perfect, that everybody is born evil. But that's wrong, Papa. You're not evil, and neither is Meredith and Garnet." The vehement whisper turned a head or two in the pew ahead.

Jacob started to shush her, tell her they would talk later. But the look of disillusionment darkening the innocent, intelligent face stopped him cold.

Yet how—sotto voce in the middle of a thundering sermon—did one explain original sin to a nine-year-old child? Taking a deep breath, he squeezed her hand. "He's talking, ah, on a spiritual level, little one," he murmured as softly as he could. "Everybody—your sisters and I, even you, Miss Muffet—are born with the ability to do bad things. Make wrong choices."

She was shaking her head. "I thought God couldn't do anything bad. He created us, so how can we be bad?"

Merciful heavens, Jacob thought, admiration for her logic warring with panic. For now, panic won. "We'll talk about it on the way home," he whispered, his insides clenching when Leah's eyes clouded and furrows marred the smooth, angelic brow. She moved away and did not speak again. It was then that Jacob accepted that, for this child at least, there would never be any easy answer.

Ah, Lord, he prayed, *You'll have to help me reach this child of mine. Of Yours. Already her mind wars with her heart, and I'm afraid the rest of her life is going to be a painful battleground.*

Aye, Jacob remembered, a bittersweet smile touching the corners of his mouth. That was when he knew what would go into the secret drawer of Leah's heirloom chest, and he prayed as he had for her two sisters, that she would someday understand.

One

ESTHER HAYS SCHOOL FOR YOUNG LADIES
RICHMOND, VIRGINIA, MAY 1895

*L*eah lifted her head and winced. Her neck muscles did not appreciate her brain's intense concentration at their expense. Absentmindedly she rubbed out the muscular kinks while she contemplated the microscope and multiple slides on the high laboratory table. Of the twenty-six slides she had chosen thus far, a handful would be too difficult for her students to identify. Four of them wouldn't challenge the brain of an earthworm, which, of course, possessed no brain at all. That left only—Leah calculated in her head while her fingers nimbly sorted slides—seventeen, satisfactory for inclusion on spring semester finals.

Unacceptable. She wanted at least twenty.

With a resigned grimace Leah slid off the high stool where she'd been camped for the past four hours. Her neck and shoulders were on fire, but she ignored the discomfort, one of the many attendant woes of a teacher, and marched across to the cabinets that held all the neat trays of slides. The science laboratory was Leah's pride and joy. Both curriculum as well as facilities had been in dire need of refurbishment when she accepted her position as teacher in residence at the Esther Hays School for Young Ladies a little over four years ago. But the Panic of '93 hit Richmond hard, and monies were scarce, interest in the school even scarcer. Mrs. Hayes had warned Leah that the school might be forced to close within a year.

Leah thrived on challenges. Her gaze wandered around the fully equipped laboratory, and the quiet glow of accomplishment offset darker currents she'd been ignoring for weeks.

"Miss Sinclair?"

"Mm? Oh, Rowena. Is it time for our tutoring session?" Leah lifted her chatelaine watch, fastened around the waist of Thursday's costume, the plaid gored skirt and pin-tucked shirtwaist. "You're forty minutes early. Something wrong?"

There was no need to ask. At a glance Leah had read the younger girl's guilt. Head tilted, she studied Rowena's flushed cheeks. "Let me guess. You'd like to arrange another time for your tutoring, because you wish to attend the Choral Festival this evening. Where, of course, you might bump into that charming young man you met at church. Geoffrey, I believe was his name?"

Rowena's mouth dropped open. "How do you know so much?"

"I'm a teacher. Teachers know everything, Rowena," Leah declared solemnly. After all, she had a reputation to maintain.

In truth, she'd learned it from Mertis Dittmore, Rowena's best friend at the school, who had also developed an affection for the hapless Geoffrey. Leah had discovered Mertis sobbing behind the rose trellis one afternoon and pried the story from her.

Rowena's lovely thick-lashed eyes searched Leah's face. "Miss Sinclair, why don't you come to the festival too? I-I'd like for you to meet Geoffrey."

"Thank you, but I'd better stay here. Remember it's my calling to torture students through their finals. I only hope you'll be able to adequately prepare, since you'll miss your tutoring session."

"Oh." Rowena gnawed on her lower lip, looking suddenly far younger than her fifteen years. "I want to do well for you, Miss Sinclair. I respect you so highly, you're the reason I'm here, because of my sister's best friend, Rachel, who said you were the best teacher she'd ever studied under. And I begged my—"

"Rowena. I'm teasing you."

Leah stepped closer and laid a hand on the flustered girl's forearm. Few persons outside the Sinclair family circle seemed able to respond in kind to Leah's subtle wit. Sighing, she offered Rowena an encouraging smile. "Have Mrs. Gribble dig an hour out of my schedule and we'll have our session then. Go enjoy the music, and your young man."

"Thank you, Miss Sinclair!" To Leah's astonishment, Rowena threw her arms around her, squeezed, then dashed from the laboratory in a swirl of white petticoats.

The melancholy struck without warning, twisting Leah's heart-strings as she listened to the fading sound of footsteps. She ignored it and turned back to the slides. She refused to wallow in wasted emotion, no matter how desperately she might miss her family. Yes, all right, Rowena's exuberant personality reminded her of Meredith, and Mertis Dittmore's sensitive nature of Garnet, but over the years there was always a student who bore a resemblance to one or both of her sisters.

Just as her sisters grew up, married and left home, so those students graduated from the Miss Esther's and departed. Occasionally one might write to Leah with the news of her impending marriage, or her entry into college, or gainful employment outside a domestic venue. But former students seldom wrote more than once. Leah was surrounded by people, but all of them drifted into her life like bright autumn leaves from the hardwoods back home, then drifted away again on a passing breeze. As Heraclitus had stated some five hundred years before Christ, nothing endured but change.

Goodness, but wasn't she gloomy today.

Leah blew out an exasperated huff of air. She could hear her father's voice as plainly as if he were standing beside her. "The love of God never changes," he would argue, his brogue thickening when he couldn't persuade Leah to his way of thinking. "The cross of Calvary never changes."

Leah selected a half-dozen slides and carried them back to her microscope. "Find me that cross." Her movements were automatic but precise as she positioned a slide on the stage. "Impossible, of course," she muttered as she peered through the eyepiece. "It disappeared nineteen hundred years ago."

For every devout believer there was a skeptic arguing with equal fervor. In Leah's experience, not a one of them, skeptic or believer, was certain of anything. Even her father. She had learned when she was a child not to hurt him by posing troublesome spiritual questions he could not answer to her satisfaction. Of course, after leaving home she had discovered that college professors and supercilious theologians stumbled over them as well.

Sometimes Leah grew so weary of her mind's relentless seeking that she longed for a knob on the top of her head, like the one on her father's pocket watch. She could press the knob on her head and have it spring open like a watch lid so she could remove her brain long enough to rest her spirit.

The simplistic trust of a child—that was the mind-set she was supposed to embrace. Accept without question a faith that demanded, to Leah's way of thinking, complete abdication of the very rational thinking process God had endowed in mankind from the beginning. He had chosen to bequeath part of His divine nature in order to elevate *Homo sapiens* above all other animals, so that they could enjoy a relationship with Him. A relationship based, however, not on one's mental acuity or logical deductions but on a nebulous spiritual reality known as faith.

All her life she had struggled to understand. And when understanding never arrived, she had struggled to conform, because she loved and respected her father more than any person on earth.

Her sisters had found that mysterious faith, had even found husbands who shared it. As always, Leah was the fifth wheel. The oddity. The ugly duckling who would never grow into a beautiful swan.

"Miss Sinclair?"

Relieved, Leah glanced up at the school's longtime secretary. Mrs. Gribble was a lonely but tiresome woman, who like the English Queen Victoria persisted in wearing widow's weeds even after seventeen years. Leah suppressed the urge to embrace her in a Rowena-like hug. "Hello, Mrs. Gribble. I take it Rowena dropped by?"

"A most annoying girl. Flighty, with that irritating breathlessness to her voice common among young, impressionable females."

Everyone at the school—including Esther Hays herself—approached Mrs. Gribble gingerly. Everyone except Leah, who understood the secretary's fanatical discipline and need for order.

"Impressionable they certainly are." She lowered her voice confidingly. "Which is why I need for you to find me a spare hour somewhere. Rowena's mind must be engaged, to combat all those unruly emotions."

"That, Miss Sinclair, should be the responsibility of a husband." Mrs. Gribble surveyed the laboratory. "I never have agreed with Miss Esther about the addition of applied sciences to the school's curriculum."

"Not all women are fortunate enough to secure a husband. And even if they do, they are not always fortunate enough to enjoy a lifelong relationship."

"I am well aware of that, Miss Sinclair. Not an hour goes by when I am not reminded of the burden of sorrow God saw fit to place upon my shoulders."

Patience, logic, and control, Leah reminded herself. Otherwise, the secretary would argue with her until the next full moon, some ten days away. She offered Mrs. Gribble a sympathetic nod and carefully returned to the reason for her appearance in the laboratory. "Were you able to fit Rowena in next week? Of course you were; you are without doubt the most capable staff member at the School for Young Ladies. It was thoughtful of you to climb all those stairs to let me know. Here"—she tore a piece of paper from the back of a tablet—"if you'll write down the time, I'll pin it on the calendar in my sitting room so I won't forget."

"You need your own office, Miss Sinclair," Mrs. Gribble said. "I've made such a recommendation to Miss Esther. Of course, as merely the secretary I'm sure my counsel is considered of little consequence…"

Leah strolled with her over to the door, pretending to listen, and finally waved the still muttering woman down the stairs. Leah returned to the slides and was instantly absorbed.

A quarter of an hour later she was interrupted again, this time by Esther Hays herself. "My dear, I really must insist that you pry yourself away from this room. You've missed supper again. You know how I feel about that."

"I have an apple, and some bread and cheese." Leah glanced down. Still two slides short…

"Hmph. You need meat, and fresh air. Pale as a new moon, and so slight I could fold you into a foolscap envelope and still pay naught but a penny's postage. What would your father have to say?"

"That you're fretting over nothing. I took care of myself—and my family—from the time I was seven years old, and we survived quite adequately." Her movements brisk, she covered the microscope, returned slides to files, stacked books and papers while she talked.

"Leah."

Leah paused in the middle of gathering up the pencils she scattered like chicken feed about a room over the course of her day. When the headmistress addressed her in that particular tone, it was wise to pay attention, even if she disagreed. "Miss Esther, in two weeks the semester ends. I'm always a trifle…intense, at the end of a year."

"Yes. I have noticed that about you." Behind new wire-rimmed spectacles a pair of shrewd gray eyes studied Leah. "Something is troubling you. You've been even more preoccupied than usual, and don't try to persuade me that it's students or studies." She paused, watching Leah with a formidable dignity made easier by her commanding height and generations of breeding. "I seldom pry into the personal affairs of my teachers. But you know that I have a willing ear, and a deep affection for you."

"The regard is mutual." Leah contemplated her oxford tie shoes for a moment, then reluctantly admitted, "In her letter last week my sister Meredith invited me to spend a month at Stillwaters when the school year ends. I was planning to attend a series of lectures in—"

"Nonsense! I've read excellent reports of Mr. Walker's newest enterprise. In fact, according to the *Daily Dispatch,* the governor himself plans to take the waters there, come August. A summer at Stillwaters would be far more beneficial for you than sitting inside some stuffy lecture hall."

Leah could feel heat building in her cheeks. She should have heeded her instincts and kept her mouth shut. She might have wished to remove her brain for a moment or two, but not in front of witnesses.

"Leah? I'd appreciate candor, if you please."

So be it. Leah returned the headmistress's level gaze. "Not all of us are destined to be wives, Miss Esther."

"Ah. I see. Your family's matchmaking again? Your sister Meredith is rather…tenacious, isn't she?"

"She and Benjamin are happy. They can't accept that I am equally content, despite my spinster status."

"Certainly you have achieved remarkable success and fame for a young woman of twenty-five years." Miss Esther's voice was smooth as polished agate. "Seems to me that the Leah Sinclair who persuaded a dozen businesses to donate enough money for us to purchase twice that many Hammond typewriting machines…who convinced an equally strong-minded headmistress"—she paused to slide Leah a glance down the length of her rather formidable nose—"of the efficacy of a fully equipped laboratory…who has won the adoration of hundreds of undisciplined adolescent girls over the past four years…seems to me that Leah Sinclair should be able to fend off the well-meaning ploys of her loving family."

Outmaneuvered, Leah conceded graciously. "Well, when you put it that way, I suppose I'd better write Meredith and tell her when to expect me." She gathered the books in her arms, conscious of a sensation of relief. "June is a lovely time to visit the mountains."

"Precisely," Miss Esther nodded once. "Shall we?" She gestured toward the hall. "I told Cook to keep a plate warmed for you. She's also saving me an extra helping of dessert. Why don't I join you, and you can fill me in about your incorrigible nephew's latest antics."

❦

By the end of the week Leah had completed the format for final exams in each of the classes she taught—household management, botany, astronomy, physics, and geography. With Mrs. Gribble's grumbling but efficient help she compressed her schedule so that she was able to tutor a half-dozen girls, including Rowena.

She squeezed in an afternoon downtown, purchasing from Thalhimer's a new traveling suit made of fine lightweight crepon, and a pair of black kid lace-up boots with fashionably pointed toes. This visit, Meredith would have little reason to nag Leah about her regimented wardrobe and lackluster style.

Two weeks later, with the semester concluded and all students having successfully passed their examinations, Leah turned all her attention to her imminent summer sabbatical at Stillwaters. On the eve of her departure, she had just laid out the new traveling suit and shoes when

Miss Esther summoned her into the school's auditorium. There, still dressed in their white lawn commencement gowns, thirty-seven giggling students presented her with a sturdy new Gladstone traveling bag and a book on flora and fauna of the Virginia mountains. Several of the girls offered effusive speeches. Afterward, everyone clustered around Leah, proffering thank-yous and good-natured banter.

Touched, Leah stood in their midst, feeling both ancient and motherly despite the fact she was only a few years older than they. No doubt the feeling arose because she'd been destined from birth to fill the role of spinster schoolmarm. Feelings, however, as she always reminded her overemotional girls, were never reliable indicators of reality. They tended to change by the hour, or with the weather. With a mental smack, Leah thrust aside her doldrums and enjoyed the gift of the students' affirmation.

That night as she lay in her narrow bed in the teachers' wing of the school's dormitories, Leah allowed herself a final moment of self-indulgence. It was lovely, finding a niche in a profession where she was respected for who she was, instead of ignored due to her diminutive stature and unremarkable looks.

Lovely, yet amazing. And, because she knew it would please her father, Leah fell asleep whispering a formal expression of gratitude to God, to whom any acknowledgment at all by a doubting Thomas such as herself must surely cause a heavenly chuckle or two.

Two

JUNE 1895

*C*ade Beringer stood alone, one hand resting on a tree stump—the ghostly remnants of a three-hundred-year-old American chestnut. His other hand was clenched in an impotent fist at his side. It was a little past sunrise, so for the moment the torn and pillaged mountainside was silent. No sweating men wielding their saws like swords, no snorting draft horses hauling tons of logs away to be transformed into lumber.

No sound of birdsong to greet the day, or nesting passenger pigeons. No fox squirrels busily burying nuts in the dewy morning air, no white-tailed deer slipping like shadows between the trunks, no black bear or raccoons or wolves. No mountain lions—they'd been gone for fifteen years or so now.

Pain knotted Cade's insides, a raw mixture of grief and anger.

He never should have returned to the site of his defeat—what was the point, after all? He'd fought the good fight; for a decade now he had confidently gone forth in the name of the Lord to protect and preserve. To function as best he could as God's steward for this small patch of earth.

Yet over the years he'd lost more battles than he'd won. Thanks largely to the railroads, the locustlike mentality that had devoured the West was now focused on the richly blanketed wilderness of the Appalachians. Mining and logging had made steady inroads over recent years despite the vagaries of the economy. The abundant supply of natural resources, particularly lumber, fueled the attendant thirst for building. For cheap furniture that filled the pages of mail order catalogs; for acres of wood paneling that adorned walls and staircases in the mansions of the newly rich—or palaces like Vanderbilt's Biltmore.

Then there were the iron-producing furnaces and forges that further decimated the forests, choked the air with belching smoke; mines that left raw holes in the earth. Everyone was hungry for a piece of this lucrative pie.

And they gorged their appetites on the ancient forests of the Alleghenies and the Blue Ridge Mountains.

Cade's gaze roved over the clear-cut strip of land. His soul flinched along with his eyelids. *Almighty Father, Ruler of the universe...Jesus, help me here, please. Why can't they see what they're doing?*

Finally he sank to his knees and bowed his head, knowing his only recourse now was to accept. Accept and wait for the Lord to lead him to the next battleground.

Cade stopped by the post office–cum general store on his way back to Mrs. Skinner's boardinghouse. His family continually bemoaned his constant changes of address. "I couldn't locate Echo, Tennessee, in our atlas," his sister Nan complained his last trip home to North Carolina. "Where *do* you unearth these tiny boroughs?" But everyone faithfully wrote at least once a week. For nine months now it had been to Echo, but Cade sensed that was about to change.

Today, instead of a weekly epistle from a family member, a letter from Benjamin Walker was waiting. After he returned to the boardinghouse, Cade snagged a couple of corn batter cakes left over from breakfast, wheedled a cup of coffee from Mrs. Skinner, and sat down in the parlor to read the letter.

> *...and I thought you might enjoy another opportunity to wield your magic. Your landscaping genius rivals that of Fred Olmstead, my friend. So rest from your crusading for a spell. Besides, Meredith and I want you to get to know your godson before he's grown—or in prison!*

Well, Lord...that was certainly prompt. Certainly not what he'd been expecting, but—*thank You.* The deep weariness dragging at Cade's soul ebbed a bit. A landscaping project would be a dispensation of sorts. He could use his training to create beauty in nature, instead of witnessing its destruction. God in His mercy had offered a balm.

"Mr. Beringer?"

Cade glanced up. Shrouded in her ill-fitting mourning attire, Louisa Bloomquist hovered on the threshold of the parlor. Six months earlier, Milton Bloomquist, his wife, and his three-year-old daughter had taken rooms here in Mrs. Skinner's boardinghouse. A month later, an accident with the monstrous lumberman's saw chewed off half of Milt's leg; he bled to death before his fellow loggers could get him back to camp.

Cade set aside the letter and rose. "Good afternoon, Mrs. Bloomquist." He hesitated before adding, "Something's wrong. Is it Prudy?"

Louisa's mouth trembled, and she nodded jerkily. Struggling, he knew, against the ready tears.

Cade waited for a beat, but when she continued to stand mute he walked across the parlor to her. "What's the problem?" he prompted, gesturing toward the settee. "Here. Come and tell me about it."

"I-I've interrupted you."

"Just a letter from a friend. It can wait." He tucked it away, treating her with the firmness she seemed to need. "Tell me about Prudy. Is it the nightmares, or is she throwing tantrums again?"

"Both. Neither of us slept much last night." She plucked at the belt buckle of her skirt in jerky gestures. "This morning at breakfast—you'd already left, they said—she threw her oatmeal on the floor. Mrs. Skinner said if I can't control my h-hooligan child, we'll have to leave." She blinked rapidly. "Mr. Beringer, I got nowhere to go. I-I know 'twas you who made the company pay the rent here. But they might not, if I had to move. Prudy's not a bad child. She's just afraid. She wants her daddy."

Like her mother wanted her husband. "Of course she does. She's too young to understand, that's all. She'll settle down, with time. I'll have a talk with her, if you like."

"Would you? Sh-she cottoned on to you, Mr. Beringer. Talks about you all the time. And I've read that book you gave her so many times I can recite it from memory myself." A bit of color bloomed in the sallow cheeks. "Prudy likes *A Child's Garden of Verses* the best."

"Does she?" Cade smiled. "I have three nephews and two nieces, spread between my two sisters. That book is their favorite too. Now, I don't want you to fret. I'll talk to Mrs. Skinner. It's been a number of years since she lost her husband, but I'm sure she's never forgotten the pain of it."

"Why are you doing this?" Louisa's red-rimmed eyes were cloudy with confusion. "Mr. Beringer, we're nothing to you. I—my husband was destroying the woods you love. I don't understand…"

"You needed help." The back of Cade's neck felt hot. He prayed for guidance, reading beyond Louisa's honest confusion to a subterranean emotion that, if not quelled, would humiliate her and embarrass him.

He jammed his hand inside his pocket, crumpling Ben's letter. *Ah.* God's perfect timing again, he thought in relief. "There are plenty of other folks who will help you," he promised Louisa now, "Folks who will be able to offer much more than I."

"I don't need anyone else. You've been everything I need. Mr. Beringer, I—"

He cut her off, his voice gentle. "Mrs. Bloomquist, I'll be leaving in a day or two."

"Leaving?" Her voice rose.

"My work here"—*futile as it has been*—"is finished." He steeled himself. The widow Bloomquist was one quivering gasp away from Prudy-like hysteria. The warning resonated through his head: *Don't reach out to her.* Keeping his movements casual, Cade retrieved the envelope and tucked the letter inside. "I'll make sure you and Prudy are in welcoming hands. Remember the Sunday the two of you accompanied me to church?"

"They were strangers. I don't want strangers pitying me. Staring at me and Prudy like we was poor relations."

"Until a few months ago I was a stranger to you. Mrs. Bloomquist—Louisa. Look at me." He folded his arms across his chest, trying to look as well as sound like a stern parent.

Some of her panic dissipated. She quit wringing her hands. Resentment clouded her face instead of adoration, less dangerous by far than her need-born loneliness, though both were equally uncomfortable for

Cade. "Have I treated you like a poor relation?" After a truculent pause her head jerked sideways once. "How about pity? Do you think I've been helping you all these months because I feel sorry for you and Prudence?"

Her eyelids flickered, her thin lips primming, but Cade waited until she finally shook her head again. "I thought you cared about me. About us," she amended hastily.

"There are people at that church who will care for you the same way. Ladies who will be your friends, gentlemen who will offer you wise counsel. Children to play with Prudy. She needs friends just like you do."

"I don't want them, I-I want you, Mr. Beringer."

Jesus, give me the wisdom, the words. "Mrs. Bloomquist, remember the other night, when Prudy wanted another piece of Mrs. Skinner's snow-mountain cake? She loves sweets, but you knew too much would give her a tummyache." He smiled a crooked smile. "I know, having overindulged a time or two myself, on my mother's chocolate pie."

The front door banged, and outside in the hallway heavy footsteps scraped across the linoleum in Mrs. Skinner's kitchen.

Cade glanced over Louisa's shoulder. "Do you understand what I'm saying?"

Her mouth twisted in the semblance of a smile. "I sneaked Prudy another piece of that cake from the kitchen, after everyone left the table. She kept on at me about it, wore me down until I fetched some. Woke me a little past midnight, and I spent the rest of the night holding her head over the chamber bowl."

She paused, breathed a long-drawn sigh, then finished, "I understand what you're telling me, Mr. Beringer. I know you're a God-fearing man. I'd better check on Prudy now. She might have woke from her nap. I don't want her to be scared." She turned away.

"Mrs. Bloomquist?" He watched her spine stiffen before she faced him again. "God doesn't want you to be scared either. Let His arms comfort you, like you comfort your daughter."

For a long moment she pondered him in silence. "I'd rather have had yourn," she finally said. "But seein' that you're leaving, I'll try to do as you say. Never known a man like you, Mr. Beringer. You don't just say all the pious words. You believe them, don't you?"

"With all my heart."

"I reckon," her voice dropped to a near whisper, "that you've been a...a godly substitute for Jesus, to Prudy and me. God keep you on your way, Mr. Beringer."

"And you, Mrs. Bloomquist."

Long after she'd left, Cade stood in the parlor, her parting words lingering in the air. Only when several other lodgers drifted into the room and exchanged pleasantries was he able to gather his wits back into some sort of order. After stuffing Benjamin's letter in his pocket, he headed out into the street, toward the neat whitewashed church on the edge of town.

Three

$\mathcal{T}$hree days later, Cade boarded a stage for the nearest town with railroad connections. Clouds gathered and darkened during the long train journey from Tennessee to Roanoke, Virginia, which had exploded from a sleepy community formerly known as Big Lick to one of the state's fastest growing towns.

That night he fell asleep to the sound of heavy rain pounding the greasy window of his hotel room near the depot. It was still pouring the next morning when he purchased a ticket to the town of Buchanan, where he'd then switch lines to a Chesapeake and Ohio train that wound its way into the mountains on the western side of the Shenandoah Valley.

"Hear there're some delays, up north of here," the ticket agent commented as he methodically counted change. "Might better check with the agent when you debark at Buchanan." His stubby fingers passed coins and ticket through the slot. "Where'd you say you was headed?"

"Stillwaters Resort Hotel and Spa."

"Ah. Heard of it." He eyed Cade's old tweed jacket and striped gray trousers through the bars of the ticket window. "Pretty fancy place. You ever been there before?"

Cade's mouth quirked in a half-grin. "As a matter of fact, I have. You're right, it is a pretty fancy place. But guests tend to come away refreshed, because it's also a place where weary souls can find peace."

"You don't say. Well, reckon I could use some peace myself." He cleared his throat, "Have a good trip. Check with the C&O agent in Buchanan, now. These kind of summer gullywashers have been known to cause landslides and flood rivers."

North of Roanoke, the eastern branch of the Norfolk and Western

Railroad loosely followed the base of the Blue Ridge Mountains up the Shenandoah Valley, while the C&O cut a westerly path across the state from Portsmouth. From Buchanan it headed into the Alleghenies, passing within an hour's ride by stage to Stillwaters. Steady rain blurred the passing landscape to an indiscriminate gray, but by the time Cade debarked at Buchanan, sunbeams poked holes through the shredding storm clouds. He shouldered his knapsack, grasped the handle of his battered leather valise, and followed several other passengers across the footbridge that spanned a swollen James River to reach the C&O depot on the western side of the town.

Rain-and-creosote scented steam rose in heated waves, and water dripped from the platform's roof. Inside, the small depot was crowded with summer travelers, all of them looking wilted in the stifling confines of the single waiting room. Two ceiling fans circulated air thick with mildew and stale cigar smoke. Several women complained in audible voices about the lack of a ladies' waiting room, while a man dressed in a flamboyant checkered suit demanded to know the location of the nearest saloon, all the while vigorously fanning himself with his straw boater.

The station agent, seemingly inured to the weather, fended questions without pausing as he shoved traveling trunks against the wall. Cade snagged his attention long enough to inquire about the status of his train, then moved to a less crowded corner of the room.

His gaze fell upon a woman sitting apart from the rest of the passengers, at the very end of a bench. Her spine was straight as a railroad beam, her hands motionless in her lap. Somehow in this crowded, grumpy atmosphere she managed to project both serenity and aloofness. Her only concession to the suffocating humidity had been to remove her hat and gloves, which lay stacked beside her on the wooden bench, the gloves folded with military precision. On the floor next to her shiny black shoes rested an equally new-looking Gladstone bag.

It was her stillness that first caught his eye. No fussing with her person or fidgeting on the hard bench or carping about her circumstances. In the wilderness, that stillness alone would enable her to escape a predator's notice, no matter that here inside the Buchanan depot her air of stoic patience achieved the opposite effect.

When her head lifted almost as though she'd sensed his interest, Cade turned away. It was rude to stare, after all. Then, incredulous, he swiveled on his heel. Their gazes met across the length of the noisy room; he reached her in a half-dozen strides.

"Leah? Leah"—he glanced at her left hand—"Sinclair?"

"Mr. Beringer."

Her level voice and absolutely expressionless face warned Cade to tread carefully. Their few brief meetings had been less than auspicious. Something about him had rubbed Leah Sinclair the wrong way from the moment her father introduced them five years ago. Cade had never pursued the matter with Ben and Meredith; for one thing, he hadn't wanted to foster the wrong impression. He wondered now if he should have, considering Leah's cool greeting.

"It's been a long time." He smiled at her, though he kept his hands at his sides and his smile merely polite. A peculiar silence stretched between them. "I'm on my way to Stillwaters," Cade said finally, puzzling at the subtle narrowing of her eyes. "Your sister and Ben invited me to spend the summer there. In return I'll be—"

"I suppose I shouldn't be surprised," Leah Sinclair interrupted with a brusqueness that bordered on rudeness. She gestured to the seat. "You may as well sit down, Mr. Beringer. Our train isn't scheduled to arrive for another hour, which should give us sufficient time."

"Time…for what?" A widowed Louisa Bloomquist she certainly wasn't, which perhaps explained why Cade couldn't bring himself to leave her alone.

"Time for you to come up with alternative plans."

Alternative plans? After shrugging off his knapsack he joined her on the bench, turning toward her so his back would serve as a screen of sorts from the curious eyes of the travelers seated further down. He realized at once that his own frank appraisal was making her uncomfortable. Though regretful, Cade wasn't surprised. "What do you mean?"

Leah eyed him with that jaded air he still remembered, even after all these years. It was as jarring now as it had been when she was a girl of scarcely twenty years.

"It's unnecessary for either one of us to suffer simply because of my meddling sister," she said. "On second thought, never mind. I'll change my own ticket. It would serve her right."

Cade held up a hand. "I have no idea what you're talking about."

"Don't be obtuse. Surely you don't think we were both invited for a visit at the same time by coincidence."

Aha. Cade's gaze ran over her in a brief but encompassing survey. He had forgotten her diminutive stature. With the primly coiled brown hair and unadorned dark blue traveling suit, she was as neat and dainty as a Carolina wren. He remembered hearing Leah's father call her his little wren, and thought it an apt metaphor. Her temperament, on the other hand, reminded Cade more of a prickly yucca plant. Of course, she obviously believed what she was intimating, which explained most of those bristles. He hoped.

"I've never claimed to be a mind reader, though nobody's ever accused me of being obtuse. Ben invited me for a visit and asked if I'd do a bit of landscaping. I agreed. Your name never came up in our correspondence, at least in reference to my stay this summer. But I do confess that over the years they have mentioned you, along with your other sister Garnet and her husband."

His gaze dropped to her ringless left hand, then returned to her face. "You're a teacher now, I believe?"

Red bloomed across the bridge of her nose and forehead, while the rest of her complexion paled. "Yes. I am a teacher. And I'll save you further speculations by stating that I am not, and have never been, married." She hesitated. "I apologize for more or less accusing you of collusion. For some reason Meredith refuses to accept the inevitability of my spinsterhood." A flicker of humor brightened eyes the color of bitter chocolate. "I seem to remember having to apologize to you, the very first time we met."

"You were tired that day," Cade murmured. "You're tired now, aren't you?"

"Of course not, I have excellent stamina. I—"

"I'm sure you do. I wasn't, however, referring to physical fatigue." He leaned forward, ignoring how she stiffened, then finished softly, "I think you're tired on every other level of your being. Why don't you tell me about it, while we wait for the train? It's been a long time, but I think we can consider each other old friends, don't you?"

"You're impertinent, Mr. Beringer."

"Yes, I admit it. But I'm also…interested."

And he was, to his surprise. Interested, and intrigued by this touchy little martinet whose manner failed to disguise a deep loneliness Cade had sensed from all the way across the room. "Besides, the least I can do since we're headed to the same place"—he hid a smile when she all but gnashed her teeth at him—"is to ensure that you arrive safely."

"I'm quite capable of taking care of myself. Furthermore, I'm not inclined to engage in either casual or intimate conversation with you, regardless of our past association."

"I've a notion that you're used to taking care of not only yourself but everyone else around you. No wonder you're weary." He shifted a bit, giving her space while maintaining the illusion of privacy. "I promise to be a good traveling companion. If you don't feel like talking about yourself, we can talk about Ben and Meredith. We have an hour before our train arrives. And for that matter, we have the rest of the summer."

Each motion precise, Leah picked up her gloves, tucked them inside her hat, and rose to her feet. "I'd rather eat a bucketful of mud." She grabbed her bag, then stalked across the floor and disappeared outside.

Cade laced his hands around one upraised knee. Looked to be an interesting journey from this point. *You'll have to help out a bit, Lord. I'm not quite sure yet what my role is supposed to be here.*

It certainly didn't look like it was destined to be that of confidant.

Four

*L*eah slipped through the knot of passengers and townsfolk to the edge of the platform, where the square bay window of the ticket office offered an illusion of privacy. She was disgusted with herself.

She'd acted with the emotional immaturity of one of her students, simply because she'd been caught off guard. It was little consolation to remind herself that she'd never been adept at personal discourse with men. But *Cade Beringer,* of all people. Leah's hand tightened on the handle of her bag. Though long ago she had trained herself not to care what men thought of her, Mr. Beringer's unexpected appearances in her life, however fleeting and far between, had a baffling way of pulverizing all those mental defenses.

For several moments she stood in silence, waiting for the emotional whirlpool to subside. "Think instead of react," she always told her girls. "God provided you with a mind. Emotions are merely messy weeds in the fertile soil of your brain, so begin the process at once, controlling the proliferation of those weeds."

A fine example she'd set just now.

A stray crumb of humor tickled the back of her throat. He'd tried to hide it, but Mr. Beringer had been equally caught off guard by her parting salvo. Leah took a deep breath, then held it while she counted to twenty, for the third time. Her death grip on the Gladstone relaxed as she slowly exhaled. There. She was fine now, in control once more, and could spend the next moments solving the sticky dilemma of how to apologize to Cade Beringer without seeming to endorse his presumption of friendship. She was confident that a solution would present itself, so long as she refused to allow him to breach her defenses again.

Perhaps over the course of the next weeks at Stillwaters she would engage in a thorough self-examination. With understanding, she could expunge once and for all her bewildering missishness toward this man.

Behind her, the rain-drenched air filled with the scent of lilacs. Leah stiffened and kept her back turned. That would be the newlywed wife, the young woman with a head of glossy black curls and a wide smile that charmed every male in the crowded depot. Over the last hour, Leah had watched the smile wilt along with the charm, until her husband had escorted her outside, his concerned gaze never leaving his wife's wan face.

For several more moments Leah tried to pretend her new shoes were glued to the platform. She lacked the energy to engage in another conversation; she needed to formulate her strategy in dealing with Cade; she didn't feel up to bearing the burden of another person's problems. The girl's welfare was her husband's responsibility, not Leah's.

It was no use. Leah turned around.

The husband was nowhere in sight, and the young wife had slumped against the corner of the bay window, one hand curved around the window sill as though to support her weight. Her head was bowed, her eyes closed. Concern overrode Leah's disgruntlement.

"I don't mean to intrude, but is there anything I can do to help?"

The other woman opened her eyes but didn't move. "Thank you, but I'm afraid not." A drop of perspiration trickled down her temple; she made no effort to remove it. "It's just this dreadful heat. I grew up in Maine. Until this trip, I'd never been farther south than Boston. My husband has gone to fetch a cup of water, to see if that helps."

"Southern humidity is a challenge even for southerners," Leah offered sympathetically. "It would help if you removed your gloves. Not proper, I know, but far more practical. I'm convinced all the arbiters of social etiquette never visited the South in summertime."

A weak smile was the only response.

Leah studied her. "As you see, I removed my hat as well as the gloves, which earned me several disapproving glances in the waiting room. But if two of us opted for comfort, it's possible we might incite a small rebellion. My name is Leah Sinclair. I'm a teacher, and I also have two sisters, both of whom learned to care more about practicality than punishment, in matters of fashion."

"Jane Bedford—oh." A fraction of the wide smile returned. "I mean, Jane Moore. Mrs. Theodore Moore." A healthy blush deepened in the heat-splotched cheeks. "We're on our wedding trip."

"Congratulations. Now, let me help you." With nimble fingers Leah began to work the glove free of Mrs. Moore's unresisting hand. "There." After she finished she briskly wiped her fingers and palm dry with her handkerchief. "Let me see your other."

"You must be one of those advocates for rational dress. They even formed a society, in England. *Ah.*" The syllable emerged as a grateful sigh. Mrs. Moore stared down at her bare hands. "I hadn't realized."

"Might as well take your hat off too. It's only straw, and fashionably small—"

"Thank you. Are you—"

"But it traps heat nonetheless." Leah paused, one eyebrow lifted coaxingly until with a little laugh Mrs. Moore lifted her hands to her hat. "When your head and hands are too warm, the rest of your body suffers. Don't worry. We'll hear as well as see the train long before it arrives in the station. Plenty of warning to put ourselves back together, before we board."

"You must be a wonderful teacher," Mrs. Moore observed after she removed the pert straw hat. Its spray of flowers nestled inside a butter yellow bow that matched her gloves. She fluffed the thick curled fringe of hair on her forehead, then tried in vain to subdue unruly ringlets at her temples. Giving up, she eyed Leah with a return of the twinkling charm. "Though you look more like a student yourself, if you don't mind my saying so."

"It's the truth, so how could I mind? Besides, you wouldn't be the first to make the observation," Leah replied. "I've learned to compensate, as you see, with a dictatorial personality."

"Not dictatorial. Helpful. And I very much appreciate the kindness you've extended to a perfect stranger." She held out her hand. "Thank you."

"You're more than welcome, Mrs. Moore."

"Please. Call me Jane." She giggled. "I'm not used to the other yet—poor Teddy. I keep looking around for his mother when someone addresses me. Is that handsome gentleman with the golden mane of hair your husband?"

"Goodness, no! We're"—Leah hesitated, then mentally threw up her hands—"old friends. Sort of. His name is Mr. Beringer. Actually, he's the friend of my oldest sister and her husband. I've only met him twice before." And Meredith's wedding didn't count, since Leah had spent the entire afternoon avoiding Mr. Beringer.

"Oh. I beg your pardon. Must be the heat. Turns one's brain to mush. I'd assumed, from the way he was looking at you—"

"And what way was that?"

Jane blinked.

Impatient with herself, Leah forced a rueful smile. "Sorry. I didn't mean to sound cross. As you observed, the heat…please. I'd very much like to hear your explanation of Mr. Beringer's attitude toward me."

Jane's expression relaxed back into friendliness. "When Teddy and I came back inside the depot, you and Mr. Beringer were sharing a conversation. I couldn't see your face, but from the expression on his, it was plain he was…well, I think he'd like to be more than just a friend of a friend."

Leah sniffed. "I very much doubt it. Mr. Beringer and I share opposing views on a number of issues. I daresay any 'interest' on his part you detected is overshadowed by aggravation."

Its ululating wail announced a train's imminent arrival. Relieved, Leah replaced her own hat, then began tugging on her gloves. "That might be my train. It's supposed to arrive at half past two."

Jane was frantically following suit. "Mine, too. I must find my husband." Her hands froze in the process of adjusting the angle of her hat. "Where are you going, Miss Sinclair?"

"It's Leah, and I'm on the way to Stillwaters Resort Hotel and Spa. It's—"

"But that's splendid! So are we. Why don't you sit across the aisle from us? We can talk, and you can tell me all about the school where you teach."

"The trains tend to be overcrowded during the summer season, so that might not be possible. But if it is, I'd enjoy that, thank you." It might even relieve her of Cade Beringer's unwelcome attentions.

"Teddy told me that we'll have to debark and ride on a stage the final miles of the journey." Jane glanced down at her stylish costume with its leg-of-mutton sleeves and lace frill the width of her shoulders. "I fear I'll arrive in a sad state of disarray." Her eyes danced. "The social arbiters of fashion obviously haven't traveled widely either."

"Fortunately Mr. Walker, the owner, also owns the stagecoaches. They're quite spacious. My sister Meredith, his wife, is a clotheshorse, and refuses to subject female guests to anything but the best."

Yet it was amazing to Leah how hordes of people willingly endured days of wearisome travel to reach Benjamin's latest venture in the resort hotel business. Stillwaters was only three years old, but its reputation already rivaled venerable, more established spa resorts like Warm Springs and "the White"—White Sulfur Springs.

"I'd better go find Teddy." Jane reached out, clasping Leah's hand in a reassuring squeeze. "I do hope we can sit near each other." She scurried into the waiting room.

Leah remained outside and out of the way. She had her bag and her ticket. At the appropriate moment she would join the throng of passengers crowding the doorway and platform in their hurry to board.

For her, the arduous daylong trip this time was worth the effort not only because she wanted to see Meredith and her family, but because the isolated setting provided an opportunity for some soul searching. She needed to analyze this insidious melancholy, this darkening in her mind that refused to dissipate no matter how relentlessly she fought it. Hopefully a concentrated dose of introspection would provide the necessary tonic, while she communed with nature instead of humanity.

Leah was not one for mingling with the crowds of guests who spent their summers traipsing among all the mountain resorts for the lavish meals, concerts, and sporting events, and of course "taking the waters." With the ruthless pragmatism that was both blessing and curse, she acknowledged that she would avoid not only Cade but Jane Moore as well, no matter how amiable she found the young woman. After all, Jane was also a newly wedded wife.

Most people needed friends. But the friends they sought out were those with whom they were comfortable, people who shared their views, their tastes. Their raison d'être. Over the past six years since she left home, Leah had found those friends and acquaintances in academic circles. Yet even those friendships had waned with time, leaving her to wonder if the fault lay within her, or simply within circumstances.

She knew that it was vital for her to learn how to be alone, without loneliness. She refused to spend the rest of her life with the aimlessness of the summer flock of guests. Only instead of fancy resort hotels Leah would be flitting from family member to family member, making herself indispensable wherever she temporarily lighted, to compensate for the burden of her presence. In all her twenty-five years, she had never been able to find a companion outside her family, male or female, who accepted her for what she was, never known anyone comfortable enough with her personality to invite a lasting friendship. Leah was beginning to accept that lifelong solitude would be less painful, and over the summer, along with a much-needed rest, she planned to come up with ways to gracefully accept her lot in life.

Bell clanging, the train lumbered to a grinding halt. Billows of steam engulfed Leah along with the other passengers and locals who had gathered on the platform.

Mr. Beringer was nowhere in sight. Piqued by her sense of relief, Leah waited until the conductor lowered the metal steps onto the nearest passenger car. After the jostling and shoving abated and a relatively quiescent line had formed, Leah stepped forward. When one was unable to secure respect due to physical appearance, one made do with tactics and timing.

Moments later the conductor took her bag, then handed her up the steps into the coach's vestibule. As expected, the coach was crowded with summer travelers. Progress down the aisle was slow, due to the number of passengers as well as the ponderous pace of the buxom woman in front of Leah. The woman's wide-brimmed hat blocked Leah's vision, so she had no warning before she heard a mellow baritone voice explain that the empty seat next to him was already taken.

Cade Beringer. Was the exasperating man destined to be her thorn in the flesh? The plan she had devised called for a brief, warm-but-dismissive apology followed by a firm declaration of disinterest. To be trapped in forced intimacy with this man above all others filled Leah with a sensation akin to the jitters. If she hadn't been blocked from behind, she would have escaped to another car. She'd sit on a mailbag for the journey. Even the caboose would be preferable.

"Leah!" Jane Moore's face beamed up at her from the seat directly across the aisle from Mr. Beringer. "Isn't this a stroke of luck? Mr. Beringer gallantly offered to stave off any number of determined passengers to preserve you a seat across from us. He happened to overhear me telling Teddy about you, you see, while we were waiting to board. It's too bad we aren't in a car with facing seats. We could converse with each other without"—a scowling gentleman behind Leah loudly cleared his throat, then squeezed past her—"the aisle between us," Jane finished, glaring at the impatient passenger's back.

"I'm not sure," Leah muttered as she eyed the empty bench seat, "that 'stroke of luck' would be my choice of words."

Further conversation with Jane wasn't possible until the passengers behind her passed along to other cars. For several moments Leah busied herself settling into her seat, refusing to make eye contact with her seatmate. She fussed about, arranging her skirts and smoothing down her own ridiculously puffed jacket sleeves. She normally saw little value in the manner women made fools of themselves over their clothes, whose only purpose should be to cover their bodies, but at least it gave her a momentary reprieve. Next she made a production out of checking her small leather purse to ensure the presence of her ticket. Finally, with nothing left to do she pretended great interest in the antimacassar dangling over the seat back in front of her, her hip smashed against the wooden armrest to preserve as much distance as possible between her and her seatmate.

"I have a book to read," Mr. Beringer said, his voice congenial. He held it up. "If you like, we'll pretend to be perfect strangers who merit nothing beyond a courteous non sequitur about the countryside, at appropriate intervals of course. How does every hour on the half-hour strike you?"

A smile itched the corners of her mouth, forcing Leah to compress her lips so he wouldn't think she was responding to his good-humored riposte. Why couldn't he have been ill-favored, or at least a dullard? An oaf without manners or wit. Deliberately she examined her chatelaine watch, whose half-open face enabled her to quickly check the time. "The scenery along this section of the James River is breathtaking. Enjoy your book."

"Before I'm relegated to a metaphorical corner, would you answer a question for me?"

Her head whipped around. "That depends on the question."

"It's a straightforward one." Casually he crossed his arms and settled deeper into his seat. "Is my presence going to spoil the trip for you?"

"Certainly not."

Rattled, Leah barely managed the retort because the nimble brain she'd relied on all her life was unable to formulate a single supporting argument. His honesty seemed as uncompromising as her own, so she settled for reciprocal candor. "Mr. Beringer, it's apparent that any awkwardness here is all on my part, not yours. While over the years I've learned to accept my status, I do try to avoid dwelling on it. Is it asking too much for you to do the same?"

"What status would that be?" Mr. Beringer asked very quietly, any traces of humor gone.

Leah kept her chin high and her hands loose but still. She was, she reminded herself, no longer twenty years old. "Spinster schoolteacher, old maid. On the shelf. Maiden auntie. Take your pick. Regardless of the term, I have difficulty conversing with gentlemen in a social context. They dislike my candor. I dislike their condescension." She frowned at him. "Or their pity."

"I see."

Outside the conductor called "All aboard," and the train soon lurched into motion, while Leah squared off with the only man she'd ever encountered who was not intimidated by her. The only man who, instead of acting indifferent, inexplicably was all but *forcing* himself on her, when indifference would have been far simpler. Certainly more effective.

Sunlight streamed through the window over his tawny hair. He had a strong face, with broad forehead and well-defined bones. His nose was slightly crooked, and she wondered if it had been broken. Considering his rugged lifestyle, the likelihood seemed probable. Leah shifted in her seat a bit. Cade Beringer looked the sort of masculine man who would no more notice a plain bookish woman like Leah Sinclair than he would the air he breathed. Yet his behavior toward her ever since he'd pounced on her inside the waiting room belied his looks.

Leah abhorred contradictions. A lifetime of experience had proved the truth of her hypothesis about the male of the species; therefore Mr. Beringer must have an ulterior motive.

"Who fostered this impression of yourself?" he asked.

Leah blinked. "Reality is a hard but unavoidable teacher, Mr. Beringer. And unlike people, mirrors don't lie."

A comma of hair dipped over his wrinkling forehead. Absently he swept it back, his air that of a man waging some manner of internal debate. "God offers a different perspective on reality," he finally said. "And He doesn't lie either. Perhaps if you tried looking at yourself through His eyes, you might be surprised."

"Since God is responsible for who I am and how I look, I fail to see what comfort I could glean from that exercise." Leah glanced down the aisle. The conductor was a half-dozen rows away. "But your assertion reminds me of the other reason I'm uncomfortable around you. Benjamin speaks of you every now and then, you know. He very much admires your faith—claims you're responsible for changing his life."

"Leah…"

"You prefer honesty." She emphasized the word. "I'm providing it."

She dug into her purse and yanked the ticket out. "I'm satisfied with who I am. I'm satisfied with what I am. The manner in which I choose to view God is not the same as yours, but it doesn't invalidate my faith. It didn't five years ago, and it doesn't now. You tell me you're ignorant of the timing of our simultaneous visits to Stillwaters, but I confess that I find that as difficult to accept as your idealistic notions of God. Be that as it may, I'll accept these arrangements…as long as we agree to disagree about our religious views. And agree not to debate them." She drew in a deep breath, finishing flatly, "Otherwise, I'll find myself another coach."

"Don't trouble yourself to do that." His broad shoulders lifted in a comfortable shrug. "I wouldn't dream of arguing with someone over my friendship with Ben or Meredith. Nor would I appreciate someone interpreting my friendship with you as though their assumptions were the gospel."

"We are *not* friends."

Cade's slow smile broadened to a grin. "Like I said, I won't argue about it."

"Ticket, please," the conductor said above her head.

Thoughts churning, Leah waited until he'd moved to the next row, then turned back to Cade, her jaw set. He sat there, elbow propped on the window sill and his hand supporting his head, studying her with unruffled serenity.

You won't be so smug in a moment, Mr. Cade Beringer. She stared back, not speaking until he raised an eyebrow and opened his mouth.

"What are—"

"Giving you a chance to look your fill," Leah interrupted. "Now that you have, enjoy your book, and the trip. I'll be talking with Mrs. Moore."

She presented her back to him and proceeded to converse with Jane. But her spine felt as though an army of red ants were tromping up and down its length, and regardless of how charming she found the young woman across the aisle, she regretted the character flaw in herself that prevented her from sharing a…well, a *friendly* conversation with her seatmate.

Five

$\mathscr{A}$s the train wound its westward path through the Alleghenies, Cade enjoyed watching Leah Sinclair as much as he did the scenery. He admired, and was amused by, her ability to keep him at a mental distance despite their physical proximity. She was an interesting amalgam of a personality, almost motherly toward the sweet but feather-headed Jane, gentle with Jane's shy husband, Teddy. Stiff as an over-starched collar with Cade, then catching him off guard with her unaffected enthusiasm when he pointed out the window to a mother black bear and her two cubs fishing for their dinner across the river.

For some reason the train came to an abrupt halt some forty minutes after leaving Buchanan and ten minutes out of the last stop, Eagle Mountain. They were surrounded by mountains, endless rolling hills thick with forest, studded with patches of weathered granite boulders. Above them the sky was a deep enamel blue. The rains of the past few days might never have been.

Cade was about to make a teasing remark to Leah about the weather—it was almost half-past three—when the conductor, a barrel-chested man well over six feet, appeared at the head of the car.

"Ladies and gentlemen, may I have your attention, please?" He waited until silence descended, his mouth beneath the cap and white walrus mustache a grim unyielding line. "I regret to inform you that the engineer has received word via telegraph of a landslide. It has obliterated the track about four miles north of Eagle Mountain. Tool cars from Clifton Forge have been dispatched to clear the tracks, but the extent of the damage has—"

A chorus of questions and shouted demands drowned out his voice. The conductor held up a commanding hand and refused to speak again until the furor subsided. "I must ask you to exercise patience until we are able to assess the nature of our present circumstances. I will pass along information as it becomes available. For safety reasons, all passengers must remain aboard the train."

Pandemonium raged afresh as he made his way down the aisle to bear the bad tidings to the next car. After he disappeared, a number of passengers rose from their seats, some pushing their way toward the vestibules at either end of the coach car while others stood uncertainly in the middle of the aisle. Loud voices proclaimed opinions and solutions for the predicament with varying degrees of vehemence.

"Well," Leah observed practically, "I certainly would rather sit stationary in the middle of nowhere than round a curve and plow into the landslide."

Disappointment shadowed her small face, but her forbearance deepened Cade's respect. Across the aisle Ted Moore was trying in vain to console his distraught wife.

"What if they can't clear the tracks? What will we do, Teddy? However will we reach Stillwaters?"

"We'll be fine," Leah answered with a confident smile. "At any rate, I imagine we'll return to Eagle Mountain if they can't clear the tracks within an hour or two. There's an old coach road there that leads to Stillwaters." Her brow puckered. "I'm not sure of its condition. I believe it follows an even older Indian trail, and was used for hauling during the hotel's construction. But it's possible that a sturdy coach could be hired to—"

"The road's fairly rough," Cade interjected. "I traveled that way myself, on horseback, last year. It might be passable by coach, but I couldn't recommend it." In spite of the dampening pronouncement, Jane Moore's face brightened like a sunrise.

"Then we could still reach the hotel this evening." She was all but squirming in her seat. "Thank you for telling us, Leah! Ooh, why didn't the engineer remain in Eagle Mountain? We could have made immediate inquiries."

Cade waited for a pair of determined looking gentlemen to stalk between them down the aisle. Two rows ahead, a red-faced woman loudly proclaimed she wanted off this train *at once*. "It's going to be difficult riding herd on frustrated passengers," he said. "But at least if the track is cleared soon, they won't have to waste time rounding people up."

"We must be patient," Ted said. "Like Mr. Beringer said, the track might be cleared in a little while."

"But it might be *hours*."

Leah shot Cade a disapproving stare that could peel the bark off a tree. She rose. "I'll see what I can do. We'll need to send some telegrams. Don't fret, Jane. We won't be sitting here for hours, I promise."

She fluffed out the voluminous sleeves of her suit jacket and checked the angle of her neat straw hat. A militant gleam burned in her dark brown eyes. She was scarcely five feet tall, Cade figured. His knapsack probably weighed more than Leah Sinclair. Yet she chugged through the milling, ill-tempered crowd with the same unstoppable aplomb as the burly conductor.

"I've never met anyone like her," Mrs. Moore said.

Cade might have echoed the sentiment, except he couldn't shake an uncomfortable niggle warning him that Leah's tenacity smacked of potential disaster.

⇜❦⇝

At four o'clock the conductor reappeared at the same time their coach jerked once, twice, then slowly began rolling backward. Stoically he informed the passengers that clearing the track would take longer than originally hoped. As Leah had anticipated, he announced that the train was returning to Eagle Mountain. Passengers with local destinations could arrange for alternative transportation rather than wait it out, if they preferred.

Shortly after that Leah returned. A hired coach should already be waiting for them in Eagle Mountain, she announced. Several other passengers bound for Stillwaters would be joining them as well. Somehow Cade was not surprised. If Meredith's youngest sister had been put in charge of clearing the tracks, the job would probably have been accomplished within the hour. His stomach muscles tightened. A clash of wills was inevitable between them, because he felt honor-bound to dissuade her from her ill-advised proposal. If the train tracks had suffered a landslide, who knew what they would encounter on the old Indian road? Eyeing her triumphant expression, Cade entertained little hope of success.

At sixteen minutes past four, while a score of irate passengers stormed the depot's telegraph office, Leah led the Moores, a party of three couples from North Carolina, and several lone gentlemen including a reluctant Cade, beyond the depot, over to a dusty road-coach drawn by four horses. The driver vaulted to the ground at their approach. He was young, with a swaggering walk and a narrow pockmarked face beneath his dusty homburg. Cade would have trusted him about as much as he'd trust a snapping turtle.

"You the folks who need to make Stillwaters this evenin'?"

"We are," Leah answered. "I requested an experienced driver and a sturdy coach."

"*You* did? Who'd have thought it?" He hooked his thumbs through his unfastened waistcoat and scanned the knot of would-be passengers. "Lester Turpin at your service. You won't find anyone who knows that stretch of road better than me."

The party from North Carolina was skeptical. Cade watched one of the women tug her escort so she could whisper in his ear; the other men's gazes slid from the driver to his dusty, battered coach. Jane Moore looked close to weeping. Leah's face was expressionless, but Cade sensed her dismay.

"Your self-confidence is duly noted, Mr. Turpin," she said. "What do you base it upon?"

Turpin's jaw dropped. "You serious? I don't—"

Cade quietly stepped up to stand beside Leah. The driver flung him a sour look, but Cade reluctantly gave him credit for at least a modicum of self-control. "You want a driver who knows that road, I'm it," he said instead. "Spent a year hauling men and supplies over that stretch to build that fancy hotel you're so desperate to reach by suppertime. I know the way better than an old Injun guide. Ask anyone in town."

He gestured toward the sky. "Sunset's a little over two hours away. Let me know when you make up your minds. And it better be soon. I can do that road after dark, but I won't like it." Muttering, he swiveled on his heel and sauntered off toward the depot.

Chin high, Leah faced the passengers she had gathered. "He's brash, and certainly unpolished. But he knows the road, and I have every confidence he'll be sufficient for the task. I, for one, intend to risk it." The corners of her mouth flickered. "Assuming the coach is sounder than it looks. I'll verify its road worthiness now, before Mr. Turpin returns. Any of you are welcome to join me." Purpose in every stride, she marched toward the dusty monster of a road coach.

Within moments two of the men and the party of six from North Carolina elected to stay with the train rather than place themselves under Mr. Turpin's questionable care. The remaining two gentlemen, both unaccompanied, decided to risk the trip. Nathaniel Covington introduced himself after a rueful glance at the coach, and his pocket watch. He was a middle-aged lawyer from Washington finally joining the rest of his family for a summer sabbatical. "I'll risk an uncomfortable ride to an even more unpleasant night sharing a room or the depot bench while we wait for the track to be cleared," he said.

The younger man had just graduated from Princeton. He was meeting a group of fellow graduates who had arrived the previous day.

"Brewster Skaggs's the name, but call me B. W.," he said, pumping Cade's hand. "This is a bit of a gollyknocker, hmm." But he was cheerful as he loped off with Covington and the Moores to fetch the luggage.

Cade, still in possession of his own valise and knapsack, promised not to let the coach leave without them. Brow furrowed, he turned his attention to the coach, the horses...and Leah's relentlessly thorough inspection; within moments he concluded that he would not be able to change her mind. For some reason, Leah was determined to reach Stillwaters that evening. There was an aura of desperation hovering around her at odds with her temperament, as well as everything Cade had learned over the years about her character.

He wanted to know why.

"Mr. Beringer?" She'd returned to stand in front of him, fists planted on her hips. "I know it's not much to look at, but I've examined the wheels, as well as the axles, which are adequate. The seats are not in good repair, but a little discomfort for a couple more hours won't harm anyone. We should manage quite adequately."

"The party from North Carolina, along with three of the gentlemen, disagree. They bowed out of this little venture."

"Oh? Well, then the rest of us won't be as crowded, will we?"

"Leah," he hesitated, then shrugged. It had to be said; he had to try. "It might be more prudent to follow suit. After two days of rain, there's no telling what that road will be like."

Temper, and that puzzling desperation, flashed through her eyes. "Feel free to remain on the train yourself. I, however, am willing to risk it. If you change your mind after we leave, I'm sure you can scare up a livery stable and rent a horse, since you're familiar with the road."

Cade straightened, clasping his hands behind his back. "Don't like for anyone to differ with your judgment, do you?"

"I hope I'm not quite as arrogant as that." She twisted to look over her shoulder at the coach. "It's a matter of weighing all the options, and making a reasoned decision. I didn't say so earlier for fear of a ruckus, but I talked with the engineer while we were still aboard the train. He finally admitted it's unlikely the track will be cleared before midnight. Despite what you think, I'm not entirely comfortable with Mr. Turpin or his manner, but he *was* recommended by the telegraph operator."

"The horses are skittish. The bay, especially. And Mr. Turpin's placed him as the lead animal—a horse that isn't accustomed to the harness."

Leah stared at him. "How on earth could you possibly know that?"

"Observation."

"Well, he'll have a chance to grow accustomed. Besides, the horses aren't skittish, they're restless. Mr. Turpin wouldn't risk his life or those of his passengers by using unsuitable animals."

Cade chewed the inside of his cheek to mask his rising frustration. "And the condition of that old road? Has Mr. Turpin traveled over it after a heavy rain?"

"I'm sure it rained countless times over the course of the hotel's construction." Leah's brown eyes darkened until her pupils disappeared, and for an instant her lips threatened to tremble. She turned away. He could see the formidable control return as she squared her shoulders and stared into the nearby forest. "Mr. Beringer, I almost didn't come at all," she admitted quietly, still not looking at him. "I'm afraid if I take a room in a hotel here, I'll return to Richmond in the morning on the first eastbound train. But I…need to go to Stillwaters."

She shook her head. "The reasons needn't concern you. But I will try to dissuade the Moores, and the other two gentlemen. Your concerns about the driver are legitimate. I'm sure you're also right about the horses. I don't want to mislead anyone. But I—" She pressed two gloved fingers against her temple, then seemed to gather herself together again. "I need to go on," she repeated.

"Sometimes," Cade murmured, "people confuse their wants with their needs."

Leah turned to face him then, all trace of vulnerability completely erased. "Don't presume to pass judgment, though I can't say I'm surprised. Nobody passes judgment more quickly than those who flaunt their faith."

She swiveled on her heel and, skirt rustling in the packed dirt, approached the foursome heading for the coach with their luggage. Cade remained in the background, not wanting her to accuse him of adding undue pressure as well as being judgmental. He watched with a tight feeling in his chest as the four waved aside her clear warnings and dismissed each of her objections. For once, Leah's persuasive powers had not achieved her goal.

One by one they climbed aboard while Mr. Turpin stowed their luggage. Teddy Moore handed his wife into the coach, but the two other men had elected to travel outside. Brewster—B. W., Cade remembered—scrambled up into the top seat, followed by the more sedate lawyer.

Torn, Cade remained where he was while Leah allowed Turpin to hand her inside. This expedition was ill-fated; he knew it as surely as he knew the sun would slide behind the mountains to the west. He also knew that he could not walk away.

The driver climbed up to his seat. Left with no other acceptable options, Cade grabbed his valise with one hand and the side of the coach with the other. He tossed the valise inside and swung aboard with barely enough time to slam the door shut before the coach wheels spat stones and a cloud of dirt as the horses leaped into motion.

The heavy coach rattled over the tracks, and Ted wrapped an arm around his wife. "Hope the two gents up top hold on tight."

Across from Cade, Leah didn't say anything at all. Her face remained unperturbed as she grabbed the wildly swaying strap to maintain her balance. The coach lumbered around a curve, labored up a steep slope, then plunged into a narrow gorge choked with towering hardwoods and thick underbrush. Branches brushed the sides of the road-coach; within moments they were engulfed in shadows.

It was thirty-six minutes past four o'clock.

Six

As the coach rumbled along the old road, Leah concentrated on keeping her balance, her dignity, and her confidence. The road, packed with sand and gravel, had been hacked into the steep shoulder of a hill. It was also an instrument of torture. Leah was amazed that none of the gentlemen traveling topside had been flung into the trees. Through the window she could hear occasional bursts of conversation punctuated by cheerful curses when they hit the deeper ruts. The whiff of cigar smoke mingled with the stale odor of mildew and Jane's lilac-scented toilet water.

Seated next to Leah, Jane hugged Teddy's side while he kept one arm braced about her shoulders. Whenever a particularly obnoxious jolt catapulted them sideways, everyone held on to whatever support they could find. Cade sat alone on the opposite seat, directly across from Leah, his gaze fixed on the open window in an attitude of vigilance. He spoke little, and then only in response to a question or remark offered by one of the Moores. Leah might as well have been a piece of the luggage, not, of course, that she cared whether he talked to her or not.

"What *are* you looking at?" she finally asked. "You can't see the road ahead, after all."

"I'm watching for protruding branches that might poke through the window," he answered calmly. "Knew a man who lost an eye that way."

Leah blinked. "Oh." Before she caught herself, her gaze darted toward the window inches away from her face. The whispery voice inside her head had risen in volume over the past hours, direly proclaiming her monumental lapse in judgment back in Eagle Mountain. For some reason, Cade Beringer seemed to have that effect on her.

45

Since when have you shifted your mistakes onto others' backs, Leah Sinclair?

Teeth gritted, she managed a smile and dignified nod, thanking Cade for his diligence. She might be bruised from stem to stern, she might regret her course of action for the rest of the summer at the very least, and she might deplore the enforced intimacy with this man…but she would at least maintain her dignity.

"Whoa, there! *Whoa!*"

The coach skidded, rocked, then jerked to a teeth-rattling standstill. Leah slammed backward against the seat cushion, then hurtled forward, unable to keep hold of the strap. Two strong hands shot out, closing over her shoulders in an uncompromising grip. Before she found her breath, Cade was easing her back onto the seat.

"You all right?"

She nodded. After a moment she remembered to add, "Thank you."

"What's happened?" Jane asked, peering owl-eyed past her husband through the window on his side, where an unforgiving sandstone slab posed a scant six inches from Teddy's ear. "Why have we stopped?"

"Probably not to admire the scenery." Leah surreptitiously rubbed her left knee, which had banged the door handle.

Cade studied her, a frown developing between his eyes. "Why don't I—"

The door wrenched open, and Mr. Skaggs, the young Princeton graduate, thrust his head through the door. "Rockslide up ahead," he announced, his face flushed with excitement. "Road's completely covered."

Lester Turpin dropped to the ground behind Brewster. "Everyone out of the coach. We got to back up a ways."

Leah watched an indefinable look darken Mr. Beringer's face, but without comment he swung out, then turned to help Jane and Leah.

Cigar clamped between his teeth, Mr. Covington, the gray-haired gentleman from Washington, climbed down and joined them, a troubled frown creasing his broad forehead. "Looks bad," he commented, then after glancing at Jane added, "but let's not jump to conclusions."

He touched the brim of his hat and strode after the other men, who had gathered at the base of the landslide. Jane and Leah remained at the coach, listening to the men's voices rise in volume as a debate ensued about what to do.

Jane looked scared. "What *will* we do? We can't turn around. This road is too narrow."

"Well, it is a bit of a muddle," Leah agreed, "but we'll work it out."

"We should have stayed with the train, shouldn't we?" Jane's hands twined together as her eyes glistened with tears. "I never should have insisted. I—"

"It's there, I tell you!" Lester's voice exploded over the others, and the two women turned their attention toward the cluster of men. "We only need to back the horses a quarter of a mile. We passed by it not ten minutes ago."

More arguing followed, but Leah could tell from their expressions that Lester Turpin's solution remained the most viable. In spite of herself, her gaze moved beyond the clutch of men to Cade, who instead of endless debate had busied himself with calming the horses. Leah picked her way along the spongy road until she reached him, waiting quietly until he turned to her.

It was difficult, but she managed a smile. "Would you like your pound of flesh now, or later, Mr. Beringer?"

His reciprocal smile did not reach his eyes. "I'll settle for a safe arrival at Stillwaters, for all of us, hmm?"

It took awhile to back the coach and four jittery horses several hundred yards to the secondary trail. When Leah caught sight of it, fresh alarm jangled her nerves, though for Jane's sake she maintained what she hoped was a composed expression.

"Trail's pretty narrow." Cade's voice sounded noncommittal.

"It's wide enough for the coach, or I never would have suggested it." Lester glared at him. "You ever been on it?"

"No, I haven't. Have you ever taken this size coach over it, Mr. Turpin?"

The driver's face turned the color of old brick. "Sunset's less than an hour away by my reckoning. We got no more time for yammering." He stomped off and heaved himself back into the driver's seat.

Soberly the passengers trooped toward the coach.

Leah put a tentative hand on Cade's forearm. Beneath her fingers the muscles felt unyielding as the handle of her father's ax. "Please don't," she murmured. "Anything you say will just make him angrier. We'll be all right."

For a moment longer Mr. Beringer remained unmoving, his stance poised for battle. Then he blinked. "You're probably right. After you," he murmured, handing her up into the coach.

Shadows had deepened. Now it was Leah and Cade's side of the coach pressed mere inches from a solid wall of lichen-covered boulders. Teddy's side overlooked a steep drop-off that made Leah grateful to be sitting on the other side. Every so often the panels scraped against the stones. Leah sat with her gaze fixed on a dangling tufting button in the back cushion next to Cade's ear, and tried to imagine Meredith's reaction when she finally arrived at Stillwaters. Guilt was not an emotion Leah indulged overmuch, and she didn't like at all the sick stomach sensation it engendered. Why wallow in blame? she'd always counseled her sisters. If Jesus had forgiven all our sins, past, present, and future, then wasn't it more useful to acknowledge a mistake, then press on with one's life?

She decided that, in the future, she would adopt a more tolerant attitude toward those suffering from that particular emotion.

The coach rounded a curve. The rear left wheel skidded as the soggy dirt underneath it collapsed, throwing everyone sideways. Leah grabbed the strap to keep from squashing Jane. Her palms were slippery, she realized as she grappled with the cloth. Through the windows she heard the snap of the whip, and Lester's voice shouting to the horses. Then they were around the curve, the coach jolted back onto the road, and a thick silence descended inside.

It was broken when Jane began to sniffle. "I'm sorry," she took the handkerchief Teddy handed her, "I'm just—This is our wedding trip, and…" Her hand lifted in a helpless wave before she buried her face in her husband's shoulder.

Leah sat back, covertly rubbing her bruised elbow, forcing herself to focus on that twinge of pain to avoid her own anxieties.

"We'll be all right," Cade said. "Try not to be afraid. God's not going to abandon us in the wilderness."

"One might argue, Mr. Beringer, that He already has," Leah commented with a rueful smile as another bump knocked her hat askew. "Or perhaps it would be more appropriate to observe that we are the ones who—"

A shrill neigh cut her off midsentence. The coach stopped, rocking dangerously.

"Whoa! *Whoa!*" Lester's voice rang out, desperation tangled with anger.

Panicked squeals and snorts rang out in the twilight; the coach veered sideways, slamming against the wall of the mountain, splintering the door next to Leah and Cade.

"Hang on!" she heard a man's voice yell, just as the coach lurched forward, then backward. "Rabbit spooked the—"

Without warning the left front and rear wheels skidded off the track. The coach tipped sideways. There was the awful sound of cracking wood.

We're going to plunge over the side, Leah thought, a curiously detached calm settling over her. She was about to die… God *had* abandoned her.

"*Jump!*" Cade threw open the smashed door. His hands closed over Leah's arms, and she felt herself being propelled into space.

She landed on her hip, then rolled in a welter of skirts and useless limbs until her body smacked into a boulder with a force that took her breath. Disoriented, she tried to rise, but dizziness overwhelmed her, and for some reason her legs refused to function. Blinking, she lay in a pile of earth and wet leaves while the twilight exploded into screams and shouts and splintering wood.

The horses were screaming—or maybe it was one of the men. The coach tilted at a precarious angle. Cade slid across the seat, grabbing the doorjamb with one hand and bracing his legs against the tilting floor. Dirt and debris clogged the air, but he could still see Jane Moore, wrapped in a fierce embrace beneath her husband's arm.

"Jump out!" he ordered again. "Like Leah! We have to jump." Across the murky interior his gaze met Ted Moore's.

The coach tipped completely over the ledge. With the crack of a pistol shot the axle snapped. Strength flooded Cade's muscles. Clarity of purpose filled his head. Even as Ted shoved Jane upward, Cade wrapped his arm around her waist and flung her through the door. Then he turned back and reached toward Ted. "Hurry!"

His face slick with sweat, the younger man lunged upward, his fingers clamping around Cade's wrist.

Cade set his jaw. They were not going down with the coach. Muscles corded as he lifted the other man until Ted's free hand curled around the remains of the doorjamb and his scrambling feet braced against the tilted floorboards. The coach plunged down the hill, gaining speed with each second. Breathing hard, sweat pouring down his face, Cade shoved Ted from the coach, then threw himself out, tumbling over and over like a stone in an avalanche until he managed to flatten his body. His flailing hand latched on to the sinewy base of a bush. With a jerk that sent fire up his abused arm he came to a halt, dazed, breathless, and bruised. But alive.

Below him the coach flipped completely over, rattling and shuddering its way down the mountain. Cade lurched to his feet, staggered, and had to drop back to his knees until a wave of vertigo passed. The others riding topside…were they all right? Had they been able to jump to safety as well? *Merciful Father*… On his knees and utterly helpless, Cade witnessed the coach's final destruction as it catapulted toward the bottom of the ravine, crashing against trees and boulders in its deadly descent. Luggage and the battered pieces of the coach tumbled everywhere. Cade watched in horror as he caught a glimpse of Nathaniel Covington, covered with blood, one arm dangling, disappear in a boiling sea of dirt and mangled seats and shards of wood.

With a final burst of noise, the remains of the coach disintegrated against a stand of hardwoods near the bottom of the steep hill.

Seven

*S*ilence enfolded Cade, thick as the cloud of dust spiraling into the late afternoon shadows.

He staggered to his feet again, survival instincts pouring over the shock, filling him with strength. Prayer beat steady time with his pulse, and bound him within a merciful calm to face what lay ahead. He was battered and winded, but uninjured; *the others,* he thought even as his mind flinched from the possibilities. *Have to take care of the other passengers.*

"Mr. Beringer?"

His head whipped around. Enormous eyes almost black in a bone-white face, Leah Sinclair clumsily descended the torn-up slope. "Mr. Beringer…" she repeated, seeming unable to continue.

Cade hastened to reassure her. "I'm all right," he called. "Just winded, a few bruises. Careful!" he warned when she took an awkward step and almost lost her balance.

Seconds later she skidded to a halt in front of him, words tumbling forth in a flow of incomplete phrases. "We have to help Mr. Covington… I saw… But you…saved my life, the Moores. They're b-back up the hill. Mr. Covington…" Her voice dried up. "We have to try to—" She started to move past Cade, who caught her arm.

"Are *you* injured anywhere I can't see?" he asked. "Leah, look at me. We'll go after the others, but first tell me if you yourself are hurt, other than scrapes and bruises."

"I'm not injured."

She tried to pull away, her gaze on the settling cloud of dust at the bottom of the ravine. Cade hesitated only an instant before swiftly running his hands over her shoulders and arms. He ignored Leah's muffled protest. Her expression told him she was shocked, but not prostrate, and he drew in a quick, thankful breath.

"Mrs. Moore…I think she hurt her ankle," Leah whispered.

Cade glanced behind them, back up the slope where the Moores were sitting on the ground with their arms wrapped around each other. They were conscious and upright. For the moment they could take care of each other. Ted lifted a hand, waving him on. Relieved, Cade turned back to Leah.

"They'll be all right," he said. *Four of them accounted for, and miraculously unharmed. For these mercies I thank You, Lord.* "Leah," he hesitated, bracing himself as well as warning her, "I don't know what we're going to find down there." He gestured with his thumb. "Will you—"

"I can do whatever I have to." Her bottom lip trembled, then firmed. "We need to hurry."

Without another word Cade clasped her forearm, supporting her as together they picked their way down the slope. Beneath his fingers her bones felt delicate, her frame slight. A bruise was darkening on her right temple, and he'd already noted her scraped palms. But if Cade had had to choose which of the passengers to have by his side at this moment, Leah Sinclair would have been at the top of his list.

"Did you see the driver, or the Princeton fellow—was his name Skaggs?" Cade leaned to retrieve a crumpled piece of cloth from a smashed bit of shrubbery. The piece of cloth turned out to be a shawl. He tucked it beneath his arm.

"Mr. Turpin's all right, I think," Leah said. "I heard him yelling, after you threw me out of the coach." There was a pause, and Cade heard her swallow. "I'm not sure about Mr. Skaggs. If he…if he…"

"Don't think about it right now. We'll do what we have to do, and pray for the strength, whatever we find."

There was no sign of either Lester Turpin or Mr. Skaggs, but Nathaniel Covington lay in a pool of blood, half buried beneath the mangled remains of one of the coach's topside seats. Cade ordered Leah to stay back. She ignored him.

"It's my fault," she said in a dull voice. "I have to help. This is all my fault."

"Don't, Leah."

Together they cleared aside wreckage, then knelt by the bloodied form of the man who was either unconscious—or dead.

"He's alive," Cade murmured after a moment, elation swelling upward in a surging tide, filling him with renewed strength. "Leah, he's still alive."

"His arm is broken, and at least one leg. And there's a lot of blood—it's soaked through both his shirt and waistcoat."

"I can set the broken bones, but we need to stop the bleeding first."

Pale as a milkweed pod, Leah silently worked beside him, not flinching from the blood, though the wound to Covington's side, a long but shallow gash, proved to be less serious than the blood indicated. Nor did she flinch from the gruesome task of helping Cade set the bones. She did whatever he asked of her, often before he framed the request. Within moments they were able to move the lawyer to a cleared spot of ground. Leah folded the shawl up as a pillow, while Cade draped torn curtains from the coach windows over Covington's torso. He fashioned another strip as a sling for the broken arm.

"Hey! Hey down there!" Lester Turpin appeared far above them, at the top of the ravine. He descended the chewed-up hillside, pausing beside the Moores for a moment, then clambered the rest of the way down, coming to a halt in front of Cade. He was breathing hard, and beneath a day's growth of beard his complexion was ashen. "What a blamed mess. Horses like to have tore my arms out of the sockets. Blamed rabbit spooked 'em. I managed to jump when the coach went over the edge, but the fool horses got away when the axle snapped." His gaze drifted over Mr. Covington. "In a bad way, is he?"

"He'll live. Have you seen the young man? B. W. Skaggs?" Cade asked.

"The Princeton high-stepper? Jumped before me. He's still chasing after the horses. I told him I needed to check my passengers. Couple up the hill are all right, but the gent told me the little woman's got a gimpy ankle."

"I'll check her," Leah volunteered beside him. She took a step, then stopped, head bent, her pose resembling that of a lost child. "My hands. They're all bloody. I'll need to clean them somehow."

"I hear water beyond that strip of woods," Cade murmured, a frown growing as he studied Leah. "Mr. Turpin, it's pretty obvious we'll be spending the night here. How about if you start clearing us out a campground, while I check out the water situation?"

"Who put you in charge, I'd like to know."

Cade suppressed a terse retort, and scraped together a smile. "No one. You prefer to check out the water, while I clear the ground, then? If so, before you go we need to scrounge around for something to use for a washcloth, so Miss Sinclair and I can clean up a bit."

After a tense moment Turpin muttered an expletive beneath his breath. "I'll fetch water. Got me a thirst worked up, chasing them fool horses." He stomped over to a suitcase that had burst open and spilled most of its contents, grabbed a handful of cloth, and stalked off through the trees.

Cade released a pent-up breath, forcing himself to relax as he turned to an unnaturally silent Leah. She neither spoke, nor even acknowledged him, just stood motionless, staring toward Mr. Covington's recumbent form. *All right, then.* Watching her face, Cade reached for the blood-smeared hand curled in a tight ball at her side. It was icy, but when he wormed his thumb beneath her fingers to pry open the fist she pulled free and tried to turn away.

"Don't concern yourself with me. I'm fine."

A great horned owl swooped up from the trees, no doubt intent on its evening meal. Leah gasped, recoiling as though she herself were the bird's prey.

"Easy, easy," Cade said, recapturing her cold hand. "He won't hurt you."

"I know that." Her voice was small, brittle. She tugged her hand again. "You need to clear some ground. I'll help, until Mr. Turpin returns."

"In a moment. You're awfully pale. Sure you're all right?"

"I told you I am." Once again she attempted to free her hand.

Cade held her still. Sunset had turned the sky overhead a glowing burnt orange, lending enough light to ensure that she had suffered no serious blows to the head, despite the swelling bruise. The anxiety she was trying so hard to hide was another matter. "Mr. Covington will be all right. Fair amount of pain, perhaps, and certainly uncomfortable. But at least he's alive. We made a good team, didn't we?" He paused, then added softly, "I carried your brother-in-law a half a dozen miles down a mountainside once, remember? I'll take care of you, Leah Sinclair. You're not alone, and you don't have to do everything by yourself."

For a fraction of a second her lips trembled. "I should," she whispered. Resolutely she stepped back, and this time Cade let her retreat. "What happened here is my fault. If I hadn't been so desper—*determined* to reach Stillwaters tonight, this wouldn't—"

She might have changed the word, but Cade had already recognized that it was in fact desperation that had precipitated Leah's every action since the train was halted by a landslide. Someday, he resolved to find out why. Right now, however, none of them could afford the luxury of examining their feelings. "Leah, you're not responsible for the decisions of others. Don't do this to yourself. We're going to be all right, but we all need to work together, without anyone assuming blame or making accusations."

A brief flash of her old spirit flickered. "I know that quite well. And the only person I'm blaming is myself."

"Well, don't." Firmly he turned her around so that she faced the steep hillside. "Go on up to the Moores. Rest a bit. You can talk with them," he added hastily when her chin lifted, "verify that neither of them is in need of immediate doctoring. I'll bring you a wet cloth as soon as I can, and you can take care of Mrs. Moore's ankle, if her husband hasn't already done so."

"All right." She took a step, then stopped. "About where we can stay. I—perhaps Stillwaters is only a few miles down the road. One of you gentlemen could investigate. It might not be necessary to—to spend the night here."

Cade started to tell her that he'd already considered and rejected that notion, because he knew they were a hefty ten miles, possibly twelve or more, from the hotel, and at least that many from Eagle Mountain. It would be dark in less than an hour now, which made travel through unknown territory risky at best, even if one of them knew the way. But something stopped him, and instead he offered Leah a half-smile. "When Mr. Skaggs gets back here, we can have a group conference. Discuss our options," he said, keeping his voice gentle. "All right?"

After a moment Leah gave a short nod, then gathered her skirts and trudged up the slope toward the Moores.

Cade went to check on the lawyer and find the best site to make a camp, wondering how the stranded travelers would react to hard ground instead of feather mattresses, and unfettered nature instead of luxurious suites at Stillwaters Resort Hotel and Spa.

Eight

*L*eah had just finished wrapping Jane's ankle in torn strips of petticoat when Brewster Skaggs hailed them from the road above. Moments later he joined them, winded, dripping with sweat, and frustrated.

"Phew. I say, I must have run a couple of miles, but those idiotic horses never slowed down. Glad to see you two ladies escaped all right," he said with a nod. "What a state of affairs! Never want to go through anything like *that* again. I heard the Viking—"

"Cade. His name is Cade Beringer," Leah said.

"Sure. Well, I heard him yell 'jump,' so I did." He grinned, revealing a row of crooked front teeth. "I know he was talking to you folks inside the coach, but seemed a good idea to me." He finally paused, glancing around. "What about the others? Everyone else make it out okay?"

"Everyone but Mr. Covington," Leah said. "He's injured, fairly serious but not life-threatening if we can get him to a doctor within a day or two."

She was pleased with her tone. Calm, competent, not revealing in any fashion the inner turmoil. Incipient fear, and the corrosive guilt, were lashed firmly back in place. "Mr. Moore and Mr. Turpin are helping Mr. Beringer salvage our luggage. I promised to stay here with Mrs. Moore, who has a badly wrenched ankle." She paused. "The men could use your help, Mr. Skaggs."

"Call me B. W. This isn't exactly a dinner party." He tugged out a voluminous handkerchief, mopped his forehead and the back of his neck. "Can't say I relish hard physical labor after my mad dash, but can't very well leave it to the others."

57

For a moment he looked young, uncertain, more a student the age of the girls at Miss Esther's than a recent college graduate. Then he stuffed the handkerchief away and rubbed his hands together. "Guess I better quit stalling. Since I doubt anyone but our esteemed driver has used this road in years, there's no use in hoping for assistance of any kind to trundle along our way. Looks like we'll have to hike out."

After that helpful insight, Mr. Skaggs—*B. W.,* Leah reminded herself—agilely descended the rest of the hill. Within moments his figure was swallowed in the trees and rapidly approaching night.

"I wonder how much longer before Teddy will fetch us." Jane shifted about, grimacing. "It's almost dark." She leaned back on her hands to study the sky, her face a cameo-like profile. With all her combs scattered somewhere on the hillside, her ebony hair spilled in a dark cloud down her neck and shoulders. "My family used to go on lovely camping expeditions every summer. We had this wonderful blue-and-white striped tent that divided into rooms. The servants would unload huge wicker baskets full of utensils and food. It was great fun. I used to complain about the bugs, though."

"I've never been camping." Leah had fashioned a single braid for her own hair. Absently she pushed it over her shoulder, then felt beneath her sore hip to remove an annoying rock. "But it can't be too difficult, especially with everyone helping. Except you and poor Mr. Covington, of course. We need to organize a list of responsibilities and chores. Yours will be to rest your ankle for the night. Hopefully by tomorrow you'll be able to walk on it a bit. We should be able to hike to Stillwaters within, oh, a day or two at the most."

Jane was studying her in a peculiar fashion, or perhaps it was the shadows. Shadows… Leah stood and briskly shook the dirt from her skirt, ignoring the brief dizziness.

"Leah?"

"Yes?"

"You're not frightened at all, are you? It's amazing. I've never been so terrified in my entire life. But without so much as a ladylike swoon you helped Mr. Beringer save that unfortunate lawyer." She made a face. "I don't know what I would have done without my Teddy. I—well, I admire your bravery as well as your independence. Traveling alone, I mean, even if I don't understand it. I'm afraid if it had been me, I would have been weeping on Mr. Beringer's shirt front."

Leah caught a glimpse of movement in the ravine below and kept her gaze trained on that instead of looking at Jane. "Mr. Beringer needed help. And I've nursed my family as well as countless students over the years. Besides, it was the least I could do, since I'm the one who's responsible for—"

She caught herself barely in time. The dewy-eyed Jane didn't need Leah's churning guilt foisted upon her. Nobody deserved that. "Mr. Beringer has enough to do without having to nursemaid me as well," she finished firmly. "I was showing him I'm able to stand on my own, as it were, so that he felt free to attend more urgent matters that benefit everyone. That's practicality as much as independence. And speaking of practical, since you're an experienced camper, one of your chores can be to offer all manner of helpful hints when I try to cook us a meal, to keep me from looking like a bumblemuggins."

Jane brightened right up. "Of course I will. Though I doubt you could ever look anything but marvelously competent."

Leah choked back a half-hysterical laugh. Not only did she have to somehow quell this—this bushel-and-a-peck of guilt. She also had to invest everything in her power to keep Jane and everyone else, especially Cade, from learning of the fear that threatened to suffocate her. She wasn't like her sister Garnet, who actually preferred to wander about outdoors, drawing her flowers. Not for Garnet, reading a book in a cozy family parlor. Nor was Leah impulsive and adventurous like Meredith. On any given evening her oldest sister could dress like a fashion illustration from a ladies' periodical, reveling in her role as the wife of Benjamin Walker; the next morning she would yank on a pair of men's dungarees and join a party of guests for an all-day hike.

Leah was in serious trouble, possibly the worst of her life, and she knew it. There was no use prevaricating, because nightfall was imminent. In moments total darkness would surround her, unrelieved by porch lights or streetlights or lanterns or any kind of man-made lighting.

Bile burned the back of her throat; she suppressed a shudder. Jane was watching her, depending on her air of confidence. Control. And Mr. Covington would need to be monitored throughout the night. Cade couldn't be expected to nursemaid the lawyer by himself. Leah would be a poor specimen of humanity, indeed, if she gave in to this irrational fear rather than applying her will to the task of alleviating their predicament, a predicament she had brought upon them all.

The sun had disappeared completely behind the mountains. *Don't think about it, Leah.*

Matches, she realized, latching with the fervor on to the solution. Somehow she needed to unearth some matches to build a fire. Fires produced light, wonderful, comforting light.

A fire, however, could not be built on a steep hillside. "We'll need a level area," she announced firmly. "A dry, level spot to build a fire. The roadbed should suffice. It's high, and the fire can serve as a signal light as well. I'll climb up there to find a likely spot. Will you be all right for a few moments, by yourself?"

"Yes, of course. But, Leah—"

"I won't go far, certainly not out of earshot. If Teddy returns, have him give me a holler. I'll come back to share what I've discovered."

"What about Mr. Beringer?"

"I'm sure Mr. Beringer will be occupied with…doing whatever he feels needs to be done." Leah ended the discussion by heading up the hill. She refused to sit for one more minute, like a cowed puppy too afraid of its own shadow to do anything except wait for its master.

Twice on her clumsy ascent she tripped over her skirt and stumbled to her knees. The second time, she heard the distinct sound of ripping cloth. Muttering, she spared a second to staunch blood oozing from a cut on her palm. By the time she gained the top of the ravine, she was breathing heavily and sorely vexed with herself.

But at least the ground was level, so she no longer felt as though she were on a listing ship's deck, about to somersault to her doom. She was alive, relatively unharmed, in control of herself if not her circumstances, she reminded herself staunchly. And Mr. Covington would live. She would *not* have to carry anyone's death on her conscience for the rest of her life. All they would suffer was a night spent outdoors.

What if a snake slithered across the road, and she stepped on it because she could barely see the massive bulk of the mountainside a half-dozen paces away? Both the timber rattlesnake and the copperhead inhabited the Alleghenies, and their venom—

Leah froze where she stood, her pulse thundering in her ears. She was administering a scathing self-denunciation in the hopes of forcing her feet to move when she heard a scrambling, shuffling noise somewhere off to her left. Rational thought flew skyward like a flushed partridge. Leah hiked her skirts and fled in the opposite direction at a dead run.

"Leah!" A large hand clamped about her elbow, jerking her to a halt and swinging her around.

Fear, and instinct honed by years of her father's patient instructions, outraced thought by a fraction of a second. Leah brought her right fist up at the same time she raised her left foot, delivering blows to Cade Beringer's jaw and shin even as his identity registered.

"Ow! You little termagant, sheathe your weapons. Calm down." He grabbed her shoulders, holding her far enough away to prevent a repeat assault, and administered a light shake. "Leah, it's Cade."

"I know. Now." She waited until her heart returned to its normal location in her rib cage. "Don't you ever scare me like that again. I might have really hurt you."

"You did hurt me. I think my jaw's broken."

"You wouldn't be talking if it were." Though she wasn't sure about some of the bones in her hand. Mercysake, the man had the jawbone of an ox.

She caught a glimpse of white teeth, but his voice was shorn of any emotion at all. "Why did you run, much less attack? Didn't you hear me call you?"

After failing to come up with a reasonable explanation, Leah ran her tongue over her dry lips and admitted in a surly voice, "I heard a noise. By the time I realized it was you, I—" She stopped.

"I see. Remind me to congratulate your father the next time I see him. He's quite a teacher in the fine art of self-defense." He paused, then asked, "What are you doing up here, anyway? I told you to stay with Mrs. Moore."

"I'm not a trained hound, Mr. Beringer. And for your information, I was scouting out a level place for a fire."

"Already taken care of. I've even scrounged quite a bit of supplies from the wreckage, thank the Lord. With a creek on the other side of that stand of trees, we have all the water we need, and I found a good site for us to set up camp. B. W.'s gathering wood for a fire. Everything's under control, Leah."

A fire. They really would have a fire, with light. Blessed light. The relief tumbling over Leah was so intense for a moment she could only stand mute, staring up at Cade. All she could see of him now was the not-quite-comfortable bulk of his masculine silhouette, and the shining gold of his hair. "You found matches, then?" she eventually managed.

"Yes." She thought he smiled. "Mr. Covington regained consciousness for a bit. He was able to tell me that matches were in his pocket. Even joked about being the only smoker among us, and how we'd have to tell his wife so she'd quit nagging him about his evil-smelling Cuban cigars."

"Oh. Of course. Well, then…"

For some reason uncertainty shivered down her spine. She knew she was safe, that Cade Beringer would no more threaten her physically than he would take the Lord's name in vain. Yet for some reason, she sensed…warning?…and the unsettling notion that he was annoyed with her.

"Ted's with his wife. We'll need to help him get her the rest of the way down the hill, to the site where we'll camp," he said. "But I think you and I better get something out of the way before we join the others."

Leah stiffened. "What would that be?"

"We're in unusual circumstances, wouldn't you agree?" He waited until she concurred. "Unusual circumstances tend to create a different set of rules, ones that wouldn't necessarily apply elsewhere."

"Stop tiptoeing around the matter and tell me plainly, if you don't mind."

He made an exasperated sound, but answered her readily enough. "Fine. We're in a precarious situation. I'm praying that at most we'll pass an uncomfortable night, followed by a long day's hike tomorrow. But it seems prudent, and everyone else has agreed, for us to try to stick together unless we recover one or more of the horses. Since I'm the one with the most experience in wilderness living, it sort of fell to me to take charge. Mind you," he ended with a hint of humor, "Mr. Turpin wasn't so eager to load the honor on my shoulders as the others."

"And you're concerned that I won't be either, I take it?" Leah finished for him.

"In a nutshell. So, will you?"

It was logical, and inevitable. She didn't understand why she couldn't better control, or even moderate, her extreme defensiveness with Cade Beringer, but she would find a way to subdue it until they were all safe and sound at Stillwaters. At least there was a foundation of sorts, for they had worked in surprising harmony as they labored over Mr. Covington. "I won't challenge you," she said quietly. "As for leaving Jane, I was just trying to help."

"Mm. I'm relieved to hear it. But until we reach Stillwaters, you'll help more by waiting for instructions, instead of haring off on your own." He took her arm. "Come along. Let's—what is it? Why did you flinch?" Cade stilled, and in the hushed evening she sensed his heightened attention. "Leah, are you *afraid* of me?"

Yes. But I don't know why. Besides that, her palm was bleeding again, her knuckles throbbed, and her head hurt. "No, of course not. I'm just...tired. Perhaps a little bit goosey, as Meredith says."

"Goosey?"

"Nervous. Unstrung. Mercysake, I'm surprised we're all alive. I'm still surprised *I'm* alive." Flustered, Leah tried to sidle past him. "You wanted to join the others, so let's go. I'm sure there's still a lot to be done."

"Plenty. Are you hurt more seriously than you've told me?"

"No." She clamped her lips together, her gaze yearning toward the flickering flames brightening the bottom of the ravine. She took another, more tentative step.

Behind her Cade muttered something beneath his breath, then slid his hand under her elbow. This time Leah managed to control the reflexive withdrawal. In truth, she was grateful both for his guidance and for the reassuring bulk of his presence. The weight of the night was pressing around her like a pair of black-gloved hands pressing over her face; she swallowed, straightened her spine, and allowed Cade to guide her to the Moores.

To the fire. To light, light that could restrain the terror.

Nine

SINCLAIR RUN
JUNE 1895

*I*t was a fine starlit night, Jacob mused. The kind of soft evening when young girls dreamed of love, and young men dreamed of— He chuckled to himself. Well, when he'd been a young man, his notion of *love* differed a bit from the dreams of those starry-eyed young girls. He lifted the ax and brought it down on the log with a satisfying crack, splitting it neatly in two.

Nothing like chopping wood to keep a man fit. Jacob rotated his swinging arm, which these days tended to cramp a mite after an hour or so.

"Mr. Sinclair? Deacon's wanting his nightly game of dominoes."

"Aye, Effie, tell the lad I'll be along shortly." Effie Willowby had been the Sinclairs' housekeeper off and on for over twenty years now, yet the woman still insisted on calling him by his surname.

Of course, she'd only been his live-in housekeeper these past six years, since Leah left for college. Human nature being what it was, there'd been talk among the neighbors over their status, widower and widow, all alone in that big old house, which was one of the reasons Effie refused to call him by his Christian name, and why three years ago her nephew Deacon Willowby took up residence in Garnet's old bedroom.

Jacob split a half-dozen more logs, then called it a night. By the end of summer there'd be enough to last well into the winter. As he climbed the back porch steps with his arms filled with kindling, he spied Deacon hovering by the wood box.

"Can we play dominoes now, Mr. Sinclair?"

Jacob dumped the wood and straightened, wiping the sweat from his brow. He looked up into the hopeful face of the thirty-year-old man whose mind, like a broken clock, had stopped growing about the age of ten when he'd fallen from the roof and cracked open his head. "If you'll fill the rest of the wood box while I clean up a bit, I'll see about beating you three games out of five."

Deke smiled his slow, lopsided smile. "No you won't. I'll wallop you this time, Mr. Sinclair." He made his way down the steps, grabbed the handles of the wheelbarrow, and trundled an erratic path across the yard.

"You're good for him," Effie observed as she mixed fat oil varnish and some spirits of turpentine at the kitchen worktable, an unpleasant concoction she used to keep the stove from rusting. "Better than his own pa, I'm sorry to say. Ira never did want much to do with him, after the accident." She lifted the bucket and carried it across to the stove. "And his mother's no better. I'm shamed of the pair of them, and them my own flesh and blood. They treat him like a simpleton, a no-account puppy they have to tolerate."

"Deacon's still a child of God, same as you and me." Jacob strode across to the sink to wash up. "In some ways, I'd say he's closer to the Lord than the rest of us. Besides, who knows how he might have turned out, if his mind had grown up with his body? He's the faith of a child, Effie. The Lord didn't cause that awful accident, but I believe He managed to produce something mighty fine, in spite of it."

"Hmph. I'll remind you of that, next time he gets underfoot in your workshop."

"Now that's an altogether different matter, woman." He winked at her. "Except for that trifling vexation, 'tis a pleasure, having him around. A house this size needs to be filled with people."

"You still chafing over Leah spending the month in Stillwaters?"

"Wouldn't, if Garnet and Sloan hadn't taken a notion to hare off to Baltimore for two weeks, at the same time."

Effie sniffed. "And to visit Doc MacAllister's uppity mother, to boot," she said.

"You keep a civil tongue about Mrs. MacAllister. And there's nothing wrong with a father missing his girls, and his grandbabies."

"Piffle. Doctor Sloan invited you to come along. Don't think you can fool *me,* claiming you've too much work. We both know better."

"Effie…"

Unrepentant, the housekeeper folded her arms across her ample bosom. "Way I see it, you've every bit as much pride as Mrs. Hoity-Toity MacAllister. You balked about going along 'cause you don't feel comfortable rubbing elbows with all those rich folks who talk with their noses aimed at the ceiling."

Jacob rolled up the sleeves of his shirt, his movements impatient. "You don't leave a man much room, Effie. Let it be, hmm?"

Later, while he set up the game table for his and Deke's nightly ritual, he found himself reflecting over the housekeeper's words. It was true enough, he'd never cared for the superior airs of folk who believed their material wealth entitled them to look down on others less fortunate. He prayed that he himself would never be guilty of that particular sin, because, thanks largely to the work his son-in-law Benjamin Walker sent his way, his own economic status had increased dramatically over the years. Even the Panic of '93 that had devastated the Valley's already flagging economy had hardly hurt the demand for a piece of Jacob Sinclair furniture.

He'd had to hire and train a half-dozen journeymen and twice that number of apprentices; now he was saddled with a thriving business that included a three-story warehouse and factory in Woodstock. Jacob refused to work at the factory, though he did spend a day there once a month. Yet despite the quality and amount of work done in town, he still had to turn offers away.

'Tis the truth, Lord, wealth can be more curse than blessing. But he was human enough to prefer it over poverty. *Well, then, I'm grateful for the blessings and mindful of how swiftly possessions can turn to poverty.*

From down the hall he heard Deke's measured voice, telling his aunt that he'd stacked the wood and was going to wallop Mr. Sinclair at dominoes. As Jacob arranged the ivory tiles on the table, he also sensed, equally clear though inaudible, a gently chiding Voice reminding him that it wasn't the wealth that led to trouble, but one's attitude toward it.

"I'm ready." Deke lowered himself into the chair across from Jacob.

Thick strands of gingery-red hair spilled over his ears and forehead. Pale blue eyes darted from the dominoes to Jacob, sparkling in innocent delight. "You should be too tired to think, Aunt Effie said. That means you'll be easy to beat."

"Don't count on it, lad."

Deke's head tilted. "You don't look tired," he said. "You have a lot of muscles, Mr. Sinclair. Is that why you're not tired, after working so hard? Mr. Cooper's almost as old as you, and he complains every time Aunt Effie and I go to his store. Maybe it's because he's got skinny arms"—the slow crooked grin appeared—"and a lot more hair."

Jacob smacked his hand on the table. "That does it. 'Twill be three quick games this night, no mercy for you at all."

They'd been playing for almost half an hour in an air of intense concentration coupled with friendly sparring when Deke said, "I shouldn't have talked about your hair. I wish I could give you mine, Mr. Sinclair."

"You didn't hurt my feelings, Deke." Jacob reached across the board to lightly tousle the carroty strands. "It's true, I might spare a thought or two every now and again, wishing for a head of fine, thick hair."

"Like Mr. Beringer?"

"Aye. Though a Scotsman would prefer a different color, mind you."

Deke had met Cade only a few times, yet he talked about him almost as much as he talked about Sloan and Benjamin, or the neighbors he saw several times a week. What was it about Cade? Jacob shook his head, seeing in his mind's eye the quietly powerful man with his golden hair and gemstone green eyes. Deacon's unabashed hero worship of Cade Beringer chafed Leah like a chilblain, though for the life of him Jacob had never understood her aversion for the man. Except Cade—like Deke—viewed the world through a different set of lenses than Leah. Humor tickled Jacob's lips. Now there would be an interesting battle. His pragmatic youngest daughter squared off against the idealistic Cade Beringer.

And, because Jacob knew his daughters even though they were grown and no longer living at home, he had a fair idea Meredith just might have arranged for such a "battle" when she invited Leah to spend part of her summer break at Stillwaters.

"Why are you grinning like that, Mr. Sinclair? I just won the game."

Jacob blinked. "You snub-nosed scalawag! You certainly did, didn't you? Well, you won't have so easy a time with the next match. I'll be keeping my mind on the game."

He deftly gathered all the pieces and left his youngest daughter's fate where it belonged. In the Lord's hands.

Ten

ALLEGHENY MOUNTAINS

*E*ven if he was unable to enjoy it right now, there was nothing quite like a starlit summer night viewed from the cathedral of God's wilderness, Cade thought. At the moment, however, he was scouring the remains of the coach's interior for bedding material. The torches he'd fashioned from scraps of torn clothing and spokes from shattered coach wheels offered adequate but meager light, when used for scavenging purposes. He paused frequently to rest his eyes by focusing on the serenity of a black velvet sky illuminated only by stars thicker than shells on an untouched beach. *When I gaze into the night sky, and see the work of Your fingers...*

"Say, Mr. Beringer?" B. W. appeared beside him, his quick grin flashing in the darkness. "Ted and myself finished clearing the site and stacked some more firewood. Don't suppose you found anything we could eat. We're starving. And he's not saying much, but I think Mr. Covington's in a bit of pain."

"I know. But I'm afraid there's nothing to do about either of those till morning. Fill up on water tonight. That will ease the worst of the hunger pangs. When it's daylight I'll check the snares. I'll also be able to scout out edible and hopefully some medicinal plants, as well." He'd dosed the lawyer with the pain medication he carried in his knapsack for a variety of medical emergencies, but had used over half that supply already. *Sufficient unto the day,* he reminded himself, and smiled at B. W. "Don't worry. There'll be food for breakfast."

"But—plants?"

Cade's smile deepened at the doubtful tone. "It's June. Should be some berries around, along with mushrooms, wild onions. You'd be surprised."

"I'm already dumbfounded. We're all lucky you were aboard, Mr. B."

"Not lucky." He shone the torch over the neat pile of salvageables he'd been able to accumulate, picking his words carefully. "I don't place much store in luck. To my way of thinking, God had a reason, allowing all of this to happen. Perhaps one of the reasons I was here was to be able to help."

B. W. snorted. "Like to hear what poor old Mr. Covington would have to say about God's reasoning."

Inwardly Cade winced, but right now wasn't the occasion to defend his faith, particularly with a young man fresh out of college, primed to dismiss spiritual matters as so much ephemeral nonsense. On the other hand, B. W.'s frankness was easier to tolerate than Lester Turpin's barely veiled hostility, the Moores' hero worship, and Leah's brittleness. He ran a hand around the back of his neck. It was a lonely feeling at times, living his faith without compromise in a world peopled by doubters and scoffers.

Cade wiped his hands on his already filthy shirt and changed the subject. "How are the two ladies holding up?"

"Now there's a pair. I'll never understand the fairer sex," B. W. admitted. "At first Mrs. Moore seemed fine, even with her own injuries, and it was Miss Sinclair who looked green about the gills. Now it's Mrs. Moore who's close to the smelling-salts stage. I heard her carrying on while we were gathering wood and searching the wreckage. Wanted her husband, kept talking about how it could have been him trapped inside the coach. I felt sorry for poor old Ted and relieved I wasn't the one with a ring on my finger." He gave a mock shudder. "Makes a man think twice about getting himself shackled."

"Mm," Cade replied noncommittally.

"That Miss Sinclair? Not much to look at, but she's a sound enough head on her shoulders. She's the one who finally calmed Mrs. Moore down, started telling her about Stillwaters. I'll be interested to see if even half of what she said about the place is true."

Seconds before he reached them, Lester's rank body odor announced his presence. "Since the pair of you's jawing away, I take it there're no more chores. Nothing else to gather up? Fetch? Or maybe you'd like me to dig a hole or something, in case the old man decides to curl up his toes during the night."

"You know, Lester, it could have been you lying injured and helpless, dependent on the mercy of strangers."

The driver spat into the dirt, then poked a mud-caked finger at Cade's chest. "Could just as easily have been *you*, woodsman. Too bad it weren't." He stomped off, but spoiled his exit when he tripped over something in the dark and staggered wildly to keep his balance.

"Phew. What a bounder," B. W. observed. "Y'know, he seemed a decent enough fellow, when we were traveling along. Entertained us, told a lot of funny stories, 'bout when he was hauling men and supplies to build Stillwaters. He sure doesn't much care for you though, does he, Mr. Beringer?"

"Call me Cade. It's friendlier. As for Lester, well, he doesn't care for my taking charge. And I imagine he feels guilty." Like Leah, though at least her defensiveness was mostly civil. "I can't help the guilt. But when he admitted he hated camping and wouldn't know a pine tree from an oak, I didn't see that I had much choice but to assume responsibility."

"Well, I for one cheerfully dumped it in your lap," B. W. said. "Put me in a sailboat or a tennis court, and I'd give you a run for your money. Or behind a desk, balancing a ledger. I'm told I'll make a smashing accountant. Out here's another story. I'm grateful for your presence. But you might want to keep an eye on your back, come morning."

"When I'm in the woods, I always do." He clapped the younger man's shoulder. "Never know what kind of wild and surly animals are prowling about, just beyond the firelight, waiting for an opportune moment to pounce. One time—"

A small sound, like a hurriedly stifled gasp, caught his attention. Cade turned, his night-adjusted sight searching out the slight figure. "Leah. What is it?"

She hesitated, glancing from him to B. W. and back while she sidled over to stand close to the torch Cade had stuck in the ground. "I saw Mr. Turpin head over here," she finally said. "He's been…grumbling for a bit, and I thought…" Her voice trailed away. Shadows danced across her face in the fitful light, but Cade still saw the way her hands clutched her skirt. Heard her nervous swallow.

"B. W.'s already warned me about watching my back," he said, then added gently, "Don't worry about Lester Turpin. I'm sure he's mostly growl and little bite."

"I'll keep an eye on him myself, if you like," B. W. volunteered. He too studied Leah, a frown gathering on his forehead. "Say, you all right, Miss Sinclair? Not afraid of the blighter, are you?"

"I was simply concerned about preventing an altercation between Mr. Turpin and Mr. Beringer." Her voice turned stringent. "Growling dogs are unpredictable, regardless of their usual disposition."

Even in the dark B. W.'s smirk was unmistakable. "What would you have done if they'd gone at each other? Boxed their ears?"

"They're grown men. I'm sure a dose of common sense would have been sufficient. However, you, Mr. Skaggs, might benefit from such a disciplinary measure." Her chin lifted along with one of her tightly fisted hands. "So don't tempt me."

B. W. glanced sideways at Cade, the corner of his lip tipped in a smile. "No ma'am." He melted into the night, retreating toward the campfire.

Leah turned to Cade. "Well?"

Cade's brief amusement faded. He sensed that this display of pugnaciousness was deliberate rather than a reflection of her prickly nature, but he was too tired, and too preoccupied, to pursue the matter right now. "I'll walk you back," he offered. "Then I need to check on our patient."

"Yes. Of course. I—Is there anything I can do?"

"I'll let you know. You're a fine nurse. But I'm hoping he'll sleep. I gave him a hefty dose of the emergency stuff I carry. The doctor who gave it to me said it's a fairly strong sedative as well as a painkiller." He shrugged. "We'll find out. If you could continue to keep Mrs. Moore calm, that would help a lot. You've done a good job with her, according to B. W. I know Ted's grateful, and so am I."

He retrieved the dying torch and held it up, then without fuss clasped her elbow in a light grip and led her toward the campfire, holding the feeble torch to light their way through the debris and chewed-up earth.

"Cade?"

"Yes?"

"Are there—" She stopped. He heard her mutter something else under her breath. "Never mind."

"Are there what?" he asked, tightening his grasp when she would have pulled away.

"It's nothing. Nothing…"

"I promise not to laugh at you," Cade finally said in a soft tone. "Are you still worried about Lester, is that it?"

"No."

Patiently he waited without asking again.

"Wild animals," she burst out abruptly. "Are there really wild animals, in the darkness, waiting to pounce on us?"

Stunned, he realized that she must have overheard his jesting remark to B. W. Only Leah hadn't realized it was a jest. He glanced down. Her head barely reached the top of his shoulder, and he could have crushed the delicate arm he held through the strength of his fingers alone. Yet in all the years of listening to Meredith talk about her youngest sister, Cade had never once heard Leah described either as fragile or uncertain. Much less fearful. According to Meredith, Leah was a feminine version of David, capable of felling giants with a slingshot. Samson, with the strength of a dozen giants. She possessed Solomon-like wisdom.

But right now, she reminded Cade of a vulnerable child, desperately holding on to her dignity.

"There are always animals about," he told her now, keeping his voice matter-of-fact. "Most of them are far more afraid of humans than we are them. I was joking with B. W. Besides, I doubt if you'll even hear, much less see one tonight. They'll steer clear of the smell, and the unfamiliar."

At that moment the flickering torch died completely, plunging them into darkness, well beyond the campfire's light. Leah jumped, and Cade was standing close enough to feel the tremor that rippled through her.

"Leah." Just as matter-of-factly he slid his arm around her shoulders, bringing her stiff body close to his side. "Are you afraid of the dark? Is that what this is about?"

For a long moment she stood rigid within his casual embrace, her breathing shallow, too rapid. Then she inhaled on a deep sigh and released her breath in a slow exhalation. "Yes," she whispered. The simple declaration was striking for its candor. "All my life. I don't know why. But ever since I was a small child, I've been terrified of the dark."

Without warning she twisted in his arms to clutch his shirt front in a forceful grip. "Nobody else knows—not even my family. I want it to stay that way. Do you understand me, Cade Beringer? I will *not* allow you to divulge this, this weakness to *anyone,* do you hear?"

He covered the fingers fisted in his shirt with his own, keeping the trembling body close. He didn't think she even noticed. "I won't tell anyone," he promised. "But the Lord already knows that you're afraid, Leah. If you could only—"

She wrenched herself free. "I should have known you'd say something like that, but I was—" She bit back whatever else she'd intended to say. "Keep your pious prayers and platitudes to yourself. I was grateful for the comfort. Comfort, hah! Job's comforter, that's what you are. You might know about God, and you might delude yourself that you have exclusive rights to His ear, but you understand precious little about people."

She backed a step, her features nothing but a vague silhouette. "And nothing at all about me. Now if you don't mind"—her voice wobbled—"let's go back to the fire. I don't want to talk anymore."

Eleven

When they reached the camp Cade walked over to Nathaniel Covington, and Leah joined the others in setting up pallets on which to spend the night. From the coach's remains Cade and the other men had scrounged everything from window curtains to cushions; from scattered luggage the stranded travelers donated shawls and coats to spread over the collection of pine boughs Cade had gathered.

Leah's stomach churned, and her face felt hotter than the flames leaping skyward. Why, *why* couldn't she control herself around Cade? Never mind that she was choking on fear and guilt; right now Cade Beringer needed cooperation from everyone.

She was no better than Lester Turpin.

After several uncomfortable moments, Leah quietly walked across the cleared ground to where Cade sat cross-legged by the injured lawyer. She opened her mouth to tell him she would sit with Mr. Covington, but the offer died unspoken. Cade's head was bowed, and he was…yes, he was praying. Aloud. Feeling strangely detached, Leah listened to the deep voice, stirred in spite of herself. He sounded completely natural, as if every day he saved people's lives, creating calm from calamity with apparent ease. Moreover, he sounded as if he truly believed the words he was speaking. Though Leah knew she would be embarrassed if he turned around and realized she was eavesdropping, she could not bring herself to leave.

Was God really watching over them with loving-kindness and faithfulness? Perhaps so. The Bible claimed those traits as inherent to the Lord's divine nature. On the other hand Leah was equally convinced, after studying over the Hebrew nation's endless cycle of rebellion, repentance, and restoration, that God had merely allowed her own desperation to reach Stillwaters to reap the consequences. On earth, human freedom included the freedom to do the wrong thing, at the wrong time, for the wrong reasons—and end up in a desert like the Hebrews.

Or at the bottom of a ravine, badly injured and in pain like Mr. Covington.

Thanks to Leah, innocent people had been hurt, forced to spend the night on crude pallets fashioned from a motley collection of clothing and horsehair stuffing from the remains of the coach's seats. Hungry. Bruised, battered, and dirty.

Surrounded by darkness.

Leah wound her fingers together until her hands ached and bit her lip until she drew blood. When they bedded down for the night, the fire would eventually die.

If God wanted to teach her a lesson in humility, He couldn't have chosen a more effective—or cruel—way to do it.

"…and with the comfort of Your promises, and the presence of Your Spirit even now to guide us in this time of darkness, I humbly leave Mr. Covington in Your care. Grant him healing sleep, Lord, that he may better endure the journey. Grant us all the healing balm of a restful night. In the name of Jesus, amen."

In one smooth motion he rose to his feet and turned toward Leah. Somehow he had known she was there, and in a childish but unstoppable reaction Leah squeezed her eyes shut. She couldn't think of a single word to say.

"Leah?" Cade's hand closed over her arm again. For some reason the gesture no longer raised her hackles. In truth, an insidious longing to throw herself into his arms had gained momentum, doubtless in direct proportion to the rising intensity of her fear. Both emotions were irrational, as so many emotions were, but Leah was honest enough to admit she was losing ground against both the fear and the longing.

Briefly she pressed her fingers over the hand on her arm. "I didn't mean to intrude," she murmured. "I-I was going to ask if you'd like me to sit with Mr. Covington. I mean, I probably won't sleep anyway. After the fire goes out, I mean."

"I promise I'll let you know if I need you. He's drifted back off." His hand squeezed gently. "So will you. When your eyes adjust a bit to the night, you'll realize it's not quite so dark as you think it is."

"Yes, it is."

"No, it's not. Trust me, Leah. It's never as dark as you think it is."

He led her back to her pallet, keeping her so close Leah could feel the brush of his body as they walked; she didn't complain. "One last thing," he murmured. "Let go of the guilt, Leah. You've enough to cope with, without adding that needless burden."

"I'm the one who insisted, the one who made all the—"

"Shh," he told her, interrupting the protest. "I'll spare you the sermon, since you've made your feelings about such things plain. Just try to remember you're not in charge of the world, or responsible for decisions other people make."

"But I should—"

"Thank God for the good things. Try it. One of the best remedies I've found, for lighting up a dark night. I'll be back in a bit, to check on how you're doing."

He padded silently across to the Moores, and Leah knelt by her designated cushion, a bemused frown on her face. She would never understand this man. With an exhausted sigh she glanced around. Mr. Turpin was already snoring at the base of a tree, just beyond the firelight, rolled in the moldy blanket that had been stowed in the toolbox beneath the driver's seat. They hadn't found the toolbox or the tools, but the blanket had been draped over the crushed remains of some shrubbery.

B. W. had arranged a spot on the far side of the fire, away from the Moores in what Leah thought was probably a gesture of courtesy. Where did Cade plan to spread his pallet? Leah would not ask, though common sense dictated that he would want to remain close by Mr. Covington. He certainly didn't need to waste any more energy on Leah. Morbid fear was neither life-threatening nor physically harmful. She must simply endure as she always had. Her will would prevail over the fear and the need for comfort. It was bad enough that Cade was privy to her private humiliation, but even the fear was preferable to his polite refusal of a plea, or another gentle lecture. Worse yet—a look of pity.

In an effort to focus on something else, she let her attention wander back over to the Moores, with a half-formed intention of talking with Jane for a while. But Jane, calm now, was plaiting her thick black locks in a nighttime braid, all the while gazing dreamily into her husband's adoring face as though the two of them were alone in their sumptuous suite at Stillwaters. Leah turned away.

All right, then. She stared down at her bed for the night, and steeled herself for the coming ordeal, wishing without hope that the fire could burn until sunrise.

Suddenly Cade appeared. "Like to wash up a bit more thoroughly before you settle in for the night?"

The firelight outlined the strength of his profile, with its firm chin and slightly crooked nose, the cheekbones blurred by the beginnings of a honey-colored beard. His hair spilled about his ears and collar in shaggy abandon. When he smiled, Leah's unstable stomach gave a strange lurch. His gaze rested for a moment on her before lifting to encompass the Moores and B. W. "With plenty of water available, it's always a good idea to stay as clean as possible. Better for sleep, as well as hygiene. Ted, you can go with B. W. if you like. Take my canteen, bring some water back for Mrs. Moore, since it's probably better for her to stay off that ankle for the rest of the night."

"I'll just wait till morning," B. W. said. "I haven't been worn to a frazzle like this since the summer I was fourteen, when my father sent me to clean out our entire stables. Proved to be an effective punishment. I've been a model citizen ever since."

Jane and Teddy laughed, and even Leah smiled at his indefatigable humor.

"Must have been some prank," Cade said. "Be that as it may, under the present circumstances cleanliness is one of our most valuable tools." He paused.

With an uncomfortable twinge Leah realized he looked as exhausted as she felt. His clothing was streaked with stains, many of them blood, his jacket had been appropriated for bedding, and he'd used his cuffs and collar for some of Mr. Covington's bandages. The campfire's dwindling light deepened the lines of fatigue in his face.

"It's your decision," he finally said to B. W. "Unless you've any sort of an open wound, in which case I'll have to insist that you clean your-self up. We've enough facing us come morning, without an infected wound."

Even before he finished speaking, the younger man rose to his feet. He snatched up a torch from the stack arranged near the fire and thrust the bound strips of cloth into the flames to set it alight. Teddy patted his wife's hand, slung Cade's canteen over his shoulder, and the two men trundled off toward the creek, B. W. good-naturedly grousing about the lack of the amenities in this fancy hotel. Cade had melted back into the darkness, though Leah could hear him somewhere on the edge of the camp.

"I would like to wash at least my face and hands," she admitted to Jane. She dreaded the prospect of visiting the creek by herself, alone in the darkness except for a meager torch. But she couldn't bring herself to tag along after B. W. and Teddy. "If there's enough water left in the can-teen after you finish, could I share?"

"Of course, Leah. I'll make sure I leave you enough." She nodded toward the edge of the clearing. "What about Mr. Turpin?"

"He'll have to be the exception to the rule," Cade drawled as he stepped back into the light and approached Leah. "I'm too tired to risk a fight. And sure as sunrise any more suggestions from me would likely precipitate one. Especially if I woke him up to ask."

He looked down at Leah, the tone of his voice changing when he next spoke. "Under the circumstances, I think it would not only be safer, but quite proper, if I escorted you to the creek. All right? You don't need to go by yourself."

"I should say not," Jane piped up. "I'd certainly go if I were able, but not by myself. If you prefer, Cade, Teddy can escort her so she's not alone. Heavens, you could get lost in the dark before you traveled a handful of steps."

"I don't want to cause—" Leah began, but Jane cut her off.

"Now, Leah. Remember what you counseled me back at the Buchanan depot? About the heat, and ladies' clothing? Hang propriety!"

"I remember," Leah murmured, and tried not to shudder because Jane and Cade were watching her. *Lost in the dark.*

"We'll go as soon as the men return," Cade said. "Why don't you fetch what you need while I check Mr. Covington?"

After awkwardly thanking him, Leah chatted with Jane until Teddy and B. W. returned, dripping but with noticeably cleaner countenances. B. W. called a general good-night, then collapsed onto his bedding and closed his eyes.

Leah returned to her pallet to fetch her things and wait for Cade. She watched Teddy pour water from the canteen onto a square of cloth. Over the quiet crackle of the fire she heard the deep tenderness of his voice. "Here, let me wash your face for you, my dear."

She was almost grateful when Cade reappeared and held his hand out. Leah followed him across their camp into the trees, where earlier he had spent an hour clearing a path through the underbrush to the creek. Her skin chilled the deeper into the woods they progressed. When her teeth started to chatter, she tried to cover the sound with a flurry of words.

"It's amazing, isn't it, that your knapsack with all your supplies survived with little damage but a few dents, and that you were able to find it all in the wreckage."

"Isn't it?" Cade agreed equably. "Amazing, but not miraculous? Not an example of God's grace, His way of supplying all our needs?"

"Perhaps finding them might be construed as an example of His grace. But for the rest, I'd say it's more an example of your foresight and the nature of your profession. You spend most of your time in the wilderness, so it's only prudent, always having the necessary supplies with you."

"You're a provoking woman, Leah Sinclair. But I suppose you knew that."

"When a woman lacks charm and beauty and a sweet spirit, she makes use of what she does possess. I'm not provoking. I'm practical."

"Mm. Well, have it your way. Practical, you say. From what I've observed over the past several hours, you're also brave, resourceful, and kind. Far as I'm concerned, that makes you a beautiful woman. And sweet, for all your practicality." His arm dropped over her shoulders and tugged her sideways. "Careful, there's a low branch here," he said with exactly the same intonation, leaving Leah floundering between the need to singe his hair with blistering words, and the urge to bury her face against his shoulder.

They walked the rest of the way in almost companionable silence.

At the creek, Cade led her to a spot on the bank covered with thick meadow grass long as a mop, damp but not unpleasantly soggy, where the water ran scant inches from their feet. Stretched out on her stomach, for the first time since she was a child Leah experienced the pleasure of cool creek water running over her face and hands. She learned the frustration of trying to keep her clothing dry when she rolled her sleeves back to wash her wrists and at least her lower arms. The cold water stung her palms, but she thoroughly cleaned them and the cut on her arm.

"I've always loved summer nights in the mountains," Cade murmured when Leah finished and sat back up. He was sprawled nearby, his weight resting on the heels of his hands, face lifted to the sky. "Clear and cool as this creek, with stars so thick and bright a lantern or a torch isn't necessary. When there's a full moon, all white and luminous, I always feel as though I've been given a pearl of great price."

Because his voice had gone soft and dreamy, Leah found she couldn't take offense at the scriptural reference. If she was honest with herself, she'd have to admit that, for all the frankness in which he expressed his faith, Cade Beringer was a very…well, a very *nice* man. One of the few in her memory who neither demeaned her nor ignored her.

Infuriated her, definitely. Aggravated and confused her, certainly. But—since she was being honest—his imperturbability in the face of her barbs had given birth to a grudging respect for him.

"Why are you being so nice?" She made herself face him. While she might be a coward in the dark, she had never in her life avoided unpleasant realities. "Is it because you feel sorry for me?"

He quit contemplating the heavens and turned his head toward her. "You always did wade right into a matter, didn't you?"

"I've always preferred painful truths to polite fiction, yes."

"Ah. Well, this time the painful truth you're going to hear is this." He sat up, crossing his legs like an Indian and leaning closer. "Right now, I've more on my mind than puzzling out what I think about you." In a fluid move he rose to his feet. "But I will tell you it has nothing to do with pity. I'm going to wash now. Close your eyes, or turn your back. I don't mean to offend your sensibilities, but I'm about to remove my shirt."

"I believe I'll take the torch and return to camp. Remove anything you want to, Mr. Beringer."

Leah grabbed the torch he'd stuck in the moist earth near the water's edge, gathered her courage and marched toward the path that led back into the woods. She could do this; he deserved privacy. She wasn't offended, but after all she couldn't remain while he disrobed, even partially. She could do this.

"Leah?"

She stopped but didn't turn around. "What?"

"The torch is about to die. I wasn't sure you'd noticed."

Her heart convulsed. Leah passed her tongue around her lips, gaze fixed on the diminishing light as she silently retraced her steps on legs that threatened to buckle with every step. Lips pressed together, she stood rigid, watching the dying flame while Cade used the shirt he'd been wearing to wash his upper torso and face.

"I'm almost done, Leah. Try not to panic."

"I never panic," she retorted automatically, just as the torch fizzled out.

The sky was pressing down on top of her, the stars were whirling around her, through her. The night was a live thing, full of malevolence, crouching to spring, and she would—

Cade's face loomed in front of her, so close she could feel his breath against her cheek. His hand, warm, the fingertips slightly abraded, clasped her shoulder in a light but unbreakable hold.

"Easy there," he murmured when she leaped in fright. "Easy, Leah. I'm here. I won't let anything or anyone hurt you…it's all right."

He kept up a soothing patter of words, but she couldn't see him, couldn't breathe, couldn't think. *Can't see…* Nausea punched with a heavy fist. "I'm going to retch," she managed, too terrified to care.

"No, you're not. You're going to breathe. In and out, there's a good girl, slow and deep for me, Leah. Open your eyes. Look at me, you can see the stars, and the moon's rising, Leah. Open your eyes and look at the moon with me."

His hands were on both of her shoulders now, running up and down her arms, then caging her face in a warm grip. "Shall I carry you then? Back to the fire?"

"No! I'm fine. I can walk." Her voice rose, and she clamped her lips together. *Carry her?* She hadn't been carried since she was a little girl, clinging to her father's strong arms. A deep breath shuddered forth, then another. She pried her eyes open, jumping a little because Cade's face was inches away. "I can walk," she repeated, not realizing her hands were clinging to the soft folds of his shirt until one of his came up to cover them. "Oh. I beg your pardon."

"Don't be silly."

"You—You're wearing a shirt. A clean one."

"Yes. It's a bit wrinkled, but it smells better than the other one, and, as you observed, it's clean."

There was a smile in the words; the hands holding her were strong, sure. His solid bulk offered a security she couldn't help but respond to. The irrational panic faded, and Leah found herself relaxing even though that wretched torch had burned out. Somehow the night terrors lost their power to paralyze when Cade Beringer was beside her. "I'm afraid I've been nothing but silly since the sun went down. I'll do better tomorrow, I promise."

"Does that mean you're ready to return to camp now?"

"Y-yes. But if you—" She stopped.

"I'll hold your hand. I won't let go. All right?" He gently detached her fingers from his shirt, then wrapped his hand around them.

"I'll be fine in the morning."

"Of course you will."

Leah wished she could believe her own words. Unfortunately, though Cade might be at her side while they navigated this dark wood, when the campfire died she would be alone, wrapped only in her dirty shawl, a torn curtain from one of the coach's shattered windows—and her fear.

Twelve

Stillwaters Resort Hotel and Spa sprawled over two thousand acres of wooded mountains and narrow valleys. A half-dozen springs followed a ragged line up the northwestern slope of one of the ridges. The main hotel, a five-story structure built in the newly popular Queen Anne style, was situated just beneath the crest of that mountain, with breathtaking views of the ancient Alleghenies on all sides. A winding lane off the main drive led to a scattering of private cottages, men's and ladies' pool houses, bridle paths, and a concert hall that over the past three years had begun to attract artists of renown from all over the world.

The setting and the atmosphere exuded tranquility, dignity, and peace.

"It's almost midnight!" Meredith paced back and forth across the parlor of their bedroom. As with every hotel Benjamin built where they planned to live on site, he reserved half the top floor for their living quarters, with private suites at the opposite end for their personal guests and family. She stopped at the huge bay window and flung back the filmy lace panel, stabbing at the sky with her hand. "Look. Not a cloud left in the sky. The moon is up so you can see almost as well as if it were daylight, and the telegram said the railroad tracks were cleared three hours ago. All the other guests who were on that train have arrived. So where's Leah, Benjamin?"

She turned around, bumping into her husband, who for some reason had removed his tail coat and his shoes. "Why wasn't she on the stage? Where is she?"

His arms encircled her, and she allowed him to cuddle her a bit because, as had been the case for almost six years now, only Benjamin knew how to calm her temper.

"Sweetheart, Leah's twenty-five, not a helpless toddler. You've got to stop comparing her to little Sam. Whatever's happened, she can take care of herself." His hand burrowed beneath the hair at the back of her neck, massaging the taut muscles while he deftly removed hairpins. "We know she left Richmond, because she telegraphed from the station letting us know she was on the way as planned."

"Benjamin, my hair… We're supposed to meet the Corcoran party in a few minutes to toast their twenty-fifth anniversary." The halfhearted protest dwindled into a sigh when the elaborate pompadour collapsed in a mass of chestnut hair to spill around her face and shoulders.

"Hominy's delivering our excuses. I knew you weren't up to a midnight gala." The rough silk of the beard he'd grown the previous year tickled her neck as he brushed a kiss behind her ear. "Never quite perfected the art of dissembling in public, have you, sweetheart?"

Meredith punched his shoulder, then gave in and clung to his starched shirt front. "Something's wrong," she whispered. "I don't know how to explain it, Benjamin. But…something's wrong."

For a few moments he rested his chin on the top of her head. "Is this feeling of yours a bit of natural worry," he finally asked, "or the same prescience you experienced last winter, just before Sam broke his arm?"

"I don't know." Meredith pushed away, filled with a surge of restlessness.

It had never occurred to her that her youngest sister might not be impervious to harm. "I don't know! I've been asking myself that question for the past two hours. I've been asking *God* that question for the past two hours. I'm trying to listen, but sometimes there's nothing there."

She remembered vividly the anguish of caring for Sam, the helplessness of seeing her tiny son in pain. And there had been nothing she could do then but…wait. At the time she had railed at God for not protecting her innocent baby.

Her restless pacing brought her back to the window, and Meredith threw open the sash. It was a lovely night. Cool, only the hint of a breeze, stars lavished in glorious disarray in a sky the same dense hue as Hominy's skin. "Benjamin, have you ever, well…wearied, of the effort? Trying to hear God speaking to you, I mean."

"No more than twice a day, my love." He joined her at the window, looking big and imperturbable and, because she'd been married to him long enough now to recognize the look, patient. "You do know that there's little to be gained, fretting the hours away. I've sent telegrams to all the stationmasters between here and Richmond. Hominy's questioned the stage drivers. If necessary I'll send him back to the hotel station to flag the next train, even if it's a freight. But Meredith, try to accept that it might be morning before we hear anything."

Morning. Hours yet of more uncertainty. Abruptly Meredith bustled across the room, her fingers flying as she wound her hair into a Psyche knot. "I can't stay here. I'm going to go make sure Sam's all right, then I'll at least put in an appearance in the ballroom. And there's a stack of correspondence in the office that I need to go through myself. No sense trying to go to bed when I'll never sleep."

"Mrs. Walker, some husbands would look upon that as a challenge."

Even after five years, a blush climbed Meredith's cheeks at the look in his eye as he unhurriedly crossed the room. "Benjamin…"

He reached her and tucked her against his side. "Shh…I know you very well. Give me a moment to put my shoes and coat back on, and I'll come with you, all right?"

Tears welled in her eyes. Smiling, Benjamin wiped them away with the pads of his thumbs. "It's always easier to wait, when someone's with you," he murmured. "Besides, I've been needing to study up on my notes for that meeting in Clifton Forge next week."

"The one with the Allegheny Land and Development Company?"

Benjamin's jaw tensed; for a moment he resembled nothing of the easygoing hotelier. "Yes. The very same. Someone's given the impression that I'll grant permission to build an east-west line along the southern end of Stillwaters for the purpose of mine exploration. I need to disabuse them of the notion and find out who planted it in the first place."

Meredith crammed the last pin in place and lifted her hand to her husband's bearded cheek. "Cade should be along in a day or two," she reminded him. For the first time in several hours she was able to smile. "Cade and Leah, here together. Ought to be interesting, don't you think?"

"Meredith"—he crammed his feet into his black evening shoes without looking away from her—"you scheming little matchmaker. I just now realized." He shook his head, the frown he directed at her curling into a smile instead.

Meredith's reciprocal smile dimmed quickly. "Even if I was a scheming matchmaker, what good would it do at the moment? Leah's gone missing, and I wish I didn't feel as though tiny little hobgoblins were stomping up and down my spine."

The campfire had dwindled to glowing coals. Other than the wind sighing through treetops, the only sounds disturbing the night were Lester Turpin's snores, and Nathaniel Covington's occasional groans. He'd been sleeping fitfully, but Cade was encouraged by the absence of fever and the lawyer's own reassurances whenever he roused.

"Suffered worse than this in the War," he told Cade once with a grimace of discomfort. "Now, don't look like that, Mr. Beringer. The missus would be the first to tell you I've the constitution of a water buffalo."

"We'll be testing that assertion come morning. I can fashion something to transport you on, but I can't promise it will be comfortable."

Covington actually chuckled. "Don't worry about that. I'm grateful to be alive. Pain's a much more desirable companion than a cold grave." Moments later he'd drifted back to sleep.

Despite the circumstances, everyone else in their unconventional little troop had also fallen asleep within moments of bedding down.

Everyone but Cade—and Leah Sinclair.

Noiselessly Cade prowled the outskirts of the cleared area. His thoughts were somber as he gathered splintered panels of wood from the coach's remains, with which he planned to build a fire that would burn through the night.

An hour ago, he'd watched Leah paste on a confident smile and whisper good night to him before lying stiffly down on her pallet. It had required considerable discipline to keep from offering to arrange his pallet next to hers and hold her hand through the night to keep her fear at bay. She would never have allowed it, of course. For Leah, far more than an offense against propriety, such a concession would be an open admission of failure.

For a while he'd hovered nearby, creating plausible chores in a pretense of busyness, aware without seeing her face of her struggle to control the fear. As long as flames licked upward, offering light, she lay there quietly enough, hands neatly tucked beneath her chin while she watched the fire, eyes dark and unblinking. But by the time the fire dwindled to embers, she was visibly trembling, and one fist was crammed over her mouth.

He simply couldn't ignore her and call himself a man.

"I'm going to fetch more fuel," he told her. "Any rustling noises you hear will be me, all right?"

Without giving her time to answer, he'd left. Now, arms laden with wreckage and some of the larger logs B. W. had collected earlier, Cade picked his way beyond the gaunt ruins of the coach. Chopping everything up would be a challenge, though he was more concerned about the noise than about hacking off his own foot. His night vision was excellent, however, and after two decades so was his skill with a hatchet. He paused to offer a thankful prayer that he'd been able to retrieve his knapsack from the wreckage. Twenty minutes later he was back at camp, overlaying the embers with chunks of freshly split wood.

"Cade?"

He glanced down at the small, still mound of clothing that was Leah. "Hmm?"

"I would have managed." With a soft plop, a piece of board ignited. Flames leaped skyward, allowing Cade to glimpse terrified eyes and bloodless lips. "But—thank you."

"You're welcome, Leah."

"You're bleeding."

He glanced down. Glass from one of the shattered windows had made a long cut on his forearm; a jagged remnant from one of the panels had peeled some skin from the back of his hand. "Just scratches. I've endured worse. Don't worry. I'll take care of them before I bed down."

She sat up. "I feel responsible," she whispered.

"Well, you're not, any more than you were responsible for the rabbit that spooked the horses."

"Should I check Mr. Covington?"

"No. What you should do is go to sleep." Moving slowly so he didn't alarm her, Cade shifted until his knees bumped into the edge of the cushion where Leah sat. Then he placed his hands on her shoulders, and gently forced her to lie back down. "Right now I'm the one responsible," he said. "Safety and everyone's well-being rests on my shoulders, remember. Not yours."

While he talked he set himself to stoking the fire and within moments had created a slow-burning pyramid that should last until dawn. "As for the fire, the only other option was for me to sleep beside you and hold your hand all night. I chose the one I thought you'd prefer."

She gave him a look he couldn't define, then turned onto her side, away from him. "Mr. Covington needs you more than I do," he heard her murmur. Then, even more softly, "Or was it the option *you* preferred?"

It was a long time before Cade fell asleep.

He eventually drifted off in the middle of praying for guidance. Not only for the coming day, but how to decipher the uncomfortable emotional tumult Leah evoked in him.

Dawn, she thought, able to take a deep breath for the first time since the previous night. Instead of inky black, the sky lightened to more of a washed-out charcoal, spreading from the east. Soon the sun would creep over the top of the tree-covered hill above her, bringing full daylight in its glorious golden wake.

And the campfire still burned. One by one she stretched her cramped fingers, inhaling the tart scent of charred wood and the freshness of early summer morning. Leah would never admit to anyone that Cade's thoughtful gesture was all that had stood between her and hysteria.

Today, however, was a brand-new day, full of potential. Today Leah would prove to them all, especially Cade, that she was not some helpless kitten tossed among a pride of lions. Bolstered by her resolve, Leah extricated herself from the rumpled shawl and strip of curtain, and stood up. First priority of the morning was to check the status of their patient.

Mr. Covington was not only alive, he was awake. His face was lined, his hair matted with sweat, his complexion sallow, but he gave Leah a triumphant smile. "Looks like we all survived the night, hmm?"

"How do you feel?" Leah asked, resting her palm against his forehead.

"Oh, I've had better days, but thanks to you and that strapping young man, I'll live to hug my wife and kiss the grandbabies." He tried to shift and thanked Leah when she helped him find a more comfortable position. "Good thing the breaks were clean ones. Mostly ache like a—" He caught himself and apologized, finishing with a heartfelt, "But what I wouldn't give for a cup of hot coffee."

"I can't offer that, but perhaps if I wash your face and hands you'll feel better." She would enlist one of the other men to help with other matters.

The sun had cleared the ridge by the time everyone woke up, paid a visit to the creek, and was restored to wrinkled respectability. Cade returned from checking his snares with a rabbit he'd already prepared for roasting.

A bleary-eyed Lester emitted a gravel-voiced laugh. "Take back everything I said about you, woodsman." He rubbed his midriff, eyeing the limp carcass. "Got anything else? I could eat that whole critter myself."

"While it's roasting, I'm going to gather up some greens, maybe some berries. You can help."

Lester's jaw dropped. He fiddled a moment with his suspenders, then shrugged. He'd been as neatly trapped as the rabbit, and everyone knew it. "Fair enough, long as everyone else has a turn."

"Everyone will," Cade agreed cheerfully. "In my book, and the Good Book, if you want to eat, you share in the labor."

Contempt flashed across the driver's countenance before he turned away with a muttered comment that when he needed a sermon he could always attend a funeral. Leah winced.

"Tell us what to look for, Cade," B. W. hurriedly asked. He looked even younger this morning, with his hair tufted in wild cowlicks instead of neatly slicked down with pomade. Unlike the other men, his day's growth of beard was scarcely more than a faint shadow.

"How about if Leah and I cook the rabbit while you men do the hunting and gathering?" Jane's face was rosy from sleep, but in spite of her rumpled appearance and the scratch on her forehead, she looked as fresh and lovely as a Gainsborough painting. She flashed Leah a smile. "My ankle's much better, but I'd rather test its soundness on the walk to Stillwaters."

"Are you sure you'll be able to hike out, dear?" Ted hovered over her, his posture radiating anxiety. "What do we do if it's too sore, Cade? We can't haul Mr. Covington and my wife."

"Why don't we wait till after breakfast, cross that bridge when we come to it?" Cade glanced at Leah. "Willing to work your culinary magic this morning, Leah?" He looked over her shoulder to the others. "Miss Sinclair's one of the finest cooks I've ever met."

Compliment or challenge? Leah wondered. Either way, this was not the time to confess that she'd never cooked over an open fire. On the other hand, everyone in Shenandoah County raved about her rabbit stews. She inclined her head. "I'll see what I can do."

A short while later, while the men scouted for any other edibles, Leah helped Jane settle near the fire. The rabbit was roasting nicely on the spit Cade had fashioned, so she unbound Jane's ankle, and both women studied it with a critical eye.

"Swelling's down," Leah said, pressing with her fingers. "That hurt?"

"Some, but it's much better. You're a fine nurse, Leah."

"We schoolmistresses have to be a bit of everything," Leah probed a little more. "Can you turn it about?"

"Yes—oh! Ouch. Well, maybe not as much as I'd like—Leah! You need to turn the rabbit, or it will burn."

"That," Leah announced, "would certainly ruin my reputation as a fine cook. Probably also get me left behind in the coach's wreckage."

They laughed, spending the next half-hour or so in amiable conversation. The delectable odor of roasting meat filled their senses, and by the time the men returned, Leah confidently declared to Cade that she would take charge of all the cooking.

For a moment he pondered her in silence. "All right." His movements swift, practiced, he sorted piles of greens, mushrooms, and berries into piles. Leah eyed the collection in relief. From her studies she knew only a person with a fair amount of knowledge could glean the edible gold from the inedible dross in the wild. Thanks to Cade, there wasn't a poisonous berry or mushroom in the lot.

"I've got one skillet, and a coffeepot I use to heat water," Cade said when he finished. "We can let the greens and onions and mushrooms simmer in the skillet, and the wild ginger tea in the pot. If you can handle that, I'll go help the other men salvage the rest of our belongings."

Instead of leaving immediately, however, he remained by the fire, pondering Leah as though he wanted to say something else. But it was no longer dark, and she was determined to restore her reputation as a confident, composed woman, so she sent him a brisk smile and waved him away. "If I need help I'll ask," she promised, knowing she wouldn't.

Cade shook his head. "The rabbit looks and smells delicious," he said. "Ah...how about if I raise the spit so it will stay warm? Then you'll have access to the fire for the rest."

"I was about to do that. Since you offered, go ahead." She busied herself with the cache of edible foods, keeping her gaze averted until Cade left.

Within five minutes a pot of ginger tea was simmering, and the skillet's contents promised a tasty soup to complement the rabbit.

Then Leah forgot she was cooking over an open fire, and that her ruined traveling costume from Thalhimer's was combustible.

Thirteen

"*L*eah!" Jane shrieked. "Your skirts! They're on fire! Teddy! Help! *Teddy!*"

"Calm down, Jane. I can handle this. I just need to—"

Leah quit trying to talk to the screaming girl and focused on her own predicament. Trapped in a kneeling position by yards of fabric, with one hand she frantically batted at her smoldering hem, while with her other she struggled to maintain her grip on the pan handle. The pan tilted, sending its scalding hot contents perilously near the rim; with an ominous crackling sound a tongue of flame ate its way up fine blue serge toward her wrist. She automatically jerked her arm aside, then watched in mute disbelief as the pan full of greens, onions and mushrooms splattered into the fire—and her lap.

From out of nowhere hands closed around her forearms and yanked her up and away from the fire, then thrust her down, down to the ground again. She was being rolled in the dirt, Jane was screaming, men were yelling, yet through a blur of motion and distress and scalding pain Leah heard a man's voice. It was deep, calm. Authoritative. She latched on to that voice, recognizing it as Cade's, knowing she would be all right because he was telling her so, over and over in that calm, deep voice. "The fire's out. I've got you, Leah. You're all right. The fire's out."

"Thank you," she eventually managed, and coughed. She blinked, gazing woozily up into his concerned face. "Mercysake, the greens! Cade, our breakfast."

"Easy now. Don't worry about breakfast, we'll gather more."

A sea of faces crowded around Cade's, and Leah ducked her head, her pride smarting as much as her hands. Right now, if a terrestrial leviathan surged out of the earth to devour her like Jonah, Leah would have welcomed it.

"I don't think she's badly injured," Cade said. "But looks like we'll need to collect some more soup fixings, and Leah will need a different skirt, or gown. Mrs. Moore? She's fine. You saved her with your quick call for help. How about if you have your husband assist you over to our belongings, and you select something else for her to wear? And when you pass by him you might reassure Mr. Covington that Miss Sinclair's all right so he won't worry. B. W., you and Lester remember where we found the wild onions?"

"I hear you," B. W. said. "Can tell those by the odor easily enough, but we'll leave the rest of the gathering up to you. Come on, Turpin. My stomach's gnawing on my spine."

Seconds later Cade and Leah were alone.

"Let me see your hands." He examined them, then matter-of-factly rolled up the sleeves to check her arms, and lifted the singed skirt enough to verify that her ankles and lower legs were uninjured. "Looks like you escaped anything serious. I might be able to find some plantain leaves to help your pain." He traced his fingertips over her reddened palms again, a fleeting brush. "Unless you're really hurting, we ought to save the medication I have left for Mr. Covington."

"Of course. There's not much pain at all. I'll be fine." Unaccountably shy, Leah fought both the urge to pull away and that inexplicable yearning to nestle into his arms that had crept over her the previous evening. She was forty-seven kinds of an idiot to entertain such longings. It was just...Cade was being so kind, when what she deserved was a lecture, and what he deserved was the luxury of losing his temper at her. "Don't fuss over me, please," she mumbled. "It's embarrassing, the way you keep having to rescue me. I feel like such a fool."

"You're anything but that, Leah Sinclair." His voice was soft. "Don't be embarrassed. I'm on familiar ground, so to speak, here in the woods. You're not. Put me in a kitchen, however, and you'd be rescuing *me* from untold hazards."

He carefully released her hands. "I'll go fetch some more plants. Let

Mrs. Moore help you change," he said and was striding away before Leah could muster a response.

Glumly she stared down at herself, then with a defeated sigh rose to slowly make her way across to Jane. As she sidled past the fire she had to resist the urge to kick one of the stones circling it. When she finally returned to Richmond and the familiarity of her classroom, she might never venture off the school grounds again.

~~~

The interminable breakfast was over, every bite consumed with gusto and effusive praise for the cook. The cook with her scalded hands. Lester had predictably laughed throughout the meal, the one Cade had salvaged after Leah's display of incompetence, but she hadn't minded Lester's insensitivity nearly so much as everyone else's stilted efforts to preserve her dignity. When she announced her intention to clean up as penance for ruining the first round of breakfast, everyone had agreed, then immediately scattered.

Dignity, hah! Ridiculous to stand on one's dignity when six people had witnessed the spectacle she'd made of herself. Leah busied herself gathering up Cade's camping kit. The four men had consumed the meal using pieces of board, fingers, and stiff leaves curled into crudely usable spoons, courtesy of Cade's boundless creativity. Jane had used an aluminum plate, cutlery, and an enamel cup from Cade's banged-up stock of supplies, which had somehow survived the crash. Of course.

Leah insisted on feeding Mr. Covington with the other plate and cup before she herself ate. She was doubly grateful when the lawyer made no mention of her mishap and thanked her with courtly charm for taking such good care of him.

Everyone marveled over the extraordinary good fortune to have been traveling with the likes of Cade Beringer. God, Jane announced several times now, certainly had been looking out for their welfare. Cade was the quintessential guardian angel, first saving their lives, then preserving them in fine fashion. Even Lester grudgingly admitted that "the woodsman's" skills beat the tar out of an empty stomach.

In the eyes of her fellow travelers, the man could do no wrong.

And the once redoubtable Leah Sinclair could do no right.

She choked on another bitter morsel as she stacked the plates and cups. No matter where she turned or what she tried to do, it seemed as though Cade Beringer was there to plague her every move, witness her every humiliation.

Yet in all her life, no other man incited these secret longings inside her, longings more dangerous than an out-of-control coach hurtling toward destruction.

"I'll help you," he said from behind her, reaching deftly around to relieve her of the now cooled skillet. "You need to be careful of your hands. Are you sure they're all right?"

She darted him a look. "Thanks to you, yes. Like Mr. Turpin observed, you're very light on your feet." Stoically she gathered the cutlery with the dishes and started for the creek.

"You're limping."

"I'm just a tad stiff. It's nothing."

"Tell you what. Why don't I take care of the cleanup? You can keep Mr. Covington company."

"I said I'll do it." She walked faster. "I'm stiff, not injured. I've been handling kitchen duties since I was five years old, with and without scalded fingers. I believe I've at least enough fortitude—and skill—to wash a few dishes." She paused, then added with no inflection, "Unless of course you don't trust even those skills, considering what a fool I've made of myself with everything else."

"Don't be absurd." She wasn't sure, but she thought a muscle jumped in his cheek. "I was trying to be considerate. Hurt pride doesn't become you, Leah."

"Condescension doesn't become you. I'm very grateful for your"— she struggled for a moment—"for your consideration. Your...compassion. But if you're going to spoil it with a self-righteous attitude, I'd rather hike to Stillwaters by myself."

They walked the rest of the way in silence. The creek was still running fast and high from all the rain. Anger permeated her already stiff muscles, robbing her of her usual dexterity. When Leah knelt on the bank, the load of dishes wobbled. Then, as though propelled by a mischievous gust of wind, one of Cade's tin plates toppled into the creek. With a flash of metal it disappeared beneath the rushing water.

"Oh!" It was the last straw. Stiff with mortification, Leah knelt forward, head bowed, hands half curled. Her scalded palms stung, her cut arm throbbed, her bruised hip ached. In all her twenty-five years, not once had she confronted even the possibility of her own limitations. The force of her will and the power of her intellect had always conquered any obstacle.

Now she'd been defeated by...by *nature,* mercysake. Her domestic prowess had been proved useless; all her years of study had provided nothing worthwhile in the way of basic survival skills. Most humiliating of all, her will had been betrayed by her emotions.

After a while she turned, utterly defeated, hands dangling at her side as she watched in a stupor of indifference while Cade washed the remaining dishes. When he was finished he wiped his hands dry on his trousers, then sat cross-legged beside Leah. He didn't speak. Eventually she roused enough interest to glance sideways.

Cade's head was bowed, his eyes closed.

"If I wanted your prayers, I'd have asked."

The petulant remark fell between them, casting a dull film over the June morning. Shamefaced, Leah fumbled through an apology, which was marred by a garbled exposition on the reason for her churlishness.

She had to give Cade credit. He heard her out without interrupting, his attitude conveying nothing but intense concentration. Then he nodded his head. "I see. Nothing's really changed in the past five years, has it? Despite what I know of your family, and the men your sisters married, you still allow the hypocrisy of some Christians to nullify what you must know is your family's genuine faith." He paused, then shrugged. "Which leaves me in an indefensible position, between the hypocrites and the family you love. You don't talk to God like I talk to God. Therefore I offend you."

"That's not what I—"

"A question, Leah," he continued, ignoring her protest. "Knowing how you feel, why did you share your lifelong secret with me?"

"I don't think you're a hypocrite," Leah stated, her face hot. "I never have, not really. It's just that…well, I…"

"Why *did* you admit the fear to me?" He searched her face, his eyes narrowed, his focus unswerving. "Was it just because I happened to be there? With you? In the dark?"

"Because I…because I… Why did you cut your hands to pieces last night, so that I wouldn't have to sleep in the dark?" she countered, annoyed with herself.

A crooked smile slowly spread across his face. With two days' growth of honey-colored beard, he should have looked as disreputable as a brigand. But he didn't. "I'm not sure either of us is ready for the answers," he said.

Leah finally managed to break the spell by reaching to stack the clean dishes. Her hands weren't as steady as she would have wished. "I told you already that I've always preferred the truth, no matter how painful. Go ahead. It certainly can't be any worse than the past twenty-four hours," she ended with a ghost of dry humor.

Without making a fuss, Cade removed the dishes from her hands and laid them aside. "How about if the truth isn't painful, just… uncomfortable? For both of us."

For some reason her throat went tight and arid, while her pulse raced along, turbulent as the swift-running creek in front of her. Leah reminded herself that her behavior deserved retribution in kind. Mercysake, she'd endured countless verbal arrows over the years, and at least Cade thus far had spurned every opportunity for ridicule. If he needed to vent a few choice words now, well, she would survive. She had no reason for the ridiculous knots twisting her middle. She was a grown woman of twenty-five years, a professional teacher.

"Unpleasant medicine is best taken fast, and all at once," she said. "Go ahead. You've aroused my curiosity. Don't worry. I promise there'll be no emotional outburst."

" 'Emotional outburst?' " His hand lifted, and his index finger brushed the corner of her eye with a feathery touch. "What does it take to make you cry?"

"I don't cry."

"Everyone weeps for something, Leah. Even Jesus wept."

"I don't." Restless, she stood, shaking grass and sand from her wrinkled skirt. "No matter what you have to say—and I've provoked you enough that you should speak freely—you can't make me cry."

"Humiliating you is the furthest thing from my mind." He rose as well, standing over her in a relaxed but watchful pose. "But that doesn't mean you won't be uncomfortable. Nor that you'll like what I'm about to say." A flicker of some inscrutable emotion danced through his eyes. "You want to know why I kept the fire going?"

Warily she nodded.

"You were afraid, and I could do something about it," he said. "If I hadn't, I wouldn't have been doing right, either as a man or as a Christian."

"Ah. You were only doing your honorable Christian duty." Leah stared across the creek, to the mountainside thick with trees and underbrush. She kept her gaze on some age-mottled boulders. "I can't say I'm surprised."

"Neither am I, by your predictable but inaccurate response. You know, Leah Sinclair, you're thinking more like a mule with a mouthful of briars than an intelligent woman."

Here it comes, she thought, tensing.

From the corner of her eye she watched him shake his head, open his mouth, shut it, then cast an exasperated look toward the sky. Seeking divine guidance, no doubt. "Let's see if my second reason comes as an even greater surprise."

All of a sudden he stepped directly in front of her, cupped her chin, holding it so she had no choice but to meet his gaze. "I'm a man. Not just a Christian who raises your intellectual hackles every time I open my mouth. Not just a friend of your sister and her husband, one you do your best to ignore every time we meet. A man. You, Leah, whether you see it or not, are a woman. I'm not certain of what this is I'm feeling, and until we're all safely ensconced at Stillwaters, I don't plan to explore overmuch whatever these feelings are. But understand this."

His thumb stroked the underside of her chin. "I did a lot of soul-searching last night. You didn't share your secret with me just because I happened to be with you. And I didn't keep the campfire going just because I pitied you or was doing my Christian duty. God has brought us together, and I plan to give Him free rein with a different kind of fire. One I'm not sure can be doused as easily as the one I kept burning last night with pieces of wood."

His head lowered until Leah could feel his breath against her flaming cheeks. "Think about *that,* Miss Sinclair, while we're hiking today, hmm."

With that parting shot, he knelt, scooped up all the dishes, and headed off into the trees.

❦

SINCLAIR RUN

Jacob gave in and allowed Effie to shoo him out of the room so she could finish packing his clothes, though he continued to protest. "I'm not going to hobnob with the hotel guests. I'm going to find my daughter." His voice was testy, but he didn't care. Ever since the telegram from Ben that morning, all he cared about was finding out why Leah had not arrived on the Stillwaters stage.

Effie ignored him, folding his best frock coat and the gray striped trousers in tissue paper before she laid them in the case. "Your son-in-law owns the place. You can't shame him, rushing over there looking like a poor relation. Go on with you, now. I'll be finished in a flea's whisker without you glowering over my shoulder."

So Jacob took himself off. But instead of escaping to his workshop, he found himself wandering into the parlor, over to the library table in the corner where Leah's heartwood chest resided. She had refused to keep the chest with her when she accepted her position at the Esther Hays School for Young Ladies.

"Papa, we both know there's not going to be a Sloan or a Benjamin to take an interest in either me or my heartwood chest. Keep it here, use it for advertising or a decorative item."

"Leah, you don't know that, nor do I. There's a season for everything, lass. Try to remember that."

She'd given him one of her Leah-looks, a mixture of love, frustration, resignation...and weariness. "If you put an old flower bulb in my secret drawer to teach me that particular lesson, your method's faulty. They'll never be a growing season for that bulb, or any of the others you've replaced through the years, locked away from soil and water and light."

Like Leah's spirit, Jacob thought now, his fingers tracing the satin finish of the rich walnut wood. All her life, she had nourished only her mind, filling it so full of provable facts and figures that her spiritual nature—that miraculous piece of God's divine nature so real to the rest of the family—had never been able to grow.

And her heart... He swallowed hard, quelling the lump of emotion that balled in his chest. *Lord? Don't give up on my Leah.*

"Mr. Sinclair? I've hitched the wagon."

Deke shuffled across the parlor to Jacob's side, bending his knees a little so he could peer into Jacob's face. "Don't worry, Mr. Sinclair. Leah can do anything. She'll be all right, wherever she is." He straightened, rocking a little on his heels like he did when he was thinking hard. "Besides, we're not supposed to worry. That's what you told me, when I lost your keyhole saw, remember? You said it would turn up, and that fretting about it wouldn't help. You said there was even a verse in the Bible about being careful but that it really meant we're not supposed to worry. You read it to me, remember, Mr. Sinclair?"

"Aye, lad. I remember. *'Be careful for nothing...let your requests be made known unto God.'*" Jacob tousled the sweat-matted carroty hair with a fond hand. And God's peace would keep his heart and mind. Trust Deke to put things in perspective. "You're right. Reckon I better read that verse again. Thanks for hitching the horses. Did you remember to place Pete on the right side this time?"

Deke nodded, his mouth splitting in a wide grin. "Because he always pulls to the left, and now he can't because Raspberry's in the way, right?"

"There's a lad. Tell you what, I'll let you do the driving this time, on the way to the station." He held up a hand when Deke let out a whoop of delight. "But you'll have to listen to your Aunt Effie on the way home, else you'll be eating cold soup and stale crackers for a spell."

"I promise. Mr. Sinclair? You found that saw in the springhouse, and you said it was the last place you'd expected, so that's why it took so long to look there. Maybe that's what happened to Leah. She's just someplace where nobody's thinking about looking."

He clattered up the stairs, calling out to Effie that he was going to drive the wagon to the train station. Jacob stood in the parlor a moment longer, pondering Leah's heartwood chest. If his youngest daughter possessed even a portion of Deke's uncomplicated soul, she'd be less of a trial to Jacob's.

But then she wouldn't be Leah, would she? And he certainly wouldn't wish for an accident like the one Deke had suffered, trapping a grown man's body forever with a boy's mind.

Jacob cast a wry glance upward. "I hear You, Lord," he murmured softly.

All the same, before he headed out to make sure his workshop was in order, he detoured by the kitchen to fetch a pocketful of bismuth powders. Several years had passed since there'd been a flareup of his ulcer, but Sloan insisted he keep a supply of the powders on hand. Jacob prayed every one of them would remain in his pocket, regardless of what transpired at Stillwaters.

He also prayed a humble plea for the Lord's forbearance as he commenced a search for something far more precious than a keyhole saw.

Fourteen

After only an hour into what promised to be a long and exhausting hike to Stillwaters, Cade knew Jane Moore's ankle was not going to be equal to the trek. She was good-natured and tried not to complain, but the road, though largely cleared of underbrush, was boggy and uneven, more so now from the galloping hooves of four panicked coach horses. Progress was slow. Ted hovered over his wife, ready to steady her, and the other men took turns dragging Nathaniel Covington's dead weight on one of the travois Cade had fashioned, along with another stacked with luggage and supplies.

"Seems like the harness trappings would have slowed the horses' pace," B. W. observed once. "Or at least brought 'em to a standstill before now."

"True enough," Cade said. He glanced at the sullen, sweating Lester Turpin. "Unfortunately, it's possible those same trappings could also have caused their destruction, considering the condition of this road. We need to prepare for a long hike on foot, I'm afraid."

"Leave me here," Covington offered groggily. "I'm the one slowing everyone down. For all we know, the hotel's only a couple of hours down the way. I can manage till someone comes back for me."

"Don't waste your breath," Cade shot back, his tone terse. "By my reckoning we've at least ten miles to travel, if not more. We'll stick together. Nobody gets left behind."

After that, no one spoke.

The carriage never would have made it. And unless they came upon the horses, at least one of them in riding condition, neither would they. Not today.

"We're going to stop here, rest a bit," he finally said, carefully lowering Covington to the ground.

He conducted a quick inventory of the others. He ignored a little swell of satisfaction when his gaze rested on Leah, noting that his intrepid brown wren wasn't even winded. Her temples and forehead were beaded with perspiration, but the gleam had returned to her eye. She'd remained beside Nathaniel Covington, monitoring his condition, distracting him from pain by sharing anecdotes about her students. No doubt about it, Leah Sinclair made a fine nurse, even if her wilderness skills were nonexistent.

"I'm going to rig up another travois, this one for Mrs. Moore," Cade announced when he caught his own breath. The logistics promised to be virtually insurmountable, but it was the only solution he'd come up with, unless they found the horses.

"I'll volunteer to be her packhorse," B. W. said. "Compared to Mr. Covington or this luggage, it would be like pulling a load of feathers. Pardon the personal nature of my remark, Mrs. Moore," he ended with a feeble attempt at humor, which raised equally feeble smiles. He had volunteered for the first shift with the luggage. Groaning, he dropped the poles and collapsed on the ground, back against a roll of bedding. "Sure wish we'd stumble on at least one of those fool horses. Unlike me, they're designed for hauling weighty objects."

"The horses are mine." Lester wiped the back of his hand across his mouth. "When we find 'em, be up to *me* to decide if they're in any shape to haul your stuff. Blamed nuisance, the lot of it. Maybe one for the old man..." The grumbling deteriorated to inaudible mutters. He ducked his head and plodded ahead, ignoring Cade's instructions to rest.

Cade had known since daybreak that Lester's only reason for tagging along with the rest of them was because the horses had stampeded in the general direction of the hotel. Once the animals were found, a confrontation was inevitable, because Lester had made it plain he'd be returning to Eagle Mountain. With the horses.

"He's not going to make it easy for anyone, is he?" Leah murmured.

"Nope. But there's no point stewing about it. Frankly, I'm more concerned about the horses' condition, and ours, right now."

"We're all fine, even Mr. Covington. And Jane will be too, if she can stay off that ankle. I have a pair of gloves to protect my palms, so I can help with the travois, except I can't promise to help for very long at a time."

For the first time since they set out, Cade felt a chuckle tickle the back of his throat. Plucky to her eyeteeth, was Leah, more determined than ever to prove her worth. His gaze touched on her flushed cheeks and damp temples. Gossamer strands of fine brown hair had slipped free of a braid she had fashioned and hung limply about her face. Instead of her ruined traveling suit, she now wore a shirtwaist and plain gray skirt. The severe costume all but proclaimed "spinster schoolteacher," except for a pair of sturdy hiking shoes peeking out from the skirts. Cade wondered how long she could maintain the confidence she'd donned along with fresh clothing.

"Three travois and four men make for slow going, I admit. I might have to take you up on your offer." Especially since thus far they'd only traveled a couple of miles.

Ted joined them, his expression concerned. "How far do you think it is to Stillwaters now, Cade?"

"Hard to say," he admitted. "Road's running roughly northwest, but it's not a precise parallel to the road I traveled along last year. Now, I figure we were about ten miles from the hotel on that road, from the point of the landslide. We only backtracked a quarter of a mile to take this trail, but I'm not real sure how far we traveled after." He paused, thinking hard. "Seven or eight miles left, would be my best guess." Some of it over a small but steep mountain. He decided to keep that bit of information to himself.

Despite a day's growth of beard, Ted more resembled an anxious young boy than a married man. "What if we never find the horses? Or what if they're all injured, or—or dead? Between Mr. Covington, and Jane's ankle…"

"Let's not borrow trouble," Leah said. She waved a hand skyward. "We have fine weather and supplies. If we have to walk the entire way, we'll manage, even if we have to carry Jane, Mr. Covington, and the luggage."

"Fine words, Miss Sinclair," B. W. called from where he lay sprawled on the ground. "All the same, while I echo the sentiment, you're not the one doing the hauling."

Up went Leah's chin; Cade could easily visualize her drawing a rapier and assuming the attack stance. "You're correct, Mr. Skaggs. I don't have sufficient strength to haul a travois for a very long period at a time, possibly not at all." In two quick steps she reached the travois and scooped up her Gladstone bag, lashed in place along with the rest of the recovered luggage across one of the larger coach panels. "But I can carry my own share of the luggage, at least."

Cade intervened with the wariness of a man well versed in defusing everything from a mob of angry men to overbearing lumber company executives. When tempers ran high, common sense tended to fly out the door. Leah might not possess Meredith's flash fire temper, and she was more levelheaded than most, but he knew from experience that she still made a formidable opponent. "I'm sure you could carry your own," he began in what he hoped was a good-natured voice devoid of any trace of male patronizing. "But you'll have to admit we men make better packhorses—" He stopped. Leah was ignoring him.

She had removed the torn jacket of her traveling suit from her case, and was holding it up in front of her, studying it with pursed lips. "Knife, please." She thrust out her hand, still not looking at Cade.

He caught on instantly, as did B. W., who scrambled to his feet. "I shouldn't have said what I did," the young man admitted. "Please, Miss Sinclair. Don't allow my bad manners to provoke you—"

"I'm not provoked, and your bad manners don't alter a plain truth. Mr. Beringer, either allow me the use of your hunting knife, or I'll make do with my pair of folding scissors."

"Here now, Miss Sinclair," Covington put in, feebly lifting his uninjured arm in a wobbly gesture. "Who's to entertain me with conversation, if you're too weary from your load?"

In a lightning swift appraisal of the group, Cade read everything from dismay to disbelief to consternation. While he hated to vanquish her spirit, particularly after the previous night, he could not afford to lose ground as the leader.

More troubling, Lester Turpin was completely out of sight. If he reached the horses alone, there was no doubt in Cade's mind that the driver was likely to mount the lead horse and take off with the others in tow, leaving the five travelers stranded.

Thoughtfully he removed his knife from its scabbard. "I'll make a deal with you," he said. "Fashion whatever will help you carry your bag. But if"—he waited until he had her complete attention, in his mind substituting the word *when*—"you tire, you promise not to let pride push you beyond your endurance." When her face reddened, he calmly handed her the knife, hilt first. "Be careful, it's sharp. I'll need it in a few minutes myself, but I can use the hatchet to cut some saplings for the poles of another travois."

Sometimes retreat worked more powerfully than standing one's ground.

Without waiting for a response, Cade removed his hatchet from its sheath. "B. W., how about heading down the road far enough to see if you can catch sight of Lester? Don't try to catch up, just see if you can still spot him." Then he motioned to Ted, and the two of them loped off toward a stand of smaller trees a dozen yards off the trail. "A couple of branches from this hophornbeam ought to do the trick. It's a good, tough wood and should support your wife without danger of cracking."

When they were ready to set out once more, Ted was hauling Jane on one of the coach's seat cushions, balanced on the frame of branches. B. W. had returned to the group to report that Lester was taking a nap a quarter of a mile ahead; without fuss he positioned himself by Covington's travois, leaving Cade with the lighter load of luggage. When they reached Lester the driver joined them for a while, but soon bored of the laborious pace. He refused to help with any of the travois and soon left the slower moving party behind. Privately concerned, Cade nonetheless made light of Lester's defection.

Leah had created a sling of sorts from her jacket, which allowed her to tote her Gladstone on her back. Now she chugged along beside Jane, chatting with the girl as though they were merely out for a stroll. Cade surreptitiously watched her, but unless she collapsed, he had decided to let her be. They composed a bedraggled little party, doomed by the terrain as well as circumstances to slow progress, and another night under the stars if they didn't find those horses. And Lester Turpin couldn't be persuaded to share.

They'd been hiking for another hour when the sound of a neigh echoed in the bright sunshiny morning.

"Eureka!" B. W. turned to Cade. "How about if we take another break, Cade?" He paused, massaging his hands. "I can run ahead. Ah... 'Help' Lester, so to speak."

"Good idea. I'll join you in a moment, and Ted can stay here with the ladies and Mr. Covington."

"I hope the horses are all right," Jane said. She'd been quiet for some time; Cade had a hunch her ankle hurt more than she'd let on.

"I do hope Lester decides to cooperate." Leah rotated her shoulders, grimacing. "If he doesn't..." Her voice trailed away.

Cade watched B. W. jog eagerly down the weed-infested track. "He'll cooperate. He's a bit of an attitude, and I'm not sure he'll be gentlemanly about it, but I don't think Lester's going to abandon us."

If he did attempt a wholesale desertion, Cade prayed for the wisdom to defuse the situation before it exploded in his face. Yes, he knew the horses belonged to Turpin, but it was obvious to everyone that they needed the animals desperately. They would eventually reach Stillwaters on foot, carrying the injured on their travois. But there was no way of knowing for sure how many days it would take, or how long the mild weather would hold, which meant they needed to keep all the supplies on the third travois. Cade would abandon the supplies only if there was no alternative.

Grimly he forced himself to confront the most disquieting of his motivations: He wanted the use of the horses because he didn't want Leah to endure another night of terror.

"We'll talk it out," he reiterated, keeping his voice cheerful. Positive. "Lester will come around."

Leah's eyes sparked. "As I've said before, one day you're going to fall flat on your face when you trip over your idealistic notions of human nature. You are familiar with the scripture that reminds us that not a single person is righteous? That certainly applies to Mr. Turpin, in my opinion."

"Leah!" Jane exclaimed. "Must you bait Cade like that? You sound almost irreverent."

The spark vanished. "That was not my intention." She squared her shoulders. "Why don't I catch up with B. W.? Between the two of us, perhaps we can convince Mr. Turpin to live up to Mr. Beringer's hopes, instead of down to my expectations." Her step quickened, and without another word she forged ahead, heavy Gladstone and all, following B. W.'s rapidly diminishing figure.

There was a sinking sensation in the pit of Cade's stomach. Forget the Moores and B. W., Nathaniel Covington. Forget the unrelenting hostility of Lester Turpin. In this moment, more than anything Cade yearned to focus all his energy on a difficult woman, a woman whose facade was cracking wide enough to reveal the wounded soul of a vulnerable little girl.

Lord? This is not what I expected at all.

It was a fallen tree that had at last halted the panicked horses' flight. The lead pair successfully made the jump, but the rear pair remained on the other side, probably due to their snarled harnessing. Miraculously not one of the animals had broken a leg, despite yards of trailing reins, flapping harnesses, and the splintered shaft. Even the metal latch hooking the pairs together had held. They were covered with dried lather, and in need of food and water, but even the skittish bay seemed to welcome human touch. Other than shoulders chafed from their collars, and a slight stone bruise on one hind hoof, the team remarkably had suffered no damage that precluded their further use.

By the time everyone was assembled together again, Lester, Leah, and Cade had freed all four animals. At Cade's request, B. W. scouted out the creek they had camped by the previous night, some two hundred yards away. Fortunately, the trail had descended to the foot of the mountain, and with a minimum of fuss the horses were watered and returned to the old road.

"Reckon it's time to discuss terms," Lester announced then, looking around the group.

"Terms?" Cade asked.

"Like I told you, these are my animals. I aim to head back to Eagle Mountain with 'em." He paused, looking vastly pleased with himself. "But I might be persuaded to consider some other arrangement." His gaze moved among the others, then settled on Cade. "Depends on the offer, and how nicely you ask me."

Ted shushed Jane's incredulous protest, and from the corner of his eye Cade saw Leah whip out a cautionary hand on B. W.'s forearm. *You've given me words and wisdom in the past, gracious Father.* He prayed this occasion would be no different.

"You've seen for yourself the strenuous nature of our task, especially facing a long hike of uncertain duration, over fairly rugged terrain. You know we need the horses. I was hoping that asking wouldn't be necessary."

"Looks like you placed your hope with the wrong team, woodsman. You like to pray. So pray to God all you want, ask *Him* to get you out of the wilderness." He slapped his thigh and chuckled. "Don't fancy yourself as Moses? Well then, I reckon you're stuck asking someone who's in a position to answer your prayers." The derisive laughter died as he stepped so close to Cade the toes of their boots brushed. "So ask me, woodsman. Beg me. Show me how humble a Christian you really are."

"Mr. Turpin, I'll pay—"

"No, Leah," Cade cut across her words without looking away from Turpin. "He wants his pound of flesh. Let him have it. Tell me, Lester, will you loan us the horses if I get down on my knees?" he continued without inflection.

"Won't know till you try it, will you?" Plainly enjoying himself, the driver rocked back on his heels and folded his arms across his chest.

"Cade, you don't have to play Little Lord Fauntleroy," B. W. sputtered. "It's three to one. We can—" he broke off with a muffled curse when Cade dropped to one knee.

"Well, Lester?" he asked calmly. "I'm on my knee. Want to tell me how to phrase the question as well?"

The driver's face turned red as an autumn maple leaf. He blinked rapidly; Cade read the temper, and the threat, and tensed in reaction. When Lester lashed out with a booted foot Cade was ready. In a blur of movement he caught the boot in his hands and twisted, throwing Lester to the ground. Then he straddled him, hands poised to help the winded man back up—or knock him back to the ground.

Glowering, Lester shook his head; Cade stepped back, watching closely while Turpin clambered to his feet. When he made no further move to attack, Cade dropped his hands. "I don't want to fight," he said. "And you don't want to make a mistake you'll regret for the rest of your life. Do you?"

"You'll be sorry for this." Lester jerked his chin toward the horses. "Use three of them then, blast you. But I'm taking the one I want and heading back to Eagle Mountain. You see I get them others back in good condition, or you'll be paying for the lot. You got five days, woodsman, starting now, or I'll set the law on you for stealing."

"You'll get your horses back, Mr. Turpin." Cade might have won a battle, but the taste of disillusionment filled his mouth like ashes. "The threat wasn't necessary."

Lester Turpin spat, missing Cade's boot by inches. Then he swiveled on his heel and stomped over to the lead horse, the high-spirited bay least suitable for a long hike with injured and inexperienced riders. *Thank You, Lord.* Cade watched without moving a muscle and prayed his relief didn't show.

After gathering the reins, Lester used the hame of the harness collar to haul himself onto the horse's back. Then he looked across at Cade. "Someday someone's going to ram that holier-than-thou attitude down your throat. Maybe then you'll learn what it's like, living down here in the dirt with the rest of us."

He kneed the horse's flanks and without a backward glance headed back down the trail at a canter.

Cade ran a tired hand around the back of his neck. He wished he didn't feel the unnerving sensation of having had a gauntlet hurled at his feet.

Fifteen

*W*ith transport available and Lester gone, the atmosphere lightened almost to jocularity. Leah allowed herself the first easy breath of the long morning as she paused to reassure Mr. Covington, then followed the other men over to the travois to help unload the luggage. Forty minutes later, they were ready to resume their trek.

"Too bad these critters weren't in postilion harness. Leastways I'd have myself a saddle and stirrups." B. W. eyed the most docile of the three coach horses, a sturdy mare previously paired with the spirited lead horse Lester had commandeered. "Say, Cade? What if he shies because a rabbit or squirrel darts out in front of him?"

"As long as you grip with your legs, not just your knees, and pay attention, you won't have a problem," Cade said. "And B. W., your mount's a mare."

The young man flushed, then took the reins Cade held out to him. "Well, if *she* runs away with me, at least you'll be forced to give chase since I'm carrying half the supplies."

Everyone laughed, but Leah empathized with B. W.'s insecurity, not only because they were riding without saddles and stirrups. She was equally unnerved by Cade's solution for the dilemma of three horses and five riders.

Instead of the impersonal security of leather and metal harness trappings, it would be Cade's arms holding her steady, Cade's solid bulk supporting her back.

There was no other practical solution, and Leah was too pragmatic to argue. Of course they would make better time with everyone mounted, and the coach horses were certainly strong enough to support the weight of two riders and a couple of pieces of luggage. Cade and

Leah's mount, a large-boned animal with the stocky build of a draft horse, would also bear the burden of hauling Mr. Covington on his travois. Ted and Jane would ride together; since B. W. was an inexperienced horseman at best, prudence dictated that Leah ride with Cade. Leah smiled an encouraging smile at Mr. Covington. He was definitely weaker, and suffering a fair amount of pain. Cade had administered the last of the medicine from his knapsack, in the hope that with the horses they would reach Stillwaters that day, but the circumstances had taken their toll.

"Try to sleep," she urged him now. "We'll be at the hotel before you know it. Mr. Beringer will see to it, I'm sure."

"He's a good man, is Cade," Mr. Covington replied before closing his eyes.

Cade. Leah watched him give B. W. a leg up, then patiently instruct him by walking the horse up and down the trail, until the younger man laughed and promised he would manage. "Never rode a lot," he said with a shrug. "Buggies are more comfortable, particularly in bad weather. Besides, boarding a horse at school was too much trouble."

"We'll be keeping to a walk," Cade reminded him. He checked the pile of cases lashed together with extra leading reins, then grinned up at B. W. "And we'll place you in the middle, all right? Offer a bit more security."

Next he helped Ted settle behind Jane. After double-checking their pieces of baggage and tightening one of the straps, Cade finally approached Leah. After reassuring himself of Mr. Covington's security and the security of his travois, Cade turned to her. Leah fixed what she hoped was a confident expression on her face and tried to ignore her frantically pounding heart.

"It's time," he said, his eyes in the bright sunlight shimmering with humor and understanding. "Don't worry. I won't let you fall."

"That's not what I'm worried about."

Casually he put his hands on either side of her waist. "No?" As easily as though she weighed no more than a roll of bread dough, he lifted and lowered her onto the horse's broad back. "What, then?"

She could no more help the embarrassed blush than she could prevent the wind from blowing. "I'm not used to this," she muttered. "Riding double. Being picked up…I still think I should walk, to keep from burdening the poor horse."

"This fellow's strong enough to pull a road-coach all by himself." Cade patted the animal's well-muscled neck, eyes gleaming up at Leah. "Relax."

She yanked down the ribboned hem of her dove gray skirt, which was supposed to be part of Monday's costume, along with the striped shirtwaist that was part of her Saturday ensemble. It was depressing, this sensation of uncertainty, simply because her orderly routine had been disordered. If only she had been able to dress in the proper day's costume, perhaps the annoying tremulousness would have dissipated. But the skirt's gored panels and light weight allowed plenty of room for walking, and Leah above all things prided herself on her common sense. Unfortunately she hadn't considered riding astride with her limbs exposed, sitting in front of Cade Beringer.

"You really do need to relax," he repeated. "Helps your balance and the horse's. Think of it as dancing with a gentleman." He shrugged into his knapsack, then vaulted behind her with the skill of a seasoned horseman, easily maneuvering around the poles that supported the travois.

Leah couldn't help it. She stiffened like an overstarched collar. "I've danced precisely three times with gentlemen, my entire life." Her father. Benjamin. An octogenarian at a debutante's ball in Richmond she'd chaperoned the previous year. None of those brief moments could have prepared her for this.

When she felt the heat and pressure of Cade's torso against her back, she couldn't suppress an instinctive flinch. Mercysake, why must he feel so, well, manly? Then he picked up the reins and his arms brushed her sides. Leah froze. She felt as though she'd swallowed a tub full of butterflies. "Your analogy is absurd," she managed, because she had to say something. "You can't compare dancing to riding a horse."

His breath stirred the hair on the crown of her head. Was he *laughing?* "All right, I might have been stretching it a bit." His weight shifted, and they set off down the trail, followed by B. W. and the Moores. "Let's try this. How about if you focus on our surroundings. If you like, I'll point out flora and any fauna that cross our path. If you prefer our ground rules from the train, I'll limit my comments to every half-hour."

For some reason his lighthearted teasing softened Leah's self-consciousness. Cade was right. The only rational response under these circumstances was humor. She opened her mouth to offer an equally lighthearted retort, and a bubble of laughter burst out.

Leah clapped a hand over her mouth. Giggles? *Giggles?* She had never giggled in her life. Every convention of the day demanded vociferous protest. Not this…this inexplicable hilarity.

Perhaps the explanation lay in the sheer incongruity of it: She was virtually surrounded by the most masculine yet the most overtly religious man she had ever met, outside of her family. And her reaction contradicted her self-image of a professional, practical spinster schoolmarm. Her gaze fell upon her bunched skirts and exposed stockings. Another laugh floated up.

"You have a charming laugh. You should share it more often."

"I can't imagine circumstances *less* conducive to laughter."

"Oh, I can think of one or two."

Jarred, Leah half twisted so she could see Cade's face. When had he shaved? "Well, I can't. I think I've passed a horrific night and survived a horrific accident. I'm riding double with a man—and I'm wearing half of Monday's costume and half of Saturday's, on Friday!"

She must be hysterical, that was the only logical explanation, Leah concluded, listening to the idiocy of her chatter. Cade was gawking at her as though she'd sprouted fuzzy antennae from her ears, which made her smile widen. Good. Predictable people were boring. "Meredith is not going to believe this."

"I'm not so sure as I wouldn't blame Meredith," he replied, very slowly.

In a heartbeat the air around them seemed to crackle. For some reason his muscles had turned to iron. She knew this because she could feel most of them pressed against her back and arms. The horse's tail swished, and the animal jigged sideways. Leah clamped both hands around the hames on the harness collar, and concentrated on keeping her balance. And not only her balance atop a saddle-less horse.

"Whoa, now, boy. Take it easy, hmm," Cade said. After a moment the arms on either side of Leah seemed to relax, and he expelled his breath on a long sigh. "You all right, Leah?" She felt his torso twist as he turned to check Mr. Covington.

"Certainly." She cleared her throat. "But I'll try to stifle any further levity until I'm on the ground."

There was another crackling span of time. Then Leah felt a fleeting pressure against the crown of her head, as though Cade had—

No. *Don't be absurd, Leah.* Regardless of his words by the creek she refused to consider the possibility that Cade Beringer was truly attracted to her, just as she refused to take seriously his assertion. God hadn't "brought them together," hadn't "lit any fires." Typical of the man, of course, attributing every bump and hiccup of life to God's master hand. Doubtless Cade felt sorry for her, and hadn't wanted to aggravate her already raw feelings. That was the only reasonable explanation. She was being ridiculous. Proximity had pulverized her mind.

Then his hand, still holding the rein, came down over hers, a brief contact completed almost before she knew it had happened. "I hadn't realized," he murmured, his voice low in her ear, "how difficult this would be, resisting temptation."

For the rest of that long day, Leah wondered if the sensation that tightened her rib cage and set loose all those butterflies mirrored the bemusement she'd heard in Cade's voice.

Sixteen

At a little past five, almost exactly twenty-four hours after they departed on the fateful coach ride, the exhausted party pulled their equally weary horses to a halt in front of the main hotel. Groomed and coiffured guests strolling the grounds gaped as the travelers plodded up the crushed oyster shell drive, and several children who had been playing croquet on the common tagged along after the horses, pointing and whispering.

Leah adopted her most forbidding expression and ignored the stares, the murmurs, and excited questions until she caught sight of Hominy Hawes, Benjamin's longtime manservant and companion. The shock of the past twenty-four hours swept over her in a flood tide. They had all survived. They were all safe. Mr. Covington, though gravely injured, was still alive and soon would be in a physician's care. *She* was alive. Safe. And yet, something profound had taken place, somewhere deep inside, just beyond the reach of her mind. She swallowed hard, fighting panic.

"Miss Sinclair...Mr. Beringer!" For once the stolid black man seemed bereft of speech as he descended the piazza stairs three at a time.

Cade dismounted to shake hands, then clapped his hand on Hominy's massive back.

"Mr. Beringer! Never expected to see you, not like this. You're...are you all right?" Chocolate eyes darted from Leah to the now unconscious Mr. Covington, to Cade. "We've had the fantods hereabouts ever since Miss Sinclair didn't come in on the stage last night. I...ah... You were with her? These other folk? What happened?"

"We suffered a mishap." Leah replied in a massive understatement. "Mr. Covington there urgently needs a physician. He's the worst. Mrs.

Moore has a sprained ankle. All of us suffered a few cuts and bruises, but we're all right. I'm all right." She nodded her head decisively to add credibility to the lie. "I'll tell you everything, I promise. But first we need to fetch the doctor." She gathered her shredding composure. "Where are Meredith and Benjamin?"

Hominy gestured to a bellboy and ordered him to find Dr. Savoy on the double. Then he turned back to Leah, studying her with a doubtful expression. *Well, then.* Without thinking, she swung her cramped leg over the horse's back and slid to the ground. Her knees buckled. She would have collapsed in an undignified heap if Cade's arm hadn't wrapped around her waist and hauled her to his side.

"You'll need to find your balance again," he said easily, as though holding her close among a crowd of gawking strangers was as natural as tipping a hat. "Those ten-minute rest breaks we took won't make up for an almost seven-hour ride."

"Seven hours?" Hominy tugged on his misshapen ear, then ran his hand through the head of close-cropped kinky curls, which had gone almost completely gray since the previous year. "You've been with Miss Sinclair, and these other folks all along, then? We knew you were coming. Just never expected—" He shook his head again. "Mr. Ben's out with a band of searchers since noon. They took the old road, after he learned from the railroad dispatcher that a party hired a coach yesterday when a landslide blocked the railroad track."

"A landslide blocked the old road as well, about five miles out of Eagle Mountain, as Ben will discover," Leah said. "We took...a different route." She glanced across to the Moores and B. W., who appeared as awkward and uncertain as she felt.

At that moment the bellboy returned with a short man wearing a neat black suit and carrying a doctor's bag. Alarm filled his face at the sight of the injured man, but without a word he pulled out a stethoscope and set to work.

"Hominy, could someone fetch an invalid chair for Mrs. Moore?" Cade asked, casually taking hold of Leah's elbow. "And a couple of bellboys, to help unload the luggage? And someone needs to let Nathaniel Covington's family know that he's here, and what's happened."

"Right away, Mr. Cade." He lifted a hand toward the clutch of uniformed boys hovering at the top of the stairs.

"Where's Meredith, Hominy?" Leah asked again as she tried to discreetly edge away from Cade. She might as well have tried to shift an anvil.

After instructing the bellboys, Hominy turned back to her. "Miz Walker's in the office with little Sam. She's been in a bad way, Miss Sinclair. I'll never understand Christians. Told me she was trying to trust God, but she didn't know what had happened to you, so she's fretting over feeling guilty because she's not trusting like she thinks she ought to. Don't make sense to me, no sir. You and Mr. Cade best go speak with her, while I help these other folks. I'll hear all about it later." He moved with his measured dignity across to greet the Moores, leaving Leah alone with Cade.

"You don't have to," she began, but he cut her off.

"I'll go with you," he murmured. "Might be easier if we're both there."

"Thank you," Leah said, meaning it. Then, "As you see, my legs are functioning now. I can walk on my own."

"I'm relieved to hear it. I'm too tired to carry you."

He calmly ushered her up the sweeping steps and into the cool lobby, steadying her with his hand. Astonished whispers rippled outward as they passed, but Leah was beyond caring. Her limbs still felt like overcooked noodles, and for some reason, now that she was finally safe, her insides seemed to be quivering.

Cade's arm tightened. "Just a few more steps."

The hotel offices occupied a suite of rooms that overlooked a finger-width valley to the southwest. When Cade opened the door, the first thing Leah saw was Meredith and little Samuel, silhouetted against the floor-to-ceiling windows on the other side of the room. Meredith, as always, looked beautiful, her thick chestnut hair piled high, her gown an elegant concoction of white lawn and lace. Yet despite the stylish elegance, she looked more mother than society matron. The toddler's plump cheek was nestled in the yoke of lace covering his mother's shoulder; his eyes were half closed, and stubby fingers crumpled the fabric of Meredith's expensive gown.

Leah had difficult forcing her tongue to frame a single word. "Meredith?"

She whirled around. "Leah?" She started forward as though in a dream, clutching her son so tightly he whimpered in protest. *"Leah!"* Quick tears flooded her eyes as she flew across the room. "We were so worried, oh, you're really here! Thank You, Lord, thank You. Are you all right? Mercysake, you look dreadful—what happened? And Cade, you're here, too. You...were with Leah? Another of God's mercies... Oh, this is too much. Benjamin's been out since morning, looking for you. I've been— Never mind." Laughing, crying, she surrendered a protesting Samuel to Cade, then hugged Leah hard enough to crack her ribs. "I've never seen you look so..." She swiped one hand over her eyes, dashing away tears while she gushed forth with sisterly admonitions, reproaches, and exclamations of relief, all the while patting Leah as though Leah were the same age as two-year-old Samuel.

"Enough!" Leah finally managed, taking hold of Meredith's shoulders and giving her a gentle shake. "I'm fine."

She downplayed the trauma of her experience out of habit as much as self-protection. The eldest by three years, Meredith was the dramatist of the three sisters, her emotions hovering near the surface. In comparison Leah always felt like a dried persimmon. She wondered wearily if her own deep reserve could be attributed in part to her need to balance not only Meredith's extravagant emotional displays but also Garnet's wild gypsy streak.

After a final steadying hug, she released Meredith's shoulders and stepped back, dredging up a smile. "I'm a bit tired, as you might imagine. I did have a new traveling costume to show off, but I'm afraid it's ruined. On the other hand, though I'm sure I must look and smell like the horse, I'm perfectly fine."

"Ha! You're a mess. And you've hurt...your arm, isn't it? And there's a bruise on your noggin. What else? Oh, my, your hands...never mind. Tell me the rest later. You're pale as a bleached pillowcase, and your hair...I haven't seen you with your hair in a braid down your back since we were children. As for your attire..."

She rolled her eyes and turned to Cade, who was playing one-handed pat-a-cake with Samuel. She kissed her son's waving fingers and gave Cade a hug. "Of course you look as rugged and healthy as you always do. Still in need of a haircut…"

"You're babbling, Meredith," Leah said. "Please calm down. It's exhausting, and I'm already exhausted."

She scarcely noticed her sister's flash of temper because the floor felt as though it were undulating to the gentle rhythm of a walking horse. If she didn't sit down, she would fall on her nose. Her gaze on her goal, she made her way over to a striped lounge chair and stiffly lowered herself onto the cushion. "One of the guests, a Mr. Covington, was injured in the crash."

"Oh! Oh no." Concern replaced the temper as Meredith came across to Leah's chair. "Leah, what a dreadful thing. I am sorry, for all of it." Fresh tears brightened her eyes. "He's all right? Did Hominy summon Dr. Savoy?"

"Yes. And yes. When do you expect Benjamin to return?"

"Shouldn't be long," Cade answered. He set the squirming Samuel down on the carpeted floor. "But might be wise to send a rider after them." He was studying Leah, a frown knitting his forehead. Leah frowned back. "Meredith, I think your sister could use a hand with a hot bath. You're right about her arm. She's a nasty scratch that might need to be checked by the doctor, when he's available."

"It's clean and too shallow to need stitching. You really are the bossiest man I've ever known," she murmured without heat. Her mouth curved in a tired smile. "But I doubt I'd be here at all, without your help. Thank you, Cade."

"Knowing what I do about you," he returned, "you'd have found a way."

Suddenly he was directly in front of her. Leah's heart jerked once when his fingers enfolded hers. His thumb smoothed over her knuckles. "I see what you're doing, dismissing me. It's not going to work," he said under his breath. "We both know better now. Give up the act, Miss Sinclair."

He straightened. "Take care of that arm," he finished in a normal voice. "Meredith, I need to ensure that the horses are stabled and taken care of properly. They belong to the driver of our one-time coach. Have someone send for me, please, when Ben returns?" He gently tweaked little Samuel's nose, sent Leah a last inscrutable glance, and left.

Meredith was looking at her strangely. If Cade had still been standing in front of Leah's chair, she would have kicked his shin. Either way, whatever hopes bubbled inside Meredith's head would soon be popped. Leah refused to allow her to build castles of air that tomorrow's brisk wind of reality would blow away. An abrupt change of subject, designed to startle, worked best. "This will be a shock for Mr. Covington's family. By the way, you didn't notify Papa, did you?"

Right on cue, Meredith's jaw dropped. "Papa? Mercysake, I forgot. I was so glad to see you that I completely forgot. Of course we notified Papa that you were missing. He needed to know. Besides, I wanted him here, especially if something awful had happened. I, well, I needed him. Praying with us, for you. I know talking about it makes you uncomfortable, and I'm sorry. But it's the truth. We received his return telegram this morning. He's on the way, should be here on today's six o'clock stage run." Dry humor kindled her hazel eyes, turning them almost as green as Cade's. "The one you should have been on yesterday evening."

Leah creaked to her feet. "Then you better show me to my room, sister dear. If Papa sees me in this state, it might bring on an ulcer attack."

"Mercysake, yes! So." Her manner turned brisk. "Did you salvage any of your luggage? Good. All my gowns would be far too big for you, unfortunately. Yours are sure to need pressing, at the very least. Let me fetch Gabby—that's Sam's new mammy, who's wonderful, by the way. She's a friend of Hominy's. Then I'll take you right up. You're in the same suite as last year." She fiddled with the sash at her waist for a moment, looking all of a sudden uncertain. "Leah?"

"Yes?"

"I— We were praying for you. I just wondered..." she made a face, then with typical Meredith impulsiveness blurted it straight out, "Did you *know*? Sense it? Feel God's Presence with you, taking care of you? I know you don't like talking about, well, spiritual matters. I just...I just needed to know. Because Papa would never mention it but he's, well, you know what he's like. And I keep—Sam! No, you don't…"

Leah watched her sister rescue Samuel from climbing up the back of a chair, her actions swift but unalarmed. Her expression softened as she lovingly scolded her son.

Fatigue, bone-deep and laden with helplessness, threatened to suck Leah into a bottomless whirlpool. At the moment, she and her sister were separated by a far wider distance than a few yards of oriental carpet. "I'm sorry, Meredith." Her voice was leaden. "I wanted to"—she'd always wanted to—"but no. I didn't hear God's voice, didn't sense His Presence, not the way you and Benjamin and Garnet and Sloan do. And Papa."

And Cade. Above all…Cade.

It wasn't fair. Wasn't fair… No matter how hard she tried, how many nights through the years she obediently tried to "talk to the Lord," tried to listen until she thought the silence would deafen her, God had not deemed her worthy of an audience. And her family considered her…lacking. Jesus might have died for her sins, but His Spirit filled the lives of her sisters, their husbands, her father…Cade. Not Leah. Apparently never Leah. She was who and what she always had been. Alone. All her life, faith for her had consisted solely of the deep determination of her will to believe in something and Someone whose existence could not be proven or logically explained utilizing any known scientific method.

"I'm sorry," she told Meredith again, wincing at the disappointment shadowing her sister's face. "But I won't lie about it."

"I wouldn't want you to lie. And I don't want to push. It's just that I couldn't have made it through this past night without knowing, somewhere deep inside, that not only was God here, giving me strength. Hope. He was also with you." She searched Leah's face with anxious eyes, heavy-handed in her love. "You believe that, don't you, Leah? Even if you can't feel God, you do know He's there?"

"Yes, Meredith. I know God is there."

But the only person whose presence she had felt watching over her, whose voice she had heard, had been Cade Beringer's.

Seventeen

or Jacob, the reunion with his youngest daughter was marred only by one small imperfection. 'Twas a little thing, in comparison with her relative good health, of course. But all the same, Jacob thought as he waited after supper for Leah to join him for a quiet walk, he wished he'd not been the only one of them shedding tears of joy.

"I'm here, Papa."

He turned, smiling a bit. "You look lovely, lass. You sure you're wanting to stroll? We could go on up to the family suite. There's a pair of comfortable chairs in the sitting room, if you're tired."

"I'm not too tired. And I look presentable, not lovely," she corrected him, reaching up to brush a kiss against his cheek. "I prefer a stroll. It's a little more private. Do you know, by the time we finished supper I was almost ready to return to the campground Cade made for us last night. At least it was quiet." She stopped abruptly, then gestured toward the door. "Shall we?"

Now what was that all about? Lips pursed, Jacob escorted her across the small parlor on the main floor, where he'd been waiting. "Where would you like to stroll, then? 'Tis a fine night again, just as last night." The doorman ushered them onto the front porch. Piazza, Ben and Meredith called it, though to Jacob's way of thinking a front porch was a front porch, regardless of whether it fronted a house or a grand hotel the length of a city block. "Another bit of God's grace, such good weather."

The silence all but deafened him. He shook his head, then took her arm as they descended the stairs. For several moments they walked in silence down the broad elliptical drive, eschewing the many walking paths that led to the springs or wandered through peaceful woods.

125

Though the main drive was well lighted with ironwork post lamps that haloed the silhouettes of other strolling guests, an air of seclusion enfolded them; Jacob's heart filled once more with a tranquillity that had been absent since Benjamin's telegram arrived.

"Tell me what's troubling you, lass," he said after allowing sufficient time for Leah to organize her thoughts.

Daughters, Jacob had learned, taught a man patience. And the blessed Lord knew Jacob had needed a bucketful of it for his three, Meredith with her stubbornness, Garnet with a core of insecurity born of an ugly summer afternoon her sixteenth year…and Leah. Och, Leah with her fearful intelligence and servant's heart. For most of his life his youngest had left Jacob floundering as he struggled to understand her.

"You've something to tell me," he continued now after a sideways perusal. "And contrary to your dinner table blandishments, 'tis not merely to reassure me yet again that you're hale and hearty. We'd already determined that, from the moment I held you in my arms when I stepped off the stage."

"There wasn't an opportunity at dinner. Meredith was hovering. Benjamin was—brotherly. Hominy was ready to track down Lester Turpin. And Samuel was crawling under the table. He pulled my napkin out of my lap and smeared peas all over my shoes."

Jacob chuckled. She sounded outraged, her notion of children's proper behavior sorely tried. "He's a braw one and more of a handful than his mother at that age. The next years will be interesting. What they need is a passel of wee ones to give Master Sam a bit of competition." He paused. "So, Leah, were you wanting to complain about your sister's mothering? Is that what this is all about?"

"Of course not, Papa."

"Don't assume that tone with me, lass." He stopped directly beneath one of the lamps, turning Leah so that he could see her expression, difficult even in daylight due to her formidable control. "You're a grown woman on your own now, with a life and a profession that has granted you power, and a fair amount of authority. But don't ever forget that I'm your father, not one of your students."

"Papa, I'm sorry. I do need to talk with you. But what I have to ask

you is difficult for me, for all I'm twenty-five and ought to know better."
She pinched the bridge of her nose. "Especially since I seem to spend as
much time counseling young ladies on the matter as I do teaching them
physics and household management."

"Ah." Jacob brushed a lock of fine brown hair from her forehead,
then stepped away to clasp his hands behind his back. "Cade Beringer."

He waited, and had in truth resigned himself to failure when she
lifted a hand in a futile gesture and simply said, "Yes."

In one accord they resumed their stroll, occasionally nodding to
other guests.

"It's not because he saved my life," Leah murmured after a while,
almost to herself. "If nothing else, I've at least convinced myself this isn't
gratitude, or mere hero worship." Then, "I can't make sense of it all,
there's no reason. It's not logical."

"What isn't, lass?"

"I wish he'd accepted Meredith's invitation to join us for supper. I
could have watched, could have reached some form of a conclusion
from the way he treated me when family members were present."

Jacob's benign patience faltered. "And how, may I ask, would that
differ from the way he treats you when you're no' with family?"

"It's all right, Papa. You won't have to fetch Great-grandfather's clay-
more from the attic. Cade was a perfect gen—" She broke off, her
breath rippling with impatience. "No. He wasn't so much a perfect
gentleman, as he was a-a caring man. Competent, composed, compassionate. We were all of us fortunate to have had him along as guardian
and guide."

Jacob grunted assent. He knew better than to start an argument
over their differing perspectives on *fortunate*. "Then why the long face?"

"Because"—she plucked a leaf from one of the trees flanking the
lane, twirling it between her fingers—"I don't know what to do about
this surfeit of emotion that seems to fill me up, whenever I'm around
him. It's ridiculous for me to entertain any sort of feeling for Cade
Beringer other than gratitude." She practically hurled the words.

A fringed surrey approached, and Jacob waited until the sound of
clip-clopping hooves and laughing voices faded into the night. "Why

not? You're not still harboring those old thoughts, are you? Comparing yourself to your sisters and coming up lacking?"

"It's not necessary to compare, only to accept who and what I am. That's what you've always taught us, what the Bible itself teaches." She thrust the leaf under Jacob's nose. "Do you see this leaf? It's a yellow poplar. *Liriodendron tulipifera.* Whether it grows here at a fancy resort hotel in the southern Appalachians, or in the back yard of a sharecropper's two-room shanty, it will always be a yellow poplar."

"Leah, that's not—"

"Unusual leaf, with this broad tip and a base that almost resembles a square. It's not saw-toothed and long-pointed like a slippery elm or pinnately compound like a black locust. God created this poplar, Papa, to be what it is." Lightly she brushed the leaf over her face. "The same way He created me."

Ah, Lord. Give me the words. "You saw I brought along your heartwood chest?" All the way from home Jacob had held the chest on his lap, on the train, then the stage. It was a part of Leah, and he had needed to keep it with him to survive not knowing where she was. "Did you open the secret drawer, before you came down for supper?"

"No. I saw no purpose in it. Why? This year did you replace the flower bulb with something other than another bulb? One of these leaves would provide an appropriate object lesson."

Sadly Jacob shook his head.

"Then there's no need to belabor the point. And certainly no need to have toted the thing all the way up here. Obviously I still fail to grasp what you've been trying to communicate all these years."

Suddenly she stopped dead, whirled toward Jacob. The leaf drifted forgotten into the darkness. "Papa, did you know that Cade was going to be here? At the same time I was invited?"

"And if I did?"

Leah froze, the pale oval face as distant and chilly as a winter moon. "Then whatever hopes you and Meredith and Benjamin and—and *God* concocted among yourselves about Cade and me are a waste of energy. Meredith I can ignore. I'd halfway anticipated her handiwork. But you of all people should know better. If not for the accident, Cade and I would already have gone our separate ways." Something dark, riddled with pain, stirred in her eyes. "This infatuation of his will die a natural death as well, now that we're here. If you must—"

"Infatuated, is he?" Jacob interrupted. "Cade's not a man to allow his interest in a lass to show if she was merely a passing fancy. And you've plainly told me that he stirs feelings in you. Good can come of tragedy, remember. It's possible, to my way of thinking, that the Lord has had a hand in bringing the two of you back together." He ignored her groan of frustration. "Why not give the lad a chance?"

"A chance to do what? Papa, think. Cade's a wanderer like Garnet. He needs open spaces, to commune with nature, as it were. My life is in a classroom, in a city. His faith moves mountains. Mine at best could move a grain of sand in a high wind. He's an idealist who harbors illusions about human nature that, frankly, appall me." For a second, desperation tightened her jaw. Then she ducked her head so Jacob could no longer read her face.

After an uncomfortable silence she cleared her throat, lifted her head, and smiled a bittersweet smile that would haunt Jacob for weeks. "You've always loved analogies, Papa. Let me phrase it this way for you. I'd rather stay like the bulb you stuff inside my heartwood chest. It may be ugly and dried up, but at least it's safe, in a familiar place. It won't ever be crushed by a storm or wither from lack of water, after a drop or two coaxed it into budding."

"Och, little wren…" He cupped her cheeks in his scarred workman's hands. "All these years, it's the wrong lesson you've learned. *The wrong one.* That's not why I put the bulb in your drawer. Think on it. What would happen if you planted that bulb in good rich soil? If you kept it watered, nurtured it as it grew? It would grow into a beautiful flower, no longer that ugly bulb. But that's not why I—"

She shook her head so vehemently Jacob cut himself off. Peering through the darkness, it came to him how she was suffering, suffering more deeply than he would have thought possible. *Why, she's as vulnerable as Garnet and Meredith ever were.* The shock was a fist in Jacob's belly, because he'd never seen it, not once in all these years. Until now, Leah had never allowed him a glimpse of her inmost soul. She'd built her walls sturdy and strong, shielding herself not only from the rest of a cruel world, but from her own father.

What have I done to this daughter of mine, when my only prayer was to bring her up in the way she needed to go, to become the woman You designed her to be? He opened his mouth, desperate with love, clumsy from the magnitude of his error. All he had intended was to explain his motivation for placing a flower bulb in the secret drawer of her heart-wood chest. He would have done anything, anything at all to erase that look of grief and pain.

Instead, Leah leaned into him, brushed a kiss against his cheek, then gently tugged his hands away. "I'm sure the bulb would make a beautiful flower," she said. "But I'm way beyond the season for bloom-ing, Papa. I'm sorry I'm such a disappointment to you. No matter how hard I try to keep it watered, my faith will never equal yours or Mered-ith's and Garnet's. If the results aren't to our liking, you'll have to do what you always do, with such success. Talk to God. When He gives you any insight, I wouldn't mind if you passed it along."

Wrought-iron benches were placed about the manicured expanse of lawn surrounded by the main drive. After Leah returned inside the hotel, Jacob sought out one of the benches, where he then spent a goodly time in prayer, mindful of Leah's parting words.

He had failed her, he now knew. Failed his youngest daughter in so many ways, because for too long—all her life?—he'd not made the effort to see beyond her implacably cheerful facade or the thirst for knowledge she substituted for a thirst for God.

Father, forgive me.

Now he knew it was because Leah felt she had no other choice. How could she trust the One she held responsible for her very nature?

Jacob braced his elbows on his knees and buried his face in his hands. This had to be his doing, his fault. His fault, not hers, that she felt unworthy to be loved. There was a burning deep in his belly, but he almost welcomed the pain. It was only justice that he suffer for the arro-gance of his heart, so smug in his role of wise father that he'd been blinded to a fundamental lesson of parenthood: Right lessons could still be learned wrongly, with children suffering lifelong consequences.

The eight-year-old Leah who demanded an explanation for the flower bulb was no longer a child. In some ways, unlike Meredith and Garnet, she never had been. And Mary…Mary had died when Leah was not even four years old. For all intents and purposes his youngest daughter had grown up with no memory of a mother's love to soften a father's mistakes, however well-intentioned.

Jesus. Jesus. I have not been a good example of Your love.

A breeze stirred the branches of the trees that screened the bench on three sides, setting the leaves to whispering. Jacob lifted his head. The splinter of a moonbeam sliced through the darkness directly onto his face, flooding him with the sensation of absolution and affirmation. His eyes dampened with tears. Borne on the soundless melody of the breeze, familiar words filled him up, bringing him back to a place of peace once more. The Lord knew, had always known, the intention of Jacob's heart… Good things could still result from man's sinful nature, because with God all things, in all ways, were working together for the good of those who loved Him.

But does Leah love You? Love you enough…

Even as the question nudged at his mind, Jacob knew it was not a question to which he deserved an answer. Leah's relationship with God was between her and the Lord. God's love was an everlasting love, and Jacob's but a poor reflection.

He sensed the Lord's forgiveness with more certainty, and was humbly grateful for it. But it would take a long, long time before Jacob would forgive himself for his part in locking his youngest daughter in a cage with invisible bars.

He spent another quiet hour wandering the grounds, away from the well-lighted paths, depending solely on moonlight for his guide. It was late, going for midnight, when he finally retraced his steps. He was weary, albeit spiritually refreshed.

As he trod quietly past one of the secluded benches, he heard a light gasp and the startled rustle of skirts. Jacob checked his stride, just able to make out the shrouded figure of a woman. Unlike most of the ladies who summered at Stillwaters, her costume was as dark as the night; if she hadn't gasped he never would have seen her.

"I beg your pardon," he said, taking a step closer. She seemed to be wearing some sort of veil. "I didn't mean to startle you."

"I didn't hear you," she admitted in a soft but cultured Tidewater drawl.

Jacob glanced around, but neither saw nor heard the presence of anyone else. "Are you all right? Would you like an escort?"

"No. I merely came out to enjoy the night." She rose, and he caught the faint scent of gardenia. "Excuse me. I must go."

Without another word she vanished into the darkness, heading away from the hotel. There was the soft swish of footsteps in the cool grass, then silence.

For some reason Jacob found himself thinking of Garnet, who as a child used to slip outside at night to count stars. Sometimes Meredith joined her, but counting stars bored her, and she would soon be off chasing lightning bugs or sneaking about trying to scare her sister.

As for Leah…

Jacob frowned. He couldn't remember a single night where Leah had joined her sisters in their innocent nocturnal play. The girls were of course supposed to be tucked in their beds, but Jacob had seen little harm in the occasional lapses, though he had made them promise never to go beyond the old sycamore at the edge of the yard. Even Meredith had curbed her natural rebelliousness enough not to test Jacob's resolve, so much had she and Garnet enjoyed those nightly excursions.

But not Leah.

It came to him now that, upon investigation, usually he would discover Leah in her bed, with a book and a small lamp. "You said we weren't supposed to go outside after bedtime," she'd told him once, her large doe eyes dominating her small face. "I don't want to disobey."

Och, but the picture filled his mind now. Jacob remembered tweaking her nose, explaining that he'd created a different set of rules for when that particular household rule was broken; he remembered trying to tease a smile from his solemn brown wren. But it was there the memory faded, for all that came to mind was her obdurate refusal. "I don't want to," she'd repeated. "I don't like it."

At the time, he'd attributed it to her overly conscientious sense of right and wrong, black and white, a facet of her character already well defined despite her tender years. He'd tucked the bedclothes around her chin and let her be. Now Jacob found himself wondering if there had been a deeper motive than simple obedience. He just wished that all those years ago he'd taken the time to find out.

Eighteen

wo days after their arrival at Stillwaters, Cade hitched Lester Turpin's horses, now rested and fit for travel, behind Ben's runabout and drove to Eagle Mountain, this time following the main road. Surprisingly, Lester Turpin wasn't in town.

Nobody seemed to know exactly where he'd gone, or when he'd be back, so in craven relief Cade left the horses at the livery stable. The antipathy between him and Lester had been instant and intense on Turpin's part, apparently irreconcilable. Cade was sorry for it, and sheepish because he truthfully hoped never to see the man again. His own conscience was clear, however; time to shrug aside questions for which there were no answers and regrets for what might have been.

It was late, after dark and after dinner, by the time he returned to Stillwaters. He was hot, tired, coated with road dust, and hungry as a mother bear with twin cubs. But at last he had discharged all his obligations and was now free to concentrate on more pleasant matters.

Like landscaping. And Leah.

His movements impatient, Cade pulled on a clean shirt and fastened the buttons. He'd grab a late bite of supper from the cold buffet available for guests until midnight, then track Jacob down. It was past time for the "lengthy chat" Jacob had requested the previous evening, the only occasion he and Cade had managed to speak more than two sentences to each other.

Cade knew the chat involved Leah, which was fine by him. He would have preferred to talk with Leah herself, but a determined man learned to avail himself of all opportunities. He needed that talk with Jacob, and soon.

Because Leah was avoiding him. In fact, her strategy had proved so successful that Cade hadn't spoken to her, much less seen her, since he'd left her with Meredith the night they arrived. The circumstances would have been amusing, had Cade been in a frame of mind to appreciate the irony.

After spending the last ten years in devotion to his calling, fending off advances, Cade decided his fascination over a woman who wanted nothing to do with him could only be the Lord's divine sense of humor. And—near as he could figure it—Leah wanted nothing to do with God, either.

Oh, she was devout, after a fashion—but it was an intellectual faith that allowed little room for growth or grace. What had happened, that she remained blind to the richness of a deeper faith? He wanted to know her, wanted to understand the convoluted workings of her mind, needed to unlock the secrets stored in her heart.

Most of all, he wanted to know why she was avoiding him. Coyness and cowardice were not part of Leah's makeup. Cade wrestled with the very *un*-Christlike urge to waylay the woman, then spirit her back into the wilderness where all her considerable defenses had collapsed, allowing him to see for the first time a hint of the undefended Leah Sinclair. She'd stayed in the back of his mind for years, he realized, ever since the first time they'd met when she'd challenged him with her disdain—and her honesty.

If this is the helpmeet You've designed for me, You've certainly chosen a peculiar way to achieve Your ends, Lord.

Cade could almost hear an echo of patient amusement in the reply that had drifted across his mind: God's ways were not Cade's, and Cade would do well to remember it. And wait patiently. Like the Lord.

His patience was further tested when he learned that the entire family was attending a concert, and wouldn't return for several more hours. And Ben had left a note asking Cade to meet him at the stables first thing in the morning.

Resigned but peaceful—after all, he would have the rest of the month—Cade spent a dreamless night, and as requested met Ben at the stables the following morning. They saddled a pair of horses and headed out for what Cade assumed was an early morning ride to discuss landscaping possibilities. But instead of exploring the grounds, ten minutes later Ben reined his mount to a halt on the edge of the road. "I want to show you something," he said, "unless you're too tired after the past several days for a bit of a rough ride?"

"If I said yes, would you change whatever plans you've made?"

Ben's head tipped sideways, a half-smile curving one corner of his mouth. "Nope. Any man who spends more nights under the stars than he does in a comfortable bed can handle an hour of rough trail."

"I'll try not to slow you down."

Ben laughed, pointing to a barely discernible path heading roughly southwest, straight up the side of a mountain. "That's where we're headed. Nugget, your horse, knows the trail, so you can give him his head."

"You going to tell me what's on your mind while we ride, or do I have to guess?" Cade asked dryly, eyeing the narrow trail that more resembled a goat path. "Or maybe you'd better fill me in now, so you won't have to shout. I take it our little jaunt is not public knowledge."

"Meaning Meredith doesn't know? Precisely. For one thing, I don't want to worry her." His eyes, the same intense shade of blue as his mischievous young son's, crinkled at the corners. "More to the point, I don't want her meddling, not until I'm certain of what's going on."

"This sounds serious, my friend." Cade settled back in the saddle and waited.

Ben's amusement vanished. " 'Fraid it is. There's a company— Allegheny Land and Development. They're buying land or mineral rights left and right, so they can mine the mountains along the southern edge of Stillwaters. To do so, they need to build a feeder line to the main track. I've been trying to block it." His horse tossed its head, chafing at the bit as though the animal sensed Ben's tension. "Opinion's about half and half, some folks seeing the beauty of the land disappearing in sludge and smoke, some seeing nothing beyond the possibility of economic growth. Trouble is, I think they're going to mine it regardless of public opinion or even legality. I want you to see the site, tell me if I'm reading this right."

"What can you do about it if you are?" Cade felt a chilly hand brush the back of his neck. "Ben, some of those boys play rough. I know of a consortium over in West Virginia. When the landowners dragged their heels about granting mining rights, there was bloodshed before it was all over." And it wasn't just human beings who'd been wounded; the land, always the land suffered.

I don't want this, Lord. I came here to rest.

"I know," Ben said grimly. "It's a ticklish dilemma, Cade. This is one of the most economically depressed regions in the state. I can't blame folks for wanting a piece of the pie. It's just this time…" A muscle twitched in his jaw. "I was hoping I'd bought enough land, that even if they sold mineral and timber rights, I'd have enough of a buffer to ignore it. We can't save every tree in the wilderness, Cade."

"So why are you fighting this time?" Cade listened to the bitterness underlying his reply and tried to moderate his tone. "Ben, we've been friends a long time. How about if you just tell me what's going on, leave me to wrestle with my conscience and you with yours."

"I know you didn't come here for this, and I'm sorry," Ben said quietly. "If it just concerned Stillwaters, I'd do what I could on my own. But a lot of other people, good people, could get hurt—and not just economically. I can't send Hominy out to gather information. He's too recognizable, like me. I couldn't think of anyone else…safe, whom I trust with my life, except you."

Cade ran a thumb along the supple leather rein. "This means that much to you? To others?"

"Yes."

The warning chill had intensified. "Then let's get it done. I've plans of my own—and I don't need any more obstacles blocking the way."

"Ah. Would any of those plans involve a strong-minded schoolteacher with big brown eyes?"

"Stay out of it, Ben. Someday you can tell me how much of this you and Meredith arranged. But for now…nobody likes to be manipulated, even when it's done out of love, for what you think is their own good."

"I hear you." Ben kneed his mount off the road and headed up the trail.

"Just for the record," he remarked some time later, when the path broadened and they were riding abreast, "I'm not sure how I feel about you with Leah. But if you think she's the one, then don't let anything stand in your way. Even family. Love's a risk. But you've been alone a long time. Take it from one who knows. The love of a good woman is worth far more than all the gems in all the world."

Fifty minutes later they reached their destination. With little warning, the narrow trail ended at the top of a bluff. Below them, a small meadow lay like a brilliant green thumbprint amid the thick hardwood forests. Beyond the forests endless rows of an ancient mountain chain loomed like sentinels over the hidden meadow. For several moments Cade sat motionless astride his horse, soaking up the panoramic beauty while a southerly wind brought a welcome coolness—and the faintest hint of smoke.

Somewhere in the distance, on the other side of the ridge beyond the meadow, a train whistle blew.

"Track's been laid to the foot of the mountain," Ben said, pointing. "According to one of the reports I got hold of, the mountain is riddled with top-grade iron ore. According to a different report, there's nothing there but an odd vein or two, not worth pursuing."

"Hmm. Interesting." Cade lifted a hand to shade his eyes. "Where's the Stillwaters boundary?"

"Runs a half-mile below the ridgeline for five miles, then cuts diag-onally down and across to this mountain we're on. At the time, that was the best I could do to ensure the sanctity of my vision for Stillwaters. I hired a surveyor from Washington, one I knew I could trust, back in April. He was supposed to have marked the boundaries with iron stakes, driven deeply into rocky ground. Hard to move those."

"Good thinking. Who owns the land on the other side, at the base of the mountain?"

When Ben didn't answer immediately, the chilly hand that earlier had brushed the back of Cade's neck clamped down. He studied his friend. Like Cade, Ben was hatless, and the wind had tousled his hair a bit, giving him a casual air at odds with his usual impeccably styled sophistication. His blue eyes were narrowed against the sun, and beneath his new, neatly trimmed beard, a corner of his mouth was curled in a faintly ironic smile.

"I only found out the day Leah went missing," he finally said. "I've been sitting on the information ever since—haven't even told Hominy. Frankly, I wasn't sure how he'd react if he knew, which is the other reason I haven't set him to investigating any further." He reached to pat his horse's neck, adding too casually, "It's Preston Clarke, Cade. J. Preston Clarke, my dear old *friend* from Winchester." For a moment his eyes flared hot as blue flame. "You remember Clarke, don't you?"

Cade expelled his breath in a long sigh. "I remember."

A little over five years earlier, J. Preston Clarke, one of the wealthiest men in the state, with family roots in Virginia all the way back before the Revolution, had decided that Benjamin Walker was a threat. He'd set out to destroy him and had almost succeeded. The fire that had mysteriously demolished Ben's hotel had killed ten people. Meredith had almost been one of them. And all evidence for that fire pointed to Clarke.

"It's not a coincidence, then, that he's nosing around your neighborhood?" he asked after a while.

"I doubt I could prove it, any more than I could prove he was responsible for that fire five years ago." Ben's voice was curt. "I didn't fight him then, Cade. I lost the Excelsior, but I didn't fight. Lost Poplar Springs Resort, but I let it go. Why? Because I'd decided to trust God to turn my life around. In all these years, I've never regretted that decision. My life, and my marriage, have been the stronger for it. But I'll say this plainly, so there won't be any misunderstanding between us. God's will or not, this time J. Preston Clarke is not going to win."

"Ben, I understand how you feel. But you're risking—"

"I know what I'm risking." The saddle creaked as Ben sat back, his movements impatient. "There's a meeting in Clifton Forge tomorrow. I'm not supposed to know about it." A thin smile flickered. "Some real estate developers and local businessmen—incited by Clarke through Allegheny Land and Development—plan to revive a speculative boom of 1890 that ended up practically destroying the town."

"And you think Clarke would sacrifice an entire town to destroy you?" Cade asked.

Ben lifted an eyebrow. "Yes. And no. He doesn't like the success we've enjoyed with Stillwaters. And strange as it may seem considering his behavior, he doesn't like the fact that he lost Meredith to me. Hominy found out that much. But with Preston, the final motivation remains power and wealth, and this area's ripe for the plucking. It's easy to pack a person's head full of lies when you fill it with dreams of instant riches. I don't want the town to suffer another financial fiasco like the one five years ago. And I absolutely will not allow anyone to despoil Stillwaters."

Another gust of wind seemed to snatch the words and hurl them like a gauntlet over the valley below. "I want you to attend the meeting," he said then, confirming Cade's suspicions. "One of the city council members is a friend of mine. He's going to be there, and I can persuade him to take you along in the guise of his assistant. You don't have to say a word. Just listen. Observe. You know people, and you can assess situations better than any man I've ever known."

Lately, that particular ability hadn't done a whole lot of good. "Ben, what good will it do? What are you truly hoping to accomplish here?"

Temper, quickly masked, sparked behind Ben's eyes. "I want you to verify that my fears are grounded in fact, and see if you can judge the tenor of the crowd. It would help to ferret out some of the opposition who agree with me to my face, then invest thousands of dollars in speculative real estate on either side of Preston Clarke's proposed feeder line. That's all. Just—sit there. Listen."

"Sit still and keep my mouth shut, hmm?"

"Don't, Cade. I'm not in the mood right now for your sense of humor."

"I can see that." He lifted a placating hand and struggled to keep the disappointment and frustration from showing on his own face. "What I can't see is how you—"

"I've already told Meredith I'm going to Clifton Forge this evening, for a meeting first thing in the morning. All you have to do is come along for the ride. I'll introduce you to Chester, then make myself scarce so nobody can connect you with me. That's it. We'll be home by late afternoon tomorrow, if the weather holds. And I promise, you can focus all your attention on landscaping."

For a long time Cade did not respond, mostly because he was afraid Ben's plan bordered on the absurd, and Cade didn't want to tell him so to his face. He'd learned through soul-shriveling experience that in the world of business, trying to do the right thing, for noble reasons, seldom produced hoped-for results. And doing what might be the wrong thing, even for the right reason—*Lord? Where's the boundary between laying down one's life for a friend and gently correcting a brother you believe is blinded to inappropriate actions?*

"Ben, I have to tell you I'm not real comfortable with this," he finally admitted. "I've done a lot of things over the years, fighting to preserve the mountains from lumber and mining interests. But what you're doing… It strikes me as awfully personal. What are you going to do if everyone at that meeting agrees with Preston Clarke?"

"I don't see how you can say that. There's not an honest bone in the blackguard's body."

"I also know you told me not five minutes ago that regardless of God's intent in all this, you're out for blood."

"Out for blood?" Ben stared at him, no longer disguising the anger. "What if I am? You haven't lost every single member of your family, haven't had your heritage stolen from you. You're so consumed with saving the wilderness that you deny any need for roots. When you fight your battles it's not for *your* land, *your* home, the home you want to preserve for *your* children." His horse shifted, pawing a restless foot. "And you're so consumed with your love of God that you have no concept of what it feels like to love a woman. To have the woman you would die for be played for a fool, by the same immoral cur who plans to turn that mountain into a treeless slag heap."

Wind set the branches behind them to swaying. Ben abruptly reined his horse backward and swiveled him around. "Forget it. I don't need you to do a blasted thing for me."

He rode his mount back down the trail without looking back.

Nineteen

*B*ecause Cade knew he'd hurt Ben's feelings, he didn't bother trying to apologize after they returned to the hotel. Instead, he hunted Hominy down and asked him what time Ben planned to leave that evening, and was waiting for him when Ben swung inside the coach, a little past eight o'clock.

"I appreciate the gesture, but it isn't necessary," Ben said, settling onto the opposite seat back with a tired sigh. He tossed aside his homburg and gloves. "You're welcome to come along for the ride if you like, but don't think I'm expecting anything else. I never should have tried to pull you into my problems." He paused, then added gruffly, "And I'm sorry for what I said this morning, Cade."

Wary but relieved, Cade waved his hand. "Forget it. I was about to apologize to you, for not being the kind of friend you've been to me. Now that we've dispensed with the apologies, you can spend the rest of the journey filling me in on everything."

"Cade, I told you I was wrong to involve—"

"Do we waste time arguing about it all the way to Clifton Forge or spend it more constructively by filling me in?"

Ben shook his head and gave a short laugh. "I reckon I can manage that," he drawled as the carriage started down the drive. "But you have to promise me that if you change your mind come morning, you'll tell me. I never meant to back you into a corner."

"God's been faithful over the years, helping me to wriggle out of quite a few of those." Cade ran his hand over the goatskin cushion. "Let's pray He'll see fit to do so again."

❧❧❧

CLIFTON FORGE

After a quiet night in a small hotel near the edge of town, the next morning Cade followed Ben down Main Street to an unpretentious clapboard building, which housed an insurance company on the main floor. Ben introduced him to Chester Wilcox, a beefy gentleman with shrewd gray eyes and a handshake like a stevedore's.

"Good of you to do this, Mr. Beringer. I'll be square with you both. I hear what Ben and others I respect have to say about Clarke. But there're equal voices claiming the opposite. Never met the man myself, you see, and that makes it hard."

"Preston Clarke's careful," Ben said. "Careful like a cockroach, only scuttling around in the dark. And I doubt you'll see him today, Chester. He wouldn't want to risk attending this meeting, because he doesn't want anyone to know the level of his influence until he's confident that he can have whatever he wants."

Wilcox tugged out his watch. "Best get on with it, then. Meeting's upstairs, first room on the right."

Ben nodded. "I'll be off. I'm supposed to meet with Eddie Sanders at nine over in West Clifton, to—"

"Eddie's here," Chester Wilcox interrupted. "He arrived for the meeting upstairs not five minutes ago."

The two men exchanged quick glances, in which Cade read equal parts frustration and concern. "Want me to bring him down here, let the two of you sort it out?" Wilcox offered.

Tight-lipped, Ben shook his head. "I'll come up. Why don't you introduce Cade around while I ask Eddie if he'd step out for a moment? He can tell me to my face why he's breaking our appointment without letting me know."

Cade opened his mouth, then shut it as he followed the two men upstairs. Though both he and Ben had apologized to each other, Cade still smarted a bit from yesterday's dressing down. Ben had spoken in anger, yes, but his words carried enough truth for them to sting. Over the years Cade's crusades against the destruction of the wilderness might have been fought with passion, but it was a passion without a personal stake.

Ben's involvement with J. Preston Clarke, on the other hand, was about as personal as it came. Ben was normally an even-tempered, fair-minded man, except with anything concerning J. Preston Clarke. Cade would do well to remember it. He was on unfamiliar ground here, along for silent observation and assessment only. Discretion dictated that he hold his peace, so he did. But as he climbed the stairs behind his friend, he struggled against a rising tide of uneasiness.

They reached the top just as the door to the meeting room opened.

"And though I'd rather stay here, offer my support, I'd already committed to this outing." Laughter floated into the hall as a slender man dressed informally in bicycling knee breeches appeared in the doorway, his back to the group on the stairs. He exchanged cheerful good-byes, then turned around.

Wilcox, in the lead, moved aside with a nod. Cade almost plowed into Ben, who had stopped dead in his tracks. The skin at the base of Cade's neck rose as he glanced up in surprise. Ben's face had turned to stone, with a look of naked enmity that chilled Cade's blood.

"Well, well. Mr. Walker," the unknown man said. Without looking away he pushed the door behind him until it shut, isolating the four of them in a menacing tableau. "What an…unexpected surprise, after all these years. I knew you were in the area, of course, but I've been too busy to look you up." Dark eyes the color of tar flicked from Ben to Cade, to a flabbergasted Chester Wilcox. Beneath a pencil-thin mustache his lips stretched in a mocking smile. "Joining the meeting, are you? What a shame I can't stay. We could catch up on old times. But before I go to meet my party, you must introduce me to your friends."

"Chester Wilcox, J. Preston Clarke." Each word emerged like the flick of a whip. Ben's chest swelled, and the vein in his temple darkened as blood suffused his face. He didn't acknowledge Cade. "Don't know this gent."

Above them Wilcox flushed, his bewilderment as obvious as the malicious speculation leaping from J. Preston Clarke's eyes. "You're a poor liar, Mr. Walker. An admirable quality, particularly in these times."

For the first time he focused fully on Cade, and a sinister smile grew over his sun-darkened face. "I'd very much like to know the man my old friend Benjamin Walker doesn't want to acknowledge." He lifted his hand. "J. Preston Clarke. And you are—?"

Cade sensed Ben's stiffening, and from the corner of his eye caught the slight warning shake of his head. Slowly he lifted his own hand. "I'm an old friend as well," he murmured, gripping Clarke's fingers firmly. "Known Ben for a very long time. Years."

"Ah. Years, you say?" The light tone frosted Cade's skin. "Someday we'll have to get together for a chat. I'm sure we'd find a lot of interesting things to discuss. Perhaps you could fill me in on the antics of his delectable wife. Until then." With a final measuring look he brushed past Ben and Chester Wilcox without another word, descending the stairs with an equally measured tread.

A moment later the outside door banged shut, and stale silence coated the hallway.

"So that was your Mr. Clarke. Seemed a pleasant enough fellow to me."

Chester Wilcox's voice seemed unnaturally loud. Cade shrugged his shoulders, but was unable to dispel the lurking aura of menace. He and Ben exchanged somber looks.

Wilcox cleared his throat. "Listen, I need to speak to a few folks before the meeting starts. Mr. Beringer, I'll save you a seat."

"Appreciate it, Mr. Wilcox." After he was gone Cade blew out a long breath. "Don't worry about it, Ben. I'll still attend this meeting, be your eyes and ears. Nothing's changed fundamentally from what we discussed."

"Except for one thing, my friend." Ben contemplated the scraped floorboards for a long time, his expression grave. "Now Preston knows your face, and it won't take him long to learn your name as well."

⊰❦⊱

Leah paused in her hike up a hillside, needing to catch her breath. She'd left the walking path choked with fashionably dressed guests and rambunctious children, all of them strolling along as though they owned the path if not the whole place. Though the resort was designed to provide guests an atmosphere of isolation and serenity, at the height of the season it was difficult to find a quiet spot despite the careful layout.

Wryly Leah admitted they had as much right to be there as she did, possibly more so since they had had to pay the exorbitant rates Benjamin charged them.

Sighing, she brushed off bits of bark and a dead leaf clinging to her sleeve, then dabbed perspiration from her temples and upper lip. At least she had finally escaped from the smothering scrutiny of her family. Their concern was well meaning but still annoying. Despite her obvious health after the brush with death, they persisted in mollycoddling her like an invalid.

Brush with death… If only they knew. But of course they couldn't, because she wasn't Meredith, spewing her feelings about with abandon. Or even Garnet, who for all her independent ways was able to share her needs and insecurities. Doggedly Leah resumed her climb, slipping often despite her hiking boots because there was no trail, only earth and leaves, crumbled pieces of limestone, and an occasional patch of soft green moss, a variety she regrettably couldn't identify. She had no idea where she was going, but she could still hear voices on the path below her, so she wasn't worried about becoming lost.

Lost.

She had come to Stillwaters for a spot of soul-searching, to exorcise the melancholy of these past months. Until the conversation with her father, Leah had not grasped the bloody nature of the battle. Bloody for her at least, from the knowledge that even when she'd been a child, Jacob had been disappointed in her.

Head bent, lost in her dismal musings, she paid scant attention to her surroundings until she all but plowed into a man. Leah grabbed the slender trunk of a nearby sapling to steady herself. Her gaze traveled from his worn hiking boots up to his face. She supposed she should have been surprised, but uppermost in her mind as she and Cade stared at each other was a sense of inevitability.

"It's time to have a talk," he said.

"I thought you were in Clifton Forge, with Benjamin."

A grimace of pain unexpectedly shadowed his face. "I was. We returned an hour ago." He paused, his hand idly stroking the trunk of the black gum he'd been leaning against when Leah almost ran into him. "I've been wondering for the past two days if God used Ben to get my attention, about a lot of things. But mostly—about you."

Leah took a deep breath. "Let's not mince words. It isn't necessary with me. You've no need to worry I'll chase after you like all those other ladies you've fought off through the years. Don't look so astonished. Meredith teases you about it, doesn't she? She's tossed excerpts of your life at me ever since she and Benjamin married, though lately she's tried hard—for Meredith—to be more subtle about it. Until this week, nothing she ever told me changed my initial impression of you."

She paused. It was more awkward than she had expected, with Cade actually standing there. In a war of words she might win. But on every other level, Leah could not wiggle out from under her ineptitude.

Cade, however, would *not* be privy to that weakness. Leah hauled herself farther up the hill above him until they were eye to eye and plunged in. "Over the past week I've come to better understand you, and my opinion has changed. You're an honorable man. I might not quite agree with everything you believe, but I have come to…to admire you, and the depth of your faith, very much. I can see, even if you don't, that the feelings you expressed toward me were generated from your kindness. Your compassion and decency."

For some reason the words didn't want to come out. She passed her tongue around her dry lips and cleared her throat. "Doubtless you feel trapped at the moment by that very decency. So let me assure you, again, that I have completely discounted everything you said in the heat of the moment. I'm under no illusions about myself"—the image of a dried flower bulb was forever burned into her brain—"and release you from any lingering obligations you might feel toward me."

A muscle jumped at the corner of Cade's mouth. Mildly puzzled, Leah stopped, searching his face. He hadn't moved, and certainly there was nothing alarming about his casual pose. And yet…

"Are you finished?" he asked then, in a lazy, almost amused drawl.

Leah nodded, frowning a little. "I'm sorry that I've been deliberately avoiding you, but I needed to analyze the matter. Formulate my thoughts. It's been difficult, as you might imagine, with Meredith and Benjamin and my father—Cade! What are you *doing?*"

He had scooped her completely off her feet, settling her high against his chest. "You might want to wrap your arms around my neck. Otherwise I'll have to sling you over my shoulder like a sack of grain."

"Put me down!" She squirmed, outraged.

"Not a chance." He gave her a look that shut her mouth and stilled her squirming, though her heartbeat accelerated to a gallop. "I've had a rough couple of days, what with Ben informing me that I use my faith as a shield to protect me from living, and your thinking I use it for protection against feminine wiles."

"I wasn't criticizing—"

He squeezed her, and his head lowered until their noses almost brushed. His eyes, Leah noted dizzily, were the same vivid green as a patch of moss she'd trod upon earlier. "Be quiet," he murmured, with a softness that sparked tingles from the nape of her neck to her toes. "Be still, and be quiet. In a few moments, we'll discover together what happens when I lay aside that shield."

He ascended the hill with a swiftness that belied the steepness of the climb and Leah's weight, then plunged down the other side, into dense woods that enfolded them in graveyard silence.

Twenty

Leah was defenseless against the sensations that now buffeted her. She yearned to maintain the righteous indignation, but Cade was carrying her in his arms, once again surrounding her with his strength, reminding her afresh of the long hours she had ridden double with him. Only this time they were completely alone. Leah could no longer pretend to be engrossed in friendly conversation with the Moores and B. W., no longer ignore those sensations.

More disconcerting than the lack of outrage, however, was the resurgence of a strange anticipation that set her pulse to thrumming. For Leah, an inchoate longing to be swept off her feet had become stark reality instead of a romantic notion. A notion Leah had derided—and denied—for over twenty years.

Mercysake, she'd placed herself in a fine pickle.

"This ought to do."

Cade lowered her feet to the surface of a slab of boulder so their faces remained inches apart. He clasped her hands, returned them to his shoulders, then wrapped his fingers around the base of her neck. His thumbs stroked a burning path back and forth across the line of her clenched jaw. "Since you think you know me so well now, want to tell me what I have on my mind?" he asked, his voice a shade breathless. "Don't worry. Neither of us has any use for subterfuge, remember. And I sure don't want you to misunderstand my intentions."

His eyes were blazing, the depth of his anger jarring. Leah had not taken into consideration the possibility that Cade possessed a temper. It was a mistake on her part, though she reminded herself that even when he'd thrown Lester Turpin, Cade hadn't exhibited anger.

Don't be such a coward. Temper or no, he wouldn't hurt her physically.

"You're only angry because your pride's been smacked. And apparently your feelings hurt because of my remarks about your faith. You want to"—she had to clear her throat, finishing thinly—"teach me a lesson."

Oddly enough, Cade looked stunned. He went still, so still Leah couldn't even hear him breathing. Then he blinked, shook his head, and his thumbs resumed those unnerving caresses along her jaw and throat. "You think I'm *angry?* Has no man ever declared an interest in pursuing you, then?" he murmured, half to himself. "Never even flirted with you? When you were in school, didn't some eager young boy ever steal a kiss, profess undying love for you?"

"You're confusing me with my sisters." Humiliated, Leah lost the battle and closed her eyes, since he wouldn't let her turn away. "Boys had no use for a plain brown wren, even to tease. That's what everyone called me, even my father. The wren. Small, nondescript, unnoticed. The young men I met occasionally at a lecture while I was attending Mary Baldwin were impressed by my intellect and used to challenge me to debates. But there was never any romantic interest. I'm not the kind of person who inspires such in a man."

"I believe we've had this discussion, the one that establishes me as a man. Not some sort of ascetic monk just because I talk to God with an ease you can't understand. Since we're being honest, I have a confession of my own."

For some reason his gaze had dropped to her mouth. "I might not understand why God brought you into my life, but I accept—finally—that He has. No matter what scheme your sister may have hatched, this has nothing to do with her. Because she didn't 'arrange' our meeting in the Buchanan depot." His thumb moved to beneath her chin, then pressed lightly against the pulse fluttering in her neck. "And what I'm feeling now"—slowly he drew her closer—"has nothing to do with anger. Or kindness and compassion, at the opposite end of your skewed dissection of my character traits."

"Teaching me a lesson?" Leah whispered. "This is a lesson, then, to remind me not to ridicule your faith?" Even to her own ears the explanation sounded implausible, but she couldn't help it. For the first time in her life, her mind was...mush.

"Hmm. Definitely more of a challenge than I realized. No, Leah, my behavior is definitely not motivated by revenge, either. But it might involve a lesson of sorts." Cade lowered his head. "I take it then, that no man ever kissed you?"

"I've never been kissed by anyone but family," she heard herself confess numbly.

"Ah." For just a moment the stroking fingers stilled. "That honesty…" Then his thumb slid up her jaw to brush over her lips. Leah jumped. A softness drifted over Cade's face. "Know something?" he murmured. "Wrens have always been among my favorite birds. Close your eyes again, little wren. You're about to receive your first kiss."

She obeyed without thought and a second later felt Cade's lips against her own. It was a careful kiss, she realized even in her spinning confusion, as though he were coaxing her into lowering her defenses, like the warmth of the sun rather than a violent wind pushing a storm over the mountains.

When he lifted his head Leah's eyes fluttered. She blinked up at him, dazedly lifting her fingers to her lips. "Oh."

The pulse in Cade's neck was throbbing. Her other hand seemed to have found its way to his chest, and beneath her fingertips she could feel his heart beating. "Your heart's pounding," she said, and he laughed.

"It is, isn't it? And how about yours, sweet Leah?"

For the first time in her life, Leah blushed scarlet. "Well, yes," she mumbled, automatically analyzing, cataloguing—and marveling at herself. "And my lips are tingling, my limbs are… Why, I believe they're trembling." Confused, she would have backed away except she realized she would have collapsed in a boneless heap. "I don't understand. I'm not a blushing young girl, not a beautiful—*Mmph.*"

His second kiss rendered her speechless as well as mindless. This time, when Cade lifted his head, Leah was so dizzy she laid her head over his thundering heart. Cade's arms tightened, and she felt his fingers in her hair.

"You're a woman, Leah Sinclair. Very much a woman—look." He tugged her head back and held his hand in front of her face. "See? I'm trembling too." He lifted her fingers and pressed them against his mouth. "And my lips are tingling. Leah"—his arms wrapped back around her, pulling her close as he rested his chin on her head—"I've never felt like this, with any other woman. Do you believe me?"

"No," she told his shirt front, even as her head was nodding assent. "I don't know." A sigh shuddered up from the soles of her feet. "This is not…logical."

A laughing groan gusted past her ear. "Never is, wren. It never is— to humans. But God sees things a bit differently than we do."

Leah allowed herself the luxury of drifting on a sea of uncertain euphoria. For a moment longer she savored the warmth and strength, the dangerous *need* to believe. Then she brought her palms up to Cade's chest and pushed.

He released her, his reluctance plain.

For the first time she studied him like a woman, a woman who had just been thoroughly kissed. It was not a salutary exercise, because what she really wanted instead of a verbal analysis was for Cade to kiss her again.

"I've always looked for a rational explanation," she began, a shade desperately, "for why God created mankind with free will because He needed us to come before Him without coercion. Then He gives us all these emotions. Emotions that keep us separated from Him throughout our mortal existence. Bodies that trick those emotions through the power of physical passion. Not all attraction is ordained by God. But how does one tell the difference?"

"I can't speak for others, but for me…it's not so much explaining the difference as it is acknowledging it, when you kiss the woman that God has designed to be your mate."

Alarm shrieked through Leah, shattering the euphoria. "Cade, you mustn't say things like that. Not to me. I'm not like you. I have no basis for comparison. For years I've counseled young girls in the throes of what they were convinced was love, only to discover a week, or a month, or perhaps even a year later that they had mistaken physical attraction, and their own longings, for love."

"There's a difference between a young girl of fifteen or sixteen, and a grown woman."

"And your explanation for the countless adult men and women, supposedly more mature, who engage in illicit and promiscuous behavior? If they claim it's 'love,' does that make it from God and therefore acceptable?"

"Of course not." He gave her earlobe a teasing tug. "Impossible woman. I'm not talking about the rest of the world. I'm talking about believers, people who honor God with their lives as well as their lips, people who seek His will with all their hearts, people who have the Spirit of Christ to help them discern whether a path, or a person, is the right one. Leah, I'm talking about you and me."

"How noble." A fiery thorn of temper stabbed deep, drawing blood. Leah stood on tiptoe and thrust her face next to his. "I don't have that kind of relationship with God!" The pain of it, the humiliation of years of struggle and searching and buried longings boiled up in a tirade. "I never will. My faith has always been a matter of choosing to believe, with my will, because I find the alternative abhorrent. That's not enough for a man like you. Don't try to placate me, or deny it—I can read it in your face. You're just like my father. Both of you are good men, godly men, men like King David with a heart for God. 'A man after God's own heart,' wasn't that David? Well, God didn't give me a heart like that. Ask my father. My heart's a dried-up flower bulb."

"Leah…"

"No." She jumped from the boulder to the ground and backed away, wrapping her hand around the low-hanging branch of a tree and squeezing until her fingers went numb. "I will never forget your—the kiss. Thank you for making me feel like…" She couldn't finish it, couldn't tell him that for the first time in her life she'd felt an equal with her sisters. A woman, capable of not only inciting passion but experiencing it herself.

But if she was capable only of physical passion for a man, without a corresponding spiritual passion for God, she was limited forever to…to lust. Not love. Or at least not the godly manifestation of love between male and female that God intended.

She would never be an equal with her sisters, much less with her father and Cade, in spiritual matters. Matters of the heart, so contrary to the logic of the mind.

Calm settled back over her. Calm, and iron control. "Perhaps God did bring us together," she murmured, not quite able to look up at him. "You sound so sure. I envy that. I envy your trust in a heavenly Father who blesses you with such insight. I have neither insight, nor proof that builds confidence." Gathering every scrap of resolution, Leah finished it. "I do possess enough insight, however, to know what you're looking for. You're hoping for a union like my sisters share with their husbands. For that, you'll have to find another woman."

Cade folded his arms across his chest. "I don't think so. You may not be able to compare your feelings with past experience. But I can." He hesitated, then continued simply, "When I was nineteen, I asked a young woman to marry me. I loved Patricia, and she loved me. She was the daughter of our minister, and we both felt God's divine hand in bringing us together, filling our hearts with love for each other. But four months before the wedding, while I was finishing my final year at Harvard, Patricia was struck and killed by a runaway freight wagon."

He absorbed Leah's open-mouthed astonishment with matter-of-fact patience. "I'm sorry," she managed after a moment.

One shoulder lifted. "It was a bad time. But I understand better now, some of the good God was able to bring out of a senseless tragedy I'm convinced was never part of His ideal will. For years, I believed it was because He wanted me to be like the apostle Paul, devoting my heart and life in service for His kingdom. Only for me, it was as a steward of His creation, if you will."

"From everything I've heard and seen, you've been very successful," Leah said, her voice still sounding weightless. *Cade Beringer, engaged?*

"Mm. Might debate my 'success' with you. Later. Right now, I plan to have my say. And that is, I know how it feels to love a woman, Leah. Equally important, though harder to admit, I know how it feels when God's leading is *not* a part of the relationship. I mourned Patricia for almost three years, then decided I didn't want to spend the rest of my life as a bachelor." A band of red deepened the bronze cast of his tanned cheeks. "Out of loneliness and determination, I convinced myself a time or two that what I felt was love. It wasn't."

"You don't have to explain," Leah began, a corresponding heat climbing into her own cheeks.

"With any other woman, I wouldn't. But Leah, I do love you. And I need for you to believe that, even if *you* don't understand the difference, I do."

He loved her? How could he just trot out the words as easily as if he'd remarked on the weather? Hadn't the man listened to a word she'd said? Leah clasped her slippery hands behind her back, planted her feet on the uneven ground, and prepared for a siege of unknown duration. "How can you say it's different, especially after what I just told you?"

"It's different," Cade said, "because of God. Like I told *you*, I think that when people seek after God first, with all their hearts, the love He returns in response spills over into all their human relationships. Friends. Family. Strangers. Husbands and wives—especially them. My parents have been married over forty years. Their love is"—he ran a hand around the back of his neck—"their love for each other, well, for me, that's the best illustration of how God desires to work in all human lives, at least in our spiritual lives. Honesty and trust. Fidelity and intimacy. Communication. I'm convinced I would have shared that with Patricia, if we'd married. I'm even more convinced that you and I—"

"Not all marriages reflect *my* notion of God's love," Leah interrupted, fresh panic warring with determination. "In fact few of them ever achieve that exalted status. Most marriages I'm aware of are arranged to accommodate base human desires. In many of them, God doesn't enter into the arrangement at all."

"I know, I know. But the ones like Meredith and Ben, and your sister Garnet and her husband—those do." He gave her a peaceful smile.

She wanted to slap it clean off his face. "I'm not like my sisters. I'm not like my father, or you. I've told you a number of times, God doesn't 'speak' to me like He does the rest of you. Whether that's His choice, or a character flaw on my part, I've given up trying to understand. You claim you love me, and that it's a love given to you by God. Don't you find it strange that God didn't condescend to share His plan with me?

"If I were you, I'd do everything in my power to excise that love you feel toward me. We'd be unequally yoked, Cade. My faith isn't strong enough for us to pull a marriage together. Find yourself a woman who better characterizes your analogy of Christian marriage and God's love."

Her body had frozen into ice, except for her eyes. They burned, stinging as hot as though she'd rubbed them with chili peppers. "I already have to live with the knowledge that my father is disappointed in me. I don't need another devout man of God praying in vain for a dried-up flower bulb that's never going to bloom."

But she wasn't a coward. She wasn't, so she kept her gaze glued to Cade's.

It was almost as difficult as watching the campfire die.

He stood in front of her looking as austere and unapproachable as the slab of limestone she'd been standing on. No more gentleness, or the quiet good humor and bone-deep confidence he'd always manifested. His seemingly relaxed stance was deceptive: His shoulders were rigid, the hand at his side uncurling and curling into a fist.

"You're very good with words, Leah," he told her. "No doubt you win every debate. But there are a few words I haven't heard in all your explanations and suppositions." His chest lifted and fell. "I told you that I loved you. It wasn't easy. Right now, I feel like I've been carved up pretty good, by someone who knows how to wield words like knives. Trouble is, you failed to deliver the mortal blow. The one to my heart, in case you're not following my analogy." A smile shorn of humor flickered and died. "You haven't told me that you're not in love with me."

Leah opened her mouth, but the denial refused to take shape. She didn't know what it felt like to love a man. How could she know, how could anyone who had spent a quarter of a century resigned to spinsterhood grapple with such an indefinable emotion?

She couldn't deny that feelings for Cade existed that in no way resembled love for her father, for Benjamin or Sloan. Familial. Sisterly. Friendly. Her feelings for Cade were more volatile. More painful. Impossible to analyze with any success.

"I'm waiting, Leah."

"I don't…" The memory of the tenderness with which he'd kissed her locked her jaw, paralyzed her lungs. "Don't…" She pressed a fist against her breastbone and tried in vain to take a breath, "I don't know."

"Ah." So swiftly she wondered if she'd imagined it, a sliver of light winked through his eyes, chasing away the shadows. "Not knowing's better than not caring at all." He took a step toward her, his arm lifting. "Come here, love."

Leah jerked backward. "Don't call me that."

Cade was having none of it. Firmly he drew her to him, his fingers burning through the fine lisle of Friday's pale pink shirtwaist. He might as well have clasped her bare skin. "Why not? You are. And one day you'll believe it. I'm a patient man, remember. Patient and persistent. And I want you to be my wife, for the rest of our lives. I want you to marry me, Leah."

"It's no use." Her tongue felt swollen, clumsy. "Cade…no use."

" 'What God hath joined together,' " he quoted softly, his gaze relentless. "Don't be afraid of it, Leah. Remember the night in the wilderness? I kept the fire going for you then, didn't I? Trust me, if you can't bring yourself to trust God yet. I can't promise all the answers. But I promise to help keep the darkness away."

His free hand rose to cup her cheek. "Ben was only partially right about me, you see. I have been consumed with doing what I feel God has called me to do. But I also know how it feels to love a woman. Give me a chance to show you. Give us a chance to have what God has given Ben and Meredith. And yes, that's the kind of marriage I want, Leah. One day, I believe you'll be brave enough to admit it's what you want as well."

"Courage has little enough to do with it," Leah said. "Mrs. Willowby, our housekeeper, had a saying when we were growing up. 'You're not too old for your wants to hurt you,' she'd tell us when there was something we really wanted, but she knew better than to provide."

With her last scrap of strength she brought her own hand up to Cade's, still cradling her cheek, and pressed her fingers against his. Then she stepped back, her eyes dry, burning like the fires of perdition as she stared into his. "I'm returning to Richmond, as soon as possible. Let's see how long your love, and my wants, linger when there're two hundred miles and two mountain ranges between us."

Twenty-One

It was a little past nine in the evening. Guests wandered about the main lobby, some headed for the dining room, some the ballroom, where a string quartet played gentle melodies designed to suit the peaceful atmosphere. Others lounged about the alcoves and parlors, enjoying the people along with the ambience of cool mountain breezes and quiet conversations.

Here at Stillwaters, contentment was promoted over clamor.

Cade had been invited to join the Walkers in a private parlor overlooking a small lake. Since the dining room overlooked it as well, Cade was supposed to study landscaping possibilities to complement the view. Unfortunately, this evening Cade's mind was more on the absent family members than landscaping.

"If you're going to keep eyeing the door," Meredith finally said, "then give Samkins to his papa or me, before both of you come to grief."

Cade looked up from his cross-legged seat on the floor, where he and Sam had been fitting pieces of a wooden train set together. "Sorry. But he's fine, aren't you, growly bear?" He flicked the unruly chestnut locks and winked.

"T'ains!" Sam smiled a beatific smile, held up a finished caboose—and flung it with gleeful abandon, missing Cade's ear by a whisker. The toy smacked into the spindle leg of an antique table and disintegrated in a shower of wooden pieces.

"Samuel." Ben leaned over from a nearby chair, his face stern. "What did I tell you about throwing things inside?"

Sam ducked his head, glancing sideways toward Cade, his bottom lip pooched out in an uncanny Meredith-like pout. Cade bit the inside of his cheek as he rose. "Sorry, sprout. Can't help you this time. House rules."

He watched Ben scoop up his son and march toward the door, thinking with a pang about the responsibilities that accompanied the joys of fatherhood.

"Ben's much better with discipline," Meredith commented from the black walnut escritoire where she'd been writing a letter. "All Sam has to do is gaze solemnly at me with those big blue eyes, and I melt. He looks just like his father, doesn't he?"

"Except when he pouts. Then he's the image of his mama."

Meredith crumpled a piece of paper and tossed it across the room, her aim far more accurate than her son's. Cade turned sideways, snatching the missile out of the air just before it hit his face. "Now I see where Sam learned to throw things."

Meredith laughed. "Oops. I concede the point."

She pushed her chair back and stood, walking toward Cade with the poised grace of a duchess. She was wearing a frothy white lace concoction that she'd told Cade with a mischievous grin was called a *lingerie* dress when he complimented her appearance. Glistening pearl and diamond bobs dangled from her ears. She...glowed with life, and love, Cade thought. No wonder she'd captivated J. Preston Clarke as well as Ben.

He pictured Leah at dinner earlier, in her unadorned dark green skirt and white shirtwaist, her only jewelry a simple bar pin attached at her throat. His heart ached for the plain little girl surrounded by her two striking sisters.

Leah's mental toughness awed Cade even as it brought him to his knees. She'd sat next to Meredith at dinner, calmly eating while Meredith exhausted everyone at the table with her efforts to prevent Leah from leaving.

"If you're waiting for her, you'll wait in vain," Meredith murmured at his elbow now. She laid a hand on his arm and gave it a commiserating squeeze. "But I thought it was a good sign, of sorts, that she refused to look at you for the entire meal, even though you sat directly across from her."

Cade lifted her hand and brushed a kiss across her knuckles. "I'm not waiting for Leah. I'm waiting for Jacob."

"Oh." A gleam turned her hazel eyes to gold-shot green. "Going to ask him about her heartwood chest, perhaps?"

"You're incorrigible. You know that, don't you?"

"One of my most endearing traits." She pondered him, putting one finger to her cheek. "You've seen my heartwood chest?"

Cade nodded, thinking of the crudely finished box she kept proudly on display in the parlor of their private quarters. It bore little resemblance to her sisters' heartwood chests, because Benjamin, not Jacob, had made the one in Meredith's parlor.

"You remember the story, don't you?" When he nodded again, Meredith shook her head at him. "Don't look so patient, I promise not to bore you with it again. Suffice it to say that, like Leah—like Garnet —I, too, did not understand Papa's reasoning."

"But you have a better grasp of it now that you're a parent yourself, don't you lass?" Jacob answered her.

He strolled into the room, but Cade instantly divined the older man's distracted air. The body was present, but his mind seemed engaged elsewhere. *Leah.* Had she spoken with her father, perhaps begged him to tell Cade to leave her alone? Cade's hands fisted.

"And you delight in pointing it out to me," Meredith said, swatting Jacob's forearm, then pressing a kiss to his cheek. "What is it? You've got that wrinkle between your eyes." Alarm flooded her face. "Your ulcer? Papa, are you in pain?"

"I'm hale and hearty as English oak." He glanced across at Cade, shaking his head. "Except for the occasional twinge, I've *been* hale these past six years. Your sister's little adventure might have added a gray hair or two, but other than that, I plan to be waltzing at wee Sam's wedding, thank you very much."

"I'm glad to hear it, Papa."

"Now that we've settled my health, I've a question about one of your guests." There followed a sheepish sort of pause. "The veiled lady. Mostly only see her about at night, and alone. Who might she be? And before you go to reading aught into it, my girl, I'm asking only because I came upon her just now, when I was returning from my evening perambulations. I started to wish her a bonny evening, but she fled as if I'd aimed a pistol at her."

"Poor Papa. Not used to ladies running from you, are you?" Meredith walked across to the pocket doors and pulled them shut before returning to Cade and Jacob. "That's Mrs. Carlton, Fiona Carlton. Every time I see her, my heart hurts."

"Name's familiar," Cade murmured, relieved. He flexed his shoulders and with a lighter heart decided to look for an opportune moment to maneuver Meredith out of the room.

Jacob was impatiently telling his daughter to stop being melodramatic and answer his question.

"She was a famous concert pianist, after the war," Meredith said. "But according to Benjamin it's been over twenty years since she played publicly. He heard her once, when he was about twelve or thirteen, he told me, working in an opera house in New York. Her husband was a famous conductor but also managed her engagements. Mrs. Carlton has this scar on her face. Doubtless the reason she wears that veil, and perhaps the reason she no longer performs. I don't know the details. Like I said, it all happened over twenty years ago."

Her movements graceful but distracted, Meredith wandered about the room gathering scattered pieces of caboose. "She wrote a letter three years ago—our first season here?—requesting a room for the season, through October. She's returned every year. She's the most private person I've ever met. Takes all her meals in her room, doesn't mingle. We seldom see her, but she's always wearing a veil when we do. Reminds me of Garnet when she never ventured out in public without those awful bonnets."

"And you don't know how she came by the scar?" Cade asked. He'd heard the story behind Garnet and her bonnets.

"No. Mrs. Carlton is a wonderful guest in one sense, because she makes few demands on the staff. But other guests have commented on her reticence. It does seem extreme. You needn't take her response personally, Papa, is what I'm trying to tell you. It would appear she's like that with everyone."

"Ah. Good to hear 'tis nothing I've said or done. It's a sorry day, watching every woman I inquire after flee in the opposite direction."

They all laughed, but there was a sadness in Jacob's eyes at odds with his jovial non sequitur. He was referring to Leah. Cade knew it, yet he couldn't figure out why she would feel it necessary to run from her own father. He was chewing over that when Meredith announced she probably needed to check on Sam and Benjamin. "It's also Samkin's bedtime, and he'll want his mama."

"Ten o'clock's a bit late, isn't it?" Cade ventured.

"Of course it is. But if we put him down at seven-thirty or eight, he's up at four. I'm not even *human* at four in the morning, and I figure it's not fair to expect Gabby to be either."

With a parting nose-rub for her father and a gamine smile for Cade, Meredith glided from the room, her arms laden with a wooden train.

"Life here is certainly never dull." Jacob rocked a bit on his heels. "But I'm thinking you're not particularly interested in jabbering about life here at Stillwaters, now are you?"

"No." Cade gestured toward the door. "Care for another stroll? I'd prefer to keep a pair of interfering matchmakers out of this, if you don't mind."

"Aye, lad. I can see where your patience has been tested to the limit."

Once they reached the main drive, Cade suggested a path that led to a small glade, where a tiny waterfall scarcely as wide as his palm tumbled from moss-draped boulders into an equally narrow rocky creek that melted into the darkness. Scattered about the glade were several natural wood chairs of the design Jacob had created some years earlier, for another of Benjamin's hotels.

"I enjoy sitting here," Cade murmured. "Especially when it's dark, or very early in the morning when there's nobody else around. I like to listen to the music of the wind and the water. It's almost like listening to the Lord..." He ran his palm over the smooth-sanded slats that formed the chair's back. "These chairs of yours make it even more of a pleasure. They're very comfortable, Jacob."

"Every craftsman enjoys a bit of praise," he responded, dropping into one of the chairs and resting his arms along the chair's. "But 'tis more of a joy, hearing the love of the Lord in the words you speak."

Cade had decided on the short walk that there was little time for polite evasions. "Leah would argue with you. My faith…seems to annoy her."

"Och, not annoy, lad. Confuse. Faith without sight, without proof, has always confused the girl. I've often asked the Lord why He blessed her with such a fine brain, when He knew she'd have a struggle all her life over how to reconcile the miraculous with the mundane."

In the opalescent white of a full moon, pain swirled darkly in Jacob's eyes. "Do you know, she quit asking me questions about God when she was but nine years old? Not because she wasn't interested—but because I didn't have the intellect to communicate with hers. 'Tis a humbling truth, but there you have it."

"I want to marry her. "

Silence fell between them, punctuated by a sigh from Jacob with what sounded like utter weariness.

"She told me," he said finally.

"And?" Cade shifted in the seat. When Jacob didn't elaborate he leaned forward, propping his elbows on his knees. "Never mind. Let me guess. She told you that it was impossible, that we were nothing alike. That once she was gone, I would realize my feelings had deluded me, masking Christian compassion as love."

The hurt and, yes, the anger of it had been kicking him like a loco mule ever since. "Tell me something if you can, Jacob."

"What is it you want to know? I'm on your side, son. Remember that. Whatever comes of this, I'm not out to stay the Lord's hand."

Cade worried his hair with restless fingers for a while. Then he looked across at Jacob and asked simply, "Why doesn't Leah cry?"

"Ah." Moonlit shadows played over Jacob's face as he leaned against the chair back and closed his eyes. "Now there's a question. One I can't answer, Cade. 'Tis God's truth that I don't know." Cade watched his chest rise and fall beneath the neat sack coat he wore tonight. "And I'll admit to you, and you alone, that the reason I don't know is likely my doing. I've failed my daughter, in ways that make my soul bleed. Didn't realize it until just recently. But I have…" He stopped, crossing and recrossing his legs. "I'll share a piece of memory with you, one that came to me, these past few days. It's the day we buried Mary, my blessed wife. The girls' mother…" He stopped again.

Cade waited unmoving, praying for insight. For the strength to accept whatever he learned.

"It wasn't raining that day," Jacob continued at last. "They say a good funeral needs a good rain shower, but Mary did love the sun. I remember thinking that the Lord was allowing it to shine, that cold March day, just for her."

He stopped again, so Cade made an encouraging sound, and with another deep inhalation, Jacob continued.

"I was concerned for the girls. Grieving myself, of course, felt like an awl was buried in my breastbone, don't you know. But I was after all a man grown. The girls…" His voice softened with memory. "Meredith was certainly the most vocal. She was seven, and sobbed hysterically for most of the service, clinging to my hand like a little monkey. But by suppertime, she was dogging the neighbor women in the kitchen, telling them she had to be the mama now. And she was hungry, so we were all going to eat supper right that very minute."

Cade smiled. That was Meredith, all right.

"Garnet, now…Garnet was six, like Meredith just old enough to understand the finality of death. Garnet wept too. But it was slow, soundless. Wrenching tears that twist a body's heartstrings. She stood there by her mother's grave, a handful of Mary's favorite flowers clutched in her wee hands, and wouldn't budge. I had to carry her away in the end. And until she married, during their season she laid a spray of black-eyed Susans on Mary's grave every Sunday."

Another silence followed, this one dark as the inside of a coffin. "And Leah?" Cade managed after a moment.

"Leah wasn't quite four. At the time, I thought her too young to understand, and her reaction did naught to show me the folly of my thinking. How could I have known—"

In an abrupt motion he shoved up from the chair and strode to the silvery waterfall.

Cade waited, watching Jacob's shoulders lift and square, much the way Leah's had when she was preparing to lay bare her soul. *Help us both, Lord. Whatever the burden, help us both to understand.*

"I was wrong," Jacob said, still with his back turned. Then he swiveled on his heel, returned to his chair and dropped heavily back down. "Stupid, and wrong. Complacent. Incredibly blind toward my youngest daughter."

"Jacob, you'd just buried your wife."

"Aye, that's what I told myself. But, Cade...the last time I saw Leah cry was the day we buried her mother."

The two men stared at each other, while the moon hung above the quiet glade and the waterfall splashed its delicate melody in the cool summer night.

"I didn't realize it, at the time." For the first time Jacob's voice sounded every one of the man's fifty-odd years. "She wept on my shoulder, then went to sleep. I suppose I thought that a natural reaction, for such a wee lass. Truth be known, those first months are still not clear. I remember how grateful I was for such an intelligent and well-behaved little girl. Meredith and Garnet were a handful for a widowed father, don't you know. You might expect my baby girl would be more troublesome. But she never was. Intense, to be sure, and oh so serious." His voice turned husky. "She was my baby, yet Leah tried to mother us all."

A half-gasp, half-groan burst from his throat, and he hid his face in the palm of his hand. "Dear Father in heaven," he ground out hoarsely, "we let her mother us all, and I never saw that what she needed more than any of us was to be mothered herself. I should hae known better, but I was a blind, arrogant dolt of a man."

Cade leaned to grip his shoulder, amazed at the strength of muscles rigid at the moment with deep emotion. "Jacob, don't carve yourself up about it, my friend. You gave her love, you gave all your daughters love. You showed them by living it, the love of God. I doubt anyone could ask for a better father. Someday I hope you'll meet mine. You're very much alike."

"I doubt that. A better father would have understood sooner." His hand lightly pummeled the chair arm. "'Tis my fault Leah's unable to grasp the incomparable love of her heavenly Father, because of my blundering ways. Then—and now. Most likely she's running away because of me, not you, lad."

Jacob's suffering was undeniable, his guilt over whatever happened between him and Leah plainly eating away at him. But Cade was burdened with trials of his own; it took a moment or two before he accepted that, to win the daughter, he must understand the father and possibly reconcile the two of them.

He sat back and folded his arms. "Why don't you tell me about it? Perhaps I can help. We have all night, if need be."

"You promise me that you love her?"

God help him, was there no one willing to take his word? *Must I prove myself to Jacob as well, Lord?* "Yes." The declaration rang out in the night. "She isn't an easy woman to love. But, God as my witness, what I feel for your daughter is love. Not pity. Not responsibility. Not lust." A forced laugh burst free. "Though you may as well know that it's a temptation to carry her off into the wilderness, and not just because I desire her. She's a completely different woman there. She can't hide, Jacob. From me, or herself."

"Hmph. Then perhaps 'tis just as well the lass *is* fleeing from you."

At least he hadn't threatened to come after Cade with a hammer. "Jacob, I'm letting her go for now. But I will go after her." And if the Lord was merciful, sooner rather than later. *I've been patient for a long time, You know.*

Jacob cleared his throat. "Well, then, that being the case, I'd better share with you about the secret drawer of my youngest daughter's heartwood chest. While I'm about it, I'll need to share as well what I'm thinking is the greatest mistake of my life."

Twenty-Two

*S*he didn't know why she was stopping by Sinclair Run instead of returning straight to Richmond. Nothing to be found at the old homeplace but a houseful of memories, a nosy housekeeper, and Deacon, who pestered the life out of her. And yet…something had pulled Leah home.

She was annoyed with her unwelcome indecisiveness and sat stiffly beside the station agent's nephew, Michael Hoffelmeyer, in his rattletrap wagon. He'd been leaving for Cooper's Mercantile when Leah arrived and had offered her a ride to Sinclair Run. At the moment, Leah wished she'd remained aboard the train. Dust clogged her nostrils and filmed her clothing, her hair—even her teeth.

This is a mistake. She should never have yielded to a momentary impulse. She knew better.

"Glad to see you're all right, Miss Sinclair. Jacob was right tore up, what with you disappearing and all. So what in tarnation happened, anyways?"

"An accident. I was not injured. Thank you for your inquiry, but I'm very weary. From the trip." She managed a civil smile but avoided meeting his gaze.

"Yes'm." Mr. Hoffelmeyer jiggled the reins, tugged his cap lower, and for the rest of the journey remained silent.

Within a mile Leah regretted her churlishness—No. *Call it what it is.* Rudeness. She'd been unforgivably rude to a nice man who had done nothing to deserve it because her own life was a quagmire. Mindlessly she ran her thumb over the seams in her gloves, while a thick lump lodged halfway down her throat that no amount of swallowing or discreet throat clearing managed to dissolve.

167

For the second and third mile, she mentally labeled every plant and animal species they passed, common name as well as the Latin classification.

As a distraction, the exercise was a tactical error.

The redstart, *Setophaga ruticilla,* swooping after insects in the hedge, reminded her of the long afternoon trek to Stillwaters, riding double with Cade. A teasing Cade who diverted her from her extreme self-consciousness by challenging her to a lively contest. Which of them, he'd mused, could identify the most species over the course of an hour?

Leah turned her head so she could no longer see the splashy black-and-orange bird. All right, she would find some other way to occupy her mind. But a moment later they passed a massive black gum tree whose branches cast a welcome patch of shade over the Valley Pike. Cade had been leaning against a black gum that day, the day he'd swooped her up into his arms and carried her off. He'd kissed her, told her he loved her.

A wash of feverish heat that had little to do with the hot June day built in Leah's cheeks; she spent the final three miles mentally reorganizing her teaching syllabus for the fall semester.

Mrs. Willowby was hanging laundry when Mr. Hoffelmeyer pulled up in front of the house. They met at the foot of the porch steps, and Leah found herself enveloped in a firm hug. "Well, miss, and aren't you a sight for sore eyes!" The housekeeper stepped back. Her gray bun was slipping, her weathered cheeks were flushed from the sun and exertion, but there was an assessing gleam in her eye that reminded Leah of Miss Esther's. "Where's your father?"

"Still at the hotel. After satisfying himself of my well-being, he decided to spend some time with his grandson. I'm on my way back to Richmond," Leah said. "I decided to stop here, for a day or two."

"Needed to remember your roots a bit, did you, after nearly losing your life?"

Leah's eyelids flinched. She turned to thank Mr. Hoffelmeyer, who tipped his hat and departed back down the lane. Silently Leah studied the big old house with its steep gables and welcoming porch. Her home. Why did she continue to feed the longing, when it hurt so much? "I see Papa wrote you a page or two of overdramatic explanations," she finally said.

"Hmph. Wouldn't know about that. You should have seen him before he left. Talk about melodrama... On the other hand, you're here now, all your limbs and teeth intact. But your father wasn't to know you'd be in Mr. Beringer's care when he went racing off to search for you, now was he?"

Abruptly the housekeeper dabbed perspiration from her face with the hem of her apron and patted Leah's arm. "Well. You're thin as a blade of grass, and your face brown as an Indian savage. But we can thank God you're all right and leave off with the rest. I'm mighty pleased you stopped by. Where'd Deke get to? He can fetch your bag inside. I've just finished bleaching the linens. That lazy laundry girl your papa hired isn't worth a Confederate dollar. I've been doing most of it myself, so I know it's done right." She turned. "Deke! Where are you, son?"

"I'm here, Aunt Effie."

He sidled around the corner of the house, this peculiar man-child who even after three years remained as wary of her as Leah was of him. Leah never knew what to say, how to treat him. He was as tall as Cade, a man full grown in both size and years, and her first instinct remained an automatic bristling. It was difficult to reconcile his appearance with the arrested mental development that made him, inside, a good-natured boy with a generous heart.

"Take Leah's bag on up to her room, if you would," Mrs. Willowby instructed.

"She doesn't like me. She won't want me touching her bag," Deke replied, his pale blue eyes skittering away from Leah's.

"I like you just fine, Deke." She winced as she scraped up another smile. "And I'd appreciate it very much if you'd carry my bag."

His expression brightened like a sunrise. "All right." Deke snatched up the heavy Gladstone as though it weighed no more than a pound of sugar. "Did Mr. Beringer really save your life?"

"Yes."

"Aunt Effie read me the letter Mr. Sinclair wrote. He says God used Mr. Beringer, and how he planned to thank Him—God, I mean—for the rest of his days, for rescuing you. Why didn't Mr. Beringer and Mr. Sinclair come home with you, Leah?"

"You're going to weigh her ears down with so many questions they'll fall off," Mrs. Willowby scolded her nephew with a good-natured buffet. "Go along with you now. Time enough to pester her with gibber-jabber when she's tucked away some of my coleslaw and stewed chicken."

"Meredith had the cook in the hotel kitchen pack me a lunch," Leah said. "I don't want you to go to any trouble, especially since I've descended without warning." She lifted her skirts and began climbing the porch steps. "After I change, I'll just fix myself a glass of lemonade, if you've any lemons. I'd like to—"

"Made some yesterday. I'll fetch it from the springhouse. But you really ought to try my—"

"Go for a walk. Clear my throat of all the smoke and cinders from the trip."

Leah could hear the housekeeper muttering behind her, but she had learned over the years that sometimes the only way to deal with Effie Willowby was to smile politely and keep going. Mercysake, but the woman still treated her as though she were as helpless as the child she'd been when her mother died.

An hour later Leah climbed to the top of the small hillock next to the run, where a wrought-iron fence protected her mother's grave from stray cows. The sky had turned gray, the air hazy and cloying so that her garments clung damply to her skin. When she breathed, it was like inhaling a mildewed rain cloud.

The mountains had been cooler, the air fresh, especially early morning, and just after sunrise. Cade had—

With an impatient huff she opened the gate and went to stand at the foot of the grave. A bouquet of wilted black-eyed Susans lay in scattered disarray just beneath the plain headstone. Garnet, of course. She was the only one of them, after all these years, who faithfully placed the fresh flowers on their mother's grave.

"I wish I could remember you, Mama." Sighing a little, Leah stood for many moments, pensive and uncertain.

Eventually she sank down, spreading her ruffled skirt and petticoats over grass cooled by a clump of fragrant cedar and the gigantic chestnut oak that protected the site from the worst of the sun. Only then did she allow this morning's memories to return full force. She needed to examine them, pick apart each phrase her father had spoken before he handed her onto the train. Settle them in her mind.

He had apologized to her. Her father had *apologized*.

"I should have done better," he'd told her, his eyes dark with regret. "You needed a mother, not two pesky sisters and a distracted father. Then you'd not be so uncertain in your heart about Cade."

For some reason, her father seemed to think that the loss of her mother at such a tender age contributed to her present inner turmoil. Leah stared at the weathered gravestone and asked herself why.

Her only memory of her mother was that of cloudy eyes full of tears, in a bone-white face. Her father took Leah into their bedroom, and told her to give her mother a kiss. She'd been two months shy of her fourth birthday, but Leah could still remember the terrified pounding of her heart, her agonized wish that her mother would smile, pat her head. Promise she'd be all right again. But nobody said a word. Leah had been too scared to speak, her mother too weak, though at the time Leah had not been able to comprehend the lack of response.

Before she fell asleep, she talked to Jesus like Papa did, because Papa had read the story in the Bible where Jesus made a sick girl well again. Jesus, Papa had told her, healed lots of sick people, because He loved everyone. But in the morning, Papa told them their mother had gone to heaven, to be with the Lord there. "Why didn't the Lord come down here to heal her, like He did the little girl in the Bible?" Leah asked. "If He wanted to talk to Mama, why didn't He come down here, where Mama is?" Jacob had only shaken his head and held her close.

Only two months shy of four years old, Leah thought again with a ghost of a smile. But after that long night she'd never been a child again. It was difficult to hug innocence, when in her heart she felt betrayed by the one Person her father loved more than he had their mother, or even his daughters.

Oh, she might understand better now, and in her mind she knew that Jacob's faith was all that he'd had to cling to those first years, an unquenchable faith that poured from him into his girls. She even knew it was not God who had taken Mary Sinclair away in the prime of her life, but an ugly disease. Nonetheless the cruel separation could never be explained to Leah's satisfaction. Not then. Not now.

Perhaps her father was right.

She lifted her gaze, scanning the ochre-tinted sky, the thickening clouds that promised an evening storm. Then, feeling silly, she laid her hand on top of her mother's grave. "I think I know why Papa felt he had to apologize," she murmured. "All these years…I think I've not quite forgiven him for loving God even though you died." And her father, being the man he was, instead of lecturing or casting blame, had taken the burden of Leah's lifelong disapprobation upon himself.

She might have considered him a splendid example of Christlike behavior if he'd chosen any other object for the secret drawer of her heartwood chest.

In this case, an object had spoken more loudly than a lifetime of loving lectures.

"Leah?"

She jumped, so violently that Deke himself jumped as well, almost tumbling back down the hill.

Leah scrambled to her feet, a barrage of words primed to spew from her lips, all of them designed to send Deke off like a cowed puppy. "Don't startle me like that! What are you doing up here, anyway? I wanted—Needed to—"

Something stopped her short, almost as if she'd been physically restrained. The growling dog brought up short by a choke collar and tugged leash. What—?

Deke lowered his head, studying her through carroty red strands of stick-straight hair. "I'm sorry," he said, the toe of his shoe nudging a loose stone. "I-I wanted to tell you something. To help you. Aunt Effie said you were unhappy, and that it was because of Mr. Beringer."

The strange sensation of a firm hand gently covering her mouth dissolved in a gush of mortification. Why in the name of Socrates, Galileo, and Plutarch had she yielded to the impulse to come home? "Your aunt has no business talking about other people to you."

"You're not other people. You're family. And I like Mr. Beringer. He talks to me just like Mr. Sinclair, as though I'm a man. Instead of…" His voice trailed off, and the toe scuffling intensified. Then, "I know I'm different. But Mr. Beringer helped me to see it doesn't matter. He told me Jesus doesn't care if I look like a man on the outside, because inside I'm a child of God, and that's just like what Jesus wants everyone to be."

"Deke, let's not do this again." Leah opened the gate, carefully latched it, her stomach churning. "Every time you and I talk about God, we end up quarreling."

"I don't quarrel. Mr. Sinclair says Christians can disagree, but they shouldn't argue."

The childish statements, delivered as they were in a deep, resonant adult male's voice, caused an already off-balance Leah to feel as though she were being swatted by a capricious whirlwind. "Fine." She remained at the gate, her hands curled over the wrought-iron spike. Deke towered over her by a good eight inches. "We don't quarrel. We just…disagree. On most everything."

"Why don't you like Mr. Beringer? Is it because he loves God, too? I heard Aunt Effie tell your pa once that you have no use for pious people and that was all right by her. But that you shouldn't—" His forehead creased in concentration, then a broad smile spread over his face. "You shouldn't lump the godly with the overrighteous because that just made you one of the overrighteous."

Pale blue eyes searched hers with a surprising streak of adult awareness. "Mr. Beringer wouldn't do anything to hurt you. That's all I wanted to tell you. I'll leave you alone now."

He loped halfway down the hill, then paused to look over his shoulder. "Supper's ready, but I'll tell Aunt Effie you don't want to be around people yet." He swiped the hair out of his eyes. "That's what I like about Jesus. Being with Him isn't the same as being around people. He's just…there, when you need Him."

Long after Deke returned to the house, Leah remained on the hill, mulling his words—and the faint possibility that, for the first time in her life, God had manifested His Presence in her life.

Twenty-Three

STILLWATERS

*I*t was late, past two in the morning, but Jacob couldn't sleep. Restless, skin feeling itchy as new woolen union suit, he finally gave up trying to pray himself to sleep and rose. He pulled on his clothes and tiptoed down the long hall, grateful for the thick pile of blue and gold carpet that muffled his tread.

When he reached the ground floor he paused, head tilted. From somewhere he could hear the faint sound of music playing. A piano? Soft and slow, the sounds drifted through the deserted lobby like a wraith. Though Jacob possessed an insensitive ear and was devoid of any musical knowledge, for some reason moisture burned the corners of his eyes in response to that haunting, slow song.

Quietly he searched for the source, listening while he padded through the empty lobby, down shadowed corridors, all the parlors and secluded alcoves void of human life at this hour. The music was sporadic, and after a while it came to him that the melody was repeating itself, over and over, with long pauses in between.

Eventually he reached the conservatory at the far end of the main floor. It was a popular gathering place, enclosed almost entirely in glass to exploit the magnificent western view of the mountains. Jacob, however, found the room a maze of greenery and stuffed furniture. On his visits to Meredith and Ben, he seldom ventured down there, though he did remember that one corner of the room was dominated by a massive grand piano. He wandered down the hall and poked his head through the doorway.

The piano bench was unoccupied. Puzzled, Jacob entered the

174

room, head tilted to one side as he pondered where the music, still playing, was coming from. The place was naught but shapes and shadows. A rolling ocean of storm clouds had inked the sky at sunset, and the only light visible in the conservatory on this rainy night was electric: a yellow circle of lamplight faintly illuminated a sitting area in the corner farthest from the doorway.

Ah. Now he recognized the sound. Someone was listening to a phonograph.

Back in '93, Benjamin had taken Meredith to the World's Columbian Exposition in Chicago. After a visit to the Electric Building, for months all Meredith had talked about was a mechanical device called a phonograph, a machine capable of reproducing sounds, including musical ones. Nothing would do but that they purchase one for Stillwaters, their newest resort hotel.

Because the contraption was an ugly monster of a thing with its metal tone arm and huge flared horn, Meredith had bedeviled Jacob until he designed a cabinet that disguised much of the phonograph's unsavory appearance. The final result might not have been one of Jacob's personal favorites, but the phonograph, with its attendant collection of flat plates upon which musical selections were recorded, was nonetheless one of the reasons for the conservatory's popularity.

Feeling like an intruder but unable to withdraw, Jacob maneuvered a silent path between potted plants and tasseled armchairs until he caught sight of a motionless figure sitting in a wing chair next to the phonograph.

Mrs. Carlton.

Reluctantly Jacob turned to leave, then hesitated. The lady had made her feelings plain enough, on the few occasions they had encountered each other. *Och, Lord. What would You have me to do?* There was something wrenching about the tableau, a solitary woman hiding in the middle of the night like a lost soul, listening to what he assumed to be some work of classical music.

The poignancy of it was more than a man who had reared three daughters could bear. He stepped forward, into the light.

"Mrs. Carlton? Forgive me, but I was unable to sleep myself, out wandering the hall I was, and heard—" The words caught in his throat when she leaped to her feet, her hand knocking against the protruding horn, jarring the phonograph.

The needle made a tearing sound like the rending of cloth, arresting the plaintive melody. Quick as a flash of heat lightning she yanked the veil over her face, but not before Jacob's eyes registered the puckered scar that disfigured her right cheek from temple to jaw.

"How dare you?" Her voice emerged in a hoarse whisper full of outrage. "How dare you creep up, spy on me, like a nasty little boy peeking under a lady's skirts?"

"I didna mean—I was no' meaning to intrude," Jacob began, then had to stop so he could swallow down the thickened burr before he choked on it in his embarrassment.

"Then you should have left."

She was backing away from him, he realized with a fresh jolt. Fingers fumbling over the backs of furniture, her footsteps clumsy, she retreated step by step, her breath rasping in the suddenly quiet room.

Why, she *was* afraid of him! Jacob closed his eyes, his stomach churning. The need to reassure her rose fast and hot, blistering in its intensity. "Lass, I'm not going to hurt you. Don't be afraid. Please. My name is Jacob Sinclair. 'Tis my daughter and son-in-law who own Stillwaters, don't you know. I've two other daughters as well…I'd cut off my hand before I'd hurt a woman."

"Just go away."

She couldn't retreat further without leaping through a plate-glass window. Her tension rolled toward Jacob like a thick cloud; her long fingers were curved like claws over the back of the chair she all but cowered behind.

"I'll go away," he promised, keeping his voice low, soothing, "as soon as you can reassure me that you're calm. And that you do not fear me any longer."

"I'm not afraid of you. I just want you to leave me alone."

"Och, but I'm not sure I can do that." He paused, torn between the need to comfort and the need to honor her request. "Will you at least allow me to fetch my daughter, someone you might talk to?"

She was beyond the lamp's light, and he couldn't see her face at all. From her frozen stillness Jacob deduced she was either stunned—or about to bolt. Then she spoke, and he heard not fear, but anger. A chilly, controlled anger that frosted the air.

"What gives you the right to assume I'm in need of counsel? Why should you care?"

Jacob thought for a moment, then replied, simply. "Because God cares. And for whatever reason, I find I can do no less myself. It bothers me, you see, that you feel the need to run. I'd like to know why, and I'd like to help, if I can."

"You can't help me. Nobody can, not even God Himself."

She closed the distance between them and in a single brutal motion whipped the veil away again. "I bear what may as well be the mark of Cain, Mr. Sinclair. For the rest of my life, every time I look in the mirror I am forced to relive a memory. One that has come close to driving me to end my life." Another swift movement, and the black gauze fluttered back in place. "Now you can remember as well. I hope the memory is sufficient inducement for you to leave me alone. Please, Mr. Sinclair, for the love of God, leave me alone!"

This time, instead of fleeing, she stood almost defiantly, her posture rigid, no doubt with the effort not to run yet again. Jacob waited a moment longer, hands dangling at his sides like a cloddish lad. He was grieved by his inability to reach her. *Lord?*

There was no answer, no direction. Defeated, Jacob ran a hand through his hair. "I ask your pardon, madam." He offered a stiff nod, then walked away.

When the rains increased an hour before dawn, Jacob still lay abed, sleepless. Miserable.

Mrs. Carlton was right. Eyes open or closed, all he could see was a brutal scar that looked as though a knife had carved into her from temple to chin.

But...who would do such a monstrous thing? And why?

Twenty-Four

*O*n a blistering afternoon several weeks later, Cade pulled the rental buggy to a halt in front of a cast-iron hitching post, conveniently situated in the shade of a stately elm. For several moments he remained in the buggy, studying the two-story brick building that housed the teaching staff. There was a parlor on the ground level to receive visitors, Mrs. Hays had told him.

Then she'd paused, fingering a set of keys at her waist before adding slowly, "Leah's living quarters include a small personal parlor. Last year she convinced me to let her knock out the adjoining wall of the room next to hers, which was vacant, to allow her more room for her books. It also allowed her a cozy sitting room."

Esther Hays was a formidable looking woman in her deep mauve gown and a triple strand of pearls adorning an equally imposing bosom. Yet a light twinkled in the headmistress's eyes as she and Cade exchanged looks of perfect understanding. "Leah is a very private person. But I think, Mr. Beringer, that she is also a very lonely woman. I trust you plan to do something about it."

She'd provided directions, then waved him out of her office.

Cade set his jaw. After securing the horse, he carefully lifted a box from the buggy seat, then strode down the uneven brick path to, God willing, "do something about it."

When she opened the door, the faintly puzzled expression on her face went blank with shock. "Cade?"

178

He smiled down at her. "May I come in? I received tacit permission from Mrs. Hays, so we needn't fret about propriety."

"I do not fret." She stepped back, gesturing him in with a delightful shade of pink tinting her cheeks. "Why are you here? I had a letter yesterday from Meredith. She said you were so involved in landscaping that she never saw you."

Landscaping was his and Benjamin's fabrication for what Cade had really been doing the past several weeks. He had no intention of risking a prolonged discussion on the subject, so merely shrugged. "I like Thursday's costume," he murmured. "Family tartan?"

Her blush deepened. "Yes. These are the hunting plaid colors— more subdued tones. According to my father, they were worn at the Battle of Flodden, in—"

"Sweetheart, at the moment I'm not really interested in a history lesson."

"I wish you wouldn't call me that." She walked several steps away, then turned in a rustle of plaid skirts, her chin lifted. "How did you know about my system of— Never mind." She pressed two fingers against her temples. "Why are you here, Cade? I'm very busy, planning the curriculum for this coming semester."

"I had to be in Richmond. And...I brought you a present." He walked across the room to a library table covered with books and papers, which he proceeded to stack in a neat pile so he could set the box down. "Come and see."

She was already there, of course, fussing because he had disarranged everything and he had no business taking over here. They weren't in the wilderness now...

Cade stemmed the lecture by clasping her hands and tugging her close. "I won't stay long," He thrust aside his restiveness over the evening appointment with a member of the state legislature. "Open the box."

But she didn't move, other than to stare down at their clasped hands. "It hasn't changed," she whispered, lifting her head to search his face.

"Of course it hasn't. It won't next month or next year, either." He slid his hands up her arms, gripped her shoulders and turned her toward the box. What he wanted to do, badly, was to kiss her. "Open it."

While she fumbled with the string he'd used to keep the flaps closed, Cade fought the need crawling through his bloodstream. Almost three weeks had passed since he'd held her in his arms, first experienced the explosive wonder of kissing her. Known irrevocably that Leah Sinclair was the woman God intended to be his mate.

You could have made this a little less of a struggle, Lord.

With a gust of love, something fluttered deep inside, then ruffled over his skin with both amusement and admonishment. *I know,* Cade acknowledged resignedly, *You never promise to make something easy, only that You'll be present to lend Your strength, Your wisdom—*

"A flowerpot filled with dirt?" Leah's dry voice recalled his full attention. "You've been talking to Papa, I take it. What 'lesson' would this be? You want me to plant something, perhaps some bleeding heart? That would make for appropriate symbolism, don't you agree?"

She removed the earthenware pot, swept the cardboard box to the floor, and with a testy thud plunked the flowerpot down on the table. "Thank you. Now please go away. I'm busy."

"Hopefully after twenty or thirty years of marriage, I'll come to understand how a woman with your intelligence and perceptiveness about almost everything else can remain so blind about love."

She stiffened, her head rearing back, but Cade had been watching her closely. "Don't be afraid of it, Leah," he said, softening his voice as he lifted her hand to his mouth and brushed a kiss against her knuckles. "I haven't changed my mind. I still love you, more than ever. We've been— how did you put it?—separated by two hundred miles and two mountain ranges, but absence has only intensified the need. How about you, little wren? Have you been able to immerse yourself in your studies enough to forget me?"

"Yes."

Cade fought a smile. "Mm. Shall I kiss you again to prove you're wrong, before I explain your gift?"

Her head actually bobbed up and down even as she whipped out a resounding "No!" Then, "I can't believe Miss Esther encouraged you, when she knew I was—" Her eyes darkened to the shade of old walnut, the same deep brown as the heartwood chest Jacob had made for her two decades earlier.

"Knew you were what, my love?" With one finger, he traced a featherlight path from the corner of those bruised-looking eyes to the fine hairs at her temple. He knew better than to take such liberties. But the need to touch her, to…*heal* the deep wounding in her spirit, had burned his discipline to ash.

Even at nineteen and in the first passion of manhood for his fiancée, Cade had never experienced this fiery blend of desire and tenderness. *Jesus, give me strength. And control.*

Leah ignored his question. "That's as bad as calling me 'sweetheart,'" she said, her tone lugubrious but her mouth curving upward. "You think you're so clever, don't you? If I tell you not to call me your love, or your sweetheart, what's next?"

"Something even more sloppy and sentimental," Cade promised. "Stop trying to change the subject. I have to leave in a few moments. And I have a feeling it's going to take me that long to secure a promise from you."

Warily she scooted sideways, her fingers trailing over the rim of the pot. "What promise might that be?" she asked, so casually Cade had to suppress another chuckle.

"Not what you think. I want you to promise to follow a procedure, and watch. There's already a bulb planted, Leah. The one from the secret drawer of your heartwood chest."

All the color drained from her face, then returned with a feverish cast that should have raised blisters. "My bulb?" she whispered. "I can't believe you would be this cruel. That my father—"

"Your father is ashamed to face you, to write you, to come visit you, Leah. He blames himself because what he was hoping to teach you with a flower bulb was not at all what you learned. He asked me to try, because—unlike you—he believes me when I tell him I love you."

When she would have turned away Cade caught her elbow, holding her still. "You're going to listen to me."

He gentled his voice, his heart twisting at the pain she was struggling to hide. "Jacob never intended for you to compare yourself to that bulb, the way you apparently shared with him at Stillwaters. Shh...don't look like that. Your father wasn't betraying a trust. He loves you. He knows I love you. That's why he shared with me. Leah, he was trying to teach you the mystery of faith, using the bulb for an example. He was *not* pointing out flaws in your character. Between you and me, he probably should have picked something else, more like the objects for your sisters that he didn't have to replace every year."

Her expression caused an ache deep inside his chest. "I told him the same thing, when I was twelve and handed him the rotten bulb. Papa didn't even blink. He patted my head, said not to worry, and the next day the secret drawer held a new bulb. Now he replaces them every New Year's Day. Papa has an abiding love for symbolism."

"He told me about replacing the bulbs," Cade murmured. "Said it was his first lesson in botany. He learned his lesson. Now he wants you to learn yours."

"I teach classes in botany," she said. "There's no mystery. A bulb is just the embryonic bud of a flower. I"—her eyelashes fluttered down—"don't understand."

He shifted his gentle grip to her wrist, then pressed her palm against the rich black earth with which he'd filled the flowerpot. "Good. That's the lesson. Faith springs from belief *without* complete understanding. Beneath your hand is a bulb. We both know from years of study that inside it lies a closely protected bud, with all the secrets that enable it to burst free of this soil. Eventually it will bloom, just as God intended. Both of us can name the parts and describe the process. But, Leah, my love, can you explain *how* that process occurs? Can you bury yourself inside that bulb and watch it happen, so that you could create a bulb in your laboratory?"

Slowly she shook her head. Beneath his hand, her slender fingers felt fragile. "Yet you know that with proper care and nourishment, the bulb I've buried in this soil will eventually become a flower. You believe this."

"Yes. But—"

He pressed her fingers, halting her automatic rebuttal. "That knowledge is the foundation of your confident belief in the scientific process. You have a college education, and a lifetime of experience, yet even you can still only understand to a certain point. Science retains its mysteries. Like God. You have faith in the scientific process. Have equal faith in its Creator."

"Science provides observable evidence from which to draw logical conclusions. You cannot prove God's existence using a scientific or mathematical formula."

"If we mortals could explain Him, God wouldn't be omnipotent, omniscient—supreme," Cade returned, patiently. "Some things—perhaps most things—about God will never be understood, not by humans. We just learn to accept, on faith alone."

He released her and stepped back, giving her room. "Jacob wanted the bulb to symbolize his hope that one day your trust in a God you've never seen and don't understand would equal your trust in provable scientific truths, which nonetheless continue to hold a mystery or two."

"Always the contradiction." She walked past him to the bookshelves overflowing with books, her back to Cade. "He creates us so that it is impossible for us to understand Him."

"Not contradiction. Paradox." Cade paused until she turned around. "God in the flesh, but not of the flesh. Providing for our salvation by sacrificing His own mortal life, so that in our spiritual bodies we can live with Him forever. Can't ever be proven scientifically. Never explained to our satisfaction. But believers in Jesus as the Christ accept the paradox. We learn to believe with our hearts and feel with our minds. Accept the mystery of a miracle."

"The mystery of the miracle," Leah repeated, half under her breath. She retraced her steps until she stood by Cade once more, staring down at the flowerpot.

He dug into the rich black earth. "In about six weeks a tiny shoot will push up through this soil. Somehow, nurtured by water and light and warmth, this shoot will transform into a beautiful flower. I believe it will happen." Heart pounding, Cade brushed his fingers clean with his handkerchief, never looking away from her. "Leah?"

"What..." He waited with shredding patience while he watched her struggle to frame the question, "What happens, if it *doesn't* grow?

You're wanting me to force the bulb to bloom out of season. It needs the cold period, it needs special care that I might not be able to adequately provide. Your analogy is flawed. You can't force faith on a person, Cade, any more than you should force God's timing."

He wanted to bash his head against the wall in frustration. Instead Cade released Leah and prowled her sitting room. A Morris chair and tapestry-covered footstool were stationed near the window. Next to the chair was a small, handsomely finished revolving bookcase—one of Jacob's creations, from the look of it. The entire setting shouted its function as the isolated lair of a person who seldom if ever entertained callers.

She's so lonely she's breaking my heart, Lord. Fresh resolve coursed through him; Cade swiveled on his heel. "All right, Leah. It's all right. I've told you before I won't push you, and I'm not. I just hadn't realized…" His muscles ached with the effort it took not to cross the room and pull her into a close embrace. "Don't be afraid, Leah. Trust me." He hesitated and after a moment added, "Trust God. Trust yourself."

"I don't know if I can." Her fingers had begun to pleat the navy, green, and black plaid skirt. "The last time I trusted God like that, my mother died."

Cade clasped his hands behind his back. His palms were sweating. *Jesus? Help me reach her.* "You're twenty-five now. That's a long enough time to hang on to a childish grudge, don't you think?"

One eyebrow lifted in an ironic arch. "You're beginning to sound self-righteous again—no. I'm sorry. I don't want to argue, Cade. I am trying, you see, to accept what you're telling me. I just don't under—" She broke off with a sigh, then finished in a driven undertone, "I want to believe you. I do. I want it almost as desperately as I wanted my mother to be well again, the night I prayed for her when I was three and a half years old. But what if I'm let down again? Feel the same betrayal I did that night? By God, by my father?" Her anguish rolled over him in waves. "What if my lack of faith is the root cause, not the effect?"

Cade took a step toward her, but Leah retreated, bumping into the library table.

"Don't. Don't hold me again or kiss me or ask me to trust you.

You're right, I am afraid. I don't know if I can survive, if I trust you, and you betray that trust. Please. Don't make me hope."

"Leah. Sweetheart. That's what faith is all about." Now the sweat was pooling at the base of his spine, beneath his armpits, as though he were dangling from the top of a ship-mast pine. Doubt and fear sawed like a couple of leering lumberjacks through the base of the tree trunk. "When your mother died, you were so young. Too young for Jacob to explain. You've been afraid of the dark ever since. But you don't need to fear the darkness."

Carefully, slowly, he took a second step, never taking his gaze from Leah's. "Because faith is born in the darkness, like the miracle of a dried-up bulb buried in the ground, somehow producing a living green shoot that pushes upward, seeking the light."

He inched forward another step.

"All you have to do is trust the process. Wait. Water it, watch. You have faith in the order of God's nature. Apply the same faith to my love for you. To God's love of us both. Please, Leah, do this for me. I can't prove my love, only pledge the truth of its existence. I can't prove that God loves you far more than I do."

Why wasn't she saying something, anything? Arguing with him? Emotion clogged Cade's throat. Leah wasn't the only one who struggled against fear of rejection. Of betrayal. He'd lost one woman to whom he'd given his heart. Was he doomed to lose another?

Surely God would not promise a loaf of bread, then crush him with a stone. For the first time since he'd dedicated his life to Jesus, Cade experienced a soul-corroding doubt that almost brought him to his knees. *Father God, blessed Jesus...* In a flash of pained insight he understood how Leah felt. Had felt, and fought, for most of her life.

Cade closed his eyes.

At first he thought the light touch on his arm was a current of air. "Cade?"

The tentative whisper drifted into his ears. He opened his eyes and saw Leah standing in front of him. Her fingers lightly rested on his forearm. Her face was very pale. She lifted her fingers from his arm and brushed the corner of his eye.

"You... You're..." She stared at her fingertip, which was undeniably damp. Something stirred in her countenance, something deep, powerful as a riptide. As though chunks of emotional flotsam were being swept away, so the fear and the control, the doubt and taint of cynicism, the loneliness and the brittleness that had left their mark on Leah's face ever since Cade had known her, all washed away.

In its wake spread the dawning wonder of a child, with light filling the darkness in her eyes.

Without looking away from her, Cade spoke. "I love you," he managed hoarsely. "Give me a chance to show you. Leah, give me a chance."

"All right," she replied, her voice mirroring the wonder reflected in her shining eyes. "I'll take care of the bulb. For you. For...us." She half turned toward the library table. "And perhaps, perhaps for my father. And my faith."

❦

He was in the buggy, gathering the reins to back the horse, when the door to the dormitory flew open and she came racing down the brick walk. "Cade!"

"What is it?" Swiftly he set the brake.

Breathless, she glanced around, then balanced a dainty foot on the longstep and lifted herself until her face was almost level with Cade's. "It's just that, you know I don't, that I don't...cry. But I-I want..."

"Want—?" Mindful of their surroundings, Cade contented himself with laying a calming hand over hers, which was gripping the door hard enough to whiten her knuckles. "Say whatever you want to. It's all right."

"Yes, I know that." For some reason, she was flustered. And shy. "I wish I could—oh, never mind. This is ridiculous."

Cade grabbed her wrist to prevent her from leaping down and scurrying back to her hidey-hole.

"No, it's not," he said, helpless against the silly grin that spread across his face. He was hopelessly, utterly, madly in love. "It's wonderful. And so are you."

186

Twenty-Five

*F*or Leah, summer's passage was marked not by days on the calendar but by a meticulous schedule as carefully plotted as her teaching syllabus. She had labored over this particular schedule the day after Cade stopped by with his pot full of soil and a promise that an out-of-season bulb would send a shoot up in October.

To her relief, Cade wrote sporadically, sometimes a handful of pages, more often than not a handful of words, to reassure Leah that his heart was with hers. For some reason he was traveling a lot, which puzzled Leah until she realized he was doubtless visiting nurseries, gathering ideas along with plants; the postmarks on his infrequent correspondence included such disparate cities as Clifton Forge, Washington, and Front Royal.

It wasn't until September arrived in a series of rainy days and a new school year that Meredith wrote to tell her that Cade had *not* been landscaping the hotel grounds for the past two months. In conjunction with a private detective agency, he was helping with an investigation of a consortium headed by none other than J. Preston Clarke.

> *...so when Benjamin finally confessed his part in all this, I confess I lost my temper. It was a magnificent display, I promise. Regrettably, all I achieved for my efforts was a sore throat, and a great deal of contrition. Benjamin reminded me that Cade has spent most of the last ten years bringing to heel a number of powerful lumber barons and greedy mine owners. I must trust both him*

and Benjamin, and God. Well, of course I do! But those
other villains Cade brought to heel—they weren't J. Pre-
ston Clarke.

Leah laid the letter aside. She sat in her chair, watching rain smear the windowpane, her fingers tapping the chair arm. Her gaze wandered across the room, to the earthenware pot. That morning she had observed an infinitesimal disturbance, the hint of a pending eruption in the center of it, and it reminded Leah of her growing feelings for Cade, pushing their way to the surface. If Meredith's fears were well founded, there existed a strong possibility that Cade could—Leah huffed impatiently.

His idealistic notions and inexhaustible persistence had given her a glimmer of hope about the future. About herself, and Cade. She wasn't about to allow those notions and his persistence to aid in his destruction. Not now. *Mr. Beringer, you need to rearrange your priorities.*

The following Saturday morning she borrowed Miss Esther's buggy, returning from the city late in the afternoon. After supper that evening, she requested a private conference with the headmistress, then told her that due to a matter of grave urgency she needed to take a personal leave. "I've made inquiries, and have a list of suitable interim teachers. Here are their addresses and credentials. As the semester has only entered the second week, the disruption to students will be minimal. I have prepared, as you know, a thorough outline which any capable instructor can follow."

Miss Esther waited until she finished, her austere face revealing nothing. She asked only one question. "Are you returning, Leah, when this personal matter of grave urgency is resolved?"

"Of course," she said, surprised. "Why would you think otherwise?"

"Ah." The headmistress rose from the settee, crossed the room to a corner whatnot shelf and picked up an oval photograph, staring down at it for a long time. "If Mr. Hays had lived, this year we would have celebrated our forty-third anniversary."

Sorrow and resolution filled the narrow patrician face. "For thirty years I have dedicated my life to this school because I had nothing else.

It has brought me a fair amount of satisfaction, but I will miss my husband until I join him in the hereafter." She crossed the room again, sat back down, and in an extraordinary gesture completely out of character laid her hand on Leah's forearm, then pressed a softly wrinkled cheek against hers. "Go with my blessing. I liked your young man, very much. However things turn out, there will always be a place for you at the Esther Hays School for Young Ladies."

❧❧

Jacob met her as she stepped onto the platform of the Woodstock depot. She hadn't seen her father for over three months; with the memory of Cade's words resting heavily between them, Leah had alternately dreaded and yearned for this reunion.

"Papa." The high collar of Wednesday's gown was suddenly much too tight. Around them the noise and activity seemed to recede.

"Leah." He didn't speak further, just stood there on the platform looking hot and ill at ease in his suit and a bow tie.

The conductor closed up the step, calling "All aboard!" as the engine blasted a departing whistle.

Leah opened her mouth, closed it, unwilling to engage in mindless chatter. Why was he standing there, treating her like some strange woman he'd just met?

The answer came to her in a starburst, and she wanted to smack her palm against her forehead: He felt as unsure as Leah, though perhaps for a different reason. *Her father was afraid she would reject him.* A freshet of peace trickled through her. Peace, and new awareness that she was not the only one to have been suffering these past months. Suddenly the words were easy. "I've missed you," she told him. "Very much."

Behind them, with clanging metal and a powerful shudder the train rolled down the track. In moments the rumbling faded away, leaving behind a poised silence.

"Missed you too, little wren," Jacob finally said. He searched her face. "Och, Leah, but I've missed you too." His gaze dropped to the box cradled in her arms. "Shall I take that for you?"

"It's for you. But let me carry it until we reach home. It's...very precious to me." Because a queer tightness seemed to be crushing her chest, Leah started walking toward the row of parked buggies. "You can fetch my Gladstone bag from the baggage cart, if you like."

Some time later, when they turned from the Pike onto the lane leading to the house, she asked him to stop the buggy. This moment was between her and her father. Leah wanted neither witnesses nor interruptions of any kind, no matter how well intentioned. Impatient now, she untied the string, her fingers all but twitching from anticipation, then lifted the bowl out as though it were made of the finest crystal and its contents more precious than gold. For Leah, they were.

"I'm on my way to Stillwaters," she said. "I want you to keep this for me, while I'm gone." Solemnly she placed the bowl in her father's hands. "Cade brought it to me, back in July. Papa...he planted my bulb, the one from the drawer of my heartwood chest. It should be blooming in a few more weeks."

"Lass..." The endearment emerged as a gravelly whisper. The strong hands, scarred and toughened from years of labor, cradled the bowl as though he held a newborn babe. Once again he seemed to be at a loss for words.

"I want you to know that I've realized a lot of things, all these weeks of waiting. Of watering and watching," Leah tried next. She still wasn't used to the sensations jiggering about inside whenever she pondered such matters, as if her mind and heart were hot kernels of corn popping over a fire. "I've realized"—*because of Cade*—"why you thought a flower bulb would be the best object to choose for me."

Pain flashed through Jacob's eyes and thickened her tongue. "Don't," she hurriedly continued, almost stumbling over words. "Don't think about what happened at Stillwaters, because it no longer matters. You do understand me, better than either of us realized, Papa. But I didn't help you at all back then, did I? When I was a girl? I wasn't like Meredith or Garnet."

"I never wanted you to be, never asked or expected such. You were *you*, a unique and precious gift from the Lord." He reached up to skim her cheek with the backs of his knuckles. "As you still are, to me, to all who know you."

"I know," Leah murmured. "I know, Papa. It's all right. Listen to me, please." On a quick flutter of breath, she slid her fingers over the surface of the soil, feeling again the leap of fearful anticipation at the sight and feel of the tiny green nubbin of a stalk, just above the surface now. The promise of spring in the middle of autumn. "Cade and I... Between us we could doubtless fill a small library with what we know about botany and biology. From a scientific perspective, forcing this bulb requires only a bit of knowledge. Not a mystery, nor a miracle. Yet...yet..."

Her eyes burned, her nostrils stung, and a gelatinous lump in her throat was dissolving. But tears she yearned to spill dried up, and the lump transformed to the texture of coal as her emotions once again lost the battle against the stranglehold of her will.

Something must have shown on her face, for suddenly Jacob carefully set the flowerpot on the floorboards between his feet and wrapped his arm around her shoulders. "It's all right," he whispered, and he leaned over so they could rub noses. "Everything will be all right, now."

"I...believe you." With a little sigh Leah relaxed against the comforting wall of his chest, not so broad as Cade's but surprisingly solid. The words emerged on a sigh. "Cade helped me a lot. His faith... I love you, Papa."

"Aye, I know that. Have you forgiven me, then, for hurting you?"

"It was my own blindness that hurt me, Papa." She raised her head. "But I'm learning how to see. And what I see at the moment is a very wise father, whom I trust with all my heart." She hesitated, and added softly, "I'm trying to learn how to trust God as well. That's why I'm going to Stillwaters."

The arm around her shoulders tightened, but Jacob didn't speak.

"That's why I brought the bulb home, where it belongs," she finished. "Will you take care of it for me, while I'm gone?"

"Aye, lass. As though it were a wee girl, needing the care of her mother."

Leah brushed a kiss against his freshly shaved cheek, inhaling the familiar scent of wood shavings and linseed oil that would forever remind her of her father, despite his natty suit. "You mustn't compare me to the bulb. That's not the reason you selected it for my secret drawer, remember? You wanted to teach me the miracle and mystery of God's love. Papa, I want you to know. You, and Cade—you're both helping me to understand. No," she corrected herself instantly, "you've helped me to *believe*. In the mystery, and the miracle."

Her father shifted, his hands closing over both her upper arms to hold her a little ways away, while he stared down into her face with his eyes blazing. "Och...Leah. Leah..."

"But since it's taken me the first quarter-century of my life to learn, it's plain I'm going to need a lot of help for the rest of my life, to remind me whenever I suffer an occasional lapse. That's why I have to go to Stillwaters. I have to rescue a noble-minded, much too idealistic man who needs to learn a lesson or two himself." She lifted her chin. "I've been told I'm an excellent teacher."

⇜❧⇝

STILLWATERS RESORT HOTEL AND SPA
SEPTEMBER 1895
Leah patiently waited through Meredith's welcome and endured Benjamin's air of disapproval. "Does Cade know you planned to come?" he asked when Meredith's barrage of questions, tears, and ramblings wound down.

"Why would you ask?" Leah returned, peeling off gloves and hat. "Where is he, anyway? Obviously not here in the hotel."

Benjamin gestured for the bellboy to carry her luggage to her room, then contemplated Leah with the sort of air she herself would utilize with a difficult student. Well, her brother-in-law might tower over her by almost twelve inches, but Leah's schoolteacher stare had been honed to perfection by the time she reached her twentieth year. She leveled it at Benjamin and waited him out.

"Cade should be back sometime soon," he finally admitted. "I doubt he'll be pleased to see you."

"His disapproval of my actions can equal mine of his. And yours. You had no right to involve him, Benjamin."

"You're right," Benjamin astonished her by admitting. "In my defense, all I intended for him to do was a little fact gathering, just enough to support my suspicions. But you know Cade. The more he discovered, the more determined he was to strap on his sword and wade into battle."

"A battle where the enemy fires cannonballs at sword-carrying idiots," Meredith snapped after throwing Leah a worried look. "Leah, I don't like your expression. What are you planning to do?"

"What I've always done. Whatever I have to."

Cade's footsteps dragged as he made his way from the stables up the path to the hotel's kitchen entrance. It was three in the morning, and fatigue coated his bones like a film of coal dust. Fatigue, and an insidious sort of disillusionment. *It never stops, Lord.* For every square foot of ground spared, another hundred was lost forever.

"You're late. I was beginning to worry."

The fatigue must have dulled his senses. It had certainly dulled his reflexes, because Ben's voice coming out of nowhere produced little beyond a sluggish flexing of his muscles.

"I was with Flanders. He's a good man, so you can relax. We spent the day in Eagle Mountain. Ben…we may have found something that will send Preston Clarke to prison for the rest of his life." He sat down opposite Ben, at the end of a huge rectangular table where the kitchen staff ate. A plate full of sloppily prepared sandwiches made his mouth water. "Thanks, friend. I could eat a side of beef."

"I'll summon the butcher." He waited peacefully, not pumping Cade for details.

Cade wolfed down two sandwiches and three glasses of tea, his spirits reviving along with his energy by the time he reached for the third sandwich. "Want me to fill you in, or do you need to tell me what compelled you to wait up for me at this hour?"

Ben stretched his arms behind his head and contemplated the ceiling. "Suppose I better tell you why I had to sneak down here in the dead of night, after I was sure Meredith was sound asleep and that nobody followed me." A strange smile hovered around his lips. "Leah's here, Cade."

"What?" There were any number of things Cade had steeled himself for. Leah's presence was not one of them. "Here? At the hotel?"

"Arrived on the six-thirty stage, the light of battle in her eye. Meredith cornered Flanders last week and wrested our secret from him. Then she collared me." He dropped his arms, shaking his head. "Haven't seen that kind of fireworks since I thought she'd betrayed me, all those years ago. For a while I was afraid her hair would catch fire. Mine, too."

"She wrote Leah, didn't she?" Cade finished on a groan. He set down the half-eaten sandwich. "Ben...this changes things. Until I can convince her to leave, I don't want to—"

"Your part in this is over," Ben interrupted. "In her own quiet way, Leah ripped another strip off my hide. Told me I had no right to involve you. She was right. Ever since Preston Clarke met you in Clifton Forge, you've been at risk. Cade, you know what happened to me five years ago, in Winchester. That man doesn't care who gets in his way, and he definitely doesn't care how he gets rid of them when they do. I've been selfish. Convinced myself you'd spent the last ten years taking care of yourself, and could do it again this time. But as of now, we're going to let the authorities do their job. So. You and Leah...ah...are free to spend however long you need, resolving matters between yourselves." He cocked an eyebrow at Cade. "Has she admitted she's in love with you yet?"

"I promised not to press her." Too tired to think, he scrubbed his stubble-covered chin. "Besides, there was this business with Clarke. You need to hear what we found out. He's organized a group of hired cutthroats, not just a few out-of-work drunks. Ben, Flanders thinks one of them is wanted for murder. That's what he and I were trying to track down. If we—"

"Not your job, my friend. Frankly, it never was." Ben leaned forward and planted his palms on the table. "I meant what I said. Your part in this is over. In fact, why don't you take Leah and go visit Jacob or your folks?"

"I'll do my best to convince Leah to go home. But I'm not leaving you hanging in the wind, not when we're this close to seeing justice done."

"Don't be foolish, Cade. Listen to me. You've somehow stayed out of trouble these past few months, but I have a feeling that could change any day. Especially if you and Flanders have unearthed concrete evidence." He smacked a fist against his palm. "I'm telling you that you might be in danger here, and now that Leah's—"

"I've been flirting with dangerous situations for years. God hasn't abandoned me yet. He's not going to fail me now." All of a sudden he grinned. "Know what I just figured out? Leah wouldn't have abandoned her students to come chasing after me, if she didn't care. See the good that God can tuck inside the worst of a bad situation?"

Ben didn't return his smile. "Just watch your back, Cade." He rose. "The last time I considered my blessings a reward for my faith, I lost almost everything I cherished."

Twenty-Six

The next morning found Cade deep in thought, wandering the hotel paths. For weeks now he'd been honoring the promise he made to Ben, gathering information about J. Preston Clarke. What he'd discovered had dismayed, even alarmed him, but until last night he'd never seriously considered that he himself might be in danger. Ben, or even Meredith, yes. Preston Clarke was a menacing presence hovering just outside Stillwaters's borders; but never had Cade feared for his own life.

Now Leah had arrived, rushing to his supposed rescue, and instead landing herself in a mire of wickedness. If something happened to Leah, because of him—Cade stopped the thought, demoralized by the tumble from self-confidence to arrogance. He needed to clear his head, to listen, and—particularly after Ben's none too subtle censure the night before—to prayerfully restore his walk with his Lord. But even after an hour of trying to pray, he still felt restless. Disjointed. Unable to maintain his focus.

A dozen yards from the main hotel Meredith stepped from behind an ancient hemlock, catching him off guard as Ben had the night before. *I'm not in good shape here, Lord.*

"Cade?" Her face was determined, her tone apologetic. "I must talk with you. I'm sorry for disturbing your walk, but this was the only opportunity I could think of to see you, before…well, before."

"What is it, Meredith?" he asked, taken aback by her ramshackle appearance. Even her hair had been sloppily gathered at the back of her neck with a clip, and tumbled over one shoulder in a mass of uncombed waves. "Or—let me see if I can help you. I've already talked with Ben. I know Leah's here."

"He told me." Her face pinkened. "I, ah, when he returned to our rooms, in the middle of the night, I woke up, demanded where he'd been. I was a trifle undone, I suppose, and Benjamin had to—to calm me down, you see."

"I see." More than he wanted to, perhaps, because it intensified the longing to know that special intimacy with Leah. "Tell me what's troubling you."

"Do you promise me that you love my sister, as much—or almost as much, as Benjamin loves me?"

Yet *another* family member, trying to protect a woman Cade once would have maintained would never require protection. Did Leah have any idea what lengths her family went to, to protect her? "I ought to tell you it's none of your business," he said. "But I won't, since I know it springs from love for your sister." He stared up through branches outlined in gold by the pearly shell of a dawn sky. Regardless of Preston Clarke's schemes, Cade determined to find a place where he and Leah enjoy an uninterrupted talk. Alone. His jaw flexed. "I love her," he admitted to Meredith now. "I want to marry her. Is that what you wanted to hear? Good. Now tell me why you're asking."

Her flush deepened. "I'm sorry, Cade. It's just...I've never seen Leah like this. She's determined to 'remove you from the influence and possibly injurious circumstances associated with Preston'—doesn't that sound just like her? But Cade, she's afraid. I know that's a strong word, but I can see it. She, well, actually she reminds me of Sam. I never thought I'd compare my youngest sister to a little child, yet it's the most accurate analogy. Even when we were children ourselves, Leah always behaved more like an adult. Now she doesn't. I'm not sure what's going on in her heart—never have been, truthfully. But I don't want her to be hurt."

"If anyone's at risk of being hurt here, I'm afraid it's going to be me." Cade watched her levelly for a long moment. "Leave us alone, Meredith. Allow Leah and me to muddle our way through whatever purpose God has in mind for us."

"I think she's in love with you. It shouldn't be that hard."

"Mm. Like you and Ben? As I recall, you put him through a bad moment or two yourself."

"Compared to what Garnet endured with Sloan, our courtship progressed as smoothly as a hot knife through a pad of butter. Very well." She shivered, and tugged her wrapper closer. "I'll behave. Just be patient with her."

"Patience," Cade muttered after Meredith scurried away down the path, "is a commodity I'm about to run out of, Lord."

❦

Dry-mouthed, pacing the hotel piazza, Leah waited for Cade to bring the buggy around. Their initial reunion had not gone well. Her fault, of course. She had been far too conscious of the stares of other guests, of Meredith's unsubtle matchmaking, and especially of Cade himself. All her earlier confidence had fled.

She'd wanted him to kiss her. There. She admitted it to herself while she paced, the confession somehow allowing her to take a deeper breath. But when they had met in one of the lobby's many parlors, all Cade had done was to smile that slow, lopsided smile of his, hold her hand for too brief a moment, then tell her he was very glad to see her, but why was she here so soon after the school year had begun? Hadn't she left Mrs. Hays and all her students in the lurch?

Even now, she winced at her reaction. She had been crushed. Unprepared despite Benjamin's warning. Even worse, Cade had known.

"This is not what either of us needs," he stated flatly. "Fetch a coat—a warm one. We're going for a ride. Meredith, tell your husband I'm borrowing one of the gigs."

"Cade, are you sure a buggy ride is a good idea?" Meredith asked, hovering at Leah's side. "Remember what Benjamin said? About being recognized?"

Cade ignored the question. "I'll bring the buggy up front. We won't need a driver. I'll handle the reins myself." His gaze dropped to Leah's mouth, then lifted back to her eyes. "We'll be back in time for dinner. That all right with you, Leah?"

Uncomprehending, all she could do was nod. Obviously she had lost the ability to veil her expression, along with her levelheadedness. Like that nascent flower pushing its way to the surface, so a crop of emotions buried deep inside for years were inexorably making their presence known. It had taken all Leah's discipline not to hike her skirts and flee up the stairs. If he loved her as much as he claimed, he wouldn't have been this offhand after not seeing her for two and a half months. Or would he? What did *she* know about men, after all?

She dodged a party of guests dressed in hiking clothes, then peered down the drive.

On the other hand, there was that look, when he'd stared so hard at her mouth, like he'd done that long ago day when he'd swept her up into his arms and carried her off… Leah felt her face heat with the memory. Perhaps Cade's subsequent actions should reassure her somewhat.

A piano box buggy with the top folded behind the seat pulled to a smooth halt in the drive. Cade hopped down as Leah descended the steps. He stood there, looking up at her with the afternoon sun gilding his tousled hair, and an expression she still couldn't decipher. All of a sudden his hands closed around her waist; he lifted her completely off her feet, swung around, and gently deposited her on the buggy seat, then climbed back aboard with a swift grace that left Leah blinking at him in astonishment.

He picked up the reins and set the horse down the drive at a brisk trot. "You looked," he told her with a sideways grin, "like a woman who needed to be swept off her feet."

"I did?" She turned the comment around in her mind for a bit, trying, mostly in vain, to ignore the melting sensation that transformed her limbs to the consistency of damp velvet. "How, exactly, does a woman who wants to be swept off her feet look?"

"Are you by any chance flirting with me, Miss Sinclair?"

"What? Of course not. Flirting is an unbecoming social convention designed to make females look and sound like featherheads."

Cade laughed, a joyful, uninhibited sound that made it impossible for her to take offense, especially when he took the reins in one hand so he could tweak the flat brim of her straw hat. "I do love you, Leah Sinclair," he said. "There is absolutely no other woman in the world like you, no other woman God could have designed who I could love like I love you." His mirth faded. "Smile," he commanded softly. "Everything's all right—we'll make it all right. You're safe with me, little wren. With me, you can be whatever and whoever you feel like being, say whatever's on your heart. Or"—he winked at her—"on your mind. Smile, Leah. It's a perfect Indian summer afternoon, and we're together."

Smile? He wanted her to smile, when her stomach was tied in enough knots to frustrate a dedicated sailor? "Cade, I—" Distractedly she checked the buttons on her coat, making sure they were all fastened while she at last decided simply to take him at his word. "I have something I need to say to you. But I'm nervous. I don't know if I can smile right now."

She didn't realize all the possible connotations of that announcement until out of the corner of her eye she saw Cade's complexion lose its healthy outdoor robustness. The arm brushing hers turned rigid as a hitching post. "Not something bad," she blurted. "Cade, it's not bad, I beg your pardon. I'm not used to attacks of nerves, and I can tell I'm handling this poorly. It's just that I wanted to tell you that I love you, but I've never said the words before and I'm—Oh."

The buggy lurched to a halt, but from behind them came the sound of hoofbeats, and voices; a wagon filled with guests was approaching.

Once again Cade took the reins in one hand, and the horse resumed a light trot. Hands damp, heart skittering, Leah watched Cade tug the leather driving glove off with his teeth, then let it drop. "Leah, love," he murmured in a deep tone. "Leah. Thank You, Lord." His fingers brushed against her cheek, her chin. "Say it again. Please." With only the lightest of pressure he coaxed her to turn her head toward him. "Practice makes perfect. Try it and see."

"I...love you." Color rushed into her cheeks at the heat kindling in his gaze, inches from hers. But—he was right. Repetition did lend a magical confidence. "I love you, Cade Beringer."

"Now smile for me, and pretend we're all alone, about to seal the declaration with a kiss." His fingers brushed the back of her neck, just beneath the wide lapels of her jacket and the lace collar of her gown. Seconds later the party of six guests rolled by with a clattering of hooves and a chorus of congenial greetings and nods. Then they were gone, and

Cade urged their own horses back into a trot. He picked up the discarded glove. "Will you help—?"

"Certainly."

Mercysake, was that shaken, smoky voice hers? Leah clutched Cade's glove, the heat in her cheeks intensifying as she worked it back over his hand. It was a plebeian task, one she had performed thousands of times over the years, for her sisters, for her students. Yet imbued in the simple act now was a wealth of meaning and a veritable cascade of feeling that poured through her like a revelation. "Cade? This being in love... It takes getting used to, doesn't it?"

"A lifetime." Glove back in place, he resumed driving the buggy with both hands.

"Is that why you commandeered the buggy and me? So we could get used to these feelings?"

"Partly. Mostly I wanted to restore a bit of color to your cheeks. And help you overcome whatever it was that was making you afraid in the middle of the day."

"Oh." She blinked at him, studying the rugged masculinity of his profile, so at odds with his gentleness. "You keep surprising me. But"—buoyed by newfound assurance, Leah gave his forearm a light rap—"I'm not always fond of surprises. This business of J. Preston Clarke? Now that I'm here, we're going to conduct things a bit differently."

"What way would that be?"

Leah was not fooled. "We can discuss it with Meredith and Benjamin, over dinner. Right now, I'd like to enjoy my first buggy ride with an eligible gentleman for an escort."

"I think I can go along with that suggestion, even though the gentleman is no longer eligible. His heart belongs irretrievably to a certain schoolteacher."

She hesitated. "Cade? We're safe, aren't we? I mean, Preston wouldn't try anything here, at Stillwaters."

"I doubt it. Too much of a risk. Besides"—briefly he rested his palm against her cheek—"while I admit I was desperate to be alone with you, I would never do anything to deliberately endanger the woman I love."

"Oh…" The stray niggle of doubt dissolved, and Leah settled back against the seat, content for the first time in months.

For the next several hours they drove without regard to a destination. Cade told Leah not to worry about becoming lost, then steered the horse apparently at random down Stillwaters's side roads, which wound through woods-choked valleys and around the flanks of steep, rocky hills. For a while they continued to meet riders, parties of hikers, or other hotel gigs, driven by uniformed Stillwaters employees. But as time passed they met fewer guests. When Leah commented on it, Cade grinned and told her he'd deliberately chosen the less traveled areas, farther from the hotel's main road.

"All well and good," Leah retorted, "but I don't want to find ourselves lost again."

"Trust me, sweetheart. Over the past three months I've trod almost every inch of the resort grounds. Did you know it took Ben two years to widen the roads just enough to accommodate a carriage? He insisted on disrupting the surroundings as little as possible, so he made changes inch by inch."

"Sounds like something you and Benjamin would insist upon." Privately she thought the trees loomed over the road, and she could have done with more openness. Then, because she was determined to thoroughly test the strength of Cade's promise that she could say whatever she liked, she told him so.

"Some guests have the same reaction," he said peacefully. "Can't please everybody. That's why we haven't seen anyone for the past half-hour. You complaining about that, too?"

Leah considered for a moment. "No."

"I'm glad. Besides, this road we're on now loops back around to the main drive to the hotel, just a ways down from where we left it three hours ago."

With a mischievous grin he then launched into a scientific discourse on the variety of flora and fauna he'd discovered at Stillwaters, and the possibility that man-made disruptions would upset the ecological balance. Naturally Leah felt compelled to respond, often with the opposite point of view, for the delight of hearing Cade's passionate response.

While the horse ambled along, she and Cade talked about anything and everything—except the immediate future, especially concerning J. Preston Clarke and the cloud of danger that lurked on the horizon. By unspoken agreement, both of them adopted Jesus' admonition to take no thought for the morrow, leaving it where it belonged—in the Lord's capable hands.

It was a glorious late September day, with a bright blue sky, mild temperatures, and all the colors in God's autumnal palette seeping through the trees. Afternoon sunbeams shot streaks of pinkish gold across the western mountains, and the deep blue sky was smeared with orange and purple overtones. Leah couldn't remember a day when she'd been so content.

They were approaching a curve when four men leaped from the trees, converging upon the buggy like a swarm of hornets.

They had no time to prepare, no time to react or truly defend themselves.

Leah managed a single healthy scream as two of the men dragged Cade from the buggy. Then the third man yanked her down as well, his hand clamping over her jaw. Leah bit the filthy, malodorous fingers, and was rewarded by an instant's freedom before her captor backhanded her so hard the pain momentarily blinded her.

"*Leah!*"

She heard Cade's agonized shout, and as in the worst of nightmares she tried to reach him but she couldn't run fast enough, couldn't help him. She sensed a dark malevolent presence, felt brutish hands wrap about her middle, her throat. Heard in spiraling terror the deafening report of a pistol. Denial screamed through her in a spasm of uncontrollable rage, and she surged upward, her hands curved like claws.

Something exploded against the side of her head, and she plummeted into darkness.

She would never know what brought her back to consciousness, disoriented, her teeth chattering from pain and shock. She just knew that she was awake—and that she could hear the sound of voices. Arguing, they were arguing about something. She wanted to moan, needed to move, but something ordered her to stay still. To keep quiet. To wait.

So she did, because the jumbled words abruptly registered in her bruised brain: The men who had attacked them were debating what to do about *her*.

"…weren't paid but for the one…"

"…too much of a risk, I tell ye…"

"…might die, leave her here. She wasn't supposed to be part of this. I didn't agree to hurt a woman. What'll…"

"…ain't our problem. Can't prove nothing, 'specially iffen you keep your trap shut. Now git the big bruiser in the buggy. It's a couple of miles to the cave, and I plan to be shed of this place afore moonrise."

It was not difficult to feign stillness. She'd recognized one of those voices. If they realized it—if *he* realized she was conscious, the question of her fate would be decided on the spot, and Leah entertained little doubt about its finality.

Twenty-Seven

*L*eah lay motionless on the dirt road long after the sound of the departing buggy and jumbled male voices faded into the distance. Eyes closed, teeth gritted against the increasingly violent urge to move, she counted to five thousand, slowly. Then, fighting the fear, she opened her eyes. All she heard was the loud hum of insects and her pulse roaring in her ears. All she saw was a patch of goldenrod, inches from her nose, and beyond the powdery fronds, an empty road.

She was alone, for the moment. *Don't forget that, Leah.* Those men might very well be returning by the same route. Coming back for her. Regardless, she could not lie here in the weeds, passively waiting. She had to do something, had to. *Cade.*

Dizziness assailed her when she staggered to her feet, but Leah ignored the physical discomforts. Those fiends had Cade. He was being taken to a cave—and Leah was going to find him and rescue him. He was injured, she knew that, she had heard the shot. But he was not dead. *He was not dead.*

Time passed according to the height of the setting sun, disappearing over her left shoulder behind the uneven line of the mountain. Doggedly Leah ignored the lengthening shadows, concentrating instead on following the buggy wheels' parallel trail, trying to keep alert.

By the time she reached a two-track path that disappeared in some woods to the left of the road, dusk draped the world in ominous tones of sepia and smudged gray. She could scarcely discern the marks left by the horses' hooves and buggy wheels, wheels that sank deep under the weight of five men.

Soon it would be completely dark, making even the most obvious trail impossible to follow without a light.

Her breath hitched. The terror weighted her footsteps, clawed her back like a live thing. Fear of the dark, fear for Cade... *Don't think about it, Leah. Think about the task before you.*

Logic told her that the men would not bother to post a guard, that her only danger lay in the possibility of their return after they presumably dumped Cade in whatever cave they'd found. But the manner of man who would attack a helpless woman and shoot an unarmed man likely was ruled by something other than logic.

Trees closed in around her, their thickly leaved branches whispering, reaching down toward her. Had it been only a few hours ago that she and Cade engaged in good-natured debate over her dislike for looming trees? Something darted across the road, scattering leaves and underbrush in a panicked rustle. Leah barely stifled a shriek. She froze, hand clasped over her mouth, her heart racing, ears straining to hear. Nobody jumped out of hiding. No shouts of alarm erupted.

The need to hurry propelled her forward once again.

Moments later she rounded a bend—and heard a horse's snort, the creak of springs, a burst of coarse laughter. Quick as a flea Leah dived under cover, dropping flat on her face behind a concealing thicket of sumac. Seconds later she heard the men pass by, still laughing and talking. As oblivious to Leah as she was conscious of them.

But—how many were there? All four men—or had they left one, possibly two on guard? If Lester Turpin was the guard, would he actually harm Leah? Of course he would. His participation in Cade's abduction left no room to hope otherwise. And it was an abduction, not a murder. He wasn't dead. She refused to believe they had killed him. *Cade was not dead.*

Once again she waited unmoving, waited with skittering heartbeat and rising urgency until the encroaching darkness simply became more than she could bear. Leah rolled to her knees, breathing through her nose, far too rapidly.

By the time she wound her way to the mouth of the cave the only light left in the sky was a dirty orange glow on the western horizon. The cave itself was an obscene black hole yawning out of brutish, lichen-covered boulders. For several demoralizing moments Leah cowered in the trees, while her stomach roiled and shudders reverberated down her spine. There was no sign of a guard, no sound of shuffling or coughing. No odor of cigar smoke or unwashed bodies. No indication at all that the band of villains had left anyone behind except Cade, who most probably was grievously injured. Or—

Her stomach heaved. Leah dropped to her knees and vomited. Then, after using her handkerchief to wipe her face and mouth, she squared her shoulders and approached the cave.

A lantern had been left just inside the entrance, along with a box of matches that she pounced upon as though the items offered the difference between life and death. *Don't light it yet, Leah.* The counsel seemed to spring from the deepest recesses of her mind, but she fought the wisdom because she didn't want, she absolutely *did not want* to take another step into the bowels of this implacably black hole.

The longer she hesitated, the greater the risk to Cade's life.

Leah bit the inside of her cheek until she tasted blood, stuffed the matches in the pocket of her skirt and clutched the lantern in one hand with disembodied fingers. Bracing her free hand on the rough stone wall of the cave, step by step she allowed herself to be swallowed up by the darkness.

The childish cry for help welled up from a source she would have sworn had dried up twenty years earlier. But without conscious urging she found herself breathing snatches of prayer, verses of scripture… pleading for God's mercy, for Cade, for herself. Her only contact with anything solid was the unyielding coldness of stone.

She was alone in the darkness. Suffocated by fear for the man she had come to love, and by a terror that had ruled her nights for over twenty years. And yet, though blackness pulsated around her, beating at her like bat wings, something was happening…inside. A calm drifted over her, into and through her. There was no light, *no light* at all, whether her eyes remained open or shut. Yet somehow the fear was receding.

Didn't make sense. This did not make sense. She couldn't see, yet she was aware of a lightness filling her from the inside out, aware of—light. Of a knowledge that hovered just on the threshold of her heart, yearning to come in and fill her up.

Was this God's Presence? Or was she crumbling into terror-induced hysteria?

No. She was not hysterical. She was afraid—but she possessed all her faculties, save her sight. *Lord? Are You...here?*

There was no answer, but she hadn't expected one. Yet the sensation of calm, the prescience of light strengthened within her being, a thin trickle to be sure. Insubstantial, unprovable, and most definitely illogical. But very much felt.

Then close by someone groaned.

Leah almost dropped the lantern. "C-Cade?" The word was a barely audible croak. Her heart staggered in her chest, threatening to crack her rib cage. "Cade?"

There was another, louder moan, and a muffled thud.

Leah fumbled in her pocket for the matches; she didn't know whether Cade was alone or if she was far enough inside the cave to hide a light. But she did know that, without the aid of this lantern, she could not help Cade.

After three tries she managed to get the job done. A blessed yellow circle bloomed, illuminating the rough-hewn walls of a cave not more than eight feet high. Emboldened as well as desperate, Leah hurried forward, holding the lantern high. Not a dozen steps later the light spilled over a prone body, tied hand and foot; a gag bound his mouth. His eyes were closed.

"Cade!"

Joy, anger, and fear exploded inside her chest. Leah rushed forward, dropped to her knees beside his head, and set the lantern down. His eyelids lifted, and their gazes met. As long as she lived, she would never forget the expression in those glazed green eyes above the gag.

"Hold on. I'll free you. We'll be out of here soon."

He nodded, urgency radiating from every straining muscle.

Her fingers shook badly, and the knot in the filthy bandanna used for the gag was stubborn, tangled and matted in Cade's hair. Impatiently she worked his mouth free; she would deal with the knot later. "Cade? I heard a shot. Did they…are you—?"

"Flesh wound. Side. It burns, but not…significant." He paused, flexing his jaw. "They…didn't want to kill. Using for…leverage. Blackmail. Telling—Ben…"

The effort to speak seemed to exhaust him. Leah had never seen Cade like this—bound, helpless, the strength of his personality vanquished. More shaken than she cared to admit, she hurriedly unbuttoned her coat and wadded it up for a pillow beneath his head. "It's all right. I'll get us out of here. We'll have to be quiet. I don't know if they left a lookout posted. I didn't see a guard." She glanced at the lantern. "After I untie you, and we start back out, we…shouldn't use the lantern."

"Leah…love. Can't believe you're here." In the fitful lantern light his eyes gleamed wetly. "Thought they'd—I was afraid they—"

"Shh. I'm fine, I'm all right—drat these knots!" she muttered, her fingers furiously tugging at the cord that bound his wrists behind his back. The callous cruelty of it filled her with rage. "I was terrified about you," she told him between mutterings, the boggy sound of her voice startling. "So afraid…don't need this stupid rope to…"

"Pocketknife," Cade said. "I still have my pocketknife. They were careless, never checked."

She had to roll him onto his injured side to retrieve it, and the pain she caused him couldn't have been more acute if she herself had been shot. "I'm sorry, sorry," she murmured again and again while she worked over him.

The knife was small but lethally sharp; within moments Cade was finally free. Leah massaged his arms to restore circulation, her mumbling litany unabated. She helped him sit up, propping his back against the cave wall where he simply rested, arms limp, eyes closed. It was imperative to leave as quickly as possible, but it was obvious that Cade would need time to recover enough strength to walk. Leah was strong, but not strong enough to support a man of Cade's size.

How long before someone came to check the prisoner? How far could she and Cade travel in the dark, on foot, with Cade injured?

She jumped when his hand lifted and brushed against her cheek.

"Leah…" her name emerged in a wondering sigh. "Sweetheart. Look." His fingers traced her face, over her eyelids.

She blinked, trying to understand why his face was blurred, why her nose and throat had clogged up. Then he fumbled for her fingers and lifted her own hand to her face.

"I'm…why, I'm crying." Bewildered, she stared down at her wet fingers, then lifted them back to wipe her eyes, which unbelievably streamed with tears. "Cade, I'm really crying."

"Yes." The haggard, dirt-smeared face seemed to melt. Was he smiling? "Well, I sort of got the impression you wanted to, that day at the school. Remember?" It was only when he stirred and grimaced that Leah's miraculous weeping faltered. Cade's eyelids fluttered, his gaze lost focus, and he tilted sideways.

"Cade. Stay with me." She swallowed noisily and braced her hands on his shoulders. "You stay with me, do you hear? We have to walk— you have to walk out of here, and we have to leave now. You have to help me."

Beneath her hands she felt his muscles ripple with effort. Coaxing, bullying, all but boxing his ears, Leah brought him back to full consciousness and somehow to his feet. He stood, wavering like a newborn colt, while she fetched the lantern. "Need light…" He made an attempt to hug her when she wrapped her arm about his waist and urged him forward. "Don't be afraid. Not alone. Not alone in the dark, Leah."

"I know." She bullied him forward, a shambling step at the time. "Perhaps later, when it's safe to stop for the night, I'll tell you about it."

"Don't be 'fraid. Love… Love gives light. My love for you—God's. Light for feet…lamp for path… Leah, don't be—"

She doused the lantern, plunging them into total darkness. "We'll be spiritual later," she hissed, reaching up until she found his lips and pressed her hand across them. "Right now, we need to be quiet."

She felt him nod against her restricting hand. "Quietness and confidence our strength. Little wren…strength of an eagle."

"Am I going to have to gag you again?"

It was strange. Though deprived of her visual faculty, Leah could see as though they were in the noon sun Cade's astonishment and amusement; sense his determination, his effort to regain full awareness. Above all, she could *feel* the power of his love soaking into her, like water soaking into black soil, to a bulb hidden in the darkness.

They gained the entrance unmolested. Awed, Leah marveled at the miracle of the mild September night. Stars so thick they peppered the blue-black heaven in a swirling storm, and a glistening half-moon that spilled silver light onto the earth below.

Cade was right. It truly never was as dark as it seemed.

Especially when, against all empirical evidence to the contrary, the almighty Creator had spoken to her in darkness, filling her with the light of His love.

"You're not afraid," Cade whispered. "You're truly not afraid."

Fresh tears spurted from her eyes. "Not about the dark." She stumbled and banged his injured side, causing him to groan. Hurriedly she shifted her grip. "Only about what might happen if we get caught." But she knew—though only time would be able to prove the truth of her knowledge—that she would never be truly afraid of the darkness again.

⇜❊⇝

Cade remembered little of his and Leah's stumbling journey from the cave, down a winding path, then straight up the side of a mountain. Time condensed and expanded in disjointed fragments of lucidity. He remembered Leah warning him when they reached the mouth of the cave that she had no way of knowing when their attackers might reappear. She had decided their safest course was to put a mountain between them, so she could light a fire and tend his wounds. After that, he remembered little but the sound of his labored breathing, and Leah's.

He was weak as water, with a pulsing headache and blurred vision that thankfully improved somewhat as the night wore on. He might have a slight concussion, but not a bad one, which was fortunate since Leah insisted that they hike up a mountainside in the middle of the night. His side throbbed at odd moments; once, when he started to fall, Leah's hands clamped directly into the long furrow the bullet left when it seared his skin, and a strangled yelp escaped before he could stop it. Oh yes, he remembered that particular moment.

Mostly, though, he remembered Leah. Dainty and delicately boned she might be, his little wren, but Meredith had been right: Her youngest sister possessed the courage of a Daniel, and her will...her will—

"Hold on to this tree trunk and rest for a bit." Her face, wreathed in star points and a cloud of fine hair that spilled free in wispy strands down her shoulders, loomed close to his. "Just a little farther, Cade. We're almost to the top."

Her will was that of a warrior. "My warrior wren," he told her, smiling a little because a bar of moonlight illuminated the shyness she covered quickly with a scowl. "Don't worry. I'm not losing my senses. You're wonderful, and I love you. We'll make it, don't worry."

The moon was at its height when the ground beneath Cade's feet began to tilt downward. Beside him, Leah's labored breaths had grown louder, and even in his near stupor he could feel the tremors that were almost constant now.

Yet she never faltered. Once they descended far enough that a small fire could not be spotted, it was Leah who found a level patch of ground, Leah who heard the gurgling sound of a tiny runoff creek, Leah who gathered the makings of a fire and coaxed it to life.

Amazing, isn't it, Lord?

Cade lay quietly while she cleaned and bandaged his various scrapes, burns, and scratches with the cut-up flounce of her petticoat; he reveled in the loving gentleness of her touch as he finally drifted into the sanctuary of sleep. His last awareness was the tingling comfort that one didn't need a burning bush, or a Damascus road, to experience God's Presence.

Twenty-Eight

The morning dawned cool and clear, then warmed as the sun rose with autumn's fiery profusion of scarlet and burnt orange and gold. Refreshed despite their circumstances, after a filling but unappetizing breakfast of sassafras tea and roasted chestnuts, Leah and Cade set out for Stillwaters.

At first Leah focused more attention on Cade than on the beauty of the day. "I told you, the bullet scarcely grazed me," he repeated with commendable patience after her third inquiry. "And my head's too hard to be affected overmuch by a knock or two. Frankly, I'm more concerned about you."

"My head's even harder than yours."

It was a little past high noon by the time they reached the base of the mountainside, and started across the floor of another hollow. The hotel was just over the next ridge, Cade told her. Leah nodded, smiling up at him as she surreptitiously pressed her palm against the stitch in her side. Not ten minutes later, he spotted Hominy Hawes, high above them on the lip of the craggy ridge. Though his commanding height and dark skin made him easy to identify, he was too far away and too high up to hail. Undeterred, Leah started to dash from the cover of the woods into the meadow they'd been paralleling as they crossed the valley.

Cade caught her arm, then winced. Leah's elation instantly turned to concern. "Be careful! Your side…I told you we should have set a slower pace."

Cade pressed two fingers over her lips, halting the lecture. "My side isn't the issue. You are. As for the pace, I deliberately slowed it for *you*, my heart. On my own, I would have moved twice as fast." He chuckled when Leah punched his shoulder. "I'll just remember to grab you with

213

my other arm next time. As for dashing into the meadow—I don't want to risk exposure. Not yet."

"Oh." She bit her lip, annoyed with her naiveté as well as Cade's revelation.

He'd set a slower pace for her? The man had been shot, tied, and whacked on the head. Yet he acted as though *she* were the one in need of cosseting.

Leah scowled at him, not understanding why he took her arms and carefully sat her down until she stared at her knees, which for some reason were wobbling back and forth. And, botheration, her own head felt as though someone had walloped it with an iron skillet. "We're safe now. Aren't we safe?"

Cade nodded. "Benjamin's probably notified the authorities. I imagine that ridge is swarming with searchers, including Ben. But we're still not taking chances."

"I suppose you're right. I just know how frantic they must be. Meredith..." Sighing, Leah massaged her temples. "Knowing Meredith, she's looking as well. Mercysake, we'll never hear the end of this."

"We have put them through some bad nights, haven't we?" He lifted her hand to his lips and dropped a kiss on her skinned and sweaty knuckles. "Wait here. I'll be back in a moment."

"What? Why?"

"Because I'm going to alert Hominy and at the same time warn him to be careful." He paused, watching her, waiting Leah knew, for her to debate the matter or demand further details.

Awash in sloppy emotions, Leah offered a compliant smile. It still seemed a miracle of sorts, that the injured, semiconscious man she had all but bullied up a mountainside the previous night was the same man as the one standing in front of her now. "Hurry up," she said. "And...you be careful too."

The green gaze sparked with tenderness as he skimmed his knuckles along her cheekbone. But his only reply was a soft, "I won't be far, not out of your sight. Rest, sweetheart."

She watched him slip noiselessly through the trees and wondered if it was exhaustion or love that filled her with this *floaty* feeling. Had to be love, she decided, leaning back against the tree and closing her eyes. Felt too good to be exhaustion. An even more miraculous truth seeped into her mind, her heart: She wasn't alone any longer. *Thank You*, she whispered with the grateful wonder of a child, to the God who loved her.

Drifting in the euphoric haze, she jumped with a little yelp of surprise when a piercing whistle rent the peaceful meadow. The sound varied in pitch, and Leah listened in open-mouthed astonishment while Cade repeated the call three times, then stopped.

From high above, a return whistle sounded, floating down to them on a current of air.

Leah staggered to her feet. "How did you do that?" she demanded the instant Cade returned. "Can you teach me? Will Hominy know it was you?"

This time he hushed her with a kiss. Flustered and breathless when he finally released her, Leah had to blink a time or two before she realized he was holding a small hand-carved wooden whistle in front of her face.

"This is how I made the sounds," he said. "Like I told you last night, those four men were careless."

"In the Bible, the Lord used a jackass to teach Balaam a lesson," Leah murmured. "I suppose God can use whatever means are at His disposal to accomplish His purpose. Even a pack of careless villains." Hesitantly she touched the cricket-size whistle.

Cade dropped a kiss on the tip of her nose. "We use them to signal each other when we're out exploring." The whistle disappeared in his pocket. "Come on. There's a path up those cliffs you should be able to manage, even in those long skirts. With a bit more of God's grace, we'll be back at the hotel in time for afternoon tea."

"A pot of hot tea's just what I need. Unfortunately, it's likely to be accompanied by something less palatable. You do know the worst is yet to come?" Leah said as they started off through the trees, toward the base of the cliff.

"Whatever happens, we'll face it together. Don't be afraid. Ben knows we're safe now, so the authorities can descend on Preston Clarke. Certainly there's more than sufficient evidence after this to finally put that man behind bars." He wrapped his fingers around hers. "Leah, I never thought Lester would be in on it, even though I'd seen him with the others once before, months ago... Should've put two and two together, but I didn't." He sighed heavily. "I'm sorry, sweetheart, for putting you in harm's way. Will you be afraid of him? It won't be long until he's behind bars with Clarke."

"Not of Lester. But a little for you. I might not be around the next time you need rescuing."

"Then I'll have to take special care of myself, won't I?" Without warning he stopped, hauling Leah into a close embrace. "We'll add a codicil to our marriage vows, if you like."

A smile bloomed as the last of Leah's uncertainty evaporated. He loved her. Cade loved *her*. The reality of it radiated from his face in a nimbus. He'd been telling her for months, only she had been too blind to see. Until now.

"Cade?" Heart racing, she gathered her courage. "Are you by any chance finally *asking* me to marry you, instead of telling me?"

"Mm. Sounds that way, doesn't it? I was planning to phrase it properly, you know. I suppose I should have waited for more appropriate surroundings," he admitted.

His gaze drifted beyond her, to a bower of brick red and golden leaves shimmering within a stand of Virginia pine. Nearby, a crop of hay-scented fern gleamed bright as newly minted pennies, while beneath their feet pine needles, leaves, and patches of velvety green moss offered the most elegant of carpets. "Although what could be more appropriate than one of God's forest cathedrals?"

"Nothing." She reached to brush a single pine needle from the lapel of his impossibly soiled coat, her fingers lingering over a dried bloodstain. "I— My answer is yes, but..." she wavered, her newly sprung emotions fighting the logistical complications that crowded her mind. "I have— I'm a teacher. And you...I couldn't ask you to live in a city, or even a town."

"Do you trust me, Leah?"

Slowly she nodded. "Yes. Because I love you."

"And you've learned to trust that God loves you, regardless of any and all evidence to the contrary?"

"It doesn't make sense," she said, "and I doubt I'll ever find adequate words to explain…" A blush heated her cheeks when Cade's eyes rolled and he shook his head. "But I know it's true."

Abruptly he lifted her off her feet and twirled her around as though he'd suffered no injuries, and she weighed no more than a handful of mustard seed. Then he set her back down and brushed a kiss across each of her eyelids. "We'll work out all the details," he murmured, "and it will be as God intended. How could it not, with the perfect Matchmaker on our side, overseeing the arrangement?"

Indeed!

The sense of childlike abandon, of wonder bubbled up all over again. *Thank You. Thank You for not giving up on me.*

"You're right," she said then, trailing her fingers along the bump on Cade's nose. "Actually, compared to what's sure to happen in the immediate future, working out the rest of our lives will be positively mundane."

"Sweetheart, there's truly no need to be afraid of Preston Clarke, or his bungling henchmen. I've promised you—"

"Oh, I'm not talking about them," Leah interrupted with a smile. "I'm talking about Meredith. It occurs to me that it might be easier to survive another round with those four villains than this coming reunion with my oldest sister."

Their laughter drifted up through the trees into the warm autumn day. Then, hand in hand, they set off to climb the mountain.

Part II

JACOB

Interlude

SINCLAIR RUN
OCTOBER 1895

*T*endrils of mist hovered waist high in the chilly autumn morning. Jacob stepped out on the front porch and moved carefully across to his favorite corner, avoiding the creaking floorboards he never seemed to have time to repair. His mood pensive as the fog-draped surroundings, he studied an earthenware bowl cradled in his arms.

'Twas October, far past the growing season. Both spring and summer were but a memory, yet the rich fragrance of a hyacinth freshly bloomed filled his nostrils and permeated the mist, suffusing the air with—a miracle.

Gently Jacob placed the bowl on the corner railing. His eyes feasted upon the gaudy purple flower that had burst into full bloom over the past twenty-four hours. "So many lessons, Lord," he whispered. The miracle of God's creation, combined with properly applied scientific knowledge, had resulted in this wondrous sight.

If only Leah were here to see it.

His gaze drifted out toward a sugar maple he and Mary had planted more than thirty years ago. When the tree matured, Mary had planned to try her hand at syrup-making. They'd laughed as they planted the finger-width sapling, knowing it would take years… Jacob smiled sadly.

Over the past week the leaves had exploded with color, delighting both eyes and soul. He enjoyed all the seasons, but for some reason, autumn always seemed to tug his heartstrings the most. Perhaps it was because on this day, thirty-two years ago, he and Mary had exchanged their vows, pledging their lives together forever. Though it was a dark year for the beleaguered Confederacy, with the huge losses at Gettysburg and Chickamauga, the Valley had been relatively quiet except for the odd skirmish or two.

Jacob and Mary had been full of plans for their future, plans not even a bloody war could tarnish. So many unrealized dreams… Instead of soldiering, he'd stayed busy building wagons for General Jackson's army. But after the war ended he built furniture, like his father and grandfather before him.

'Tis our anniversary, Mary. Why do you suppose I can't seem to let go of it, when you've been with the Lord far longer than you were allowed to be wedded to me?

Mist washed the world in shimmering white-gold as the morning sun ascended over Massanutten Mountain; within moments the thick fog began to dissipate, thinning until all that remained was a translucent veil of heavy dew ripe with the odors of damp earth and wood smoke and resin.

And hyacinth.

What would Mary say about their daughters? About their heartwood chests? Jacob propped his elbows on the railing, beside the earthenware pot, and rested his chin in his hands. She had teased him about that particular dream, her laughter like delicate chiming bells. "You've the soul of a poet, or perhaps a scholar," she'd told him, her eyes soft with indulgence. "My Jacob of the strong hands and brawny shoulders, with a head full of romantical notions. And his heart"—she'd flung her slender arms about his neck and pressed a kiss to his cheek—"his heart is much more attuned to the Lord than mine can ever hope to be. Build your chests for our wee girls, then. Perhaps one day they will appreciate that their papa likes to think in parables, like Jesus."

Aye, that he did, true enough. But good had come of it, had it not, for Garnet, for Meredith? And now, for Leah. It had been a long and painful awakening for her—for Jacob as well, but 'twas well worth the wait, and the pain. *Cade Beringer.* Who would have thought, all those years ago, that a devout believer like Cade would win the pragmatic heart of Jacob's youngest daughter?

He inhaled deeply, reveling in the heavy floral scent while he imagined Leah and Cade's reactions, when they arrived this afternoon. *There's to be another wedding at last, Mary.* With the love of three fine men, his daughters had in God's good time learned how to see through their father's eyes into his heart. *And I learned a lesson or two myself with our Leah.*

A bar of radiant sunlight spiked across the front yard. Somewhere in the trees a bird trilled a good morning; soon Effie or Deacon would be poking a head through the door, if he wasn't careful. Jacob lifted the pot and deposited it on the floor under the parlor window. 'Twould be safer there, while he completed the task he'd set for himself this day.

Hands clasped behind his back, Jacob set off across the yard. He took the long way, following the winding run until he reached the base of the small hill. Then he climbed to the top, to the graveyard, where with bowed head he stood over his wife's grave.

"They're all grown up, Mary, with men of their own. My job is finished." He stopped, throat working as he fought the thickening moisture gathering there. "And, Mary, dear, I think it's time…" He stopped again, gasping a little. "Time to let go of you, as well."

All these years, he'd carried the emptiness left by her passing even though God's grace long ago had healed the grief. But he'd never completely let her go. Look at him now, talking to her as though she hadn't been gone these past two decades. Aye, it was time.

But the years ahead of him stretched long and uncertain, with naught but his work to fill the time. *Lord, 'tis hard, this matter of aging.* He was too old for adventure, chasing after fresh horizons—yet far too busy with his craft to join the old-timers around the stove at Cooper's, playing checkers and jawing the day away. Shaking his head, Jacob studied the simple gravestone for a final moment, then turned away.

The Lord had instructed His human creatures to enjoy the good in their labor, which after all, *was* from the hand of God. Yet 'twas a puzzle nonetheless, this business of love, and loving. Of loss and gain; of faith —and faltering.

Ah yes, Jacob thought now, a bittersweet smile touching the corners of his mouth. Even a simple cabinetmaker such as himself could be plagued with the mysteries of life, and all he could do was pray that someday he, too, would understand.

Twenty-Nine

STILLWATERS
OCTOBER 1895

*F*iona Carlton came awake with a smothered gasp, fighting the bedclothes even as her hands clutched them beneath her neck. Like an oily residue, a remnant of nightmare clung to her sleep-drugged mind; it was the third such occasion since the encounter in the conservatory with that man, back in June. She was grateful that the nightmare had thus far returned only three times.

For several moments she lay against the pillows, listening to the rat-a-tat patter of the rain against the windows until her breathing quieted, and she was able to stretch and turn on the banquet lamp on the nightstand. Sighing, she wondered what time it was, not that it mattered. Hours slid past, becoming days, which drifted into weeks and then months. Years. How many of them had faded away, like the once honey-eyed blond braid that now lay across her breast in nondescript shades of silvery gray and flax.

Fiona sat up, wincing a little. As always, in her nightmares she was frozen stiff as a corpse; when she finally roused her muscles would be locked and aching. Her joints had been less forgiving of late, though usually by the time she finished breakfast she could assume her daily routine. At home in Richmond, that was a merciful blessing, since so many people depended on her there.

She could limber her hands if she played the piano.

Still caught between nightmare and reality, Fiona held her hands straight out in front of her, studying them as though they were strange appendages of unknown origin. The hands of a pianist, Gerald had told her, many times. Long-fingered and strong. Strange, he'd said, for a willowy girl with the bones of a greyhound to have such strong fingers.

Well, she certainly was no longer a girl, and however strong her fingers might be, she had not played the piano since 1873. Gerald would never again gloat or rage about the fame and fortune her powerful musician's hands had brought them both.

Gerald would never do anything again, except perhaps haunt her nightmares, however fleetingly. Long ago Fiona had forgiven her husband for his unwitting part in the tragedy of their lives. But Henry, dear little Henry…

This pain, Lord—will it be with me until I die?

One hand lifted to the scar, a reflexive gesture Fiona couldn't seem to stem when she was distraught—or freshly wakened from a nightmare. Provoked with herself, she rose and padded across to the small sitting area where she spent most of her daylight hours. It was so peaceful, here at Stillwaters, and her private cottage offered the perfect summer retreat—especially for Fiona. The half-dozen other cottages were all accessible to a hard-packed dirt lane wide enough to accommodate a carriage, yet they were far enough apart, tucked beneath trees and shrubs, to give the illusion of utter privacy.

Maisie, her housekeeper and companion, was the unlikely instigator of these yearly sabbaticals. "You need to take time to rest, take care of yourself. What good does it do, pouring yourself out for good works if you wind up buried in the ground?"

She'd tucked the advertisement for Stillwaters beside Fiona's dinner plate one evening three years earlier. Fiona's interest had initially been captured by the resort's isolated location. But she spent subsequent summers here for other reasons, one of which was the man who had built it. The other could be found in the verse from the Twenty-third Psalm, which was printed in the brochure beneath the hotel's name.

Stillwaters offered much more than luxurious accommodations for its guests.

Rest for the soul, Lord. How I've come to cherish the peace of a restful soul.

Tomorrow she would return to Richmond.

For the first time in years, the prospect failed to buoy Fiona's spirits. It was that incident in the conservatory, of course. She'd been caught off guard, her poise in shambles, her behavior unforgivable. How *could* she have been so cruel to the gentleman, with his compassionate eyes and the charming hint of a Scottish burr in his low voice? Over the years, Fiona had learned to perfection how to differentiate morbid fascination from genuine kindness, particularly from what the Europeans considered the upper classes. Regardless of her startlement, she should have recognized the kindness in Mr. Sinclair.

Worse than cruelty, however, she had allowed her shame—and habit—to forestall the needed apology until it was too late.

The nightmares that infrequently awakened her might be the product of a twenty-year-old tragedy, but there was little doubt in Fiona's mind that these last few occurrences arose from the depths of a guilty conscience.

She switched on the floor lamp beside the chair and settled herself against the plush cushions, then picked up the Irish lace collar she'd been working on after supper. It was a particularly difficult pattern in Cork crochet, one of her namesake grandmother's favorites. Not only had Fiona always thrived on challenge, right now she needed the distraction.

He'd said he was Mrs. Walker's father.

She blew out an exasperated breath, retrieved her reading glasses, and concentrated her attention on finishing the collar's scalloped border. Regret made for a mighty poor bedfellow, though it had taken years of pillow-soaking prayers to learn that particular truth.

His name was Sinclair. She could ask the lively Mrs. Walker for her father's address, and write him a note, however belated. Not only did Mr. Sinclair deserve it, but by extension she owed his family the same respect they had always afforded to Fiona.

For three years the Walkers had gone out of their way to accommodate her needs. They had treated her with respect, and no matter how bizarre they must have found her requests, on the few occasions when Fiona talked to them they displayed nothing but courtesy. The well-trained staff had obviously taken their cue from the Walkers, for not once had she been subjected to poor service, sly looks, or—worst of all—pity.

Definitely a note to Mr. Sinclair was called for. That was all, just a heartfelt note of apology.

With the thorny issue settled in her mind, Fiona relaxed. For several moments she worked in quiet contentment, her movements gradually recovering dexterity and speed.

Abruptly, in the middle of tying a knot, she dropped the collar onto her lap, a thought imprinting itself with such unmistakable clarity that she accepted the truth of it without question.

It wasn't a note that was called for, but a personal apology, delivered verbally.

She didn't understand why, but even as her mind rebelled against the notion, her heart accepted the inevitable: If she ignored the inner urging, she would ultimately lose the peace she had struggled to gain. It was outlandish and likely a waste of time. But she had been told the way—now it was up to her to walk down the path, with the grace of God to give her the courage she was going to need.

Of course, come morning she might feel differently, especially if making a personal visit entailed more than an extra day of travel. Decisions should never be reached in the middle of the night, in the wake of nightmares.

After a long time, Fiona resumed her needlework. Dawn had lightened the sky to a dreary gray before she laid it aside again, and allowed herself another few hours of troubled rest.

❧

SINCLAIR RUN

Cade watched the wind-stung pink of Leah's complexion fade when he turned the rental buggy onto the lane leading to her house. He smiled across at her.

"There's some Moth Mullein in the ditch over here. That makes forty-seven for me, forty-five for you."

"Only because you cheated when we stopped the buggy to verify that *my* identification of that rat snake was in truth correct. If we hadn't stopped, you would have missed the fawn mushroom and the chipmunk." Even under the harsh glare of a pewter gray sky the love shining out of her eyes bathed Cade's world in a luminous gold. "Of course, if we hadn't stopped, that chipmunk probably would have become the snake's lunch. Cade, please don't worry about me. Whether my hyacinth bloomed or died, I'll be all right."

"Of course you will," he returned comfortingly.

Cade was learning that for Leah, living out her faith would always be a struggle, doubtless even more of one now that long suppressed emotions were crowding her heart like the weeds and wildflowers that proliferated here in the Valley. He wondered whether or not he should kiss her, thoroughly enough to restore the bloom in her cheeks, and distract her from her anxiety.

"Cade? Are we going to tell Papa the news about Preston Clarke?"

Thoughts of a rosy romantic interlude evaporated. Cade's hands tightened on the reins; his mouth thinned. "Let's enjoy the reunion first, think about the rest later, hmm?"

Gloved fingers suddenly brushed his cheek. "I'm sorry. Now you're the one in need of a diversion." The buggy seat creaked as she scooted closer and tipped her head so that he could feel the warmth of her breath against his ear. "A beaver just slipped into the run, and right over there"—she pointed—"is some Three-leaved Rosinweed. Since animals count for two points each, that means *I* win."

"I don't think so, madam fiancée." Cade flicked the ostrich feather of her fancy braid hat, a parting gift from Meredith. He gestured grandly to the horse. "*Equus caballus,* a most valued member of the animal kingdom, and two points for me. I win, my love."

She was quietly frustrated the rest of the way up the lane leading to the house, and Cade had to bite the inside of his cheek to restrain the laughter. His beloved was many things, but a gracious loser did not number among them.

Mrs. Willowby and her nephew Deacon came out to greet the buggy. In the background Cade heard the rhythmic thump of a treadle lathe, which explained Jacob's absence from their arrival. Cade bowed over the housekeeper's hand and shook Deke's man-to-man, which of course delighted Deke, who couldn't stop talking about Cade being a member of the family now.

The small talk dwindled until they were all standing staring at one another; Cade glanced at Leah, whose arm rested in his but whose head was turned toward the workshop.

"Go on along, then," Mrs. Willowby told her brusquely. "Plain enough he didn't hear your arrival, what with all the racket he's making."

"He's been nervous all day," Deke said, swiping aside strands of red hair. "He wouldn't let me help. But I'm supposed to fetch him when I see your buggy. I forgot. It's been forever since Mr. Beringer visited."

The blatant hero worship was even more of an unnerving experience since he and Deke were the same height. Cade lightly pummeled the lanky back. "I think it would be better if Leah fetched him, don't you? Why don't you and I unhitch the livery horse?"

"Cade?" Leah asked. She glanced from the barn to Deacon and seemed to hesitate. "Would you mind very much coming with me?"

"I can do the horse by myself," Deke said, his voice dropping its boyish banter for a rare flash of adult maturity. "Leah's right. You ought to go with her, Mr. Beringer. But I want to hear all about the cave and the bad men, so promise you'll wait until I'm through."

"I'll be in the kitchen," Mrs. Willowby announced. "Made some of those pastry ramekins you taught me how to do when you were here last, Leah. I reckon we'll find out shortly if they taste as good as yours." Without another word she disappeared inside the house.

Cade's hand closed over Leah's. "Another challenge for you," he teased, then stopped abruptly when the line of her jaw seemed to quiver. "Sweetheart?"

"I never realized," she murmured, then shook her head and continued in a stronger voice, "never realized how thoughtful she could be. She was trying to divert me, like you were in the buggy, with our game." She sliced him a frustrated glance, then looked back toward the house. "Mrs. Willowby taught me how to cook, the first time she was our housekeeper. But ever since she moved back, some years ago, after Papa's ulcer attack, there's always been this…I suppose 'rivalry' is too strong.

Unvoiced competition, I'll call it. So I wasn't expecting…" Her voice trailed away.

"Ah," Cade said, stroking her fingers. "She loves you. Your whole family loves you. I love you. Keep that in mind, all right?"

"I'm trying," she whispered. "I'm trying."

A westerly breeze blew through the window Jacob had opened for some fresh air. Pausing from his labors, he lifted his head to better enjoy the wind's caress; even on a biting fall day, a man could work up a fine sweat, especially using the lathe.

Voices floated through the window. Jacob's gaze flew from the doorway to the corner of the room, to the walnut plant stand he'd fashioned. He dropped his tools, fumbling to untie the strings of his work apron as he hurried through drifts of wood shavings, and out into the yard.

"Leah!" Arms lifting, he watched her separate herself from Cade. For a single heartbreaking second she hovered, her great dark eyes uncertain. "Och, lass, come and give your father a hug then." She all but hurled herself into his arms.

Over the crown of her hat his gaze met Cade's. "In my heart, you've been my son for a good many weeks now," he said. "But thanks be to God, today I can officially welcome you to the family."

"I'm honored you'll consider me a son," Cade returned. They shook hands, Leah still firmly in Jacob's left arm. "I've written to my family in Butler's Gap as well. They've been longing for the day I'd bring home the woman they could consider a daughter."

"All a matter of timing," Jacob said, and winked. "The Lord's, that is. Your dad still a surveyor?"

Cade nodded. "Until his dying day. But he's not too busy to love another Beringer woman. My two sisters married local boys and produced a passel of nieces and nephews my mother loves to spoil. When I take Leah home, she'll be drowned in attention."

"Good. She needs it," Jacob said. *It's time.* Gently he set Leah away from him. "I've something to show you."

Her face was a study. He watched her grab Cade's hand as they trooped into his workshop, watched her eyes go wide as they fastened onto the hyacinth, blooming in all its glory on the plant stand. Swallowing hard, she crossed the room as though in a dream, her gaze never leaving the brilliant purple flowers.

"It bloomed," she finally whispered. "Cade, do you see? It really bloomed."

"I see it, sweetheart."

Jacob turned away to dab the corner of his eye. *So long, Lord. It's been so long I've prayed for my Leah.* Then he turned back around—and saw tears dripping down the face of a child he had not seen cry in twenty-two years.

"Leah." The word emerged hoarse, all but unintelligible. "You're weeping."

Cade laid a hand on his shoulder and squeezed. "Your daughter's a lot to tell you," he said. "Why don't I leave her to it for a while? I'll go help Deke and gather up our luggage."

Jacob nodded, but scarcely noticed the younger man's departure. He was too busy watching Leah touch each delicate flower in the cluster, with the wonder of a child of God blessed by the miracle of sight after years of blindness.

Thirty

*M*r. Walker, I apologize for persuading your staff to break the rules. But I've an unusual request."

"Mrs. Carlton?" The owner of the resort hotel stood on the threshold of the entrance to their personal living rooms, dressed to perfection in his silk waistcoat and gray-striped trousers. Above the standing collar his handsome face was blank with astonishment.

Beneath her veil Fiona's lips curved upward in a slight smile. She knew she had disconcerted him. Not only had she tracked him down in his private quarters—strictly forbidden to guests—but she had gained the cooperation of his personal assistant to accomplish her purpose.

"I promised Mr. Hawes I would only take a moment of your time. After he heard the nature of my request, he was gracious enough to escort me here."

"And discreet enough to leave," Mr. Walker murmured, glancing down the empty hallway. "Come in, then. Tell me how I can assist you." Concern flickered through a pair of fine blue eyes. "Has a guest, or another staff member, been troubling you?"

"Not at all." She walked passed him into the foyer, into a suite of rooms that might have graced a mansion instead of the fourth floors of a hotel. "I'm afraid it's more the opposite."

"I beg your pardon?"

"I was the one who was unforgivably rude to one of your guests. A Mr. Sinclair. Your father-in-law?" Even softened by the veil's gauzy fabric, Benjamin Walker's utter mystification was obvious. "Not recently,"

232

she clarified. "This occurred back in June, shortly after I arrived. He was…kind to me."

She was impatient with herself because nerves had made her clumsy. "I— Well, ever since then I've been troubled by my response to him. I'm leaving in an hour and was hoping to secure Mr. Sinclair's address from Mrs. Walker before I departed."

"Mrs. Carlton, you're distressing yourself over nothing." His voice was gentle, the blue gaze surprisingly kind for a man of his status. "Jacob mentioned meeting you on a few occasions, while he was strolling the grounds, but to my knowledge he was not offended in any way."

So. He had spoken about her to his family, but she could only thank the Lord that Mr. Sinclair had for whatever reason not mentioned the debacle of their middle-of-the-night encounter. Plain as paint, Benjamin Walker thought her overly sensitive for manifesting "distress." Fiona wasn't about to tell him she hoped Jacob Sinclair lived across the Atlantic, in Scotland, so she could vanquish her conscience and return to Richmond after penning a brief note of apology. She would also thank him for his discretion about their unpleasant encounter. "I still feel compelled to contact him," she murmured, "and convey a formal apology."

Mr. Walker studied her in silence, then inclined his head. "I'll write down his address. Please come in."

"Thank you, Mr. Walker."

"Let me fetch my wife. She's bathing our son." He grinned. "I'm sure she'd much prefer chatting with you. Sam's a handful all the time, but bath time… Well, let's say he delights in more than—" He broke off in midsentence. "Mrs. Carlton? What is it? Are you ill?" He stepped toward her, but stopped when Fiona shook her head.

"I beg your pardon," she managed after a moment. "Thank you for your gracious offer, but I've very little time. The stage…"

"Of course." A frown gathered on his forehead. "I'll only be a moment. You prefer to wait here?" Fiona nodded, marginally relaxing at last. "Very well." After a final searching look Mr. Walker strode through an open doorway off to his left, returning shortly with a piece of crisp linen stationery.

Instead of handing it to her he folded it in half, then tapped it against his palm. "Mrs. Carlton, it's plain that you're troubled about something, and equally plain that you'd rather I pretend not to notice. Under any other circumstances, especially when you're a guest in my hotel, I'd honor your wishes."

Ah, well. She should have known he wouldn't let the matter rest. His mother had been the same. Ever polite, but quietly relentless. "But since I've barged into your private quarters requesting your father-in-law's address, you feel circumstances warrant your…intervention, shall we say?"

"Not entirely." Slowly he extended the folded sheet of paper. "I'm not worried about your intentions concerning Jacob Sinclair."

"Well. Thank you." Fiona took the stationery, glancing down at the neatly printed address, and her heart gave a queer little bump. Woodstock, Virginia. Practically on the way home, with little inconvenience other than an added night spent in a ladies' hotel. Conflicting emotions tangled about her thumping heart.

Fiona had anticipated the dread and the reluctance. What confused and, yes, alarmed her, was the relief. The flicker of anticipation at the thought of seeing Jacob Sinclair again.

"I'm concerned about you," Mr. Walker admitted then, pulling her attention back to him.

"Don't worry about me," Fiona responded on a sigh. "God does provide the strength one needs, Mr. Walker." And every now and then, He also provided a message unmistakable even for the most reluctant soul. "Suffering has been a part of the human condition since Eve gave birth to her first two sons. I've often wondered which of them she grieved for the most, since both ultimately were lost to her."

What would he say, she wondered, if she told him that she was going to visit his father-in-law in person, instead of writing a brief note of apology?

The look on his face prompted her to lay a consoling hand on his forearm, an unprecedented gesture for her. He was so *young*, she thought, her heart breaking a little inside because such an observation on her part underscored her own advancing age. She would never have another child of her own. Never. *God, oh God…help me remember that I'm only growing closer to joyful reunion with You, and my son.*

"I'll leave you to your family," she managed, moving toward the door. "You have a beautiful wife. And your little boy…I've seen him a time or two. He's precious. I pray he will be able to grow into a man as fine as his father. Thank you, again, for Mr. Sinclair's address."

"Mrs. Carlton—"

"I really must go." Back straight, she waited for him to open the door.

All the way back down the corridor, she could feel his gaze burning through her spine like the searing point of a hot poker.

❦

"Coward. Where have you been?" Meredith blew a sodden lock of hair out of her eyes as she pulled on the knee pants of Sam's reefer suit, all the while deftly controlling the squirming little body. "This morning he discovered what fun it is to wriggle between our hands so he can duck his face in the bathwater and—oops!" Sam managed to pull free so he could scamper across the nursery toward his father.

Benjamin scooped him up, tossing the happily giggling boy in the air. "What have you done to your mother, you little hooligan?" Suddenly he gathered Sam close and buried his face in the damp hair. There was an expression that bordered pain on his face.

"Benjamin?" Meredith rose and hurried across the room. "Is something wrong? You look"—she hesitated, searching for words—"I'm not sure. Not quite upset, but not yourself." Abruptly the breath stuck in her throat. She clutched his arm. "Is it Cade? You heard from Cade, the sheriff? They finally arrested Preston, is that it?"

Before Benjamin could answer, Gabby bustled back into the nursery, hastily tying the strings of her bibbed apron. "Sorry to take so long, Miz Walker. I'm afraid I had to change everything. Even my shoes." The dark chocolate eyes ruefully surveyed Sam. "Lots of spring in that young un's suspenders, for sure."

"It's all right, Gabby," Meredith said. "As you see, I'm not much better. Now that you've returned, I'll go change as well. Benjamin, could we—?"

235

Benjamin handed Sam off to his mammy, but Meredith could tell he was reluctant.

"Tell me what's wrong," she demanded the moment he shut the door to their bedroom. "And this time, no charm, no evasiveness—Benjamin!" she gasped when she was hauled backward into his arms. "My gown is damp, you'll stain your—"

When her husband finally released her from his passionate kiss, Meredith was breathless and flushed. But when he laid an almost reverent hand to her cheek, his blue eyes brimming with tenderness, unaccountable tears stung her eyelids.

"I love you, and Sam, more than you can possibly imagine," he said.

"I love you too." She turned her head to kiss the palm cupping her cheek. "But you're starting to alarm me…"

"While you and Gabby were joining Sam for his morning ablutions"—they both grinned—"we had a visitor. Mrs. Carlton."

"What? Here, in our apartments? Mrs. Carlton?" Nobody was allowed access to their private rooms. Hominy saw to that. How had she circumvented Hominy? Unless… "Did someone accost her, Benjamin? She's always alone, doesn't even bring maid or companion. I've always worried that—"

"No, no. Calm down, love. She caught me off guard, I admit, because believe it or not, Hominy escorted her up here."

"Hominy did?" That in itself was unprecedented. Hominy guarded their privacy zealously. "Why?"

"All she wanted was your father's address," Benjamin replied. "She wouldn't tell me why, beyond sharing that she felt she'd been rude to him, of all things. She was so nervous, trying so hard to hide it, that I didn't have the heart to press for details. Gave her the address, and she left."

Mystified, they stood in silence for a little while. "That doesn't explain *your* behavior," Meredith finally said. "With Sam, and me. Not that I'm complaining," she added hastily, a ready blush rising. Even after five years and the birth of a child, Benjamin had only to look at her a certain way, and the rest of the world disappeared behind the wallpaper.

"I wish I could see her face without the veil," Benjamin murmured. "Read her better." He shrugged. "That veil screens more than the scar."

"Ah." Meredith moved behind the dressing screen to peel off her damp gown. "I've always wondered why she bothers with it, but doubtless you're right. Now that I think on it, she must know the veil can't completely hide her face, so its purpose must largely be security. I wonder if she wears one all the time, or just when she ventures out in public. Remember how Garnet felt compelled to wear our mother's old sunbonnets, all those years ago?"

"Mmm. Something about thinking it disguised the color of her hair, wasn't it?"

Meredith slithered out of the house gown and tossed it over the screen. With Sam, for bathing time she'd learned to wear her oldest and most easily divestible clothing. "Yes. It was most annoying. What do Mrs. Carlton and her veil have to do with your sudden demonstration of affection?"

"Nothing." His voice spoke in her ear, deep and soft as he came around the screen and encircled her waist with his hands. "It was what she said, and the pain in her voice." Slowly he turned Meredith around. "I haven't mentioned it since she's been coming here, out of respect for her privacy. Her past is her business. And yet, seeing her just now... I'm not sure she's been able to leave the scandal behind, not entirely."

"Scandal? Mrs. Carlton? All you ever told me was the time you heard her play, in New York, when you were employed as a stage worker in some opera house. What scandal?"

He shook his head, smiling a little at her incredulity. "I was only fifteen, a struggling Southern boy obsessed with recovering his family fortune. I must have been working the docks by the time it all happened. But I do recall the papers were full of the story for months, on both sides of the ocean."

His voice softened into reminiscence. "They called Fiona Carlton the Jenny Lind of piano performance. An extraordinary musician who could wring tears from marble statues. She was married to Gerald Carlton, the conductor? They made quite a sensation." The softness abruptly vanished. "But they made more of a sensation when a crazed young girl caught Mrs. Carlton in the wings. Attacked her with a knife. While Mrs. Carlton was recovering, for safety her husband took the son to his family estate, back in England. Their ship caught fire and sank. Everyone aboard was lost."

"Oh!" Quick tears sprang from Meredith's eyes. "I can't begin to imagine… Sam… Oh, Benjamin…"

She clung to the strength and safety of his arms and wondered how Fiona Carlton had survived.

❧ ❧ ❧

SINCLAIR RUN

The MacAllisters arrived for a celebratory dinner and reunion, two days after Leah and Cade's homecoming. Dusk had settled in with a chilly, misting rain. Feeling very much the patriarch, Jacob watched his daughters' tearful reunion and the easy camaraderie between Garnet's husband, Sloan, and Cade that spoke of mutual liking and respect. Then little Robbie, struck with a bout of shyness, raced over to his granda and hid his face in Jacob's shoulder after he scooped the five-year-old up into his arms.

When Garnet lifted the blanket so Leah could have her first glimpse of wee Daniel, the babe promptly set to squalling.

"Oh, dear," Garnet said, laughter in her voice, "he's such a peculiar little fellow. Robbie always hated to be covered up, but Daniel seems to prefer it. Don't take it personally, Leah."

"That's all right." Leah backed away a step. "Are you well, Garnet? Completely recovered from Daniel's birth?"

"Honestly, sister mine! You'd think I wasn't married to the best doctor in Shenandoah County."

Sloan placed a protective hand against his wife's back. "She's fine, Leah. You needn't don your maternal garb. Both she and Daniel are perfectly healthy. Here, let me have him." He lifted the wailing baby into his arms, and within seconds Daniel was cooing at his father.

Grinning like any proud parent, Sloan raised an eyebrow at Cade. "Cade, a man's supposed to protect the light of his life. Yet it seems as though all we've heard about these past months are tales that threaten to turn our hair gray. Thought my wife was going to make us cut our visit to Baltimore short and pay a visit to Stillwaters, back in June."

"If Leah had been hurt in that coach accident and needed a doctor, I thought she should have the best," Garnet defended herself good-naturedly.

Robbie stirred in Jacob's arms, whispering something Jacob didn't catch. "What's that, laddie?"

"Mama's hair is red, not gray."

Laughter filled the parlor. Jacob watched the last of Leah's awkwardness fade when Cade joined her, calmly separating her intertwined hands. Then, utterly indifferent to the presence of an audience, he dropped a kiss on her knuckles and drew her arm through his.

Leah blushed crimson. Compared to the vibrant beauty of Garnet's stunning red hair and mysterious gray-green eyes, to some Leah might appear plain, even drab. But Jacob knew differently. Though she would doubtless always be as delicate as a fairy in build, her strength of character, along with a rare contentment born of Cade's love, bequeathed Leah with a beauty equal to her sister's.

"Your mother's hair is the most beautiful hair I've ever seen," she was telling her nephew. "Except for the time she dyed it as black as your father's. She wasn't a lot older than you, Robert."

Robbie's eyes went round. "Why did Mama do that?"

Sloan stretched out an arm to one-handedly ruffle his son's hair. "Granda can tell you about it, come bedtime. Makes a good story."

"Will Mama's hair look like Phinnie's hair when she's old?"

"I hope so," Garnet told her son.

Phinnie, or Phineas, in truth, was a red fox Garnet and Sloan had rescued years earlier. Amazingly he'd turned into a pet; for the past six years his status in the MacAllister household had been the topic of oft-times heated conversation among the locals, from Tom's Brook to Woodstock.

"Look, here's Deke," Jacob said, spying the young man hovering at the kitchen doorway. "I bet he wants to play checkers with you, until time for supper."

Robbie happily relinquished Jacob for a perch on Deke's shoulders, and the pair headed for the sitting room that Jacob had built off his bedroom two years earlier.

After everyone settled in the parlor, talk turned to the saga of Cade and Leah's incredible escape from the band of hired cutthroats.

"And you say there's finally a warrant out for Preston Clarke?" Sloan asked when Cade finished the tale. "You found enough incontestable evidence to convince a sheriff to butt heads with one of the most powerful men in this end of the Valley?"

"Yes. Ben told me one of the—"

Loud knocking on the front door halted Cade midsentence. "I'll see who it is," Sloan said, looking every inch the physician as he rose to his feet. "Most likely someone looking for me."

But when he returned a few moments later he was holding what looked to be a letter. "It was Mike Hoffelmeyer," he said, handing the envelope to Jacob. "He was headed north on the Pike and told his uncle he'd drop this off, so you'd have it this evening."

Puzzled, Jacob studied the neat, plainly feminine handwriting, though it wasn't Meredith's.

"Go ahead. It's addressed to you," Sloan said, a smile glinting beneath his mustache. "Open it, before we all perish from curiosity."

"I've no idea who…" Jacob carefully tore the envelope and withdrew a single sheet of Stillwaters Hotel stationery. "Why, 'tis from Mrs. Carlton!" He blinked, scanned the few lines, then lifted his head. "She's wanting to stop by, she says, because she has something very important she needs to tell me. In person."

"Mrs. Carlton?" Garnet asked. "Who is Mrs. Carlton?"

"A guest at Stillwaters," Leah answered when Jacob, too flabbergasted to respond, could only sit and stare at the neatly penned words. "I never met her, though I believe Papa spoke with her a time or two. This is very interesting. Does she indicate what the 'something important' is, that can only be told to your face?"

"Nae." He ran his thumb over the edge of the paper. "I canna imagine what it could be. But I daresay I'll find the truth of it soon enough, for she plans to drop by sometime within the next two days."

Thirty-One

Fiona caught an eastbound C&O train out of Clifton Forge, though she had to change trains in Staunton. Instead of proceeding to Woodstock as she intended, however, she decided to find a small hotel in Staunton that catered to unescorted ladies, and spend the night there. The delay suited her purposes, and not only because she would be able to travel to Woodstock in more privacy than a day coach offered.

Perhaps it was a cowardly choice, but it had been awhile since she'd paid a strictly social call, even longer since she'd sought the company of a gentleman, regardless of the purpose. She needed extra time to prepare in her mind what to say to Jacob Sinclair. Silly perhaps, but somehow she felt better able to think when she was seventy-odd miles from Sinclair Run instead of seven. And it gave her letter time to arrive before she appeared on his doorstep.

The following morning dawned wet and dreary; Fiona was grateful Maisie had insisted on packing her mackintosh, back in June. "You'll be coming home in October. Don't want you coming home with the ague. Be more work for me," she'd stated, stuffing the long coat inside one of the three already bulging steamer trunks. "If you don't need it, fine by me. You don't have to carry these here trunks either way, so what are you fussing about?"

Dear Maisie. The young woman was a trifle unpolished, even after three years of gentle coaching in the fine art of being companion and housekeeper. But Fiona couldn't cast her back out on the street. Maisie, like Fiona herself, was one of the casualties of an unforgiving society, both of them lumped as women who had broken the Rules of Good Taste and were now considered objects of scorn—at least to the society

Fiona had once inhabited. In that world, lost innocence and damaged souls mattered little, appearances everything.

Lands, but wasn't she morbid this morning.

Of course, she was on her way to what promised to be an extremely uncomfortable encounter. She was halfway inclined to change her mind again. Yet there was that twitch between her shoulders shoving her northward. Jacob Sinclair had treated her kindly, even when she spurned his kindness and offended his decency. Why?

As the train chugged northward and the rain-blurred hills of the Shenandoah Valley rolled serenely by, Fiona sat brooding in her small private cubicle of a Wagner sleeping car. She knew the visit was unnecessary, knew there were obligations at home to resume, lonely and helpless people who no doubt had been neglected these past months due to her absence.

As in Jesus' day, there were few laborers to plow the field of the blind, the old and infirm, the indigent. *Well, they would have to wait only another day for this particular laborer.* Courtesy of her banker, wise investments over the years from hers and Gerald's estates allowed Fiona to indulge in a financially imprudent bit of whimsy like spending an extra night on the road if she chose.

She roused herself, determinedly opened her knitting bag, and spent the rest of the journey to Woodstock crocheting lace edging for the girls at the orphanage, so that each of them would have one pretty slip to wear under their dreary smocks.

Jacob Sinclair's dwelling was a surprise.

Instead of the simple farmhouse she'd pictured, the hired driver pulled to a stop in front of a neat-as-a-new-penny three-story frame house. It was finely crafted with its gables and steeply pitched roof and an inviting front porch that brought a hard knot to the base of Fiona's throat. She raised a reflexive hand, pressing her fingers against the ivory lace jabot that suddenly seemed too tight. The kindly gentleman from Stillwaters she remembered was obviously a man of some wealth, not a struggling country farmer.

Struggling country farmers did *not* pay visits to exclusive hotels to take the waters. *Fiona Carlton, your upper story's gone vacant.*

She should have known better. After all, this man's daughter was married to the last remaining member of what had been one of Virginia's oldest and finest families. A family with whom Fiona had been well acquainted, in another life, another time. One day, when the time seemed appropriate, and she had gathered enough courage to make herself that vulnerable again, she would finally share with Benjamin Walker that she had known his mother—and what the connection had meant to a bashful young girl with a heart full of dreams.

But at this particular moment, she needed to unglue her feet from the ground, climb the porch steps, and ring the buzzer. Fiona gathered her courage and her plum-colored skirts in both hands, then mounted the stairs.

A young woman who looked to be in her early to midtwenties opened the door. She was dainty in build, with brown hair and eyes, eyes that possessed both warmth and intelligence.

"You must be Mrs. Carlton," she said, her voice brisk and surprisingly refined. "We've been expecting you." She stood aside. "Come in. I'm Leah Sinclair. Here, I'll take your coat, shall I? There are only the two of us at home at the moment. By design, I confess. My father's waiting in the parlor. He's almost as nervous as he is puzzled."

Unsurprised, Fiona did not allow her expression to alter. "Thank you, Miss Sinclair. But if anyone's nervous, I'm afraid it would have to be me." Reluctantly she removed her damp coat and handed it to the daughter.

"May I take your hat?"

Fiona hesitated, through the veil assessing the young woman's tone of voice and expression. She settled for bluntness. "My face is not a pretty sight. Frankly, this veil is designed as much for the sake of other people's sensibilities as it is a sop to my vanity."

"Do you wear it all the time or just when you're in public?"

"Leah." Jacob Sinclair appeared between the tasseled portieres of the doorway behind his daughter. "That's not our concern." He frowned at her, then turned to Fiona. "Even as a child, I'm afraid Leah tended toward straightforwardness as opposed to tact. Don't worry about your hat. You're fine just as you are. Please, come in and sit down, Mrs. Carlton."

Leah Sinclair did not seem at all perturbed with her father's gentle rebuke. "I'll fetch refreshments," she said and, with a peaceful smile, disappeared through a narrow doorway down the hall.

"I tend to agree with Miss Sinclair," Fiona murmured. Hat in place, she moved past Jacob into the parlor, a comfortable room without the stifling clutter fashionable in so many parlors these days. "I've always preferred straightforward honesty to bald-faced lies, no matter how socially expedient."

They sat down, facing each other. A pool of silence fell, broken only by the quiet ticking of a ship's clock on the wall behind Jacob. Fiona arranged her skirt over her knees, smoothing the soft woolen fabric, then folded her hands in her lap while she studied Jacob Sinclair.

He was not a large man—in truth of a height only several inches above her own—but he had broad, sturdy-looking shoulders, and the scarred hands of someone well used to physical labor. She wondered what his vocation might be, or had been. His once dark hair was liberally streaked with gray; his crown was going bald, though the rest still looked thick, with a hint of wave. Like many balding men Fiona had observed over the years, Jacob attempted to disguise the thinning by carefully combing several strands over the bald spot.

It was about as effective as her veil. Vanity, and vulnerability, Fiona thought with a tiny sputter of inner amusement. Did the Lord ever grow weary of those particular human weaknesses?

Mr. Sinclair shifted in his seat. "Did you have a fine journey, then?" he asked in the manner of a schoolboy performing an unpleasant task.

"It was tolerable. Of course, even for short trips I always try to ride lines that offer cars with staterooms, or at least single-berth sleeping cars. For obvious reasons."

"Ah...umm..."

Silence fell again. Miserable, vexed with herself, Fiona glanced around the room. "You have a lovely home, Mr. Sinclair. The needlepoint cushions are superb."

"My wife's. She—when she was alive, that is, she did enjoy needlework."

"I do quite a bit myself, mostly crochet. Knotted Irish lace, actually. My maternal grandmother taught me, when I was a little girl."

"Oh. Well, 'tis a fine occupation for a pian—" He stopped. "I beg your pardon."

Fiona stiffly inclined her head. "Quite all right, Mr. Sinclair."

Relief lit his face when Leah entered the room, a large tray in her hands. "Ah, thank you, lass. Here, I'll help." He all but leaped to his feet.

"I've got it, Papa."

The daughter deftly served the refreshments as if to the manor born. Clearly, despite her blunt manners Miss Sinclair was more at home in a social setting than her father. Fiona studied the young woman's slight but skilled fingers. Interesting. No doubt Leah Sinclair's diminutive size nonetheless housed a strong-minded will. What did she do with her days, other than serve as hostess to her father? Who else lived in this big old house, the ones who had "by design" absented themselves?

After Jacob and his daughter were seated, everyone sipping a welcome cup of hot mulled cider, Leah turned to her and without preamble commented, "For years, my sister Garnet used to wear our mother's old sunbonnets every time she left the house, because she thought it was necessary. Even when she learned differently, for a long time it was a struggle for her to do without them."

Her father choked on his drink.

Leah didn't blink an eye. She leaned forward a little, toward Fiona. "It would be less bothersome to enjoy the cider without your hat and veil, Mrs. Carlton," she finished, smiling gently. "You really don't have to protect yourself, or us."

"Leah, for sure! Lass, you mustn't—"

"It's all right, Mr. Sinclair," Fiona interrupted him with a serene smile. Amazingly, Leah's straightforwardness had actually helped toughen her resolve. "I do understand the motivation behind what you consider your daughter's deplorable lack of manners." She inclined her head to Leah. "Thank you for trying to put me at ease, my dear," she said. "I…wasn't expecting such, when I came here. You see, the reason for my visit is because I owe your father an apology."

Regrettably, now that the moment had arrived, her courage seemed to have departed. She took a sip to ease her constricted throat. *Lord, I don't know if I can do this.*

"Mrs. Carlton, I don't understand. What would you need to be apologizing for?" Jacob finally asked, the hint of brogue stronger now.

For some reason, unlike Leah's bluntness, his discomfort intensified her own. Fiona had always been excruciatingly sensitive to atmosphere. Well, best to emulate Miss Sinclair's example instead of her obviously awkward father. Speak her piece and be done with it, though she would have preferred to keep the apology a private matter.

"I had no right, that night in the conservatory," she began haltingly, focusing only on Jacob Sinclair, "to…to do what I did. To expose you without warning not only to an ugly sight, but to an ugliness of character, of which I'm deeply ashamed."

"Nae, you mustn't think that," he responded instantly, a flush creeping over his face. "My fault entirely. I had no right to be intruding upon your privacy. What happened was entirely *my* fault, Mrs. Carlton. There is no need for you to apologize."

Leah Sinclair set her cup down with an audible thud. "What did happen?"

For Fiona, the question struck with the force of a thrown gauntlet. It was obvious that Jacob Sinclair had kept the encounter to himself; she should have let the already awkward incident fade into obscurity. She never should have come here.

Impulse, or her conscience, the matter was irrelevant. She was here, the question had been broached, and Fiona must respond. She owed the Walker family more than she could ever repay. By extension—and because of her own cruelty—she owed the same to the Sinclairs.

Fiona laid aside her cup and straightened herself on the edge of the settee. "Your father surprised me, late one night in the conservatory, up at Stillwaters," she said. "I was…not at my best, and did not give your father a choice as to whether he cared to be exposed to the sight of the scar, without the screen of this veil." She paused, hearing the pulse in her ears like the roar of a demanding crowd.

Just get on with it, Fiona. Swiftly she lifted her hands, then stopped, dividing her gaze between both Leah and her father. "I'm willing to remove the veil"—to open herself up to them, a risk she had been unwilling to take for more years than she could remember—"but only because you requested it. This time, it is not my intention to purposefully shock, as I did back at the hotel."

For a long moment neither of the Sinclairs spoke. The sick sensation flooded Fiona as it always did, while she waited with false poise for them to reach a decision. Either way, she knew she would pay a heavy price. *It will pass,* she reminded herself, *I can bear this.* If Christ could bear the humiliation of the cross, surely she could endure her own small mortification, here in the Sinclair family parlor.

"It's no' necessary—"

"I think it is, for all of us," Miss Sinclair said. "Communication with one another without any barriers, as it were." She glanced at Fiona, one eyebrow elevated almost in challenge.

Taken aback by the girl's perception, Fiona nonetheless did not respond. Instead, she looked across at Jacob Sinclair.

After much mumbling and even a word of two of incomprehensible Gaelic, he folded his arms across his chest and inclined his head. "Like I told you, my youngest daughter speaks her own mind," he said. "As for myself, with or without the veil matters naught to me, Mrs. Carlton. You're a grand lady, despite a scar you feel you must hide. The Lord loves you just the same. Possibly more, because of the pain of it seems to have caused you. I can do no better than to follow His example. You're welcome here, however you come," he finished simply.

"At Stillwaters, you... What I mean to say is, I know it was a shock, that you saw..." She stopped again.

"It won't be like Stillwaters," Mr. Sinclair said, his expression softening despite the chagrin in his eyes. "Come now. Take off the veil and be done with it. Let's enjoy Leah's refreshments."

"Very well." Fiona took a careful breath. Stage nerves had always disappeared once she sat down on the piano bench. These circumstances weren't so different. With the grace of long ease she lifted the veil, unpinned her hat, and laid it on the settee between her and Leah Sinclair. Head high, she managed to pick up her cup of cider without trembling. She took a careful sip, her heart kicking against her corset, while the silence scorched her skin like a thousand burning crochet hooks.

"It's not a pretty sight, you're right," Miss Sinclair murmured, her tone soft and friendly. "But—it's only a scar, after all. Garnet boasts an even longer one on her shoulder, though I'm thinking the surgeon who tended her initial wound did a better job stitching her up. What happened to you?"

For the life of her Fiona could not summon a response. In twenty-two years, no one—not her outspoken housekeeper Maisie, nor any of the unfortunates Fiona had taken on as her act of service these past two decades, nor the few families with which she retained contact—not one of them had addressed the matter of her face with Leah Sinclair's forthright kindness.

Jacob Sinclair, on the other hand, looked ready to strangle on a spate of words, all of them for his daughter. He hadn't so much as blinked at the ugly spectacle of Fiona's scar, but perhaps that was because he was glaring ferociously at Leah.

Fiona finally scraped together a smile and answered the question. "I was attacked in the wings, by a crazed young woman jealous of what she thought I was—who also fancied herself passionately in love with my husband. At the time, all I could think about was protecting my hands, my wrists." Even after all these years, she sometimes couldn't believe how dangerously obsessive her focus had become. "If the girl's aim had been a shade more accurate, she would have succeeded in cutting my throat."

"Merciful Father." Jacob Sinclair swallowed two gulps of his drink, choked, and suffered through a coughing fit.

Leah rose, hovering over him until he waved her away. "How dreadful that must have been for you," she said as she returned to her seat beside Fiona. "All Papa shared last night was that you were once a famous concert pianist, right after the War, but it was his understanding that you no longer play. Did you quit performing because of the attack?"

Fiona stilled, closing her eyes, her hand automatically rising to the uneven line of the scar. "More or less," she said after a long time. "Shortly after the attack I lost my husband and my little boy." She reached for the cider, finishing more calmly, "I spend my time on other pursuits now."

"Mrs. Carlton, my wife died of typhoid back in '74. The pain of it was like a live thing, tearing at my soul." Compassion wove like a ribbon through Jacob Sinclair's soft words. "But I had three wee girls, and it was my lasses, and the Lord, who brought me through that time. To lose not only your mate, but your child…" He shook his head, "I canna imagine."

"Try one of my cream cheese sandwiches, Mrs. Carlton," Leah said, holding the plate in front of Fiona. "You say you do Irish crochet and knotted lace? Do you prefer decorative items, such as pillows, pillow-cases, and the like, or articles of clothing, like the lace collars?"

Fiona gratefully latched on to the change of topic. "No preference. I teach the craft, actually, to women who have no other means of employment, or who are bedridden. They tell me what they wish to create, and I show them how."

"We have a bit in common, it would seem. I'm a teacher myself, though the past two weeks I had to take personal leave. I return tomorrow." She paused, frowning a little. "I've sadly neglected my students, I'm afraid."

"I understand." That explained the maturity of manner, the utter self-possession. Leah Sinclair might look like a girl, but she was very much a woman. A woman, it seemed, with a profession outside the home. "I feel the same, after the summer season. One feels a tremendous responsibility, even if the teaching is voluntary. Where do you teach, Miss Sinclair?"

"At a school for girls who desire a bit of formal education."

Fiona nodded. "There seems to be a growing need for such." Relaxing, she bit into the neat triangular sandwich and smiled. She felt almost relaxed for the first time since she'd left the station. "This is delicious. Your school, is it in Woodstock, Miss Sinclair?"

A small, almost secretive smile hovered at the corners of the younger woman's mouth. "No, in Richmond. I teach at the Esther Hays School for Young Ladies."

Fiona almost dropped the plate. "You don't mean it! Why, that's the very one I was referring to. One of my ladies was acquainted with Mrs. Hays before the War." Hesitantly she smiled at Leah. "What a happy coincidence."

"One of your ladies?" Mr. Sinclair asked, and Fiona glanced across in surprise. Lands, she'd almost forgotten he was in the room—and here the poor man was the reason she'd come all this way.

"I…well, I spend most of my time, fall through spring, visiting." She avoided discussing her life with strangers, mostly because she was afraid they would regard her as a patronizing benefactress spreading her largesse. "Hospitals, orphanages, the Home for Ladies, the Baptist Home for Aged Women. A great deal of time with the residents at the Alcorn School for the Blind."

She could feel their rising curiosity like a burn across her skin. The intimacy of her circumstances swept over her in a flood tide: She was sitting in this dignified parlor, exposing not only her naked face, but details of her private life, for public scrutiny.

All of a sudden it was too much.

"I must go." She thrust aside her plate, snatched up her hat, and rose, hurriedly pinning the hat in place and drawing the veil across her face. "My train. I don't want to miss my train." She aimed a perfunctory, no doubt graceless smile toward both father and daughter. "Thank you for your hospitality, your kindness. It was…" The words caught in her throat. It…was necessary."

She left them standing in the middle of the parlor, half-formed questions on their lips and bewilderment clouding their faces. But along with everything else Fiona had learned from her years of performing, she had also perfected the art of a swift exit.

Thirty-Two

*F*or the next several weeks, Jacob stayed busy supervising his journeymen and apprentices at his factory in Woodstock. He'd
always liked the sound of the word *journeymen.* 'Twas a good word, a
strong word rich with history, though for Jacob the meaning reached far
beyond its original medieval roots.

The men he trained in the fine craft of furniture making were not
merely workers, hired drones who filled the hours allotted to them for
the sole purpose of collecting wages. No, the men Jacob hired were
those with a deep-seated craving to learn, to improve—to one day, perhaps, earn a reputation of their own. Those who were sloppy, careless,
or indifferent soon found themselves shown the back door.

For his part, Jacob suffered the wearing of a suit only when he spent
the day in the office, going over paperwork with Eli Tubbs, his accountant and business manager. Since Eli was an honest lad, with a fine head
for business but with the creativity of a turnip, Jacob tried to limit the
days he spent in the factory office, wearing a suit. Far more rewarding
were the days he spent on the floor, with his journeymen, clad like them
in sturdy work clothes and a tool in his hand instead of a pen.

He looked about the large shop, full of the noise of creation—pieces
of furniture in various stages of completion. Ah, but the sight never
failed to awe and humble the simple Scotsman whose only dream had
been to honor his heritage and his Lord with the work of his hands.

He stopped by a workbench. "Careful, Jimmy. You don't want to
cut your pins for the dovetail too small, else you'll wind up with a
drawer that won't stand up to wear and tear."

"Sorry, Mr. Sinclair." The young man straightened, wiping his face
with his shirtsleeve. "How do I—?"

"I'll show you," Jacob promised.

As was his habit, he spent the next several moments first demonstrating the technique, then coaching Jimmy through the process. By the time the drawer was finished, they were surrounded by other journeymen. After Jimmy, Jacob was entreated to show another man how to properly cut the mortise and tenon for the rail and stile of a cabinet door, then had to correct the finish on a tabletop. When the noon whistle blew for the lunch break, he and Dean Watts, his foreman, were hard at work honing the final edges on their prized wood chisels.

"Always good to have you spend a day here," Dean commented as they sat outside, munching thick roast beef sandwiches and crisp pickles. "Not too many owners, particularly famous ones, who'll roll their sleeves up with their employees."

"Oh, get along with you, Dean. I'm about as famous as Uriah Smith."

"Who?"

Jacob grinned and slapped the foreman's back. "There you have it!"

Dean shook his head. "Think that about yourself if you care to. But I'm the one who has to fend off all the customers who stop by, wanting to see a genuine Jacob Sinclair piece even if they can't afford one. I'm the one who has to listen to Mervis and Betty complain that the orders come in faster than they can respond."

"You're supposed to be supervising the men, doing a bit of work yourself, lad. Not flirting with the secretaries." Jacob swallowed the last of the pickle. "Have you finished the cherry corner table for the Grables?"

"Last night." He fingered the brim of his flat cap, then diffidently asked, "You want to inspect it before I have it shipped out?"

The urge to personally inspect every piece of furniture that left his fledgling factory was a compulsion Jacob struggled to subdue every time he came to town. "Nae." He stood and brushed his hands on his corduroy trousers. "I didn't train you to keep you on a leash, lad. You haven't needed my approval since the dining room set you completed last year. 'Tis proud I am to have you as one of my journeymen, Master Watts. I predict they'll someday be attaching brass plates to pieces with your name on them, instead of mine."

"Doesn't that prospect bother you?" Dean asked. "The men talk about it sometimes, the way you truly don't seem to care about your own image as much as you do helping all of us to become—well, rivals."

"I don't look at it that way." Jacob tipped his head back, gazing almost dreamily up through the branches of a magnificent oak. "I look at it that there's better quality furniture being made. That I'm doing the best I can, as a servant of God, to pass along the skills He blessed me with. Aye, I can see you've little understanding. But think on it, lad. If my grandfather hadn't taught the craft to my father, and himself along to me, where would I be? Besides, I've no sons to follow in my footsteps but the men who work here. Like you, don't you see, men who love wood, love their craft more than they crave a paycheck. When I help you achieve your best, am I not doing what any good father would do for his sons?"

"Like I said, definitely a strange one." Dean settled his cap on his head and headed for the back door into the factory. He paused on the threshold, glancing over his shoulder. "Be a long time before I'll approach your stature, Mr. Sinclair. The way you have with a piece of wood in your hands—it's the difference between a scrubby cedar and a four-hundred year old chestnut."

By afternoon the late October day had cooled; Jacob set Raspberry to a steady trot after they headed down the Valley Pike for home. He found his thoughts returning to the words Dean had spoken over lunch. *Truly, Lord, 'tis a humbling feeling, that. You'll have to see to it that I don't suffer from a proud heart.*

He glanced down at his gloved hands, feeling through the leather the steady tug of the reins. For some reason, the image of Fiona Carlton flashed across his mind. Or, more specifically, Fiona Carlton's hands. There was strength in those hands, he thought. Strength, but sorrow.

Now why would *that* particular attribute float into his head?

His memory of the afternoon she had come to Sinclair Run was colored for the most part by the memory of his own discomfort, having such a famous personage sitting in his parlor. And the reason behind her visit tugged his mind like the reins tugging his hands. He still couldn't comprehend the depth of her remorse, her need to atone in person, when *he* was the one who had wronged *her.*

He'd never been able to leave a suffering person be, particularly if the person happened to be a woman. Fiona Carlton hid hers well, perhaps too well, veiled away along with that scrap of cloth behind an almost impenetrable screen of self-containment. Plainly, Mrs. Carlton suffered. Trouble was, Jacob had intruded upon her privacy with neither permission nor the privilege of familial or friendly connections.

Even more incredible than the motive behind her visit, however, was the amount of courage it must have taken for her to bare her face not in a heated moment, but deliberately. Aye, the scar was an ugly affair, one a mind could not easily dismiss, nor ever forget. Yet for Jacob, whenever he chewed over that day, what he remembered most vividly about Fiona Carlton was not that scar, but her hands.

Och, Lord, but were they not beautiful? Long-fingered and graceful, no matter what the activity, whether resting quietly in her lap, holding a cup and saucer—or ripping off hat and veil with a dramatic flair that had taken his breath away.

He could easily imagine her on stage, a thousand candles blazing above and around her as she sat before one of those monstrous pianofortes, her pale elegant hands poised above the keys.

When he imagined those hands, the obscenity of the scar faded almost completely into the background.

A pleasant surprise awaited when he pulled the buggy to a halt in front of the barn. "Cade!" he called to the man who had just emerged, lantern in hand, from the murky interior. "What brings you to the Valley? You on the way to or from Richmond?"

"Returning from. I wanted to tell you too, that the detectives Ben hired caught up with Preston Clarke in Charleston, just before he was to board a packet for South America."

"He's in jail then?"

"Without bail. All four of the men who attacked Leah and me testified against him." His movements swift and economical, his soon to be son-in-law helped Jacob unharness Raspberry. Satisfaction surrounded him as visibly as his windblown mane of wheat-colored hair. "We also managed to secure a restraining order for all the mining on Stillwaters' southeastern border, until the town council and Ben reach an accord on how to boost the economy without sacrificing the area's natural beauty." His shoulders lifted in a self-conscious shrug. "I needed to tell Leah in person, of course."

Lips pursed, Jacob pondered him a moment. "Have the two of you decided on a date for the wedding?"

Cade didn't respond at once, turning away to fuss with the harness on the peg. "Leah feels a strong obligation to both Mrs. Hays and her students," he finally said. "I can't fault her for loyalty. Nor can I rush the pace. Besides, I stay pretty busy myself, now that Ben and I are finally able to focus on some of the landscaping ideas we've been mulling over since last spring."

The lad would never be content, living in a city, surrounded by buildings instead of forests, breathing soot-choked air. Jacob led his horse to the stall, then absently grabbed a currycomb from the box of grooming supplies. When Cade joined him a few moments later, bristle brush in hand, Jacob smiled at him over the horse's broad withers. "You'll work it out," he said, injecting confidence in his voice. "I've no doubt at all that, between the two of you and the Lord, a solution will present itself all in good time."

"I know. But I will confess that this particular lesson in living out my faith hasn't been easy." He began combing out the mare's wind-blown mane. "Leah was telling me about Fiona Carlton," he said, abruptly changing the subject. "I wish I'd been here."

"Aye, well, doubtless it was as well you weren't, nor Effie and Deke. Mrs. Carlton was skittish as it was. I suppose Leah shared with you the nature of her abrupt departure."

"Mm. Said Mrs. Carlton turned white as bleached muslin all of a sudden, and was out the door before either of you could even say good-bye. Leah blames herself, you know. She said to tell you she means to find out where Mrs. Carlton lives and pay her a visit of her own when she finds a spare moment."

"Ah." Jacob chewed over that, wondering at Leah's interest in the woman, wondering as well at the sensation of relief over the prospect. "Mrs. Carlton apparently stays busy herself. But 'twould be a good thing for them both, I'm thinking."

❧❦❧

RICHMOND, VIRGINIA

"And then you tie the knot, like this." Fiona carefully guided Lally Jenkins's fingers, helping the blind girl feel the thread, the differing texture between net and cambric…the emerging pattern. "There! And can you feel how much more uniform your loops are? Soon you'll be able to try one on your own."

"No I won't." Mouth pulled down in a sullen frown, Lally thrust the needlework away, almost knocking over Fiona's bag of supplies. "I don't like working with my hands. And I hate lace. Go teach somebody else."

She shoved back her chair and lurched to her feet, clumsy in her anger, almost knocking into Fiona, who hurriedly stepped aside, her heart going out to the girl. "I know it's difficult," she began, but stopped when Lally turned toward the sound of her voice, her face distorted with rage.

"You don't know nothing! You're not blind. You think you're special, don't you, comin' here to pay us poor blind folks a visit, like some grand lady." Feeling for the back of the chair, she edged closer to Fiona. "Oh, I hear all the stories about you, the all-wonderful Mrs. Carlton. Come here every afternoon, you do. Out of the goodness of your heart. Teaching us a trade, so we won't feel useless."

"Lally Jenkins, you mind your manners," Winifred Dunwoody scolded from her seat nearby. "You might be blind, girl, but that doesn't mean you've cause to misplace all your manners."

"It's all right, Mrs. Dunwoody," Fiona said. Winifred had been a resident at the Hiram Alcorn Home since Mr. Alcorn willed the Monument Avenue residence as a haven for the blind, some eight years previously, to honor the memory of his blind wife. "Lally should have the freedom to express her frustration. Besides, she's right. I can't understand what it's like, not being able to see."

"I'm going to my room," Lally snapped. "Don't need lecturing from anyone, either."

Fiona opened her mouth to offer assistance, but managed to swallow the words. Sometimes newer residents like Lally, who still struggled against the implacable reality of their sightless state, needed time more than a helping hand. "Your cane's on the floor," she merely offered quietly. "Near your left foot, about ten o'clock."

"I can find it! Why don't you go do your good works somewhere else? Better yet, take yourself back over to all your fancy clubs with all the other hoity-toity society ladies." Stooping, hands splayed, she finally located her cane and rose, red-faced with frustration and humiliation. "I know all about them. Playing golf and tennis, riding in fancy carriages to show off, and all the time yammering how glad you're not one of the poor unfortunates—like me."

Fiona laid a tentative hand across the seething girl's forearm. "Lally, I don't—"

"Leave me alone." She jerked her arm away and shuffled an erratic path across the room. The cane tapped angrily on the floor, punctuating her rage.

"You haven't let her see your face, have you, dear?" Winifred commented a few moments later.

Sighing a little, Fiona paused from gathering up her materials. "She's still too raw, Mrs. Dunwoody. She wouldn't care, much less understand my circumstances."

Her circumstances. Bittersweet irony tickled the corners of her mouth as Fiona carefully gathered up linen-papers, threads, patterns, and sundry other crocheting accessories. Usually she was most relaxed during the hours she worked with the residents here. They couldn't see her and placed little value in her physical appearance, which allowed Fiona to interact more naturally. Unfortunately, whether sighted or blind, people wanted to know what others looked like; because of their handicap, whenever new residents needed to "see" Fiona, they were by necessity forced to rely on touch, instead of their eyes.

It took every ounce of discipline for Fiona to sit quietly, while searching hands drifted like gossamer wings over her forehead, her nose and mouth, her cheeks—both cheeks, so that they could form some manner of mental image of the woman who had made herself a part of their lives. For the first few years Fiona tried to look on the experience as penance. Eventually the horror of being touched by them diminished somewhat, though never enough for comfort.

She shuddered, and quickly finished cleaning off the library table she used as a work space. It was late. She needed to leave, before the streetcars were crowded with people going home at the end of the day.

"Come talk to me. You've been quiet ever since you returned from your summer sabbatical." Mrs. Dunwoody gestured imperiously, and after a quick glance through the windows Fiona perched on the edge of a straight chair, next to the elderly woman.

Sunken sockets of her long-worthless eyes, in a face lined like the cracked cover of an old Bible, turned toward Fiona with complete unselfconsciousness. Mrs. Dunwoody had been blind for more than sixty years; unlike poor Lally, she was long content with her circumstances. "Tell me what's wrong."

She was also extraordinarily perceptive—and protective—of Fiona.

"I suppose I've a touch of melancholy." Fiona kept her voice light. "It's a raw day outside. You know how weather has always affected my disposition."

"Balderdash! More likely that Lally's gone and hurt your feelings. You're far too sensitive for a woman of your age and experience with life."

"I'm sure you're right," Fiona murmured. She gave her a hug, hiding her concern at the twiglike frailty of Mrs. Dunwoody's once sturdy frame. "It's getting dark outside. I must go. Take care of yourself now—and no browbeating residents and staff."

"You know better than that. Who else is going to keep them on their toes?"

What a gallant creature, Fiona mused as she hurried to the corner. Sure enough, a knot of people were already waiting; automatically she distanced herself from the crowd, making a mental note to ask one of the supervisors about Mrs. Dunwoody's health. For the past couple of years, the indomitable woman had seemed to Fiona to be aging more rapidly. Or perhaps it was her own perspective that was aging. When one neared the half-century mark, one tended to view life in terms of how much of it was left, as opposed to how much one planned to accomplish. Sometimes, she wondered if—

"Look at that lady with the veil!" The little boy's childish voice echoed in the gray afternoon like a steam whistle. "It covers her whole face. Why doesn't she want people to see her face?"

"Oh, hush, honey. You shouldn't say things like that."

"She scares me." The boy's sister began to cry.

The mammy gathered her two small charges close, edging them away from Fiona. Their gazes met, and through the veil Fiona watched the colored woman's dark eyes widen in pity before she shushed the girl as well, then urged both children to the back of the sidewalk, further away from the sight of a woman who sent children screaming in terror.

A murmur swelled among the crowd, but Fiona stood stiff and silent, keeping her face turned toward an approaching streetcar. Beneath her stiff corset her heart thudded painfully, while each breath she drew threatened to choke her, so thick was the air with morbid curiosity.

And to think at one time she had reveled in the attention, craved the stares, the adulation lavished upon her. How childish that young woman had been. How hopelessly snared by the world's callous seduction.

Rattling and clacking, bell clanging, the streetcar pulled to a stop. The car was almost full, which meant Fiona would be forced to share a seat with a stranger or left standing in the center of every passenger's line of vision. Suddenly it was too much.

Chin lifted high, she brushed her way through the crowd and marched off down the street. She'd rather walk two dozen blocks on a dank and dreary afternoon than suffer another moment of an insensitive public's scrutiny.

By the time she reached the comfortable brownstone an hour later, Fiona was exhausted, chilled to the bone, her teeth practically chattering.

By the next morning she was running a fever, and Maisie was having hysterics.

Thirty-Three

*T*ime passed in blurred fragments, like bits of shattered glass swirling inside an endless tunnel. Two days, five...one time she heard church bells through the closed draperies, but for the most part Fiona either lay in feverish misery, or sank into stuporous sleep, where at least she could escape Maisie's well-meaning but useless and exhausting attentions. When awake, she choked down greasy helpings of broth the tearful girl left on the cart she'd wheeled beside the bed, or a cup of cold, weak tea. Every so often, a limp slice of toast.

Sometimes, half dozing, mostly miserable, she was vaguely aware that Maisie was in the room, furiously dusting, straightening, even shining Fiona's hammered silver brush and comb set. It was as though the girl hoped to atone for her abysmal nursing skills by doing something she *did* do well; for all her shortcomings, there was no more conscientious housekeeper in all of Richmond. The brownstone's interior always gleamed, and the last particle of dust Fiona remembered seeing had disappeared during Maisie's first day on the job.

"Ma'am?"

Fiona blinked herself out of a torpid semiconscious state and focused on her companion, who hovered over her with clouded eyes and wringing hands. "What is it, Maisie?" Speaking made her cough, but at least this time Maisie forbore from either smacking her on her back, or trying to pour some of the horehound syrup Fiona had instructed her to purchase from the druggist. After her frantic pounding almost broke one of Fiona's ribs, and after she poured half the syrup on the counterpane instead of the spoon, both of them decided it was safer to simply allow the illness to run its course.

"Ma'am, Mrs. Carlton…you have a visitor. I-I didn't know what to do. She refused to go away after I said you was too poorly to receive visitors."

A visitor? Fiona pressed a hand to her aching head, then defensively covered the scarred cheek. She couldn't remember the last time someone had called to visit. The minister of the church she attended had stopped by once, some years ago. He'd been so ill at ease he'd resorted to pomposity, which had annoyed Fiona. She'd retreated into what must have appeared to Reverend Deardon as hauteur. They'd sat in silence for a full five minutes.

"Ma'am, what shall I do?"

Do? About what? Oh, yes. A visitor. A chill that had nothing to do with the fever shuddered down her aching spine. She tried to take a deep breath, but it made her side hurt and precipitated another bout of coughing. "Who is it?" she finally managed.

"Sinclair. I forget the first name. Tiny as a whisk broom, she was, nothing much to look at. But I couldn't make her leave."

Her. Not a man, then. Not Jacob. Must be the daughter, Leah. The description certainly didn't fit Benjamin's wife Meredith. "I…I don't think I can—"

"And you shouldn't even try," Leah Sinclair's brisk voice carried across the room. "I know I'm unforgivably rude," she continued as she crossed to the bed to stand beside a flabbergasted Maisie, "but your housekeeper was visibly distraught over your health. I simply couldn't leave, not without knowing more."

As she talked she was calmly unbuttoning her long coat, removing her gloves, unpinning her hat. She tossed them across the padded bench at the foot of the bed, then laid a cool hand against Fiona's scarred cheek, and her forehead. "Your fever's high, but not alarmingly so," she said briskly, as though she hadn't even noticed Fiona's violent jerk or that she'd clumsily tried to hide her cheek in the pillow.

"What have you been feeding her?" she asked Maisie.

"I…ah…I'm not much on cooking," the poor girl stammered.

"Nor sickrooms. But Mrs. Carlton told me she just needs sleep. You shouldn't be in here. Can't you see she doesn't want you?"

"She needs more than sleep." Brown eyes as dark as the nearby bottle of syrup surveyed Fiona with nothing but a slight frown of concentration—no shock or disgust, not even pity. Fiona might as well have been a fractious child in bed with a cold, instead of a woman old enough to be her mother, without even her veil or a dab of powder to soften the hideous scar. Leah's hand reached for the bottle. "What is this stuff?"

"Medicine." Maisie snatched it away. "Hale's Honey of Horehound. I got it fer Mrs. Carlton. Leave it be." She glanced down at Fiona. "You want me to throw her out, ma'am? I could do it, you know. I watched 'em toss the drunkards out all the time, when I was working at—"

"That's all right, Maisie," Fiona managed. "Why don't you"—she paused, struggling against a cough, searching for a scrap of strength— "make some...some..." What could the poor thing prepare, that wouldn't offend Leah's internal organs, much less her sensibilities?

"Tea," Leah finished bracingly. "A pot of hot, strong tea will do for starters, Maisie. Do you have any honey? Well, never mind. I'll start a list of things, and perhaps you can fetch them from the grocer while I stay here with your employer."

"I don't go nowhere without Mrs. Carlton being the one to tell me."

Dear Maisie, big-boned and homely as a draft horse next to Leah Sinclair's petite stateliness. Her loyalty in the face of Leah's authority almost reduced Fiona to tears. "It's all right, Maisie. Miss Sinclair is a—" She hesitated, feeling as wooly-headed and presentable as a rag bag. She'd only met the girl twice, and yet...

"A concerned friend," Leah said. Head tilted, for a moment she studied Maisie, then smiled. "I promise, Maisie. I'm a capable nurse. I teach at Esther Hays's school and am often called upon to care for girls too ill to be transported to their homes. My sister is Meredith Walker, Benjamin Walker's wife? He's the owner of Stillwaters, where Mrs. Carlton spends her summers. Despite how I bullied my way into the sickroom, I'm quite respectable. And competent."

"Well, then." Relieved, Maisie nodded and took the tray Leah loaded up with used plates and cups. "Don't see why I shouldn't put on a kettle."

"Maisie?" Fiona croaked out. "Don't forget to watch the kettle. And"—she passed her tongue around her dry lips—"the strainer. Use…the strainer, for the tea…"

"Yes'm."

"Not proficient in the kitchen, I gather?" Leah observed after the other girl clattered down the back stairs. "No wonder you're poorly. How long have you been ill?"

"Frankly, I'm not sure. A week? Ten days? It's just a bad cold," Fiona insisted, albeit with little force. She couldn't remember the last time she'd taken sick and was unprepared to cope with the debilitating effects with any grace. But not for all the gold in the richest Colorado mine would she confess the fear nibbling along the fringes of her consciousness: Surely she ought to have recovered by now. "You really shouldn't be here, my dear."

"How long since the doctor stopped by?" Without fuss Leah straightened the bedcovers and fluffed pillows, never revealing by expression or action that she was affected by either Fiona's appearance or the scar, which Fiona knew was even more livid due to fever.

Fretfully she plucked the lace edging of the sheet. "Don't have a doctor. Don't need one. This is just a dreadful cold." A frog caught in her throat; this time, before the cough took her breath, Leah was supporting her shoulders, holding a glass of tepid water to her lips.

"Thank you," Fiona whispered. Her fingers fluttered, but she simply didn't have the energy to lift them. "I'm all right now."

"Hmph. Well, I don't think you should talk. And I also think, with your permission, I'll go help Maisie. After we've gotten some decent invalid food down you, we'll discuss whether or not to call a doctor." Humor twinkled across her face. "You have one of the most beautifully maintained homes I've ever seen, Mrs. Carlton. But as cook and nursing companion, I'm afraid Maisie leaves a bit to be desired."

Her eyes were burning. Fiona gave in and closed them, though she did try to smile back. "I know. But she's very loyal, as you saw. Besides, she has no one else. No place to go, but back to a life that would destroy her." The fever was rising again, she could feel it heating up inside until she was afraid her aching bones would ignite in flames. "Couldn't… allow that. I know what it's like…"

"Go to sleep, Mrs. Carlton. It's going to be all right."

❧

And since you usually come to visit Dr. McGuire at the University College of Medicine around this time, I decided to write and ask you to consider this. I realize I'm asking a lot, yet for some reason I've yet to fathom Mrs. Carlton has nobody to care for her except a devoted but uncouth housekeeper/companion who can't cook, and who is terrified in the sickroom.

Garnet looked up from the letter, watching her husband's frowning face. "From what Leah says here, Fiona has adamantly refused to see a doctor and claims she doesn't need a nurse. Here"—she riffled through the eight-page letter—

She's so colorless I'm afraid she's anemic, despite her insistence that all she needs is time. I sense that for some reason, she is possessed of either a morbid fear or intense dislike of doctors, perhaps because of her experience when she was attacked, all those years ago. But she refuses to discuss it, and if I press, Maisie all but brandishes the fireplace poker. I fear for her, Garnet. I can only visit her every other evening, and each time she seems weaker. I'd tend her myself if it were possible, but I can't afford to miss any more classes.

"What makes her think Mrs. Carlton would be any more willing for me to treat her?" Sloan's gray eyes were almost colorless at the moment, as chilling as the bleak November sky.

"I don't know. But I think Leah's desperate." Concerned, Garnet bit her lip. Desperation was not an emotion she associated with her unflappable younger sister.

"I know you'd been planning your visit with Dr. McGuire for next week. Do you think he could rearrange his schedule?"

"That's the least of this. More to the point is Mrs. Carlton. It doesn't make sense, a woman of her stature with only an inept housekeeper for staff. That woman was one of the most famous personages of her time. Her husband was a member of the British aristocracy. Her present circumstances defy logic, particularly Mrs. Carlton's attitude toward the medical profession." He ran a large hand around the back of his head, mussing the thick black hair. "If she's anemic…"

Sloan mumbled something else under his breath, but Garnet could tell he was growing more concerned—and less reluctant. Hiding her impatience, she laid the letter down on the desk, then wandered over to the basket tucked near the parlor stove, where Phineas was curled up asleep, the bushy tail draped elegantly over his body.

Garnet's rustling skirts roused the fox. He lifted his head when she knelt to scratch under his chin and behind his ears, and Garnet marveled as she had for six years at God's mysterious whimsy. A fox for a pet. She smiled down into the unblinking eyes, eyes that gazed back at her with uncanny intelligence and utter trust.

Sloan's hand thumped the top of his desk, startling both Garnet and the fox. "Ought to just arrange for her to recover at a private sanitarium, for crying out loud," he grumbled. "Instead of juggling everyone's schedules just because your sister has her knickers in a wad."

After giving Phineas a consoling pat, Garnet walked back across the room and pressed a kiss at the corner of her husband's mustache. "I'll help you pack," she murmured. "And don't worry about us. I'll ask Josie Mae Whalen to stay here until you return."

"Sweetheart, it's not that simple." He stopped, shaking his head, and reached past Garnet for the letter. Still tucked against his side, she watched him read through the pages, his frown deepening. At the end, he dropped the pages back on the desk and closed his eyes, whispering beneath his breath, "I hear You. I hear…" Then, aloud with his gaze on hers: "I'll telephone Dr. Hanover up in Strasburg this evening, to see if he'll be available should an emergency arise. If Josie Mae's willing to stay here while I'm gone, to help you with Daniel and Robbie, I'll make the trip to Richmond."

"Between you, Leah, and the Lord, Mrs. Carlton won't stand a chance."

Thirty-Four

SINCLAIR RUN

*T*hrough the windows the mid-November afternoon light cast a sullen glare over Jacob's private sitting room. Like the old desk where he sat, he was buried in paperwork. The chore was necessary, but Jacob always dreaded the afternoons when weather, or Effie's badgering, forced him to put his affairs in proper order. Today it had been his irate housekeeper.

"At the mercantile this morning Mr. Cooper stood right there with his face the color of boiled beets and mine the same, over having to tell me it's going for three months since he was able to balance your accounts. I assured him you'd be sending him what he's owed within the week. If you wish supper this night, Mr. Sinclair, you'll take the time to keep me from being a liar."

Troublesome woman. Jacob thought of the kneehole desk waiting in his shop, then set his back teeth and doggedly plowed through correspondence and bills and fliers. An hour later, he was ready to climb out the window and slip around the side of the house to escape Effie's eagle eye; every quarter-hour she poked her head through the doorway, harrumphed her satisfaction, then departed without a word.

"Granda! Granda, where are you?" Robbie burst through the door, flew across the room, and hurled himself into Jacob's startled embrace. "We're here for a visit! Father's gone, and Mama said we had to come here, that you'd want to know…to know…" His freckled face scrunched up in confusion. "I forget. We brought Phinnie. Miz Effie says she has some apple cores, but I have to give them to him in the kitchen." He pulled himself out of Jacob's arms and barreled back to the doorway. "Bye now," he called over his shoulder as he scooted into Jacob's bedroom, almost careening into his mother, then whisked down the hall.

"What a bonny sight!" For a moment Jacob simply enjoyed the picture Garnet made, with her burnished red hair lighting the dreary day and her lovely freckled face rosy with wind-stung color. He hugged her, and they rubbed noses, then he scooped his bundled up namesake out of her arms. "What's this about Sloan leaving, redbird?"

Garnet ensured that Daniel Jacob wasn't going to pucker up and squall, then began talking while she peeled off her outer garments. "He plans to be back either by tomorrow evening or the following morning."

Something in the lass's tone wasn't right, and she was avoiding his gaze. "Why would he leave— It's Leah, isn't it? Garnet, is something amiss with your sister, something medical she's afraid to tell me about?"

"No, no. Leah's fine." She tugged his arm. "Let's sit, all right? Close to the parlor stove? It's a raw day, and I'm chilly, especially since I had to do the driving."

Something chillier than the November day skimmed the base of Jacob's spine. "All right, lass. What would ye be trying *not* to tell me, then? Out with it. I'm no' in the mood for guessing games."

"I can see that." Garnet said, and took a deep breath. "I'm sorry. You remember how Sloan tries to go to Richmond several times a year, to consult with that physician who founded the University College of Medicine?"

"Aye. I thought he was to go next week."

"He…changed his mind. He left yesterday." She glanced at him, then finished in a rush. "Leah wrote us a letter. Mrs. Carlton is very ill, with influenza, she thinks. Leah's undone by the circumstances, Papa. I can't blame her. Apparently Mrs. Carlton has no family or friends to help, and she refuses to have a physician."

"Mrs. Carlton?"

"I had the same reaction myself," she said, smiling a little. "The only care she's had is her companion, who is of little value in the sickroom. Leah is—well, I've never had a letter from her quite like this one. She practically begged Sloan to come."

"Fiona Carlton?" Jacob repeated blankly, unable to reconcile his image of the woman who had sat so regally in his parlor with a woman ill enough to frighten Leah.

"You know Leah is not given to melodrama, like Meredith. Sloan was concerned enough to call the school on the telephone. After talking to Leah, he agreed to make the trip at once." Her head tilted as she contemplated Jacob. "There's a story here, isn't there?"

To give himself time, Jacob blew onto Daniel's tiny waving hands, then engaged him in an absent-minded game of pat-a-cake. "Not a story," he finally admitted. "But there is something about Mrs. Carlton that catches at one's heartstrings."

"This is so peculiar. You'd think she'd be surrounded by servants and family," Garnet said. "Fiona Carlton is a famous lady, for all she hasn't appeared in public in years. If she needs help... It's hard to fathom, but Leah wouldn't have asked if she felt there was another option."

Jacob sat back, thinking. "She's a reserved woman, very much a lady. But..." He hesitated, wondering at his own reluctance to discuss her. "She's made it more than plain, on the occasions I've been in her company, that she's a very private person. No matter how much Leah bullies, nor how persuasive Sloan's bedside manner, I'm thinking Mrs. Carlton will have little to do with either of them."

Now why in the name of bonny Prince Charlie should that probability cast him into a state of melancholy as bleak and barren as the November afternoon? Jacob rose and turned away, unwilling for Garnet to read his expression.

Truth to tell, he was even less inclined to study on the thought himself.

⤙※⤚

RICHMOND, VIRGINIA

Fiona kept her hands very still in her lap, not wanting the tall, dark-haired gentleman Leah had introduced as her brother-in-law to notice their unsteadiness. "I'm sorry you've made a needless trip." She sliced Leah a reproachful glance that the younger woman ignored. "I admit to being ill. But I'm improving daily." She managed the lie, but it took an effort of will. "There was certainly no need for you to make a special trip," she finished, belatedly realizing she was repeating herself.

"I'd planned to be here in the city anyway. It was no trouble at all," he replied calmly, as though she didn't sound like a dotty old woman.

"Last Thursday you told me you couldn't seem to regain your energy," Leah said. "You were concerned, or you wouldn't have mentioned it." She sat down on the other end of the sofa, an expression on her face that Fiona could only describe as *schoolmarmish,* though of all the costumes Fiona had seen her wear, the colorful tartan plaid shirt-waist she'd donned for today little resembled a prim schoolteacher. "Shall I tell Sloan what Maisie confessed, about the day you tried to visit the Alcorn Home for the Blind?"

Fiona went rigid. "That is neither your nor your brother-in-law's concern. I have not called on a physician because I do not care to have a physician…" Despite her determination the palpitations of her heart had intensified to the point that she involuntarily pressed one fist beneath her breast. Perspiration gathered on her brow.

"Mrs. Carlton."

She forced herself to meet the piercing gray-eyed gaze of the man who was, according to Leah, not only a physician but a compassionate man of God. Ha! Such a person did not exist, as far as she was concerned. "Dr.—I'm sorry, I've forgotten your name."

"MacAllister," he supplied, again without the slightest nuance of impatience.

"Dr. MacAllister, I'm afraid what you are suggesting is quite impossible."

She managed to slide to the edge of the settee, but was afraid to test the strength of her limbs. Her headache was almost blinding her, and the queasiness was intensifying. Pain stabbed her side. Somehow she must make them leave. Where had Maisie got to? Oh, that's right. Today was market day? No…that was—Fiona gathered her muzzy thoughts and tried to produce a clear-eyed stare. "I appreciate your concern, but I'm afraid I have an…engagement."

"With the floor?" Leah said, her voice tart. "Sloan, do something. Can't you see she's about to faint?"

"There's nothing wrong with my eyes, Leah."

In an unexpected move he knelt right down on the floor, beside Fiona. Her reflexive withdrawal cost her dearly; for a swirling moment or two she was terrified that she would indeed pass out in front of them. Only through a will honed in the furnace of intense suffering was she able to remain upright, gradually focusing on the stern masculine face.

"Mrs. Carlton, shall I tell you what you're feeling?" he said. "You've a bad headache, your heart is racing, you're so weak at the moment you lack even the energy to stand up"—beneath his thick black mustache a smile flashed, causing Fiona to blink—"so that politeness would force us to leave. If I felt your pulse, it would be pumping much too rapidly. And unless I'm badly mistaken, you're running a fever."

He paused, but Fiona refused to give him the satisfaction of telling him he was right. After a moment he continued in a deep voice all the more powerful for its utter confidence. "Mrs. Carlton, I am a doctor. I believe this is what God called me to do, and with all my heart I also believe the tenets of the Hippocratic oath. I will do you no harm. I can help you, if you'll let me. With God's help, I believe I can heal you."

That was novel. A physician who allowed the Almighty some credit. "Why?" she asked, unable to elaborate.

"Mrs. Carlton, mercysake, this is no time—"

"Easy there, Leah. Don't rush it. Let me talk with her, all right? Mrs. Carlton." His voice returned to that compelling blend of strength and compassion. "Do you believe in God?"

What kind of question was that? "Yes, of course," Fiona answered wearily. If she could just lie down. If they would just go away, leave her be.

"Try to stay with me, hmm. Would you like to lie back on the couch? It would help your head, you know. Leah, why don't you help her, since you've become friends."

"I'm quite all right," Fiona began, mustering up a scrap of forcefulness that was wasted on both her visitors. She didn't want to be touched; beyond polite handshakes, nobody but Maisie had touched her in years, except for the new residents at the Alcorn Home, who at least couldn't see her.

She might as well have been a dressmaker's dummy, for in short order she found herself supine, with a throw pillow beneath her head and an afghan tucked around her torso. Her breath sounded peculiar, like a dying bellows, and she fought against a moan of pain.

"Mrs. Carlton, may I hold your wrist, so I can count your pulse?"

"Why bother to ask?" She heard the grumpiness and was ashamed of it. She was more ashamed of the flood of longing that washed even over the embarrassment, a longing she had suppressed for years that these two had resurrected. She was also afraid, because the room was starting to blur, and nausea was a fist, hammering her to near insensibility. "Count my pulse, then leave?" she whispered.

"Mm, probably not. As both a doctor and a Christian, I'm afraid I can't walk away from someone so obviously ill."

"Suit me better if you *were* the Levite or the priest…"

"Ah. You are familiar with the Bible, then?" Without fuss his fingers wrapped around her wrist, unbuttoned the cuff, then lightly pressed her pulse. Fiona watched through drooping eyelids as he silently counted, a frown deepening in his forehead. "Then you understand perfectly why neither Leah nor I can leave you to suffer alone, with only your pride for company, and a faithful companion who's going to aid in your demise, if we do."

"Sloan!"

Dr. MacAllister ignored Leah's outraged cry. The gray-eyed gaze was too intent on dissecting Fiona. She couldn't help it. With the last of her strength her hand lifted as though tugged by strings and covered her cheek. Something flickered across the doctor's face, but without comment he rebuttoned her sleeve. Then he proceeded to examine her fingertips, and after that he gently tugged down her lower eyelids. He didn't try to force her hand away from her face, nor did his gaze ever focus on what she was trying to conceal.

Utterly spent, Fiona gave up and lay quietly, resigned to the helpless indignity. After all, it wasn't the first time. Mouth tight, she stoically waited for what would come next. The probing, intimate questions, the condescension, the inference that she was a woman and therefore prone to all manner of hysterical manifestations. The callous indifference to her modesty…

I'm going to faint, she thought on a hopeless moan.

Her last conscious sight was Sloan MacAllister's face swooping down, pulling darkness in its wake.

Thirty-Five

I t was worse than before. She'd never felt so ill, not even after the attack with her face on fire and her life in ruins. Time passed not in blurred fragments, but as monstrous chunks of darkness interspersed with terrifying shards of light. There was a man—a doctor because her parents would never allow a strange gentleman...no. She was married, Gerald had returned from his watery grave to torment her, and she kept trying to explain that she was ill, that she couldn't perform tonight.

"Swallow this, Mrs. Carlton. That's it."

Gerald? Fiona tried to say, only something vile dribbled down her throat and she had to swallow or choke. Gasping, she felt hands holding her steady, smoothing a cool cloth over her face—*not my cheek.* She cried out, flinching because she knew now they were going to hurt her again, every time she cried they hurt her. Yet a deep voice reassured her that it was all right, he wasn't going to hurt her, he was here to help her.

Maisie was weeping; she could hear the girl somewhere in the darkened room, snuffling noisily. "Am I going to die?" she wondered aloud.

"No, you're going to feel better soon, very soon," that deep voice murmured.

The sliver of light brightened, and abruptly Fiona focused on the amazing sight of the man Leah had brought to her—her brother-in-law, the doctor. The one with eyes that saw too much, but that didn't wound. Like Jacob Sinclair. She stared up into the doctor's face and almost found a smile. "You need to shave." Her voice emerged in a thin croak. "How...long?"

"How long have I been here, taking care of you?" he guessed, and his mustache twitched at Fiona's shock. "This is the fifth day."

Five days? *Five days?* "Maisie?"

"Has kept your sickroom as neat as an English butler's pantry. Leah's taught her how to brew a good cup of tea and make passable invalid nourishment, and I've persuaded her to help me care for you. Right now she's probably sleeping, however. It's a little past four in the morning."

"You've stayed here?" She couldn't grasp the enormity of it. When he slipped a hand behind her neck and eased her head up to sip liquid from a glass she docilely allowed the intimacy, too weak to resist.

"You've been very ill." The deep lines about his mouth and forehead attested to the statement, as did the rest of his appearance: The good doctor looked as though he was ready for the sickroom himself.

Dr. MacAllister. The name slipped back into place, along with a tickle of gratitude, the beginning of wonder along with the automatic revulsion for his profession. "Dr. MacAllister," Fiona whispered in her watery gruel voice, "did you…bleed me?"

"Absolutely not," came the terse response. "A barbaric custom in my opinion, now utilized solely by quacks. With any luck, by the turn of the century the practice will be relegated where it belongs, in the grave-yard of medical ignorance."

"Before…the doctors…" Her tongue felt clumsy with shamed relief. "I wasn't a good patient. When they bled me, I was weaker, didn't—resist. One of them got to where he'd threaten…"

"I'm sorry." He lifted her hand, holding it in a comforting grip. Amazed, Fiona could only gawk at the sight of her cold claw of a hand lying in Dr. MacAllister's. "No wonder you don't want anything to do with anyone in the medical profession."

"Am I… I feel so weak."

"Well, that's because your body's been fighting pneumonia along with everything else, not because you've been bled. I promise." He gently laid her hand back on the bedcovers, and stood. "You need to sleep. Your fever's finally down. The worst is past, Mrs. Carlton."

Strange. Fiona had no trouble taking Sloan MacAllister at his word. Sinking into sleep, she turned her head on the pillow, searching the shadows for his face. "Dr. MacAllister, you saved my life, I'm thinking."

A tired smile came and went in the gray eyes. "God saved your life.

I was privileged to assist. Rest now, Mrs. Carlton. That's what you need now. Lots of rest."

❦

"And Garnet's reply arrived this morning, so everyone agrees that this would be the best solution all the way around," Leah finished. She leaned forward in the chair, hands planted on her knees. "As soon as Sloan feels you're able to travel, he'll accompany you and Maisie to Tom's Brook. You can stay as long as it takes for you to completely recover your health."

"There's a room off my office for patients I need to keep an eye on," Dr. MacAllister said, watching her. "At the moment, that patient is you. Now, you've commented yourself that I need to return to my own practice, my family. I can't deny the truth of it. But unless you change your mind about hiring a nurse, or allowing me to contact a local physician here in Richmond, you face a relapse. This time, it might prove fatal."

When Fiona opened her mouth to protest, he lifted an eyebrow, then finished evenly, "Your body lacks the resources for you to take care of yourself. We might have licked the pneumonia and the influenza, but you're still anemic. I've seen that Maisie is devoted. Loyal to a fault, but…" He shrugged, stroking the ends of his mustache while Fiona reclined on her bed and fumed.

She felt trapped, not only by the two people hovering over her, but by her own intractability. The thought of calling in another physician, or even a nurse who would be privy to all her weaknesses, who would see her unveiled and vulnerable—no. She simply could not, would not agree.

If she needed the services of a doctor, she wanted Sloan MacAllister. Over the past days a strange bond had developed between them, one Fiona did not know how to categorize, which left her foundering with an anxiety she struggled to conceal. She didn't want him to leave her here, at the mercy of strangers. Yet she was hesitant to trust him enough to impose herself into his life, his family. She'd been alone for too many years; she didn't want to be a burden.

"How long before I'm completely well?"

"Some weeks, a month at the most," Dr. MacAllister answered. He smiled down at her, but the smile did not extend to his eyes. "Will you trust me?" he asked, very quietly. "You won't be a burden, I promise."

"But your wife. You have…" Small children, one of them a boy, Leah had told her. A little boy. A shudder rippled through her.

"My wife has wanted to meet you since the afternoon you stopped by to visit Jacob Sinclair." The blunt statement reduced Fiona's thoughts to chaff. "And whether or not you believe me, Garnet will enjoy your and Maisie's company. She doesn't get out as much as she used to, before the baby was born."

"A change of scenery would be good for you," Leah put in. "Good for Maisie as well."

"That's another issue," Fiona said, pinching the bridge of her nose as she scrambled to reassert a modicum of authority. "Taking in a patient might be a necessary evil of your profession. But Maisie is— Well, I don't want to leave her alone, when she's alone all summer. And it's not fair—"

"Mercysake! This isn't a children's board game, so hush up this talk of being 'fair.'" Leah's brown eyes snapped impatiently. "You want to come, I can see it in your face. And Maisie will be a tremendous help to Garnet. I do wish you'd stop torturing yourself and us and just be done with it." Leah shoved the chair back and stalked to the other side of the room.

Dr. MacAllister turned the chair around, straddled it, and propped his forearms across the back. "Don't you think it's time to be ministered to, for a change?" His head tilted sideways as he studied Fiona. "Be a Mary, instead of a Martha? It's a good thing, you know, being able to sit at the Lord's feet sometimes."

"Ha. How often do you sit there, Dr. MacAllister?"

He grinned at her. "But we're not talking about me, are we Mrs. Carlton? So…which is it to be? I can contact Dr. McGuire, have everything arranged by the end of the day. Or—a ticket to Tom's Brook?"

Fiona's resistance dribbled away. Sloan MacAllister might be an intense, intelligent man and a doctor to boot, but she had learned that he knew how to be gentle as well as compassionate. Besides, the grin was irresistible.

Sufficient unto the day, she decided, for the time being laying aside the uncertainties, the doubts. The questions and fears.

"We'll go to Tom's Brook." Even as she said it Fiona couldn't help but wonder which would turn out to be more dangerous for her peace of mind—the dread or the relief.

Thirty-Six

For much of the bitingly cold ride down the Pike, Jacob talked aloud to himself, to the Lord, even to the horse, trying to convince all of them that the only reason he was visiting Tom's Brook was to see his grandsons. After all, Garnet and Sloan had been too busy to make the trip to Sinclair Run these past weeks. "So if I want to play with the lads before spring, 'tis myself who must make the effort."

At that precise moment Raspberry snorted, probably over some roadside distraction but with what Jacob deemed a perfect example of uncommon horse sense. "Aye, you agree with me, right enough, don't you, girl?" Satisfied, he burrowed deeper inside his wool muffler, tucked the ends of his lap robe more firmly beneath his thighs, and jiggled the reins. "Pick your feet up then. Sooner we're there, the sooner you'll have a warm stall, and I'll have a pair of grandsons on my knees."

And if Fiona Carlton was of a mind to share a mug of steaming cocoa with him and the boys, why, that would be a braw thing, would it not?

He wondered how she would look today. With each subsequent visit over the past three weeks, Jacob couldn't help but notice the signs of recovery, for all that he was careful to comment only obliquely about her improved appearance. That she was staying with Garnet and Sloan at all was something of a miracle. For twoscore years the lady had guarded her privacy with a tenacity that bordered on paranoia, as Jacob well knew.

You're healing her spirit as well as her body, aren't You, Lord? Why, the last time hadn't she sat and chatted with him natural as could be, not a veil in sight? Nor had her hand lifted a single time in the pitiful gesture to cover her cheek. Best of all, perhaps, had been the bit of color blooming in her face, good, healthy color instead of the self-conscious blush or the bleached-wood paleness.

And her eyes. Doesn't she have a fine pair of eyes, Lord? Blue they were, though not a deep intense blue like Benjamin's, but more of a soft blue-gray, like a twilight winter sky. Aye, Fiona had been blessed with lovely eyes.

He was grinning when he pulled Raspberry up to Sloan's barn; after taking care of the mare, Jacob hurried across the yard, his step light as he crunched across the frost-coated earth.

When he was halfway there, Sloan burst through the back door, doctor's bag in hand. When he caught sight of Jacob the taut lines bracketing his mouth relaxed. "Jacob. A timely arrival indeed. Listen, there's an emergency out at the foundry. When the call came, Garnet and Maisie had already left to take the boys for a visit with Elmira Whitaker. It's been hard on her, cooped up with that broken leg of hers, and Mrs. Carlton insisted that they go since I was still here seeing patients. I hated leaving her alone—you're a godsend."

"Well, now," Jacob began. "I'm not sure about—"

"She's in the family's sitting room, by the fire, not her private room. You needn't worry. Help yourself to whatever you need in the kitchen. Don't let Mrs. Carlton wait on you—she's champing at the bit a little, but I'm depending on you to talk her out of any strenuous activity. Now, I might be late, but the rest of the family should be home within an hour. Thanks, Jacob." He sketched a salute, then strode rapidly for the barn.

Jacob scowled as he approached the house. Shouldn't be leaving her alone, he thought. Showed a lack of foresight, and he planned to say so to his son-in-law, who should have known better. His gaze swept over the porch, which he and Sloan had completely rebuilt the previous summer. Jacob still wasn't sure he approved of the spindlework frieze.

Once inside, realization struck. He and Fiona Carlton were alone for the first time since the night he'd cornered her in the conservatory at Stillwaters. The prospect was unsettling, but he found himself rushing to pull off his overcoat, muffler, hat and gloves, all but dumping them on the massive hall tree in the front hall.

Fiona looked up when he appeared in the doorway. Phineas, asleep at her feet, lifted his head alertly, then relaxed. "Mr. Sinclair!" Fiona said, laying her needlework aside. Jacob watched with a spurt of disappointment the way she turned her head as she leaned to pat the fox so that the scarred cheek was hidden. "I didn't realize you'd come. Garnet's out with Maisie and the boys, visiting. But they should be back soon." She glanced at the grandfather clock ponderously ticking in the corner. "Sloan's been called out on some emergency. You just missed him." She started to rise.

Jacob waved her back. "No, don't get up. I saw Sloan in the yard, on his way to the barn. I'm under strict orders to limit your activity. Please, go on with your needlework." He sat down across from her, leaning to scratch behind Phineas's ear. "A fine companion you've found here."

"I've enjoyed his company." A timid smile hovered. "Maisie certainly doesn't. She all but climbs on a chair to avoid being near him."

For a few moments they exchanged idle chitchat; Jacob watched in relief as the rigidity gradually faded from her shoulders. She picked up the lacy concoction pooled in her lap. "What's that you're working on?" he asked.

"A scarf tie, for Garnet. I'm adding a fringe to either end. Pattern's a bit complicated—it's based on laces of Italian design, but adapted for crochet." The corner of her mouth curved. "Keeps me occupied, at least. I'm not allowed to lift anything heavier than a cup of broth or expend myself beyond a ten-minute circuit up and down the hallway, three times a day. The kitchen is strictly forbidden." Her hands, those pale, elegant hands whose every movement was woven with gracefulness, resumed plying some sort of hook.

Strangely at peace, Jacob settled back to watch. "Sloan tends to be a trifle overprotective of people he cares about."

She hesitated. "I've come to respect him very much, both as a husband and father and as a doctor. He's quite skilled, isn't he? And he plainly loves Garnet and the children very much."

"Aye. He's a fine one, right enough. I've known that from the first time I met him, even though he was a seething young man at war with the world and the Lord. Yet he gave of himself to my daughter—saved her life, truth be told."

"She told me, soon after I arrived. Even showed me the scar on her shoulder. I was quite amazed." A shadow crossed her face, and for an unguarded moment Jacob witnessed a yearning so poignant it was all he could do not to sit down beside her and give her a hug. "I wish..." she murmured, then seemed to collect herself. "I wish there were some way to pay them back, for what they're doing," she finally said. "Not with money, but somehow let them know..."

"I think they already know," Jacob finished, very gently. He propped his elbows on his knees and leaned forward, his gaze steady on hers. "You've bloomed, this past month. Not just from my son-in-law's excellent doctoring skills, but from being around a loving family."

She turned her head aside, and he watched the muscles in her throat quiver. "It's difficult for me," she murmured in a voice so low he barely heard the words. "So many years...I'd forgotten. And they don't even notice—I mean, I do feel as though there's nothing wrong with me, they treat me like—" She stopped dead, and with a flash of insight Jacob realized why.

"They treat you like a member of the family," he finished for her. "Of course they would. Besides, anyone who's been subjected to Leah's managing ways is entitled to be treated like family. As for the other, you need to sand out a few rough places in your thinking, Mrs. Carlton. There's naught *wrong* with you, merely because you've a scar on your face."

"Not everyone would agree with you."

"No," Jacob agreed calmly. "I saw that, at Stillwaters. After our first encounter, I used to watch for you, though to be sure you made it difficult. But the few times you did appear when other guests were about, I saw the sidelong glances, heard the whispers. You've not had an easy time of it over the years, have you?"

"I learned quickly and thoroughly the difference between adulation—and aspersion." She sent him a quizzical look. "You've been very careful the past few weeks not to exceed the bounds of polite discourse, Mr. Sinclair. Now that we're alone, you do. I would like to know why."

Jacob wondered himself at the inexplicable urge to have a part, if he was honest about it, in Fiona Carlton's healing. But how to tell her, when he didn't fathom it himself? He tugged the drooping lock of hair on his forehead, scratched behind his ear, then gave up the struggle for discretion in favor of plain speech.

"You bother me, and have since first I came upon you that night on the grounds, draped in moonlight and shadows. 'Tis shameful of me, to be sure, to pry into your affairs when you're a captive audience." He inhaled, then let his breath out in a sustained sigh. "It seems I canna help myself. I…care about you. My family cares about you. I would like it very much if you would call me Jacob and consider me a friend. A trustworthy friend you don't turn your face away from, nor hide from behind pretense—or a veil."

"I haven't been allowed to wear that veil since I arrived." She was regarding him with that smile barely curving her lips, but a frown lurked behind her eyes. Her fingers lay statue-still amid the lacy folds of the collar she'd been fashioning.

For several moments she did not respond further, and Jacob was content enough to wait. Through the window thin winter light touched her profile, turning once golden hair to a silvery flaxen hue, softening the fine lines about her mouth and eyes. She'd braided her hair today, he saw, winding it about her head in a coronet that gave her an almost regal air.

He was seven kinds of a fool, to be entertaining these thoughts. Just as he was about to apologize, however, Fiona spoke.

"I would be honored to call you Jacob," she said, "if you will call me Fiona. As for friendship, for most of my life I've had little practice at being a friend, and few friends I wouldn't consider threats to my peace of mind."

"I beg your pardon?" The woman was daft. Or rather, she was about to make him so. "From what Leah has shared, before your illness your days were filled with people, people who like and respect you. She told me you were seldom home at all. And surely after these past weeks you don't think you've been naught but a-a patient."

The smile twisted. "There is a difference between friendship born of pity and guilt on one part, need on the other—and friendship between equals. I'm afraid what I do was never intended to cultivate friendship. That changed over the years, of course. I'm older now and, I hope, content with my lot. I do care about the people I visit, very much. I like to think I've offered a bit of brightness in their lives. But if my visits ceased, they would transfer their affections elsewhere. My life is not vital to anyone, even Maisie."

Jacob scowled. "That girl dotes on you, for all she's as rough around the edges as a shagbark hickory. You've a poor opinion of those bright-ened lives—and of yourself, I daresay."

Fiona shook her head. "I offer Maisie a modicum of respectability. But if something happened to me, she'd return to a back-alley saloon somewhere, because no one is willing to accept those rough edges, and she's too contrary to smooth them. You've a very idealistic view of humanity, if you think it would be otherwise." Placidly she resumed her needlework. "You see what a difficult sort of friend I might prove to be? My view of humanity is hopelessly jaded."

She worked her fingers to the bone, expended all her energy mak-ing rounds of no less than four different homes for the needy, Leah told him. Every week from October through May, she devoted her days to teaching blind and bedridden women how to crochet, reading to the sick and elderly, feeding the helpless…being Jesus as it were. Yet she pro-claimed herself a cynic? *Aye, Lord, she's going to make me daft.*

"So you've a jaded view, whilst I try to maintain a more hopeful one. We offset one another nicely then, don't we?" He hesitated before deliberately adding, "Fiona?"

For a moment she did not respond. Then, "Yes, we do…Jacob," she managed, the words husky. "I would very much like to count you as a friend." Her fingers fluttered in a helpless gesture. She ducked her head.

"Well, then." Brisk for both their sakes, he rubbed his hands together. " 'Tis settled. Now, until you're well enough for a buggy ride, how do you feel about checkers? Before you answer, I'd best warn you that I'll not be a gentleman. If you want to win, you'll have to earn it."

"I…why, I've never played checkers, or any other manner of game," Fiona said, looking as flustered as a girl.

"Time you learned." Pleased with himself, Jacob rose. "Finish your sandwich. You'll need your strength. I'll be back in a moment." He returned shortly with Robbie's checkerboard and a tin box of checkers.

"Jacob?"

He paused in the midst of setting everything up on the table he'd cleared of tray and food. "Yes?"

"You should know...I've a very competitive streak."

"Ah. No wonder you and Leah get along so well." He beamed at her. "That should make up for my skill."

She laid aside her needlework and sat forward, her gaze on the board, her face close enough that Jacob could brush his fingers across the long ragged line of that scar. He wondered what her reaction would be.

He knew what his own was, at the mere thought of it.

I'm too old to be feeling like this, Lord.

As he began to explain how the game was played, he could almost hear the sound of a heavenly chuckle floating light as a snowflake into his ear. A question breathed through the very pores of his skin, into his heart: *And how old does one have to be, to be too old?* The nation of Israel was born of a woman pushing the century mark, and the father of John the Baptist wasn't exactly a lad in the first bloom of manhood.

It wasn't the Lord who limited love between a man and a woman to the young.

"I'm ready," Fiona said, meeting his gaze with only a snippet of bravado shadowing her lovely light eyes.

Och, Jacob thought, awareness fogging his brain, *I'm not so sure that I am, Fiona lass. I'm not so sure that I am...*

Thirty-Seven

*T*he season's first snowfall blanketed the Valley that night. From the Turkish tufted sofa beneath her window, Fiona watched entranced as millions of madly whirling flakes transformed the earth from bleak and black to sparkling white. She was alone, having sent Maisie off to bed a half-hour earlier, and the rest of the house was quiet. Presumably the Sinclairs were tucked away as well.

Fiona could revel to her heart's content in the majestic silence of the storm.

Once, when she'd been a small child, younger than eight because by the time she turned nine Fiona had discovered that piano keys were even more magical than snow, she remembered sneaking outside in a snowstorm. Oblivious to any hazard, she'd whirled round and round, pretending to be a snowflake.

How lovely it would be to resurrect that innocent child, just for a little while, so that she could once again lose herself in a world that, for a brief instant, had become a fairyland.

"Mrs. Carlton? Are you all right?"

Surprised, she glanced over her shoulder to where Garnet hovered inside the doorway, Phineas at her feet. "I'm fine, dear. Just enjoying the snow."

Garnet joined her at the window, her expression troubled. "I'd enjoy it more if Sloan were safely home."

Fiona paused from scratching the fox's thick ruff. "I hadn't realized he was still out." It was almost eleven—Sloan had been gone for more than nine hours. She straightened, offering Garnet a comforting smile. "Try not to fret. Last week he was gone from dawn till suppertime, remember. Surely this is familiar territory for a physician's wife, but I suppose you could ask him to keep banker's hours. Or—let's be magnanimous—office hours until dusk."

"I know, I'm being silly." She hesitated.

Fiona suppressed a sigh, then gestured to the sofa. "Would you and Phineas like to keep me company for a while?" She was surprised by the lightness that filled her when Garnet's face lost much of its drawn look.

"Are you sure? You probably ought to be in bed. Rest is the most important restorative, remember." But she perched on the end of the thick cushion when Fiona moved her feet out of the way. "Mercysake, it's coming down so thick you can't see the barn." Biting her lip, she ran distracted fingers through her unbound hair, her gaze never leaving the window.

"I enjoyed visiting with your father today," Fiona said, searching for a distraction. She had plucked the words out of the air, but realized they were true, rather than merely polite. The realization was even more disconcerting than her easy acceptance of Garnet's company.

"I'm glad. I hope he didn't make a pest of himself. I wanted to box his ears for openly gloating because he beat you three checkers games out of four. I never thought Papa would be so ungallant." Phineas laid his narrow snout across his mistress's lap and whined.

"Well, I'm afraid I deserved it. I was equally annoying, the one game I managed to trounce him." Smiling down at the fox as well as the memory of Jacob's poorly concealed frustration, Fiona patted the cushion. "Come on up, there's a good boy. A little fox fur never hurt anyone."

"Not according to Maisie."

They both laughed then. If Phineas elected to nap the day away with Fiona, Maisie filled the air with dire predictions and surly grumbling.

"Phineas likes you," Garnet observed, sounding puzzled. "Always has. He's not usually so friendly to strangers."

"Nor am I. Perhaps that's why we tolerate each other." The fox nudged her hand, begging for more scratching. "I never had a pet. My parents thought animals were unsanitary. I never realized they would offer such companionship."

"Yes, they do. But your parents weren't entirely wrong. I don't normally allow him access to this room, since it's designed as a sickroom for Sloan's patients."

"Which is why I need to think about going home," Fiona began. "I'm no longer ill."

"Flumadiddle. Don't start that again. You'll stay until Sloan pronounces you fit to travel, and if that's not until spring I'd be delighted. Truly." She flashed a quick, shy smile. "I'm being selfish, you see. I've enjoyed your company, especially the time or two I've been able to draw while you crochet. It's been"—she seemed to fumble for words before finishing simply—"lovely."

All the more reason for her to leave. She was dangerously vulnerable: Affection, she was learning, could be as insidious as anger. It had taken years to rid herself of anger and reach a state of grace that allowed her a modicum of tranquillity. She wasn't sure she possessed the strength, physical or emotional, to endure the process again, especially when—this time—her heart longed to reciprocate an emotion instead of rebuff it.

This would not do. *Think of the little boy.* Did she really want to be around Robert, so like Harry in his ways her heart came near to exploding every time he reached up for a hug? *God. Dear God...I cannot.*

The armor slid into place like an old pair of slippers. Slippers fashioned from Pittsburgh steel.

"I've enjoyed my time here as well, and I wish we might have shared it under different circumstances." There. Reserved warmth, which gave no cause for offense yet shielded her from true intimacy. "Phineas is a delightful creature, even though he does make for an odd sort of pet." Fiona lifted her hand from the thick rust-colored fur and let it drop to her lap. "In my own way I suppose I'm as much of an oddity."

"No more than the rest of us," Garnet told her, a troubled frown growing between her eyes. "As you say, a fox isn't exactly a tabby cat or a lap dog, though Phineas thinks he's both on alternate days. Then of course there's my flaming hair"—she gathered a handful of red tresses and thrust the mass behind her shoulders—"Sloan's infamous temper, and Papa's Scottish burr. Of course you only hear it when his composure is rattled."

The child was a dear. Like her father, a warm, compassionate young woman who did not deserve Fiona's chilly reticence. Before she could halt the gesture, she was patting Garnet's arm. "Thank you, dear. You're quite right, of course. Everyone has his own splinter to fret over."

"You're mixing your biblical metaphors."

"So I am. Must come from being an oddity."

She may as well pray to stop the sun from rising in the east as to hope to protect herself from this family. Their warmth was too genuine, their every action imbued with the kind of unselfish caring that could only spring from an all-loving Creator. Resigned, Fiona yielded to a Will more powerful than her own, and the tension she had fostered melted away. In unspoken accord the two women turned their attention back to the snowstorm raging outside.

The mad swirl of white flakes proved hypnotic. Within moments Fiona was struggling to keep her eyes open.

"May I ask you something, Mrs. Carlton? It's rather personal, and I'll understand if you tell me to mind my own business."

Jolted awake, Fiona contemplated Garnet in silence. "Since I've been living off the goodness of your hearts for these past weeks, I'd say that entitles you to a personal question or two," she finally said. "Ask me anything you like, my dear."

"All right." She smiled sheepishly. "But I wish you wouldn't sound as though you're steeling yourself for the guillotine. I've been thinking—well, no. Actually I've been praying, for Sloan, hoping he'll return soon, and safe. Then my mind sidetracked, as it tends to do whenever I pray."

She drew in a deep breath, and shook her head. "What I wanted to ask you is—why don't you trust doctors? Don't worry, Sloan's not said a word to me," she hastily added. "But when Leah first wrote us about your illness she did comment on your...your intransigency, she called it, about summoning a physician. Considering how debilitated you were when Sloan first arrived, it seems incomprehensible. You could have died."

"Looking back, I realize that." Another sin laid at her door, though it was possible that there had been a bit of divine interference in her behalf. "Please believe that my aversion has, and had, nothing to do with your husband. He's unlike any physician I've ever encountered."

"I know." Tears brightened Garnet's eyes, but she blinked them back. "When he's doctoring he's more like the Great Physician than any man I've ever known. Of course, when he's *not* being a doctor, he can be as hardheaded as old Mrs. Pritchett's mule. And when he loses his temper, even Phineas stays out of his way. I say that," she finished with a watery smile, "so that you'll see that though I love him with all my heart, I'm certainly not blind to his faults."

"They were very much in evidence, the first time Leah dragged him into my parlor," Fiona said dryly. "He didn't want to be there, of course. As poorly as I was at the time, I could still sense it from all the way across the room. Then…" She hesitated, remembering with a sort of wonder that moment when he had leaned over her, the gray eyes warmer than a goose-down comforter. "It was a…revelation. He was the first doctor to treat me with dignity. With caring."

She gestured to her scar. "I might have been surrounded by the best physicians New York had to offer—my husband wouldn't countenance anything else—but not a single one of them treated me as though I were a person, with feelings and fears." The copper taste of that night could flood her mouth to this day.

"Will you tell me about it?"

Startled, Fiona glanced down and saw that Garnet had covered her clenched fist with a gentle hand. "I don't think—"

"It might help you." She removed her hand and sat back, waiting, her expression earnest.

At that moment Phineas sprang up, ears pricked as his head swiveled toward the doorway.

"Mama!" Robert pulled free of Maisie's hand and pelted across the room. "I woke up. I couldn't find you, so I went to Maisie like you told me. She said we would find you together." He landed in a tumble of arms and legs on the sofa, his pale, freckled face alight. "She didn't want to wake up, but I made her. Look at the snow! Can we go outside? Where's Father?"

"That varmint's likely to bite." Her eye on Phineas, Maisie stood over them with folded arms and a truculent expression. "Risking rabies, right enough. And look at you, sitting by the window with nothing but that wrapper. Catch your death…shouldn't be up in the first place."

Nobody grumbled better than Maisie.

As though he'd understood her words, Phineas hopped nimbly to the floor, then retreated in silent dignity, disappearing through the doorway. Robert burrowed between Garnet and Fiona, whispering in a voice audible to them all, "Maisie's cross. Should we pray for her, Mama?"

"Certainly, darling." Garnet cupped his chin. "Why don't you give Mrs. Carlton another good-night kiss and hug, and I'll take you back to bed. We can pray for Maisie then. You didn't wake your brother, did you?"

"Huh-uh." Shyly Robert turned to Fiona and lifted his arms.

Heart clenched, Fiona gathered him close because she could no more spurn the gift of his trust than she could restrain the weather outside. "Go to sleep," she murmured against his flushed cheek. "Morning will come faster that way, and perhaps you can make a snowman."

"Look, Mamá, I made a snow lady!" His precious face was red with cold, the straight little nose running freely. But his eyes shone with pride, so she glanced through the door as she patted his head, mindful of the effect of wet snow on the lace flounces of her silk gown. If only she didn't have the concert tonight…

"Miz Carlton! Snap out of it, ma'am. Time for you to go to bed."

Fiona shook her head but released the memory reluctantly. She focused on the blinding scarlet and royal blue dragons embroidered in Maisie's wrapper. "Yes, I suppose it is." Because she knew the girl, she rose and drew the drapes. "Go on yourself. I'm fine, I promise." Whether she slept peacefully or not was none of Maisie's affair.

"Hmph. Still pale as boiled milk. But nothing I'm not used to, I guess." Scowling, she fussed until Fiona was neatly tucked beneath the bedcovers, then stood over her with her twisting hands and shuffling feet. "You all right?" she finally managed.

"Of course I am, dear."

"Not getting any easier, no matter how long we're here, is it?"

"Good night, Maisie."

Maisie harrumphed again, then began quietly straightening the already tidy sitting area—no doubt checking for fox hair. She would leave when she was ready, and Fiona braced herself for the inevitable discussion.

"That Mr. Sinclair," the housekeeper ventured moments later, "I think he likes you, Miz Carlton."

"I like him, too." Drowsily Fiona tried to muster the energy to dismiss Maisie for the night.

"We both know I've more experience dealing with gents. And Miz Carlton?" She tucked Fiona's neatly filled workbasket into a corner by the bed, then cast a speculative eye over Fiona. "When a man looks at you the way Mr. Sinclair was watching you, when y'all was playing checkers—the liking takes on a whole new meaning. He's got courtin' on his mind, ma'am. So if I was you, I'd watch my back."

Thirty-Eight

*B*y dawn the storm had worn itself out. Bleary from a largely sleepless night, Fiona watched the sun rise with defiant brilliance in a blue china sky—a perfect setting for the sparkling drifts of white snow.

Moments after she had finished the breakfast tray Maisie brought her, Dr. MacAllister knocked on the door. Despite his pronouncement that she was well along the road to fitness, he insisted on a thorough check every morning before he opened his consulting room for office visits. On this morning, Fiona firmly told him through the door panels that as he hadn't returned home until after two in the morning, his first priority should be to himself and his family, not her.

"If you heard me come in, then you're not sleeping soundly enough," was Sloan's imperturbable response. "Don't misbehave now—open the door, why don't you? I promise, no hypodermics today."

She gave in with little grace. Sloan MacAllister might be more good-humored after a sleepless night than Maisie or herself. But the man could be more stubborn than a whole *herd* of Missouri mules.

She suffered through his gentle touch, his questions and assessing gaze, promised him that she had faithfully consumed the protein-rich breakfast Garnet had prepared for her, yes, she had taken her iron pill, and, yes, she would sit out on the porch awhile for some fresh air, since it looked as though it might turn out to be a mild day in spite of the previous night's snowstorm.

"Why aren't you sleeping?"

"Normally I do. But sometimes I'll suffer a night or two of sleeplessness. The curse of aging, Dr. MacAllister, as every doctor should know. It won't kill me as quickly as your sleepless nights might you." She met his bloodshot gaze without batting an eye; after a glowering moment he was forced to let her go, because a knock on the outer door signaled the arrival of the day's next patient.

With typical December irregularity, by noon the temperature had risen to almost fifty degrees. The snow melted rapidly, leaving behind a sea of mud and spongy earth that promised to keep Maisie busy with mop and bucket for a week of Sundays.

Contrary as a feral cat, Fiona remained stubbornly reclusive inside her room, passing the time with needlework, reading—and brooding. She wondered if Garnet would give in and hire a full-time housekeeper after she and Maisie were finally allowed to return to Richmond. After all, her hostess was the wealthy wife of a physician, and appearances must be kept, no matter that they lived in a tiny hamlet forgotten by most of the rest of the world. It was inconceivable to Fiona that the MacAllisters' only servants were a laundress who came twice a week, and a cook who left every afternoon after making preparations for their evening meal, which Garnet herself served. All right, there was the young woman with a cast to one eye who functioned as maid and nanny. But she hadn't been around since the week Fiona arrived. No doubt Maisie's blunt manner and fetish for cleaning had driven her away.

Lands, but she *was* testy today. Fiona bent over the stocking caps she was knitting for the boys at the Richmond Male Orphanage. They were Christmas presents, but she was beginning to suspect that if she wanted to hand-deliver them as usual, she would have to sneak out on foot in the dark of night. The MacAllisters were determined to keep her and Maisie in Tom's Brook through the entire holiday season.

That explained her mood, of course. The prospect of spending Christmas in the bosom of a loving family instead of Doing Good Works did little for her peace of mind.

However, her contrariness was a product of more than her present circumstances, and she may as well quit pretending otherwise. Maisie's parting remark the previous night, about Jacob's regard, had been festering ever since. At a little past three o'clock, Fiona dumped the knitting in an untidy heap, thrust her feet into a pair of boots Garnet had bought for her at the Tom's Brook Mercantile, then jerked on her coat and went outside.

Surprisingly the brief stint of exercise helped. By evening her mood, like the night's previous storm, had worn itself out. Fiona joined the family for supper with poise intact and the placid pace of her convalescence resumed. The mild temperatures and sunshine held, though her twice-daily outdoor walks remained brief; a single circuit of the house still left her exhausted. It was annoying, but Fiona forbore from querying Dr. MacAllister. Quietly determined, over the next several days she planned the timing of hers and Maisie's departure. She must leave as soon as possible, she reminded herself, because with every passing day the longing to stay intensified. It also needed to be within a fortnight in order to escape the family's Christmas celebrations. The prospect was quite simply unbearable.

Soon. It must be soon.

⥲⚬⥲

The moment he saw her, Jacob knew the plan he'd concocted on the buggy ride up here had been inspired.

"You've been cooped up too long," he announced after the greetings were over, and Robbie finally scampered off with his momentarily patient-less father. "A buggy ride's just the thing."

"That's a wonderful idea, Papa," Garnet said. She lightly bounced a fretful Daniel in her arms. "Sloan's offered a time or two, but it's not worked out."

Jacob studied Fiona, wondering what she was thinking. She was back to being wary, he'd seen instantly, with that infuriating remote politeness she affected to keep the world at bay. Yet he sensed a banked desperation as well, and with an acuity born of last week's revelation he predicted that the lady was about to bolt altogether.

"I saw a doe and two fawns in a meadow, a mile down the road," he said. "Lovely sight. The Lord's just waiting to fill us up with blessings of His bountiful nature. No telling what you might miss." He glanced at Garnet and winked. "How about if we discuss it with Sloan? He's your doctor, so perhaps we should secure his permission for—"

"I believe I'm well enough to determine whether or not I can handle a buggy ride."

"Ah. Then shall we?"

For the first few moments she sat beside him with queenly grace, not speaking, bundled up to her ears in cloak, muffler, hat, and gloves. Garnet had even tucked a blanket around her despite her protests.

"Warm enough?" Jacob asked straight-faced after they turned onto the Tom's Brook road.

"Sweltering."

"Well, we're out of sight of the house now, along with its mistress. 'Tis safe to dispense with the blanket at least."

Out of the corner of his eye he monitored her struggle to free herself from the heavy woolen fabric. After a moment he pulled Raspberry to a halt and set the brake.

"Here, we can put it under the seat." Their gloved hands brushed as he lifted the blanket away. Jacob tried not to notice the startled look in her eyes or the way she subtly flinched from his touch. "There we go. Let me know if you want it back. We'll both be in trouble if you catch a chill."

"I will. Yes."

Disheartened, he stashed the blanket, released the brake, and set the buggy in motion once more.

"Fiona."

"Yes, Jacob?"

"I meant no offense. I'm sorry if I made you feel uncomfortable."

The air between them seemed to prickle with tension-filled sparks; for a bad moment or two Jacob was afraid he'd pushed too hard, that for the whole of their outing he'd be sitting beside a marble statue. Then she spoke, her voice shifting between caution and warmth.

"You didn't offend me. I'm not accustomed to being treated with the casual familiarity of a family member, that's all."

"You're too much alone, Fiona Carlton. And since we're friends"—he turned his head so he could see her eyes—"then I see no reason why I shouldn't offer a helping hand, as it were."

"No reason at all," she murmured faintly.

They were staring at each other from a scant yard apart, yet Jacob watched in rising frustration as her gaze turned abruptly inward; he could almost feel her retreat to some distant, mist-shrouded land inside her mind, a place he could neither visit nor understand. She was so different from his Mary, who like Meredith had shared her feelings with a lavish and ofttimes indiscriminate hand.

I'm no good at this, Lord. I've lost entirely the knack for the way of a man with a maid.

That, of course, was the problem. Fiona Carlton was no longer an artless young maiden. Instead, she was very much a grand lady, with a sophistication he could never hope to attain, experience with a world he'd never seen, a lifestyle he could scarcely imagine. *She's known all over America and Europe. She played before thousands of people. Even royalty, Lord.*

"Oh, look!"

The breathless exclamation jerked him from his depressing thoughts. "What is it, then?"

"Over there—see! Just like you said. Deer, three of them. Oh, my, it's a magnificent buck. Look at the size of those antlers."

Jacob forced his gaze to follow her pointing finger, because he was far more enchanted by the rapturous joy flooding Fiona's face. "I see them. Aye, must be close to a dozen points on the big fellow." He slowed Raspberry to a walk, allowing Fiona to look her fill.

Och, but right now she more resembled that artless maiden, and precious little of the grand lady. Lovely color from the crisp bite of the wind stained her cheeks, and her eyes were alight with excitement over seeing a wild creature. The self-contained woman who had held two continents enthralled with the gift of her music had vanished in the blink of an eye.

I hear You, Jacob thought with a wry grimace heavenward. In God's eyes, Fiona Carlton was merely one of His beloved children, who for all her sophistication somehow had retained the capacity for wonder. Here, then, was the way to reach her. Not by picturing her as the grand lady he'd first met at Stillwaters, but holding in his mind a portrait of her now, with unveiled face and the uncomplicated joy of a child.

"Since you doubtless remember little of your trip from Richmond to Tom's Brook, would you like to travel along the Valley Pike for a bit, enjoy the countryside? We might not see many animals besides a herd of cows and another deer or two, but the view of the mountains is enough to bring music to even a tone-deaf soul such as myself."

"I'd like that, very much." There was a pause, then to Jacob's delight she added tartly, "Who told you that you were tone deaf? There's no such thing, merely a lack of training of the ear. Anyone may be taught to listen, and to sing even if they never play an instrument."

"Your ears would fold over themselves to muffle the sound, should you have the misfortune to hear me mangling the hymns of a Sunday at church."

"Hmph. Give me an hour with you, and a decently tuned piano, and I could have—" Silence filled the air between them again, this time so thick with atmosphere Jacob could have built a corner cupboard out of it.

He let it hover there, absently listening to the rhythmic *clip-clop* of Raspberry's hooves while he chewed over what to say to a woman who had renounced what had to have been a gift from God. Finally, he resolved that he could do no more than treat Fiona as he would have treated one of his daughters.

Or his wife.

"Can we talk about your music?" he asked her, keeping his eyes on the road and his voice comfortable. "I heard you've not played for over twenty years, since your attack. And I saw, from that night in the conservatory, that you're still grieving over the loss of it."

By the time she replied, Jacob's palms were damp inside his gloves, and he was kicking himself for his frankness. "Everyone assumed it was because of the shock of the tragedy. Do you know, not once in all these years has anyone asked me to explain?"

"Ah. And would you have explained, had they ventured to ask?"

"I don't know," she said after several more moments of nerve-stretching silence. "Nobody did."

"Until now." He allowed himself a thorough inspection of her face, lingering on the puckered white scar until her lips tightened, before he returned his attention to the road. "I'm asking you to explain, Fiona lass. Will you talk with me?"

"I— It's difficult." Flustered she was, practically stammering. Good.

"As you know, until I was brought to Tom's Brook, I tended to…to keep to myself, for the most part."

"Except for your visits, where you give only that part of yourself which cannot be wounded further."

Aye, that startled her right enough, he saw with another tug of satisfaction. "I've sore spots on my heart myself," he continued. "Matters I avoid with all the vigor of a hardheaded Scot, so I can't say I don't understand your reluctance. But over these past weeks I believe I've come to know you a wee bit better. 'Twould do you good, I'm thinking, to take out some of those old habits and examine them in the light of a crisp, clear day."

"Give them a good whack or two, like beating the dust out of a rug?"

"Precisely."

Slowly the rigidity left her shoulders. The graceful hands relaxed in her lap. She flexed the fingers, pondering them while she answered. "I haven't played a piano," she said, "because—I won't. I can't. Not anymore, not ever again, probably. But it's not the hysterical manifestation of a monstrous shock on my weak female sensibilities."

"Is that what the doctors told you?" *When she was young, injured, and terrified… Where had her fool of a husband been?*

"Yes. Bunch of pompous old windbags. Well, never mind that." She shook her head, drew in a deep breath. "For the first few years after I recovered, I would try. I needed something to fill my days, to give me a reason to live. I'd sit down on the bench, lift my hands to the keys."

She stopped, and Jacob heard her swallow several times. "I'd feel the power and the desire return, almost pulsing through my fingers. I knew I was good, you see. And that blend of knowledge and power is very seductive. It would have been so easy to immerse myself in it again, to feed upon public adoration and self-satisfaction. So I would force myself to remember the price I'd paid for that power, that desire. My husband. My looks. My *son.*" The last emerged on a strangled whisper. "That last concert, all I was thinking about was…I'll call it my technique, to spare you the details. Harry, my son, he was three-and-a-half years old. A good boy, quiet and obedient, yet so full of life. Whenever I see Robert…"

"'Tis difficult, is it?" Jacob offered quietly.

"Yes. Especially when he wants his hug. He holds his arms up, just like Harry did, that last concert. It's been twenty-two years, but I remember, as though it had happened this morning. And I—" She turned her head away, struggling for control, Jacob saw, unsurprised when it took her very little time to achieve it. "I was preoccupied. Distant. He wanted to cuddle, and I told him he could wait, that I needed to prepare myself. In effect, I placed more value in my performance than I did in my only child."

"And you've shouldered the guilt of it, ever since."

"Not as much, since I gave up the piano. I can never atone for my actions, of course, or return to the past to make a wiser choice. But choosing to renounce my career, even playing altogether, has produced a measure of peace." She smiled a peaceful enough smile to convince almost everyone.

Everyone but me, Jacob told himself with a fierceness so intense it unnerved him to the soles of his feet.

Fortunately Fiona didn't notice anything amiss. "Now I give of myself to people through spending time with them, instead of distancing myself behind an inanimate instrument," she said. "There's a different sort of satisfaction, but I like to think it's a more lasting one."

"Fiona, I feel I must tell you—the Lord does not require such a sacrifice. He's forgiven you, lass. It's no' necessary to—"

"How do you know what the Lord requires of me, Jacob?"

Stung into silence, he drove without answering for a while, staring between the horse's ears. "I overstepped," he eventually said. "You've the right of it. Your conscience is very much between yourself and the Lord. If He's told you to give up your music, why, I've no right to tell you otherwise." He cleared his throat, finishing gruffly, "It's just that as I think on it I realize I've no' half of your strength of mind. I'm thinking I could no more renounce *my* vocation than I could my faith. They're…" he fumbled for the words, "they're that bound up together, for sure."

"I'd enjoy seeing you work with your hands, Jacob." She seemed to hesitate before adding with surprising diffidence, "Would you show me your workshop?"

Right there in the middle of the road he pulled the horse to a halt and turned to Fiona. For a timeless moment they studied each other, awareness growing between them until the air was charged with sparks once more. Hot and cold prickles coursed down Jacob's spine.

They might be in a buggy, traveling south on the Valley Pike, but it had struck him deep inside, all the way to the marrow of his bones, that in truth the Lord had just set a Scottish furniture maker and a once-famous concert pianist down a different road altogether.

Thirty-Nine

SINCLAIR RUN

*W*hy on earth had she asked to see his workshop? As the buggy climbed the lane flanked by snow-tipped cedar, Fiona tried to calm her jangled nerves. It would be easier if her heart were not bumping against her rib cage and she could control the faint trembling of her limbs. Lands, but this was a fine kettle of fish for a respectable matron of her circumstances! When they rounded a curve and she caught sight of the house, a cascade of memories jammed her throat, making it difficult to swallow.

Jacob stirred beside her. "I've wondered, don't you know, what you thought of my home, that day you came to visit. 'Tis no' fancy, no' the size of Sloan's, certainly. Needs a fresh coat of paint, I'm thinking, and a new shutter on the—"

"Oh, hush now. It's beautiful," Fiona interrupted, touched and relieved by his nervousness. "Welcoming. Did you build it, Jacob?"

His face relaxed. "Aye. Took two years. Did it all myself. Now, that piece you see jutting out over there? Added it on just last year. But the rest of it's been standing there since '68. Lost the first one when that blackguard Sheridan burned the Valley."

"Even after all this time, sometimes it seems as if it happened yesterday, doesn't it? So much suffering, so much loss, on both sides," Fiona murmured. "I was studying piano theory and technique in Ohio. My father wouldn't let me come home. He said Richmond wasn't safe. I remember weeping all night into my pillow when I heard that our own men had set fire to the business district when they evacuated the city. But I also heard that one of the other girls in my boardinghouse had learned her father was a prisoner of war. In Richmond, at Libby Prison. He died two days before General Lee surrendered. *Two days.* I realized then I was not the only one suffering."

"Aye. 'Twas a terrible conflict for the whole country." He clucked to the horse, and with pricked ears the animal moved into a trot the rest of the way up the lane. "But the north lost only men. Not their lands nor their homes."

"Yes," Fiona said, her voice soft, "I know." Until Fiona herself passed on, the ravaged face of Irene Walker, Benjamin's mother—and Fiona's benefactor—would remain an aching reminder of that truth. "I've yet to tell him this, but when I was a child, my family attended the same church as your son-in-law Benjamin's family. We didn't have a piano, and my mother had talked the minister into letting me practice on an old square pianoforte at the church. One day Benjamin's mother heard me playing. Next thing I knew, I was seated in front of an ebonized grand piano in the Walkers' conservatory. I still remember the joy I felt when I heard what sound I could produce on that magnificent instrument."

Jacob pulled the horse to a halt in front of a large square building of weathered clapboard. His expression, Fiona saw in some amusement, was one of utter amazement. "You knew Benjamin's family? *Meredith's* Benjamin?"

"Yes. But I scarcely knew Benjamin. He was only a baby when I left for the conservatory in Ohio. I'm sure you know that, before the War, the Walker family was one of the finest in Virginia." *Why is it that You seem to always take the finest prematurely?* She stopped, waiting for the residue of the unbottled past to settle before continuing. "It was the Walkers' influence and generosity that gained my entrance into Professor Himmel's studio when I was only fourteen. At the time it was a miracle, to me. The professor had studied under Muzio Clementi himself."

In hindsight, of course, *miracle* was not the word she would choose. Even after all these years Fiona wondered at the workings of the Almighty. Through the munificence of one family the course of her life had been determined, for it was Professor Himmel who introduced her to Gerald. Already a prominent conductor of some renown, he shared her obsession for musical perfection in a way that seemed preordained; when Fiona finally returned to Richmond after Lee's surrender at Appomattox, it had been as his fiancée as well as his protégée.

But the Walker family was no longer there to share in the joy of the moment. And the magnificent brick mansion Horace Walker's great-grandfather had built before the Revolutionary War now belonged to strangers.

"You must tell Benjamin the story," Jacob said. "He seldom says so, but I know the loss of his entire family and his heritage still grieves him at the odd moment."

With good reason, Fiona thought. He deserved to have fine memories of them to cherish, yet every time she considered writing to him or telling him in person, something stopped her. She didn't want Benjamin to feel obligated to her in any way. He was very like his parents. Like—Jacob. Regardless of Fiona's secret fears, or perhaps because of them, she was drawn to the entire family by a force even more powerful than her entrenched fears. "I will, one day. The timing needs to be right."

"'Tis a constant marvel to me, the Lord's guiding hand in our lives," Jacob mused then, and she started in surprise. He lifted a questioning eyebrow. "Why did you jump? For sure you've marveled at it yourself, especially these past weeks, knowing already of the common bond between us all."

"Actually, it was because I was thinking the same thing, more or less." Fiona decided not to confess that her attitude toward "the Lord's guiding hand" likely differed from Jacob's. "Is this your workshop?"

"What? Oh, aye." She could tell he was reluctant to change the subject. "Here. Let me help you down. I'll show you the place, then we'll go on up to the house. Effie's been after meeting you, all these weeks."

Fiona doubted that, but she set aside her foreboding and allowed Jacob to usher her though the workshop door.

Inside the deserted building was a dusky, magical place, full of mysterious tools and pieces of wood of all shapes and sizes. Half-formed furniture that hinted of the maker's skill. The fragrant tang of wood shavings, linseed oil, and a scent Fiona could only describe as creative, twitched her nostrils. Fascinated, she prowled, indifferent to her skirts dragging through the sawdust-riddled floor, trailing her fingers over complicated bits of machinery, the smooth unfinished surface of an evolving corner table. The worn knob of a plane.

Abruptly she turned to Jacob. "Will you let me watch you work? I'd like to, very much, if it wouldn't bother you."

For a moment he stood still, one hand resting on some piece of equipment. Silvery light poured through the window behind him, shadowing his face so that she couldn't read his expression. "It wouldn't bother me at all," he finally said. "But I'm not sure it would be a good thing. I tend to, ah, lose myself in my work, as it were. I might forget you were here."

"I understand. I was the same way myself, once." She hesitated, then threw caution out the window. Something about Jacob always seemed to pull her out of herself, though for the life of her she couldn't understand why. "I want to watch your hands. I...I always notice people's hands, the way they work with them. I'd like to see you create something beautiful, something useful. It would—" She stopped again, overwhelmed that she'd been about to blurt such a deeply private need.

"It would what, Fiona?"

He stepped closer, reaching up to yank on a long string. Light from a naked bulb bathed them in a lemony glow, illuminating his face, and she realized again the source of some of that strange tugging: Jacob Sinclair might not be a striking man, as far as appearances went, but he had kind eyes. She remembered now that his kindness had lured her from the first time they'd met.

"Help me," she finished, her head tilting slightly. "It would help me."

"Ah. Because you feel as though you've lost the music in your own hands, is that it?"

"For a man who thinks of himself as a simple furniture maker with no formal education, you see people with extraordinary clarity, Jacob."

He fiddled a lock of hair that drooped over his forehead, a bittersweet smile curving his mouth. "Not always, Fiona lass. Not always, I'm afraid. Leah, especially, would be more than willing to tell you of the many times I've been naught but a dunderhead."

"Leah struggles to understand you as well. Did you know?" The constriction about her rib cage began to ease. "She told me about the heartwood chests you made for each of your daughters, about her flower bulb."

"Aye? Well, then. You see the truth of how much of a dunderhead I can be."

"What I see instead is a loving father, one who has done a fine job of rearing three beautiful daughters."

His face turned red, and he cleared his throat a time or two. "I love them, that's all. The Lord accomplished the rest."

The heartache always caught her off guard, no matter that she had struggled for two decades to cloak herself in armor thick enough to withstand it. "At least He allowed all your daughters to reach adulthood," she murmured.

"Your son, your wee son. I forgot. I'm sorry. Here I am, gloating over my blessings… Forgive me, Fiona."

He looked so abashed that Fiona found herself rushing to reassure him. "Please don't apologize. I shouldn't have said that. It wasn't fair or kind, especially when I've had the pleasure of enjoying all three of your daughters. Why, since I met her here, last summer, Leah has become a dear friend, almost, if you'll forgive me, like a daughter. Garnet as well. Your family has been very generous to me."

"And so they should," he said gruffly. "But I still ask your pardon all the same, for my insensitivity."

"I tell you again there's no need. Jacob," she stepped closer, "I don't begrudge you your life or your daughters. We live in an ugly world, where freedom of choice produces evil deeds as well as good. Why blame God, when I enjoy the same free will as you and your daughters, or even the madwoman who attacked me? My…anger against life, if you will, burned out long ago. One of the few gifts of aging, wouldn't you agree, is the flattening out of one's passions." She paused, wondering at the brief, strange flicker in his eyes. "Perhaps I should apologize to you. Listen to me, foisting my personal trials onto your shoulders."

"I've cultivated a pair of broad ones, what with three lasses and my vocation." He turned away, gesturing toward a dust-coated straight-backed chair sitting off to one side. "Here. You're looking a wee bit tired.

Sit for a spell. I'll plane a board or two, then we'll go to the house for refreshments, before I take you back."

As he spoke he grabbed a stained cloth off a worktable and wiped down the chair. Fiona thanked him and sat, sending him one last searching look he ignored by mumbling something about fetching his work apron.

I've become entirely too sensitive to atmosphere, she scolded herself. With a grateful sigh she settled back, allowing the weariness to drain out of her body and into the wide planks of the floorboards. She was so tired of that weariness. And it was so peaceful here. Dreamily she watched the jerky movements of Jacob's hands calm as he lost himself in an obviously familiar routine, until each movement became the kind of poetry in motion she loved to watch.

She fell sound asleep, her head resting against the chair's back, drifting off to the comforting lullaby of the plane scraping a piece of wood into perfection beneath a master's hands.

⤜❧⤏

"There's a full house tonight, despite this annoying rain. Are you ready?"

"Of course I'm ready. Aren't I always?" She flexed her hands, fretful because the fine trembling seemed to be growing worse. Months had passed, and the inability to discipline her inner fears both angered and dismayed her. Ever since Gerald received that first passionate note, followed by the scribbled threat to Fiona, she had been losing the battle. "Gerald? What if she's here?"

"I told you to forget about that deranged woman. I've hired guards, private detectives. You've nothing to worry about." He came back, looming over her, his thin, severely handsome face distorted by irritation. His sideburns twitched with it, betraying the clenched jaw. "We're famous, my dear. The toast of two continents, the darlings of the press. This morning we made the front page. Listen to this." He snatched up a newspaper. "They even published a reprint of the article in the London papers, from your concert there last month. 'The ongoing debate over Fiona Carlton's incredible technique. Does her playing follow the Thalberg style, or Franz Liszt? All of New York has joined the frenzy, thanks to—'"

307

Suddenly he threw the paper aside, chained her wrist in a forceful grip and lifted her hand in front of her face. "Stop it! This ridiculous fretting will damage your concentration. It will blur the brilliance. You know better."

"Gerald…that last note she wrote…she threatened Harry."

"The ravings of a lunatic, a jealous madwoman." He leaned down until their noses almost touched, his eyes hard, almost black as piano keys in their intensity. "Do you want to make a fool of yourself out there? Ruin your reputation?" Straightening, he smoothed the lapels of his swallowtail coat. "There's always another budding virtuoso in the wings, hoping to reap the rewards of your mistakes."

Her spine stiffened. "I don't make mistakes. You just see that you don't make any either. Try to remember how we practiced the Andante movement of the Beethoven. I told you not to rush it."

"You play. I'll conduct."

Harry bounded into the room ahead of his nanny, and the stolid policeman assigned to guard his every step. "Mamá! Mamá, I've come for hugs!"

"I know, darling." Mindful of the orchestra warming up, she gave him a perfunctory peck on the cheek. "There. No, don't cling, dear. You'll crush Mama's corsage." Over the small head she met Gerald's look of smothered impatience. "Go along with Nanny. I have to prepare."

"Hugs?"

"Your mother has to focus, so she can play her best." Gerald gestured to the quiet German girl he'd hired to care for their son. "Take him away. He's distracting."

Fiona watched the thin little face so like Gerald's crumple with disappointment, but heedful of her husband's warning, in her mind she was already rehearsing a difficult couple of measures in the Brahms sonata, her opening piece tonight. "You can wait," she said. "Just for a few hours. I'll wake you up for our cuddle time after we return to the hotel."

"Promise?"

"Hmm? Oh, yes, of course…"

The music reached a raucous climax in her ears until the roar throbbed inside her head. Gerald's baton swayed back and forth, up and down, faster and faster until the musicians' hands seemed to melt into their instruments. The crowd swelled, pressing around her so she couldn't move her arms, couldn't play. She ordered them back, but they shrieked in open-mouthed laughter, devouring her with their eyes. She caught sight of Harry, borne aloft in a sea of waving arms as he called to her, his voice lost in the swirling maelstrom.

Out of nowhere the knife appeared, shiny and sleek, weaving like a serpent through the crowd, growing larger and larger until it blocked her vision. She couldn't see her son, couldn't reach him. "Harry," she tried to call, but boiling waves reared up, swallowing the crowd, the piano—her son. Then they crashed over her, pouring into her throat. She was drowning, she was burning, there was nobody to help her and on a sob of utter despair she threw out a hand, begging, pleading as fire and water spilled through her.

❦

"Fiona! Wake up, there's a lass. You're all right now. Wake up, you've had a nightmare."

It was the warmth, and the voice's comforting burr that penetrated the madness, drawing Fiona up, up out of the deadly ocean. Her eyelids flickered; she couldn't breathe. Couldn't see. Panting, she tried to lift her hand.

"Shh, now. Dinna fear. 'Tis all right. Here…" A soft cloth that smelled vaguely of cedar wiped her eyes. Her cheeks.

Jacob. Jacob Sinclair. She blinked, tried to speak, but all that emerged from her locked throat muscles was a pitiful sob. Ashamed and disoriented, she made an abortive effort to rise, but the nightmare had sapped her strength.

"No," Jacob said. "Don't run."

Somehow his arm was around her shoulders, holding her in the chair while he stood above her, his voice low, his very presence both a support and a bulwark. Defenses crumbling, she finally managed to lift her hand, brushing the back of his where it curved over her upper arm.

"So long," she choked out. "It's been so long, since I've been held…" Then, because her throat was peppery with burning tears, she pressed her scarred cheek against Jacob's side and wept.

Forty

*I*t was not at all like holding one of his girls. Jacob gazed down at the silvery-gold braid wrapped about her head. Fiona Carlton. Fiona. *Lord? What is this You have planted in my heart?*

Her shoulders shook with the force of her weeping; tears soaked the linen of his shirt, burning through to his skin. He hugged her harder, his hand stroking up and down her arm while he spoke to her, random phrases of comfort, unintelligible sounds, even a word or two of Gaelic. When Fiona's hand blindly reached out, Jacob felt his heart crack open. A torrent of emotion swamped his insides as he clasped her hand in his own.

For a long time they remained thus. Even when his back commenced to ache and his knees stiffened, Jacob continued to hold Fiona in the protective shelter of his arm. He could scarcely credit that this incredibly strong, self-contained, quintessential *lady* had chosen to reveal her wounded soul to a man such as himself. Like Leah, she was not an easy weeper. The sobs torn from her were deep, wrenching, her body taut with distress.

Och, likely she would be a fine mess when she came to herself. Jacob smiled a little, knowing from experience that his greatest challenge would be to convince her he was not a whit disturbed by red noses and swollen eyes.

Against his side Fiona mumbled something incoherent.

"Dinna fash yourself," he told her, his voice tender. "Cry it out, dear one."

Her hand tightened convulsively in his. "I…can't seem to stop," she gasped. "Jacob…I can't…" Her breath wheezed as she labored to take in air between the sobs.

All right then. "Easy. No need to panic now. I'm going to lift you." He stepped in front of her, then pulled her to a standing position, supporting her with one arm. "Come along with me now, there's a lass. Walk, Fiona. One step at a time. That's it." Slowly he led her across the room to the huge galvanized sink he'd fitted against one wall. "A nice cool cloth ought to help, I'm thinking. Can you stand on your own, for only a moment? Aye, for sure you can, that's it…yes, hold on to the rim of the sink."

He kept up the easy banter while he retrieved a clean square from the stack of neatly cut up rags Effie supplied periodically, wet the cloth, then turned to Fiona, hesitating while he debated how free he should be with his care. Fiona herself decided the matter: She made no move to take the cloth, merely stood with drooped shoulders, weaving a bit on her feet, her hands clinging to the sink.

As though it were the most natural thing in the world, Jacob cupped her chin, then held the cool cloth against first one cheek, then the other. Fiona finally reacted when the tips of his fingers brushed over the scar. She flinched, trying to turn her head aside.

"Don't." Jacob placed his hand over her undamaged cheek, holding her still. "I've told you before, you don't have to hide your face from me, Fiona."

"I don't want you to touch it. It's…ugly." The words emerged still thick with tears, but he could see the worst was over.

"It's no more ugly than Garnet's freckles or these lines scoring my forehead. And I've enough scars on my hands to rival a cutting board."

She took the cloth out of his hand, backing away from his touch as she pressed it over the scar. "Leah's more honest. She didn't hesitate to admit the truth."

Something feathered the length of his spine, a burning tingle Jacob seldom experienced, though he recognized it instantly. Anger. Aye, the emotion could still ignite inside him fierce and strong when he was provoked beyond a certain point.

"Her intentions are noble, but Leah occasionally has a way of telling the truth that wounds, rather than cleanses," he said. "Everyone carries scars. I'm thinking the unseen ones are often more unsightly. More painful. But you will listen to me, Fiona, and hear me when I tell you that when I look at you, what I see is a beautiful woman. A woman of rare strength. A woman whose eyes mirror both peace and pain."

At the moment, they also mirrored incipient panic. "Jacob, what—"

"I see a woman who has done a fair job of twisting my tongue into knots and reducing my good intentions to sawdust." Deliberately he stepped close and tugged her hand away from her damaged cheek, keeping his fingers wrapped about her wrist. "I'm thinking, lass, that you and I might be needing to see if there's to be more between us than friendship."

Holding her still, Jacob cupped her face. After the anticipated jerk of her head, Fiona turned rigid as a singletree, though he could feel the pulse galloping in her wrist. Calmly, lovingly, he traced the uneven line of the scar from the corner of her temple, down her cheek. Hectic color flooded her already tear-splotched face. "This scar is a part of who you are," he said, his voice roughened by emotion. "But it does not make you ugly, any more than the scars left by cruel nails mar the body of our risen Lord."

Fiona blinked once, then slowly nodded. "In twenty-two years, nobody has touched my face," she whispered then. "Nobody who could see it. I'd forgotten…" Her voice faded into a thrumming silence.

"High time someone did." Jacob said. "Time you were reminded." He could no more prevent his next action than he could stop rain from falling. Leaning forward, he pressed a kiss against her temple, then tenderly trailed his mouth the length of the scar.

When he finally lifted his head, he could scarce draw a breath, stunned by the overwhelming urge to haul her into a complete embrace and kiss her half-parted lips with the passion of a man half his age.

Instead he released her and stepped back. Their labored breaths rattled noisily through the stillness of his workshop.

Moments passed. Neither of them moved; for Jacob, the process of recovering his control reminded him of the unpleasant sensation of surfacing from a laudanum-saturated sleep. He wondered what was going through Fiona's mind. She gazed unblinking at him with a peculiar expression in her lovely ice-blue eyes. He smiled crookedly at her. "Did you know, I haven't kissed a woman, excepting my daughters, in a score of years? I hope I haven't forgotten entirely the way of it."

Fiona didn't smile back, but he glimpsed a stirring of humor, like a sunbeam lighting a cloud-choked sky. "You haven't." She swallowed several times. Her hand lifted, her fingers touching the cheek he'd kissed. "This is very strange," she murmured.

"Aye. Sometimes the Lord likes to shake us up a bit. Push us free of the cages we build around ourselves." The scent of her still lingered, the softness of her saturated his blood until he was lightheaded with it. "Fiona, I want to kiss you again."

"Jacob." She sighed, her gaze dropping to the damp cloth still clutched in her fingers. "What you're thinking—it's too complicated. We're not young people, with their lives ahead of them. There's too much history."

"Pshaw. We may have passed springtime, but we're no' in the dead of winter." He folded his arms to keep from snatching her against his chest and demonstrating the truth of his assertion. "To my way of looking at it, there's little to compare to the blazing colors God paints the world in, come the autumn. Red and orange and gold—all the colors of fire. Look me in the eye, Fiona, and tell me you didn't feel the burning between us just now."

"I don't know." She seemed to recover some of her formidable reserve, along with a quiet resolve. "No, that's not right. I do know. I'm just not prepared to dissect the matter. You're"—her gaze wavered, steadied—"too volatile. And I'm...too vulnerable. This has caught me by surprise."

"Aye," Jacob admitted, "I can see that. Sometimes, dear one, that's how it happens. But it doesn't make the feelings any less intense. Nor," he finished evenly, "does it make them wrong. I canna believe that the Lord would bring this about, were it not in some way for our good and His glory."

"A noble sentiment. One I'm sure couples have cited to justify their passions since long before Samson met Delilah."

He could feel the skin on the back of his neck sting with the heat. Angry and hurt, Jacob swiveled on his heel and retreated several feet.

Even Leah at her most pragmatic had never jabbed at the heart of his faith. *And did she no' feel the heat, after all?* Had he misspoken, misunderstood the signs? He was at a loss, not knowing what to do, what to say to rectify what had become one of the most humiliating moments of his life.

Gradually he realized there was pressure being applied to his forearm. When he glanced down, his gaze focused on the long musician's fingers resting lightly near the buttons on the cuff of his shirt.

"I'm sorry," she said. "I had no right to say what I did."

"Why did you?" He knew his voice was more growl than grace, the rawness still too fresh.

Her hand fell to her side. "I was embarrassed, by my hysteria. And I believe I mentioned I'm not used to—to being touched. What I felt, when you kissed me…" She drew herself straight, but Jacob could hear the timbre of fear licking through her words, "I didn't know I was still capable of feeling that depth of emotion."

"Ah." Slowly his muscles began to unknot. He tried a tentative smile. "'Twould seem not all passion fades with aging, hmm?"

"No," Fiona whispered, so softly the word was more of a weary exhalation. Color deepening anew, her hand lifted to the scar. Her reflexive vulnerability never failed to move him. "You were right, about a lot of things. Even God's hand in your life, in mine. I… The expression of my faith has always been as intensely private as the rest of my life. Not at all like yours and the rest of your family. But just because I'm uncomfortable does not give me the right to belittle the honest expression of yours." The ghost of a smile finally appeared. "You're more like Leah than you realize. You don't know how to be anything *but* honest, do you? It's very disconcerting."

"No more so than you." Jacob was finally able to draw in a good deep breath. "Thank you for giving me honesty in return. You caused me a bad moment or two there."

"Jacob, I need some time. Time to assimilate what is happening between us. Will you give it to me?"

"Aye, lass. I'll give you time." He pondered her silently, then let out his breath in a long sigh. "I wouldn't force you down a path you haven't chosen of your own free will. I've known for years that the Lord does not always speak to hearts in the same way, at the same time. I forgot that, just now. What happened…" He struggled, searching for the right words, "I was not prepared for the force of it myself. So we'll take it slow, for both of us."

Fiona nodded. "You mentioned scars on the inside earlier. You need to know that I have some of those as well." She stared at their clasped hands, then lifted her gaze to his. "For more than a score of years I've been alone, not only by choice but because I thought there *was* no choice. I don't know how I feel about allowing someone in my life. But if I do, Jacob Sinclair, the end result must be—marriage. Anything less would be"—she paused, thinking for a long time—"unbearable. Do you understand what I'm telling you?"

"I do." The words rang out in an eerie mimicry of the marital vow. "Would you be willing to live here, at Sinclair Run, Fiona?"

She looked around the workshop, then back into his face. After a long time she spoke, the tone cautious, her gaze pleading. "I was an only child. Both my parents are gone. I have an aunt somewhere in Georgia, I believe. She moved, to get away from the scandal. I've heard nothing from her or her family since. Gerald's family disowned me when Gerald died. There is nothing for me in Richmond that can equal the home you have created here, with your hands and with your heart. But willing though my spirit might be, neither my flesh nor my heart is as malleable as they were when I was eighteen."

"That, dear one, will be the least of my concerns. 'Tis the Lord's business to give you a new heart and new life." He took her arm, as much to steady himself as Fiona. "If you ask Him for it, that is."

"Oh, I'll be asking, in my own way, as you will be. I'll be interested to see how, and when, God chooses to answer."

Forty-One

ESTHER HAYS SCHOOL FOR YOUNG LADIES
DECEMBER 1895

*L*eah surveyed the uniformly revolted expressions of twenty-four young ladies. "This is not pleasant," she admitted, holding up the limp carcass of a pigeon. The equally unappealing carcass of a rabbit lay waiting on the table. "But all of you who were assigned to this course are here because you've little experience in the culinary arts. Quite likely your future circumstances will not always allow you the luxury of ordering your fowl or wild game already trussed and prepared for roasting from the butcher. So today's lesson in household management will be a step-by-step demonstration, from plucking to singeing to trussing, of a pigeon"—she held the bird high—"and if there's time, a rabbit."

"If I stay here, I'm going to be sick," one of the girls wailed.

"You don't expect *us* to help, do you, Miss Sinclair?"

"I'd rather do without meat than perform such an odious task."

Leah laid the pigeon aside, washed and dried her hands, then walked around the huge working table. "You will all, before the end of the year, have the opportunity, and you will consider it as such, to perfect this aspect of cookery art. Or do you entertain the foolish hope that you will marry a rich, titled gentleman from Europe who will take you to live in a mansion with an army of servants, complete with chef and cooking staff? Is that why you're here at Miss Esther's?"

Eyes fluttered, feet shuffled, and an embarrassed giggle or two was hastily stifled. Then one of the girls raised her hand.

"Yes, Cynthia?" Leah leaned back against the worktable, keeping her expression serene. Cynthia Spauling had established herself as a bright but wearisome girl whose favorite pastime was to bait her teachers. "You wish to be my first volunteer?"

Cynthia vigorously shook her head, setting her fashionably short ringlets to bouncing. "Do you want us to learn how to do this because of what happened to you, when you had to spend the night with Mr. Beringer in the wilderness?"

A titter swept the rapt students, all of them eyeing Leah with bright, expectant eyes.

"I'll answer your question," she said, "after you rephrase it to reflect not only respect, but the entire truth."

For weeks her adventure, and subsequent engagement to Cade, had created a firestorm of gossip. Leah wondered grumpily if she would ever regain her former stature at the school. Mrs. Gribble had refused to speak to her at all for a month, and even now the school secretary's mien was likely to be full of reproach, as though she believed Leah had deliberately arranged the accident. Leah's letters to Cade more often than not reflected a growing frustration with the small-mindedness of people, particularly people who called themselves Christians.

"I wasn't trying to be disrespectful, Miss Sinclair," Cynthia returned with enough innocence to belie the assertion. "But you did spend—"

"A lot of time preparing for today's class," Leah interrupted. "Which you are now in the process of wasting." She made a show of examining the face of her chatelaine watch. "Unfortunately, due to the perishable nature of my two specimens here, we must remain in class until the lesson is learned, no matter what the hour. I do hope none of you had anything pressing for this afternoon."

Cynthia's innocent air evaporated. "The Christmas fete," she blurted. "Miss Sinclair, what about the fete at the Hotel Jefferson?"

All the older girls had been invited to attend the lavish dinner. The hotel had just opened that fall, and was purported to be the finest hotel in all the South. The prospect of a formal dinner in the city's finest hotel had kept the girls whispering and madly planning for an entire week. Now every one of them glared at the abashed Cynthia, obviously afraid that Leah would detain all of them as punishment. Leah let the hostility gather for a few moments before she briskly walked back around the table and lifted the pigeon.

"I suppose," she mused to the limp bird, "we can learn how to prepare fowl today, and I could donate the rabbit to Cook. Save wild game for another time." She smiled at her students. "Which suits me, I confess. Though I've no doubt I could have done so, I was relieved Mr. Beringer prepared the rabbit he snared for roasting, on the occasion to which Cynthia referred. But if he hadn't been available, of the other five people stranded there I was the only one with sufficient knowledge."

Then, conscientious to the end, she added, "Of course, since I never learned any other skills necessary to survive in the wilderness, I proved to be of little use at all." Which was why she was discussing a change in the curriculum with Miss Esther, to include some of those typically nonfeminine skills most boys seemed to learn almost from the cradle.

Everyone relaxed, and though there were the usual assortment of groans and gagging noises, for the rest of the class Leah enjoyed the girls' undivided attention. By the time each of twenty-four fumbling fingers had attempted to skewer the chicken, Leah's back was burning, and the smell of raw poultry was making her queasy. But she maintained an air of confident optimism as they all lined up at the sinks to clean up. She was drying her own hands, exchanging remarks with several girls, when a movement in the doorway caught her eye.

"Cade!" Surprised, caught off guard by a tumult of joy and shyness and uncertainty, Leah stood with dangling hands, frozen in place.

The girls were not so reticent. They scurried past her in an eager whirl, calling his name, their faces flushed, voices high with excitement. There was not a female alive, Leah well knew, capable of resisting Cade's charismatic blend of courtliness and unaffected masculinity.

"What a welcome!" He accepted their attentions with the long practice of a man comfortable with female company, bestowing smiles and jovial remarks though his gaze continually returned to Leah's.

Slowly she approached him, her mouth cottony and her heart stuttering. It had been five long and lonely weeks since his last visit; Leah was ashamed of the secret fear she harbored, that their separation would dim and eventually destroy his love for her. After all, she was the one who had insisted that she could not resign her position in the middle of the year, and she was the one who had insisted that Cade owed Benjamin an equal obligation.

"Hey." A long finger tipped her chin up.

He was so close her heart leapt into her throat before she realized that with his usual skillful diplomacy he had dismissed her students. The room was empty, save for Cade and herself. "I didn't even notice they'd left," she whispered.

"I'd like to think that was because all you could see was me," Cade said. Swiftly he pressed a kiss to her mouth, then stepped back, brushing her cheekbone with the back of his hand. "You're thinking too much again, I can see. What are we going to do about you, sweetheart?"

"This past spring, I remember wishing my brain was like Papa's watch, so I could press a knob and my head would pop open so I could remove my brain. Not think for a while." She looked him over from his neatly combed hair to the natty single-breasted frock coat and expertly knotted tie, to the narrow creased trousers and patent leather–capped boots. "Meredith and Benjamin picked this out?"

He laughed. "Of course. Left to me, I'd throw on the first thing I pulled off the hook. After we're married, the duty falls to you, my love. Perhaps you'll have to regiment an outfit for each day of the week, to coordinate with your—Leah? What is it?"

She shook her head, turned to straighten the worktable, stack notebooks—anything to occupy her attention.

"It was the remark about being married, wasn't it?" Cade asked, following behind her. His hands closed over her shoulders with such gentleness the ice coagulating in her veins dissolved. He turned her around, his eyes probing, yet soft with understanding. "How about if I take you to dinner somewhere, so we can talk? Remember the meeting I was to have next week, with the assemblyman from Harrisonburg? It was changed. Now it's first thing in the morning. I traveled all night, booked into my hotel two hours ago, and cleaned up. That means we have the rest of the afternoon and evening together. You're through with classes for the day, aren't you?"

"Why didn't you let me know you were coming?" Leah asked, when she was able to speak naturally. She couldn't continue. Cade knew her well, and already his bright green eyes were shadowed with disappointment. Disappointment—and a grimness so out of character the ice crystals returned to her veins. "Tonight's the Christmas banquet at the Hotel Jefferson—I wrote you about it," she continued in a brittle voice. "And after the meal, I'm making a speech in the Tea Room, for the Ladies Literary Society. If I had known—"

"There wasn't time to let you know." He shrugged, running a thumb around the knot of his tie. "I only found out about the time change for my appointment last night, by telegram. He and his family decided to go to Florida for Christmas. I barely had time to pack and catch the last eastbound train. If I don't make this appointment, there's little chance until late next spring to present my case for creating state-protected forest reserves." Not looking at her now, he stepped back, distancing himself physically as well as mentally.

In an instant the atmosphere had changed, so radically Leah couldn't grasp it. Couldn't make sense of what was happening between them, how such a trifling matter as conflicting schedules could be blown so out of proportion. She had never seen Cade like this and felt as though she had been sucked into the wrong end of a telescope, shrinking, shrinking while Cade receded out of her reach.

For the past three months she'd been deceiving herself. That must be it. Love, and Cade's persuasiveness, had fooled her into thinking that the obstacles they faced would be cleared away simply because they loved each other. Yet…wasn't she also learning to trust? God's hand *did* lend guidance, in her life as well as Cade's. Miracles did happen. Miracles required trust, not explanations.

"I wasn't accusing you of anything," she told him now. "Cade, I wish—"

"'If wishes were horses, beggars might ride.' And that's what I'm feeling like about now." He jerked at the neatly knotted tie, then expelled a frustrated breath that made Leah wince. "A beggar, pleading for crumbs of your attention. I know, I know my reaction is upsetting you. I know that, in the scheme of things, what God requires of me is to wait patiently."

"Cade, had I known you were coming—"

"Had you known I still doubt you would have said no to the Ladies Literary Society. That would mean you'd have to put me first for a change." Abruptly he stalked past her, over to the row of windows. Hands braced on the sill, he stood with his back to Leah, the broad line of his shoulders more of a reproach than a slap.

"Cade," she whispered, too low for him to hear, nor could he see the pleading hand she held out. She needed to go to him, needed to say something, *do* something to break this tension so they could communicate intelligently. She was equipped to handle masculine indifference, ridicule, resentment—even dislike—but not from Cade. His response was completely alien to his character, and the only conclusion Leah could draw left her mind a blank sheet of foolscap, her heart as trussed in knots as that worthless carcass on the worktable.

Is this the end of it, God? Had the Almighty brought them together only to teach her that logic and science could be compatible with emotion and faith? Perhaps the love she and Cade shared had been intended within God's purpose as merely *phileo,* the love of friends for each other.

Denial, white-hot in its intensity, lanced her. "That's not fair."

"What?"

She jumped, only then realizing she had spoken aloud, and that Cade had turned back around. He remained at the window, his hands behind his back gripping the sill. "What isn't fair?" he repeated. "My being here? My inability to hide my disappointment? My needs? Which of those are unfair, Leah?"

The words fell between them like stones. "None of them, Cade," she whispered. "I was…actually, I was talking to God." The astonishment that streaked across Cade's face was almost comical. Leah's chin jutted and her hands clenched. "I'm afraid of what's happening between us. Afraid of what God intends, of what He might have planned all along."

"What," he asked in a deadly quiet voice, "do you mean by that remark?"

"You're the one with all the confidence in the ways of the Lord. You're the idealist, the Christian who strides boldly into the lions' den, sure in your faith that God will close their mouths and bring you through unscathed. I'm not like that."

"I've never asked you to be."

"No, you haven't asked. But the implication is there, in every letter you write to me, every look, every gesture when we're together. You came here today without even letting me know. But when I'm unable to alter my plans to accommodate yours, you act as though I've somehow betrayed you. I love you," she burst out. "Do you think I can't *feel* the yearning inside you, can't know that your every prayer is that I will turn into a...a nineteenth-century Ruth?"

Cade's complexion turned ashen. "I don't deserve that, Leah."

"Can you deny its truth?"

"I won't deny that I want to marry you, that I detest the distance between us." His eyelids drooped, screening the searing hurt Leah had glimpsed for a moment. "And I won't apologize for loving you so much that yes, I wish you did have the urge to forsake all, follow me wherever I'm compelled to go."

When Leah started to speak, an expression filled his face that caused all feeling to leave her knees. Cade went on. "But I knew almost from the beginning, that you would never do that. You've been equally transparent in your glances and gestures. Every time our talk turns to marriage, or a wedding, you change the subject, turn pale as though contemplating some heinous act. So I've waited, I've tried to give you time. I've seen what a magnificent teacher you are, how much your students admire you. And I'd ask myself how I could ask you to give that up for a rural one-room schoolhouse. Then I'd stand at the crest of a mountain, surrounded by nothing but the sky, seeing nothing but an ocean of forest that, unless someone lifts a voice, will disappear within the next twenty years. How, I asked God, could I lift *my* hand from plowing the field I have felt called to cultivate for half my life?"

Mechanically Leah shook her head. "You can't," she said, the words almost harsh because she'd had to squeeze them past her locked-up throat. "I can't change who I am, either."

He stood in front of her, this man she loved but could not conform to, and she watched the broad shoulders flex, the jaw set as he gazed across three feet of space that seemed more like three miles. "What I want—wanted, is irrelevant now. What either of us wanted no longer matters. Perhaps it never did. That's a lesson God seems to have to teach me over and over again. With every hillside I see ravaged by greedy mine owners, with every three-hundred-year-old yellow poplar I see toppled to slice into lumber, He was trying to tell me that what I want is not as important as doing His will—"

"Doing His will?" Leah lashed back, panicked and furious that he would twist everything around. Cade was trying to corner her, make her acquiesce to *his* will, not God's! "What makes you so sure of the nature of that will? Did it ever occur to you that perhaps the Lord cares more about our attitude than He does our actions? That regardless of what we do with our lives, as long as we're trying to honor His name, is it remotely conceivable to you that God could bless us wherever we are, whatever we happen to be doing at any given moment?"

When Cade finally spoke, his voice had gone flat, shorn of emotion. "Who are you trying to apply that truth to? Me—or yourself? My faith, my vocation—or yours?"

The ugly words spewed up and out before she could halt the flow. "Ben was right, wasn't he? You hide behind God. Everything you ever told me was a lie, all designed to manipulate me where *you* wanted to go. That's not a love I want, or need." Blinded by hurt and rage, for the first time in her life Leah was out of control. She couldn't live up to Cade Beringer's expectations. After all they'd been through together, she still wasn't the woman for him. *She wasn't good enough.*

She looked him straight in the eye, ramming the words home. Suddenly she couldn't resist the desire to hurt Cade as much as he had hurt her. "I was right, too. We're mismatched. Unequally yoked within our faith. I don't want your love, because you don't really need mine. You have God and your vocation. Looks like that's all I have as well."

A terrible silence filled the room.

Then his hand made an abrupt slashing movement, the only visible sign of turmoil. "Apparently it was foolish of me all these months to assume that my commitment and willingness to sacrifice would be reciprocated. Don't worry. I won't make that mistake ever again."

Without another word, not looking at Leah, he walked across the room, opened the door, then too gently shut it behind him.

Forty-Two

RICHMOND, VIRGINIA
JANUARY 1896

$\mathcal{F}$iona was in the attic, lost in memories, when Maisie hailed her from the bottom of the narrow staircase.

"Got a visitor, Miz Carlton. Leah Sinclair."

At last! About time too. Neither of them had seen Leah since Fiona returned to Richmond, the week before Christmas. She laid aside a dust-coated collection of piano sonatas. "Tell her I'll be along," she called back. "If you're not too busy, could you see about preparing some refreshments?"

"Don't need to, ma'am. Pay her no mind, she tells me, then calm as a mortician informs me she'll help herself so's I wouldn't be disrupted from polishing the door handles. Miz Carlton? Not my place to notice, but all the same I wanted to warn you. Miss Sinclair's after pretending she's in the pink of health. But I got eyes, and I can tell you she looks as puny as you did, back when you took sick. I almost didn't let her in the door."

Hastily Fiona shook out her skirts, dusting her hands on the bibbed apron she'd donned as she stepped over piles of music, boxes of photographs, and other memorabilia. "I'm on the way. And Maisie?"

"Yes'm?"

"Don't you say or do anything that would make her leave, you hear me?"

"Yes ma'am."

She heard the girl clump back down the stairs, resignation plain in every indignant step.

Even prepared for the worst, Fiona struggled to mask her shock when Leah rose from the old high-back rocker in the sitting room. "I hope you don't mind." She gestured to the tray beside her. "I stopped by the bakery and picked up some fresh apple turnovers. The tea's from your kitchen. I'm afraid I used the last of the leaves. I'll replace them, of course."

"Don't be absurd. My home is yours, though it's been so long since you visited, I was beginning to think you'd forgotten your way,." She crossed the Oriental carpet to where Leah stood, looking strangely lost. "Have you been ill, my dear?"

"Not physically, no."

For a moment a constraint hovered in the room that pinched Fiona's heart. Then Leah grimaced and wandered over to an antique globe set in a walnut stand. "I need to talk to somebody," she murmured, her back to Fiona as though she were speaking to herself. She glanced over her shoulder. "For some reason I ended up here."

More concerned than ever, Fiona seated herself on the settee next to the rocker Leah had vacated. "Then why don't you come back and sit down, tell me what's troubling you." Unless it was something to do with Jacob. There would be, Fiona resolved, absolutely no discussion concerning her relationship with Jacob.

Leah shrugged and obeyed. But she still didn't speak, just sat on the edge of the chair, arms hugging her waist. After a few moments, with a lifted brow Fiona fetched a pillowcase she'd been edging with crochet and sat back down, quietly plying the hook while she waited for the younger woman to gather whatever tortuous thoughts had brought her here.

Time passed. Maisie poked her head through the doorway once, a question in her eyes; Fiona waved her away. Outside a cardinal *chitted* on the edge of the roof, then flew past the sitting room window in a splash of crimson. The radiator attached to the parlor stove quietly ticked as it sent out welcome heat.

"I don't know what to do."

Fiona laid aside the pillowcase. "About what, my dear?"

Another silence followed before Leah spoke, the words slow, halting. "I haven't seen Cade since the day he came to Richmond for an appointment with someone in the General Assembly, just before Christmas."

"From what I've gathered that's not so unusual." After all, she and Jacob hadn't seen each other, nor had they celebrated the holidays together. She hesitated. "I take it there are extenuating circumstances?"

Leah's lower lip trembled, but she gave a curt nod.

"Did you and Mr. Beringer quarrel?" Fiona was surprised. She did not know Cade, but Leah seemed too sensible to be undone by a lover's tiff.

Yet she sat there, stiff and prim in a severe blue serge gown, misery leaking from her pale countenance with every breath. "I suppose you could classify what happened as a quarrel. We exchanged words, but I was the only one who came close to raising my voice."

Fiona tried, but could not imagine such a scene. "People who care for each other still have the occasional snarl. Surely, though, by Christmas—"

"He wrote me a letter, a very polite letter, explaining that he felt obligated to spend the holidays with his family. He indicated that he would return soon after the New Year. I was disappointed, but I understood. I thought. I mean, he has family obligations too, and because of this misunderstanding between us I thought he might need more time. Then last week I received... I received another letter," she finished, almost gasping the words. "He told me he was sorry, for presuming too much. He..." She looked down, and Fiona watched her crumble a corner of apple tart with clumsy fingers, seeming completely unaware of her actions. "I never knew, never lost my temper before, not in my entire life. Never realized how...ugly I could be."

Heart sinking, Fiona poured herself another cup of tea. "Have you told your father that you quarreled? One of your sisters?"

"None of them would understand."

"Ah." She took a couple of healthy swallows before setting the cup down a shade too firmly. "Evidently you thought I might. Which means you must feel some responsibility for what seems to be your and Cade's estrangement. This has to do with your teaching, doesn't it?"

"I suppose." The fumbling fingers stilled, then balled into fists. "He was thinking about giving up his work, his...calling, if you will. We talked about living here, so I wouldn't have to leave Miss Esther's.

But when he implied that he was the only one doing God's will, while I…"

She lifted her head, and Fiona's breath caught at a despair that had extinguished every glimmer of hope from her face. "I said terrible things to him. Unspeakable things. I was scared. Hurt. But that's no excuse, when you love someone. I wrote him back to explain, after I received his last letter, but he never came. Never wrote again. He's left me. Mrs. Carlton… Cade left me. And—I can't blame him." The words ended in a strangled gasp. Abruptly she bowed forward, covering her face. "But I cannot bear this."

Tentatively Fiona laid her hand against the soft brown hair at the back of Leah's neck. "My dear," she whispered, vaguely recognizing a pain she hadn't experienced in two decades, the helpless pain of a mother for her hurting child. "My dear child."

"I don't know what to do. I don't know how to fix it." Leah's words came in short bursts, her gaze locked on her knees, and Fiona leaned closer. "It doesn't make sense, like trying to prove grace exists. It's not like a leaf or an insect one can examine under a microscope and then you say 'Aha! *That's* how it works.' I love him. I do. I just…I just…"

Leah lifted her head, her expression so full of entreaty that Fiona could do nothing but pass along what Jacob had offered: unquestioning comfort and loving arms. "Come here." She clasped the girl's wrists and tugged. "Sit beside me. We'll talk and sip tea, and everything will work out. There." As though Leah were four years old, her body yielding instead of taut as overtuned piano wire, Fiona wrapped her arm about the stiff shoulders and hugged. Amazing how easy it was to do. "Just because you're a wonderful teacher doesn't mean you have all the answers to the secrets of the universe."

Leah emitted a sound that was part laugh, part derision, and mostly despair. "I've come to the conclusion that I don't know the answers to anything." She swallowed hard several times, her eyes glistening with tears. "From the time I was a child I'd accepted that I would be alone," she managed finally. "Then Cade forced his way into my life. He was convinced God had arranged to bring us together. I…came to believe that myself."

Fiona stirred uncomfortably. Leah pulled a little way back, then pressed her fingers against her temples. "I'm sorry. I had no right to come here, burden you with my problems."

"And why not? I thought we were friends. Besides which, I believe I'm in love with your father, and he with me. If we can't talk to each other about affairs of the heart, the future might prove to be a trifle awkward."

Her pronouncement achieved the desired effect. Some of Leah's pasty enervation faded as the corner of her mouth tipped upward. "He told us, at Christmas. He wanted you to share the holiday with us, you know."

"Yes, I knew that. But the decision to commit my life to another man has not been an easy one, particularly after all these years. I needed distance and time. Perhaps, my dear, you and Cade need the same thing. It's a challenge, isn't it, this business of altering our perceptions about life and people. About what we're supposed to do with our own lives." She handed Leah her tea. "Here. Finish this. You need some color. While you're at it, eat one of those turnovers you brought along, instead of demolishing it with your fingers. Maisie's right. It wouldn't take even a puff of breeze to blow you away."

"Now you know how I felt last fall, when you were so ill."

"Hmph. Then I would think you'd take better care of yourself."

Both women settled back in their seats, sipping tea and munching the pastries in near-congenial silence. Then Leah spoke. "Mrs. Carlton?"

"Yes?" Fiona set aside her cup, wary of the cautious tone.

"I need to ask you something. I shouldn't, my father wouldn't like it. But…" She hunched her shoulders, not looking at Fiona.

"I assumed as much, since you came here instead of going home to your family." Sighing, Fiona contemplated the Constable landscape on the wall behind Leah while she battled almost a quarter-century's reticence. It would be a relief if only she could leap into the painting's landscape and hide away, but for the second time since the previous November, Fiona allowed her regard for another person to win. "I imagine I know what your question is."

Leah shook her head. "I'm not sure you do, at least not entirely. Yes, it concerns your past. It's—I know why you quit performing," she blurted, frustration darkening the brown eyes almost to black. "After what's happened to me I think I understand better how you felt, losing your husband, your son— No. That's not right. I haven't lost a child, and Cade's not my husband." Her voice broke on the last word. "What I wanted to ask, what I need to know, is how you bear it, with such grace."

Grace? Wryly Fiona considered the years that had passed before she allowed even a drop of that grace to soothe her parched spirit. "We're very alike, in many ways." Alike enough for her to be uncomfortable. "I'm going to share something with you, something that might be as difficult for you to hear as it is for me to say." She paused. "It was not losing them that caused me to forsake my former way of life. It was the realization that my career had cost them their lives, albeit indirectly. I will miss the piano until my last breath, but never again will I allow it to have more importance in my life than people."

The admission sounded even more condemnatory when spoken aloud. Yet Fiona didn't mind as much as she would have once. She had acknowledged her sin years ago, when she lay helpless in her bed, with her ruined cheek on fire and the hotter fire of remorse burning the lesson into her soul.

If she could spare Leah even a day's torment, she resolved to do so despite the seeming cruelty of what she was about to say. "From what you've indicated, dear, it is your choice not to have Cade for a husband, more than it was his choice not to have you for a wife."

Leah's head reared back. "I didn't come here to be reprimanded like one of my students."

The hot flash of temper in her face reminded Fiona of Gerald. Lands, how he had detested being challenged, particularly when he knew that Fiona was right. "What did you come here for, then? A pat on the head? An endorsement of your decision?"

"*I* didn't make a decision. It was made for me. I thought you of all people would be able to understand."

Poor child, Fiona thought with an inward wince. She looked as though Fiona had dropped a stone on her foot, when she'd been pleading for a crumb of bread. It was unfair of course, but then life was seldom fair, much less kind, and right now Fiona could help Leah more by forcing her to think through things for herself. "Why not Miss Esther? Surely she qualifies."

Leah's eyelids flickered, but she answered readily enough. "I didn't want to place her in an awkward position. For her, the needs of the school must come first, not her regard for me or Cade."

"I see." Fiona examined her fingernails. "And your family? You're afraid they're too…provincial?" Never mind that Fiona cherished every charming, provincial letter she received from Jacob, for they reflected his heart. Whenever the postman delivered one of those letters full of love and misspelled words, Fiona's spirits lifted.

She would not share that with Leah, however. Right now the girl needed clarity, no matter how painful; for whatever reason, it had fallen to Fiona to help her achieve it. She watched the disbelief and anger shudder through Leah's body, waited while the younger woman took a deep breath, then sat for a moment before slowly exhaling.

"You're trying to goad me into losing my temper," she murmured. "Why? Afraid I'll throw a weeping fit on your shoulder?"

Good for you, dear. "You're welcome to weep on my shoulder anytime. But you also have a father and a family who do love you, no matter what happens between you and Mr. Beringer."

"You might be surprised. Meredith and Benjamin would likely disown me. And Papa…" Despair slashed her face, leaving it raw and bleeding colorless tears. "All these years of praying for me, and he's been so…at peace. I don't want to hurt him. He loves Cade like a son. He won't understand. *I* don't understand. I want to marry Cade. I do. But he wouldn't let me explain, he wasn't willing to wait. If he loved me, he should have waited."

"I wonder what your answer would have been, if he had," Fiona murmured half under her breath, reawakened memories crowding her back into a corner of her own. "Never mind. You don't have to answer. Please believe me when I tell you I'm in no position to judge, much less offer advice." Shakily she pressed one hand against the scar, then dropped it to her lap. "That's a feeble excuse of an apology, isn't it? I've always been impatient with people who trample all over other others' feelings, then excuse their behavior by claiming they were only trying to help."

"I came to you. Forced a discussion of a subject you'd prefer not to discuss. I'm the one who should apologize, for being so defensive when— Wait." Absently she swiped her face while she studied Fiona, a frown building across her forehead. "Why are *you* so defensive? You are, aren't you?"

Why not tell her? After all, the girl had come here to make sense of a nightmare, and Fiona understood better than anyone the nature of nightmares. Especially the futility of pretending they would cease if one denied their cause long enough. "I'm going to tell you something else," she said. "Something I've never told a living soul. Not even your father, who asked me to marry him. After I share this, you might thank God that I haven't accepted his proposal."

Leah was looking faintly alarmed. Fiona toyed with one of the tassels on the throw pillow beside her. A lot more than Leah's future rested in her response to Fiona's confession. *Lord, give me Your strength.* "You know that when I married my husband, he was considered one of the most prominent conductors in both America and Europe?"

Leah nodded.

"I was eighteen years old. Flattered, and yes, a bit moonstruck, as they say. But—" She hesitated, still reluctant.

Ever since Jacob had proposed, she had realized the need to reconcile past mistakes with present circumstances, today's venture upstairs in the dusty attic only the latest of those clumsy attempts. Her marriage to Gerald certainly had nothing in common with Leah Sinclair and Cade Beringer, yet why did she hear this nagging, fretting, wretchedly *insistent* voice inside her head, demanding that she tell Leah the truth? The exercise had been intended as a private one, between herself and God. She didn't want to lose Leah's respect.

Repudiation, or reaffirmation. Which would it be? *Jacob,* she thought, imminent loss lacerating her heart. *Jacob…I didn't know until now how very much I do love you.*

Like a whirling carousel, memories spun around her head. Jacob holding her close, his comforting burr dispelling the nightmare; Jacob sitting on the MacAllisters' porch, gazing unflinching at and unaffected by her scar, his eyes full of love; Jacob presenting her with a spray of wilted leaves and shrunken berries. "It's dogwood," he told her, smiling sheepishly. "One of my favorite trees. At the height of autumn there's nothing more beautiful, when the leaves are scarlet and the berries Christmas red. That's how I think of us, dear one. At the height of our autumn."

"Never mind," Leah began stiffly. "I can see that—"

Fiona silenced her with a single gesture of her hand. "Be patient with me, my dear. I promise not to ramble." Far better to tell the tale swiftly and be done with it. The future rested, as it always did, in God's hands. Decision made, she plunged in.

"I was only eighteen, but I convinced everyone, including myself, that I married Gerald because we loved each other. Now remember that in those days, as now, love between husband and wife was not a requirement for a good match. But in order to gain my parents' consent, I needed to persuade them that our match was more than circumstances or convenience. And we did love each other, after a fashion."

She was rambling after all. *Spit it out. Quit dithering like an old woman.* "Leah, the truth is I didn't marry Gerald Carlton because I loved him. I married him because I knew he was a famous personage and the best opportunity for me to achieve the fame and fortune I thought I deserved." With great difficulty she maintained eye contact with the daughter of the man she did love, though she would have preferred to ride a crowded streetcar without her veil in place. "I was selfish, and I allowed my ambition to take over my life, as well as another person's."

Instead of a gasp of horror Leah gave an impatient sniff. "You were all of eighteen years old. Besides, if what I've heard and read is even half true, your musical ability was extraordinary enough to forgive the ambition. Knowing human nature, I daresay your husband entertained the same base motives himself. No doubt *he* was planning to use *you* to achieve even greater fame and fortune, as you put it."

She picked up her cup, but set it down before it was halfway to her lips, brown eyes flaring wide. "Wait. Are you trying to tell me that you think I've allowed ambition to blind me, as it did you? That my desire to be a good teacher, to honor my commitment…" She swallowed, not completing the sentence.

"I'm not the one who can answer that." Fiona could bear it no longer. Standing, she fussed with the tray, stacking the plates of half-eaten turnovers while Leah sat there glaring, only she more resembled a sick, fluffed-up bird buffeted by a January blizzard. "You came to see me, because you thought I would understand. Perhaps I do, perhaps I don't. Since I met your father, I believe I have come to understand what marriage ought to mean. A good marriage, with a depth of love and mutual respect on both sides that—" Heat climbed up her neck, over her cheeks.

Acutely embarrassed, she stumbled with the words. "What I mean to say is that when your father looks at me, the love…oh, *landsakes!* It's different, that's all. There's a difference in the love two men have shown for me, and me for them. I believe the reason is God."

For a moment she closed her eyes, drifting without effort in another memory: Jacob holding her close as he whispered softly in her ear, telling her not to be afraid. *Don't be afraid.* The words tickled her mind, seeped into her heart, spreading certainty—and courage.

She reopened her eyes and drew in a sustaining breath. How strange. In facing the very thing she most feared, she had been blessed with courage instead of condemnation. Hope instead of humiliation.

Jacob had given her so much more than his heart. In some myste-rious way he had also restored her own faith in God's love and the power of His forgiving nature. She looked at the young woman before her and smiled. "All I can offer you is this, Leah. You have learned to trust God. Now you must act on that faith. Use it to help you decide the nature of your love for Cade. Then perhaps you'll know why he left, and you'll know if you love him enough to forgive him, so you can win him back."

Forty-Three

SINCLAIR RUN
FEBRUARY 1896

...and whatever you do, don't badger her if she finally gathers the courage to come home. She's confused, Jacob. Confused and I would say perhaps a bit ashamed, as well as frightened.

*J*acob thrust the letter aside, then rose to stab the poker at the fire, turning logs to rekindle the flames. He was a bit confused and frightened himself. Why hadn't Leah shared Cade's desertion with her own father, was the question gnawing at his vitals. Made his heart glad, aye, that she felt free to share with Fiona. But still and all, he *was* Leah's father.

There was also anger against Cade. A rage so hot it ought to shame him, though at the moment contrition was far away from his mind. If Cade appeared on the doorstep, Jacob was more inclined to go after him with an ax. A dull one.

"Mr. Sinclair? What's the matter? You have a terrible scowl on your face. Do your innards hurt?"

"No." He gave the logs a final vicious stab. "Your aunt asked that you use the word *stomach*. It's a more refined word. When you go to work for Mr. Cooper, come spring, Mrs. Cooper will appreciate such efforts on your part." What would happen between Leah and Cade, come spring? For sure a wedding no longer seemed in the making. *Lord? There's a need for Your hand at work in these children's lives.* He thought for a moment, grudgingly added the need in his own life.

"Is it the letter from Mrs. Carlton?" Deke came to stand by the fire. "She writes a lot of letters to you. More than Ma writes to me, even." He wiped his sleeve across his nose, flashed Jacob a guilty grin. "I forgot my handkerchief again. When I go to work at Coopers', Mrs. Cooper won't like it if I use my sleeve, will she?"

"Decidedly not. Neither do I."

"Are you angry with me, Mr. Sinclair?"

Wearily Jacob shook his head. "No, lad. I'm not angry with you. But I've some weighty matters on my mind. Think I'll take myself down to the workshop for a spell."

"Aunt Effie won't like that. You might catch the ague, because it's sleeting outside. She says if I hadn't stayed outside so long last week, I wouldn't have a cold now." He sniffed again, noisily, and Jacob thrust out his own handkerchief. "Thanks. Mr. Sinclair, why hasn't Mr. Beringer come to visit us? Do you think he came down with ague or something, because he's outdoors too much?"

Jacob bit back another curt response, told Deke to keep the handkerchief, and took himself off to his workshop, where he spent the next several hours listening to the sleet splattering on the workshop's tin roof while he sanded boards. He was sweeping up when the door banged open, smacking into the wall as Deke burst dripping and bright-eyed into the room.

"Mr. Sinclair! You got a visitor!" Turning, he shut the door, then dried his hands on his plaid wool jacket. "Sorry. Knob slipped out of my hand. Aunt Effie says you'll probably want to clean up in a hurry. It's Mrs. Carlton. She wanted to come straight out here to your workshop, but Aunt Effie's made her sit down in the parlor."

Fiona is here? Elation battled with alarm. Mind spinning, he tossed aside the broom and hurriedly began to stack the sanded boards. "Tell them I'm on the way. And Deke?"

"Sir?"

"Wear that cap you've stuffed in your pocket. Won't do much good in there now, will it?"

"Not going to be outside but a minute."

"Aye. And your head's already damp, is it not, from the minute you spent dashing across the yard. Here, I'll be wearing one myself, see?" He grabbed his flat cap off the hook and jammed it on his head, then reached for his coat, his thoughts tumbling over themselves.

Deke sullenly complied before reopening the door. Cold wind and icy pellets swirled into the shop. "Mr. Sinclair?"

"Hmm?" Jacob crammed his arms through the sleeves. Why had she come? For herself or for Leah?

"You forgot to take off your work apron." With a triumphant grin Deke skedaddled out into the yard.

"Blast!" There was a sawed-off pine nubbin on the floor. Jacob snatched it up, eyed the distance to the scraps piled in the corner, and let the nubbin fly. Then he laughed. *Aye, Lord. Sometimes I act more the lad than Deacon.*

By the time he reached the house, he had himself well in hand. Or so he thought, until he walked into the parlor and saw how the firelight transformed Fiona's hair to a shimmery silver-gold halo about her head. She was holding her hands out over the fire, those long-boned hands full of goodness and grace, and Jacob's heart banged against his ribs hard enough to crack them.

"Jacob!" She rose, moving across the room, her face rosy from the heat of the flames, her eyes flooded with—distress. "I'm so sorry to descend upon you without warning. Maisie fussed at me the entire morning before I left for the station, until I closed the door in her face. I refused to bring her along, you see. I didn't want to compound my rudeness." She stopped three paces away and they stood awkwardly, staring at each other.

Then Jacob stepped forward, clasped her chilled hands in his and gave them a comforting squeeze. "You're welcome anytime, any hour. With or without warning or Maisie." Regardless of the turmoil in his heart, the woman he loved needed him. She had traveled halfway across the state because she needed to see him. And, he hoped, because she knew that he needed to see her. "It's Leah, isn't it?" Jacob said at last. "Your letter arrived just past noon."

"That wretched letter. I never should have written it, never should have posted it." She shook her head, but Jacob could see that she was relieved to have the matter out in the open. "It hurt you, didn't it, that she talked to me first."

Taken aback by her quick perception, Jacob stammered a bit. "Well, now, as to that, perhaps I was wondering why. Though of course Leah's always been more private than either of her sisters, don't you know, and then she's all the way to Richmond. Which seeing as how you're there, and the two of you great friends, why, then, it's only natural she might feel disposed to—"

He stopped, feeling a fool. "See what you've reduced me to, Fiona love. Aye, it hurt like the dickens. It shouldn't, I know that well enough. But it did." He tried to smile. "I'm no' used to my lasses not sharing their hurts with me, for all they're grown and gone."

"I know that. Something told me to come." Fiona reached to lightly brush the tips of her fingers over the back of his hand. "I'm glad I did. Jacob, Leah doesn't know I'm here. I need to tell you that, in case you'd prefer not to talk about this without her knowing. But she's suffering, and I need to help. I know I've no right—"

"You've every right, you daft woman! Haven't I asked you to be my wife? That gives you the right. More to the point, she loves you. You're the mother she's never had and always needed." When Fiona's eyes went glassy with unshed tears, Jacob wanted to rip out his tongue. "You must know you're more to her than just a friend," he finished more quietly. "You're an intelligent woman, for all your contrariness."

"I do know." Her voice was thick. "I just… The thought of coming between the two of you is frightening enough. But the pain of it, the pain of loving someone like that and not being able to help…" She pressed two fingers against her temple, then sighed. "Jacob, I need to confess this, because it has helped me understand what Cade might be feeling. There have been times these past few months when I thought about closing up the house. Leaving Virginia altogether."

The confession ripped through him like a rusty saw blade. "Leaving—me, the way Cade abandoned my daughter?"

Her head went back, and Jacob watched the flash of spirit stiffen her spine. "I told you to help you better understand both of us. Until you do, don't presume to pass judgment either on him or on me. I said only that I thought about it. I certainly have no intention of acting on those thoughts. I'm here at Sinclair Run, aren't I? Talking to a dunderhead of a Scotsman who should know better."

"So I should," Jacob agreed, relief making him lightheaded. "But then so should you, Fiona-me-love. Don't you know that, when a man's been scared out of his few wits, it's his nature to strike out at the one who caused the scare?"

"How could I have forgotten man's nature? Must be my age."

He couldn't help it. The indignation flooding her face was too much to resist, so Jacob snatched up her hand and pressed a kiss against her fire-warmed palm, then folded her fingers into a fist. "Waiting for you to agree to be my wife's not an easy thing, dear one. I don't know how—"

The revelation punched him on the chin: *This* was what Cade must have felt, all those months, loving Leah while she was unwilling to commit herself. It wasn't anger the lad needed, but understanding. Which of course was precisely what Fiona had been telling him, albeit from her own perspective. Thanks to the regal woman glaring at him now, Jacob found himself for the first time looking at Leah and Cade with a more charitable eye. *Every board has two sides, Lord. Thanks for the reminder.*

Softly he stroked Fiona's fingers, then released her. " 'Twas difficult enough enduring a lonely Christmas without you. I don't know what's happened between the two children, but promise me that, between you and me and the Lord, we'll have no more talk about running away. It's not fair to me, Fiona."

For a long moment she stood head down, not speaking; Jacob couldn't fathom her mood. Then she looked up, the scar more pronounced because her face had lost its indignant blush. "All right," she whispered, closing her eyes. "All right, Jacob. No more talk about running away." She gave a shaky little laugh. "Besides, I have no place to go."

"Your place," Jacob said, lifting her hands and holding them tightly between his, "is here with me, at Sinclair Run. You know that in your heart. This business between Leah and Cade has rattled us both, that's all. Come now, let's talk about it. Tell me what you can about Leah."

"I don't want to betray your daughter's trust, or yours." She drew in a deep breath. "First though, I have to tell you something about myself, and my marriage to Gerald. It isn't pretty, but it has to be said."

When she looked at him with her winter sky eyes full of uncertainty, all he wanted to do was kiss them closed, then press his lips against the softness of hers. "Tell me anything you want. It will not change how I feel about you," he said instead. "One day, please God, Leah will be *our* daughter, not just mine. You're not betraying anyone's trust, dear heart. It's just part of the pain of loving."

⟅⟆

"And even after I told her why I married Gerald, she still doesn't understand how to apply my mistakes to her circumstances with Cade, not completely." Fiona swallowed another sip of the mulled cider Effie had left for them. Her throat was raw from talking, but her heart felt lighter. Despite the lines deepening on either side of Jacob's mouth, it was plain the hurt Leah had unwittingly inflicted had been assuaged. It had been the right thing to do, coming here, telling him. "Of course, with Leah it's not so much ambition at the heart of it. I truly believe it's never occurred to her how deeply Cade might have been crushed by the strength of her will and by her capacity for anger."

Jacob made an exasperated sound. "How would you know that, seeing as how he's not written so much as a word since— When did you say he sent her the second note? Going for six weeks now, is it?"

He was tugging on the lock of hair that tended to dangle over his forehead, and Fiona realized with a shock of surprise how much she longed to press a tender kiss to the balding crown of his head. The novelty of it distracted her, since she had never before experienced love with tenderness. Except with her son.

"Fiona?"

She smiled painfully. "Sorry. My mind wandered for a moment. Let me see… How do I know what Cade is feeling? Well, I don't, of course. I only know how Leah believes he is feeling. The rest is conjecture on my part. You see, she's willing to admit that she can teach school anywhere and promised me up, down, and sideways that her only purpose for remaining at Miss Esther's has been to fulfill her obligation for the rest of the school year. Now, whether or not that is her sole motivation for wanting to remain in Richmond is between herself and her conscience. But she doesn't comprehend how Cade might interpret her attitude as rejection." Unless she had unknowingly revealed something less noble to Cade, which could lend credibility to his subsequent behavior. Fiona did not share that suspicion with Jacob, however.

"Why didn't she tell him all this?"

"Apparently he never gave her the chance. Which is why she has reached the conclusion that he was only using the 'conflict of their respective occupations,' as she put it, as an excuse. Naturally she, too, feels betrayed, hurt. Disillusioned. And she refuses to go after him." Fiona sat back against the settee, weariness pulling at her. "She went after him once, last fall when she was afraid for his life and determined to 'rescue' him. She won't go after him again." Not even if, like Fiona, she spent the next quarter-century alone and punishing herself because of it.

"And if Cade feels the same?" Abruptly Jacob rose to pace the room. "What's to be done?" Fiona heard him mutter.

He swiveled around. "There has to be more to it, this is not like Cade, not at all. I've known him for nigh on six years. I'll go after the lad myself. You don't call yourself a man of God, promise your love to a young woman, then leave her high and dry."

He sat again beside Fiona, gazing at her in pained confusion. "He taught her to trust. To believe with her heart, as well as her mind. Fiona, this is too much. Too much. I canna think what to do."

"Jacob." His hand was pressed palm down on his knee, the scarred, bony knuckles taut. Fiona gave in to the tenderness, the love bubbling through her like a spring of clear water.

The need to heal Jacob's hurt as he had helped to heal hers overcame all inbred reticence, along with the memories of her complicated marriage to Gerald. "All people make mistakes, especially in the heat of the moment, when they've been hurt. No matter how godly a man Cade Beringer might be, he's still just a man. If you cut him, he bleeds. He might still be bleeding, as it were. But because we don't know, perhaps right now it isn't our place to do anything—but pray. Jacob? With two of us together—"

What am I doing? Lord, what have I done?

"Together," he whispered, his head lifting. He searched her face. "The two of us? Fiona? What are you saying?"

For a moment panic squeezed her with an iron fist, and she had to look away, blind to everything but the memory of a man she had first hero-worshiped, then shamelessly used, fought with, and, for a while, feared and hated. *I'm older now. I'm forgiven.* What she was about to do was the right thing, right not merely in her own eyes, but God's, whose Presence lit the darkest cavities in human souls, offering a way out. Offering…redemption. *And Jacob isn't Gerald.*

Certainty grew with each breath and spread through her fear-stiffened limbs like heated oil massaged into each aching muscle, every strained ligament until she flowed gracefully from the settee to kneel on the floor, at Jacob's feet.

"Jacob Sinclair." She reached up, clasping both of his strong, scarred hands, not only to gain strength, but to give it. "Will you have me for your wife?" When the words wobbled, she paused to catch her breath. "I can't promise to always be a comfortable mate, but I promise to be devoted. To you and to your daughters."

His throat muscles were working. Fiona watched him blink rapidly, watched stupefaction transform to gladness. "Aye, dear one. I will have you for my wife." He slid his hands to her forearms and helped her rise, both of them smiling when one of her knees gave an unromantic creak. After urging her back down on the settee, close to his side, he laid his palm over the scar. "I'll be your husband. Can you accept that without shame or fear?"

For a moment Fiona closed her eyes, unable to bear the burning kindness in Jacob's. His compassion had beckoned to her from the moment of their first meeting. Jesus would have eyes like Jacob Sinclair's, she was certain.

After a while, when her heartbeat calmed and she was sure she could do so composedly, she spoke. "Gerald was not a…cruel man. I wouldn't want you to think that, Jacob. It's just that I was so young. So passionate about my music, blinded by the ambition and the attention. It took me several years to realize that God had allowed me in effect to reap what I had sown. It was my musical ability Gerald loved—not me. We were well matched, after all."

"Pshaw. The man was twice a fool."

"Twice a—? Jacob, didn't you hear me? I might have felt love for Gerald, but I still married him for all the wrong reasons."

"He was a man twice your age, past old enough to know better and therefore twice a fool," Jacob repeated more forcefully. "First for not loving that young girl, then for not loving the woman she became."

"You didn't know me then." She laughed a little. "Lands, but I was single-minded and certainly selfish. When I realized I could never earn my husband's love, I decided I would become more famous than him. Every time I received top billing, I took great pleasure in flaunting it. We had some terrific rows."

His fingers drifted from the scar to the corner of her mouth. "What happened?"

"Harry." For the first time she could remember, the name fell easily from her lips. "I discovered the joy of being loved, not because I was a famous concert pianist rivaling Jenny Lind in the crowd numbers, not for the fame and fortune I brought. Harry loved me simply because I was his mama." Her voice trembled on the last word. She gave in and allowed herself to be pulled into Jacob's embrace. "Oh, Jacob. How I wish I had been a better mother!"

"You were a fine mother. Hush, now. No tears. This is a moment I've prayed for for months." He jostled her a bit. "Know what I'd like very much, right now?"

Fiona searched his craggy face and blushed. There was no mistaking that particular desire. "'We may have passed springtime, but we're not in the dead of winter'?" she managed, glancing over his shoulder to the bleak January dusk.

"Does a man good, having the woman he loves remember his words. Aye, love. All the blazing colors of autumn, that's you and me."

When he tugged her closer, his head tilting, as with a will of their own Fiona's hands crept over his shoulders. "If Effie returns, we'll both be in for a scolding."

"No we won't." He smiled into her eyes. "She's been waiting

impatiently for you to come to your senses. Under the circumstances, she's more likely to scold if we *don't* seal the declaration with a kiss."

"I see. Now I understand why she hasn't so much as creaked a floorboard in the past hour." Lands, she was trembling like a girl, dizzy with anticipation. "Jacob?"

"I know." The smile in his eyes turned wry. "I know, dear. It's all right. Close your eyes." She obeyed and felt the warmth of his breath, the miraculous softness of his lips feathering across her lids. "I do love you, Fiona Carlton," he breathed into her ear. His lips returned to her face, brushing along the scar as on that momentous afternoon the previous November. "For all you were. For all you are."

Then he gathered her close, and for the first time in more years than she cared to remember, Fiona found herself fully embraced by a man with love for her in his heart.

And she gave herself over to the miracle of his kiss.

Forty-Four

Washington, D.C.
March 1896

*C*ade exited the Capitol onto the upper terrace, into the silence of a bitingly frigid day. Out of the pewter sky, pinhead snowflakes were already drifting down; one of them landed on his cheekbone, stinging like the frozen point of a needle. His mood as bleak as the weather, Cade stood for a time, staring blankly at the broad swath of lawn sloping downward from the Capitol steps, the clusters of trees in Seaton Park and the Botanical Gardens, block upon block of imposing buildings lining either side of the Mall, with the obelisk dedicated to Washington ten years earlier a blurred outline against the lowering sky. Well over a million dollars and thirty years spent for that one, Cade recalled.

Monuments to human greed and national pride, that's what they all were, regardless of the worthiness of the men honored.

His hands clenched; he lifted his face to the wind and indifferent sky, fighting the hopelessness of defeat. *Why can't they see? Why won't they listen?*

Below him a buggy pulled to a halt. A man descended, his black overcoat billowing. He donned his top hat and took the steps two at a time, brushing past Cade without acknowledgment as though Cade were one of the marble statues filling the Statuary Hall inside.

Cade had felt equally invisible throughout his fruitless meeting with Senator Martin.

"While I appreciate your concern, now is not the appropriate time to consider such altruistic endeavors. Virginia, particularly the western regions, suffered staggering losses in the Panic of '93. We need to recover the spirit of the New South, where prosperity lies in commerce and manufacturing. What you're suggesting would be a waste of natural resources, Mr. Beringer."

"Not everyone in Congress agrees," Cade pointed out. "I realize it was before you were elected, but Congress did pass the Forest Reserve Act back in '91. And President Harrison set aside land tracts in both Wyoming and Alaska as forest reservations."

"Lands with little population and even less potential for development. People are starving in the mountains as well as the Valley, Mr. Beringer. It's the railroads, and the wealth to be gleaned from our natural resources, that can restore Virginia to her former glory. Preserving forest for the sake of preservation strikes me as remarkably short-sighted."

"If we don't take the time to be good stewards of those natural resources, within a generation there won't be anything left of them."

There had been little point in prolonging the meeting, and both men knew it. "Look," the Senator said after shaking Cade's hand, "I heard about a young fellow, Yale graduate, name of Pinchot. Apparently in line for some committee on forest management. He's been down in North Carolina working with Olmstead, on the grounds of Vanderbilt's estate."

"Thanks," Cade replied, trying to hide his indifference. He'd been passed along, shunted aside, and fobbed off on too many occasions over the years not to recognize the tactic.

Senator Martin's eyes gleamed. "Way I heard it, Pinchot talked Vanderbilt into buying over a hundred thousand acres of land, so he could have himself a forest. There's your preserve, Mr. Beringer. Created not through government regulation, but courtesy of a private individual with money. Money earned from railroads. Understand what I'm saying, Mr. Beringer?"

"Perfectly," Cade said, and escaped.

With a renunciatory shrug he forced himself to leave the Capitol's upper terrace and descend the steps. Snow fell thick and fast now, but he eschewed the comfort of hiring a hack, instead walking the half-mile to the Baltimore and Potomac Station. On his last visit to Stillwaters, Benjamin had given him a letter of introduction to the governor; with no hope of help from the federal quarter, Cade once more resolutely set his face toward Richmond—the last place he wanted to visit.

To this day, the breath-stealing punch of that afternoon in Leah's classroom, and her utter indifference to his last letter, filled him with a stew of disbelief and outrage. So much hurt the only way he'd survived had been to throw himself back into his own life's work.

And for what?

Head down against the bite of the wind, Cade tried to close his mind against the cold as well the crippling pain. With every day that passed, every defeat he met at the hands of indifferent, opportunistic politicians, every memory of Leah stabbing his heart, he faltered a little more. Surely there had to be a reason for God's seeming defection. He'd pored over pages of Scripture, his thumb tracing verses that promised the Lord's ongoing Presence in the life of those with faith. Jesus Himself had prepared the disciples for the Comforter. His Spirit would be part not only of their lives, but of the lives of all who believed that Jesus was the Christ.

Yet spiritual silence bound him in lonely isolation.

He was surrounded by magnificent buildings, paved walkways, and cobbled streets. A sea of humanity—businessmen and beggars, women, servants and tradesmen, soldiers and ex-slaves. Conveyances of every make. Buggies, carriages, curricles, drays, wagons. All the noise and jangle of a city, yet loneliness was killing Cade slowly, a breath at the time.

A gust of wind blinded him with a barrage of snowflakes and rattled the trees planted around the grounds of the Library of Congress. Trees…Cade swiped at the flakes, then sent a grudging acknowledgment skyward. To be sure, there *were* patches of nature in the nation's capital, particularly here in the heart of it. Trees and gardens and the promise of great beauty arising from the fifty acres surrounding the Capitol upon which Frederick Olmstead had bestowed his extraordinary vision.

Fine. Cade was man enough to admit that Washington wasn't a treeless desert.

But he still felt more isolated than if he'd been dropped in the middle of one, with no hope of an oasis. He pulled up his coat collar, shivering at the growing dampness. Perhaps cast adrift in the North Atlantic would be a more apt metaphor. Either way, he was out of his element. And there would be no lifeboat to save him, much less a helping hand to keep him afloat. *Leah. Leah...*

He was lost at sea. Regardless of where he turned, no matter how he strained to keep his eyes focused on Jesus, right now all he saw were the waves.

Am I wrong, Lord? Is that it? For weeks he'd been struggling against the possibility that he might have wasted his life, that his present circumstances resulted from pride and possibly spiritual blindness. Something he'd done, or not done, had—

No.

He refused to believe that the almighty, omniscient Creator of the universe would allow the complete ruination of His planet earth at the hands of corrupt people.

Leah might be lost to him forever, but Cade lifted his shoulders and quickened his step. His train left in an hour. While he had breath in his body, he would fight not to lose the only remaining source of purpose in his life.

❧❧❧

RICHMOND

"And much as I admire your dedication, Mr. Beringer, I trust you can appreciate my precarious position. Voter apathy has reached record highs; it would be self-defeating for me to adopt a stance that has the potential to create more conflict with the railroads and the business community."

"Regardless of their spurious ethics? Remember the Kent Bill four years ago? The bill that was supposed to provide stricter controls over the railroads, and was very popular among voters across the state? Correct me if I'm wrong, but the watered-down version that eventually passed might have contributed to some of that voter apathy."

The governor flushed, clearing his throat. "Mr. Beringer, it would appear that the two of us are unable to find any common ground upon which to base an understanding." He drummed his fingers on the top of his desk. "From what your good friend Benjamin Walker told me in his introductory letter, you're obviously a man of character, and I do regret your needless journey. Unfortunately, these days it takes more than a sterling reputation to accomplish one's goals."

"Perhaps for you," Cade replied.

He'd left quickly, almost abruptly, because his control was tenuous at best. It was humbling to realize that his once legendary patience had disappeared of late, along with every other spiritual fruit he'd spent his entire adult life trying to cultivate.

For an indeterminate time he wandered the snow-dusted streets, a cottony numbness isolating him from crowds and cold and noise. Eventually he boarded a streetcar that ended up at Monroe Park, where he sat awhile on a wrought-iron bench. There were few strollers about the park, no doubt due to the wintry weather. It was snowing again, but only halfheartedly, with crumb-size flakes that drifted down in lazy spirals. Hands dangling between his knees, indifferent to the weather, Cade gazed unseeingly at the statue of a Confederate general. *Can't have a park without a monument, can we?*

When it dawned on him that his ears were aching from the cold and he couldn't feel his toes, he forced himself to rise. No sense freezing to death the week before spring officially arrived.

Less than a dozen blocks away, Leah would be inside her classroom. Or, since he had no idea of the time, perhaps classes were over for the day, and she was in her neat sitting room in that chair by the window. Did she ever think of him? His eyes stung; the scenery blurred. He scrubbed the moisture from his cheeks and told himself to quit acting like a grieving puppy abandoned by its mistress. He was supposed to be a man, a man whose faith enabled him to accomplish whatever was asked of him, regardless of travail and woe.

Where are You?

A chilly breeze stung his wet cheeks, the only response. Like Leah, the Lord had withdrawn His Presence from Cade.

He wasn't consciously aware of where he was headed until he arrived at the two brick pillars that flanked the drive leading to the Esther Hays School for Young Ladies. *Don't do this, man.* The pain wasn't worth it. He thought of all the other letters he'd written, then crumpled and tossed in the trash, thought of the sleepless nights reconstructing that agonizing afternoon, when she'd cut him off at the knees.

To this day he didn't understand how it had happened, what he had done to precipitate Leah's vitriolic attack. He had laid his heart and his life at her feet. She had sliced both open and left him bleeding, then stepped over the carcass so she could go where *she* wanted to go. Four months had passed, yet time had not eased the suffering. He still didn't know how he could have been so wrong, how he had misinterpreted Leah's feelings and missed completely the will of God for their lives.

Not wanting to believe it, at first he'd tried to give her more time. Certainly they had been acquainted for years, but their love was too new, therefore misunderstandings were possible. So he'd nobly spent a miserable Christmas, dodging the questions and concern of his family, praying all the while that Leah would come to her senses. She'd write him, tell him she'd been wrong… *Wasn't that a better way, Lord?* If he'd crowded her or tried to persuade her, then he would have deprived her of the opportunity to freely examine her feelings, choose for herself whether she wanted to follow God's plan for her life—or her own.

It had taken him weeks to accept the truth: God's will or not, Leah apparently wanted out of Cade's life. She'd never responded to the letter he'd sent in January, not even with a terse note. He'd promised to give up his wandering, live in Richmond if after she finished out the year at the school they could move to a town nearer the mountains. Her reply had been—silence. Total, devastating silence.

A carriage approached, jammed with bright-faced young girls. Cade realized with an unpleasant jolt that he had entered the school grounds and was in fact less than a block away from the teachers' dormitory. He turned his back to avoid recognition and, after the carriage rolled past, ordered his feet to retrace their steps.

On the other hand, there could be no harm in strolling past the building. In fact, perhaps what he needed to begin healing was a kind of official renunciation. A final farewell. She would never know he'd been there, so the gesture offered no risk.

By the time he reached the commons across from the dormitory, he was sweating like a wet dog despite the temperature, and his insides were cramping. There was the hitching post where he'd tied his horse— he remembered how Leah had come flying through the door, looking flustered and shy. She'd balanced her dainty foot on the longstep and lifted her face…

Jesus, this is too much. Too much. With a muffled groan he turned aside, groping for the solid trunk of a nearby tree and bracing his palm against the cold wet bark. His shoulders heaved; tears spilled from his eyes. She was gone. Though her body might be present, less than a stone's throw from where he stood, Leah was as lost to him as if she were dead.

The snow was falling thick and fast now, transforming the world to shades of white and gray and black. Somewhere in the distance a bell clanged; a treble voice called out, was answered. Unless Cade wanted to be found standing out here in the cold, playing to perfection the part of rejected suitor, he needed to scrape himself together and get out. Get away. Far away.

Back to the mountains, where he belonged. He began walking, numb to everything but the grief.

Like a wounded animal, he was returning to his territory, not to lick his wounds, but to learn how to endure the rest of his life when inside he felt defeated and dead.

Forty-Five

*J*acob longed to shout the good news of his and Fiona's engagement from the top of Massanutten Mountain, but Fiona persuaded him to wait.

"Give Leah a chance to heal, Cade a bit longer to return. You've been patient all these months, dear. Surely now that you know I'm yours"—she tilted her head imperiously—"and you're mine, you can keep our news a secret for another month or two."

"Aye, love," Jacob admitted. "It won't be easy, mind you, though you've the way of it. I love you both dearly, but this one last time I'll put my daughter's feelings before yours." He heaved a longsuffering sigh, prayed for patience, then added a wistful entreaty that perhaps the Lord might consider nudging Fiona to change her mind. *And while You're about it, perhaps Cade, too?*

It was the end of March before Fiona finally admitted her own patience was at an end. Neither Cade nor Leah had made any further efforts at reconciliation, so Fiona returned to Sinclair Run, where she and Jacob formally announced their engagement. Jacob fired off a telegram to Stillwaters, then drove his betrothed to Tom's Brook. Garnet hugged them both, shedding quiet tears of joy.

Sloan winked at Fiona. "We saw it happening the day you managed to beat him at checkers," he said while he shook Jacob's hand. "If he'd had his mind on the game, he would have trounced you four times instead of three."

From Benjamin and Meredith came a return telegram with a half-dozen lines of eloquent blandishments and rhapsodizing. Some things about his eldest daughter would likely never change.

Tempering the joy, however, was their lingering helplessness over Leah. A week later, Jacob and Fiona boarded the train for Richmond.

"I'm not looking forward to this," Fiona confessed quietly after they changed trains in Staunton. "She's going to try to be happy for us, Jacob. But…"

"But inside she'll be tearing herself to pieces, grieving over her own loss." Jacob mulled over the decision not to tell Leah they were coming. "Should we have written her first?" he asked, not for the first time.

"She would have suffered alone that much longer," Fiona responded. Jacob felt her hand burrow between his elbow and waist, a secret yet bold show of affection that delighted him. "Jacob, we're all of us on a journey here on earth. And we're not always in the same place. There's a season for everything, remember. For whatever purpose, this seems to be Leah's time to mourn. But it's ours to dance, as it were. She won't begrudge us our joy. We mustn't begrudge her the time to grieve."

"Still think I should write to Cade," Jacob grumbled. Never mind that nobody, not even Benjamin, knew where the boy had taken himself off to, though at Christmas Ben speculated that likely he was chasing after politicians and influential businessmen. *Some weeks ago I wrote a couple of letters of introduction for him, but he got preoccupied with more important matters, and I'm not talking about Preston Clarke. Meredith likes to tease about being matchmaker, but you know what I think? I think Cade's had his eye on her for years. It's a shame they can't be together for the holiday, but you can't fault the man for honoring his family.*

Honoring his family, then jilting the woman he'd asked to marry him? It didn't make sense. Restless, Jacob crossed and uncrossed his legs, remembering now what he hadn't paid attention to then: Leah had been unusually quiet throughout the holiday. At the time, he had attributed it to missing Cade, only natural when one's affianced was hundreds of miles away. He'd felt much the same himself. "It doesn't make sense," he exclaimed aloud. In a more reasonable tone he added, "Cade's not the sort of man to leave a lass at the altar. Oh, now don't be looking at me like that, love. I know they hadn't even set the wedding date, but he had announced his intentions. Cade wouldn't have done so, had he not been settled in his heart. This shouldn't have happened at all." Absently he reached to pat her gloved hand. "I told you about the hyacinth?"

"Yes, Jacob."

"And how I never knew she was afraid of the dark, but Cade discovered it, and—"

"Yes, Jacob. You've told me. And I'll tell you again"—through the gauzy veil compassion flowed from her lovely eyes, bathing him in its stream—"that human behavior doesn't always make sense, even when those involved are good people, people who try to live their faith. What happened, happened. Leah's your daughter, but that doesn't absolve her of all responsibility in this. Jacob, we can love her unconditionally, but we can't tie all the blame on Cade's back."

"Oh, aye…" With a brisk head shake Jacob let the matter lie. For the moment, anyway. When they arrived in Richmond, however, he and his youngest were going to have a father-daughter talk.

Because it was a balmy spring evening in dramatic contrast to the previous week's freakish snowstorm, Jacob coaxed Leah into taking a walk about the school grounds with him after they finished supper. He'd spent a restless afternoon in his hotel room after he escorted Fiona home from the station, waiting for Leah to finish her classes for the day, wondering whether he and Fiona were doing the right thing, descending upon Leah without any warning. Fiona serenely stood her ground, and not only about surprising Leah.

"The two of you need time together, just the two of you. I also want her to feel free in her response, when you tell her about us. If there's to be a problem, I'd rather know now, than six months after we're wed."

So Jacob had waited alone in the formidable headmistress's office, hat in hand and nerves as raw as the end of a sawed-off board.

"I'm very glad to see you, Papa," Leah said beside him now. The sky had turned a rosy peach shade, tinged on the edges with deep purple; they passed a bed of bright yellow flowers, but she didn't spare them even a glance. "You're looking well, better than I've seen you in a long time."

Her voice, like her manner, was brisk; Jacob stole a sideways look and then was sorry. In contrast to the array of early spring colors, Leah was pale, her brown eyes chillingly empty. "And since you consumed a hearty meal just now," she continued, "that would seem to infer you're not here to alert me to a health problem. It doesn't take much of a stretch to deduce that you're therefore here because you're...concerned about me."

"And can't a man drop in to see his beloved daughter if he takes a mind to?"

"Mm. When was the last time you yielded to impulse, Papa? We're very alike that way—we like to plan things out." They reached a stone bench. Without warning Leah dropped down on the seat; her chin lifted. "You know what's happened, don't you?"

Caught off guard, Jacob scowled, joined her on the bench, and tried to stall. *Och, Fiona. This is why you should be here.* What was he supposed to do, pretend he didn't know? Or ignore the question and just blurt out his own news? For the moment, ignorance seemed safer. "Oh, aye? And what is it I'm supposed to know?"

Impatience tightened her lips. Her eyes darkened. "Don't pretend, Papa. Not right now. I've known ever since the day I talked to Fiona that she would feel constrained to write you. That's what brought you here, isn't it? She told you about"—for the first time the brisk schoolteacher's voice faltered—"about Cade. Didn't she?" She looked away then.

"Aye, lass," he admitted gently. He reached to cover her hand, which had balled into a fist in her lap. Now that the moment had arrived, he felt the wash of love, the overwhelming urge to comfort, displace his awkwardness.

He also knew that his and Fiona's news must wait. There would be plenty of opportunity for celebration—later. "She wrote to me. But because she cares for you like a mother for a daughter, she did something else as well. She came to see me in person." Leah's head jerked up, her lips half-parted in astonishment. "Aye, she did. She wants to help. So do I."

Her eyelids flinched. "There's nothing you can do," she whispered. "Papa? Are you... Are you very disappointed in me?"

"Never. And don't be saying such a thing again, do you hear? I'll no' have any child of mind allowing a despicable thought like that one to even cross her mind." Turning, he gripped her shoulders and firmly drew her close. "If I'm disappointed in anyone, 'tis Cade. No matter what was said, he should not have done this thing."

"Don't be angry at him, Papa. It only hurts you in the end. I've tried that, so I know." A pathetic smile barely lifted the corners of her mouth. "I just wish I could understand why. I've had to accept that God doesn't owe us explanations, that the nature of faith demands trust without proof. But…" A shudder rippled through her body and she laid her head on his shoulder. Jacob felt all the rigidity dissolve, like a child on the verge of exhaustion. "I'm still not sure I'm going to survive the lesson."

Jacob rested his cheek on the crown of her head and held her tight. For a few moments they sat in silence, and he prayed that somehow the Lord would give him comforting words—and Leah the grace to endure.

Footsteps scraped nearby, an irksome intrusion. Jacob didn't release Leah, tightening his arm to prevent her from moving. But whoever was approaching had the sensitivity of a buffalo, for the steps continued to approach the bench.

A moment later a throat was noisily cleared. " 'Scuse me. Ah, Miss Sinclair?"

Leah straightened, lifting her gaze to the weather-beaten man who now stood in front of them. He was carrying a rake, and a little way behind the bench Jacob spotted a wheelbarrow filled with dirt.

"Mr. O'Keefe." In the wink of an eye his daughter was transformed from forlorn waif to authoritative schoolmarm. "Is there something you needed from me?"

Mr. O'Keefe whipped off his cap, then stood there looking miserable and uncertain. "Didn't mean to intrude, ma'am. I beg your pardon. I just wondered…" A flush crept into already ruddy cheeks.

"What is it?" Leah asked him, her voice softening. She stood. "Don't worry. Here, let me introduce my father, Jacob Sinclair. He's come to visit me." Jacob rose as well, and the two men nodded. It was an effort, but Jacob kept his mouth closed, allowing Leah to handle the ill-timed interruption. "Did you need me to pass a message along to Mrs. Hays?"

"No'm." He shifted the rake to his other hand, wiped his mouth, and offered a tentative smile. "It's— Well, when Mr. Beringer returns next, could you tell him I appreciate the advice he gave me last fall, on the Wild Gardening? The daffodils and winter iris are coming up mighty fine, just like he said. And I sowed them foxglove and primrose seeds, too, like he told me. Be pretty as God's own garden by next year. And you tell him Mr. O'Keefe said so."

Leah's managed to nod, her complexion waxen as she promised that yes, she would be sure to pass along Mr. O'Keefe's gratitude.

"Would've told him myself last week when he was here. But I was across the grounds there. He didn't hear when I hailed him, and it was snowing, so likely he didn't see me. We always enjoyed a good natter, Mr. Beringer and I. 'Tis sorry I am to have missed him."

Leah swayed on her feet. Jacob grabbed her arm. "Mr. Beringer was here—last week?" he asked, forcing his voice to casualness.

The gardener was looking perplexed. "Well, and why would you be questioning that? He was standing under that elm yonder, the one in front of Miss Sinclair's dormitory, like he was waiting for Miss Sinclair. Does that a lot, I learned last summer. Likes to listen to the leaves rustle, he told me."

He cleared his throat again, as though aware he'd been rambling. "I started across when he didn't hear me. He's a mighty fine man, Miss Sinclair, never treats me like I was a shantytown mick. We've had some fine discussions—Miss Sinclair?" He broke off, glancing from her to Jacob. "Is something amiss? Is she ill?"

"Aye, she's feeling a bit poorly." Carefully Jacob pressed her boneless form back down on the bench, keeping his hand on her arm while he searched O'Keefe's bewildered face. "The day you saw Mr. Beringer, that was last week, did you say?"

"Aye. Day of the snowstorm. I don't understand."

"Don't worry, Mr. O'Keefe. I, ah, I'll be sure Mr. Beringer gets your message, but right now I need to see to my daughter." Hoping the gardener would take the hint, Jacob turned his back and focused all his attention on Leah. He was afraid she might pass out at his feet. *Och*, he needed Fiona.

"Well, I'll be returning to my work then," Mr. O'Keefe mumbled above them, and Jacob hurriedly lifted a hand in acknowledgment. Then, "You'll tell me it's none o' my affair, but I'm thinking I need to say this."

"Mr. O'Keefe, my daughter's ill, you can plainly see that she—"

"No. It's all right, Papa." Her voice was unnervingly thin, but her fingers pressed against his arm with enough force to give Jacob pause. She lifted her head to face the gardener. "What is it you need to tell me?"

"I just thought— Begging your pardon, miss, but is Mr. Beringer himself ill?" He scuffled his feet, looking so anxious and miserable Jacob felt a pang of contrition. "What I mean to say is, I only saw him from a distance that day. But I mentioned it in passing to Nolly—he's the boy from the orphanage who helps me? Nolly saw Mr. Beringer as well, and told me…" He hesitated, his gaze darting between Jacob and Leah.

"Spit it out, then," Jacob ordered, his hold tightening when Leah swayed against him. "I need to take her inside."

O'Keefe flushed. "Aye. I can see that. And I wouldn't cause Miss Sinclair any trouble for the world. It's just that what Nolly told me, it might be a bit distressing. What I mean to say is, he wondered to me if Mr. Beringer was ill, seeing as how Mr. Beringer never even noticed Nolly, and the boy standing less than two yards away when he passed. It was snowing that hard, so I'm thinking when he told me he thought Mr. Beringer was…weeping, it was naught but melted snow. But seeing Miss Sinclair now…"

His lips clamped together when he caught Jacob's warning look. "I ask your pardon, miss. Sir," he said, and carefully replaced his cap. "I'll not bother you again."

"Mr. O'Keefe." Leah raised her arm, reaching her hand toward the man. Tears were streaming down her cheeks. "Thank you."

The gardener's stiffness vanished. He bowed with the grace of an earl, then plodded across to his wheelbarrow.

"Come along, lass." Jacob handed her his handkerchief as he helped her to her feet. "What you need right now is a good weep yourself. Afterward, we'll decide what to do."

"He was here," she choked, pressing the linen square over her mouth as the tears poured unabated. "C-Cade was here. Why…"

"Don't talk. Don't wonder, little wren. I'm thinking the Lord's sent along a message just now, and we both need to let the message sink into our hearts. Into our spirits."

Forty-Six

*A*nd I particularly wanted you to know," Fiona finished in an artificially bright tone. She had been looking forward to this visit to the Alcorn Home for the Blind, because of Winifred Dunwoody. To be sure, she had known Winifred's health was failing, but Fiona had only been gone for a week.

She dabbed the corners of her eyes with her hanky, relieved that Mrs. Dunwoody would not know that Fiona was shedding a sorrowful tear. "Jacob's sharing the good news with Leah now," she said. "Which is why I decided to pay you a visit and do the same."

"The staff assures me that you've never worn black bombazine, so it's about time you gave up your mental widow's weeds." The once imperious dowager lay beneath the covers of her narrow bed, her frame so wasted now the outline of her body scarcely raised a ripple. Her voice was thin as embroidery thread, but she was smiling, her spirit undaunted as ever. "Never did ask my advice, did you, no matter that I've been telling you all these years what you needed was a good man in your life, not orphans and indigents, nor a bunch of blind folk."

"Now you know you could never be one of a bunch," Fiona teased, earning a rattling chuckle.

For a time they sat in companionable silence, while Fiona felt a spasm of grief as well as gratitude for the opportunity she would have missed, had she gone with Jacob to visit Leah.

"Mrs. Dunwoody." She reached for the shriveled hand and folded her fingers around the elderly woman's. "You'd want to know that one of Jacob's sons-in-law is Benjamin Walker. Horace and Irene Walker's youngest boy?"

"Ah…" Her breath seemed to escape on a prolonged sigh. "How…

fitting. The eternal circle of life. Not always comfortable perhaps—but always reassuring on a divine scale. I'm glad for you, child. The Walkers as you yourself know were fine people. I lost track of the little boy after Irene died. Turned out all right, did he?"

"Yes. Quite all right, though he's the only one of the entire Walker family left. You'd be proud of him, Mrs. Dunwoody. I know I am. He's a credit to his parents." She hesitated, then finished firmly because the time, at last, was right. "I plan to tell him so, the next opportunity."

"You do that. And you'll be a credit to yours as well, if your Jacob Sinclair is even half the man you've made him out to be." The bony fingers gave Fiona's a feeble squeeze. "Lots better than that puffed-up peacock you married after the war. Your parents were never easy in their minds about him. Finally feel like you've paid your penance, don't you?"

Fiona started to offer a chastened reply, but Mrs. Dunwoody wasn't finished.

"Figured out life is worth a sight more than crying over past mistakes and putting yourself in bondage because you're afraid of making more. You be happy with this man, Fiona Carlton. Don't disappoint me—or your folks. I'll be joining them and my own dear Lucius soon enough, I expect. Good Lord willing, we can all celebrate together."

"Mrs. Dunwoody, I wish—"

"Now don't start making a fuss over me, child." She drew in another rasping breath. "I've been ready for a long time. Fact is, I'm impatient to get on with it. So I want no tears shed." Her head turned on the pillow, the white fluff of her hair framing the lined, sunken face. "Just remember, I'll be able to see. Been waiting a long time, for that."

"I'm going to miss you," Fiona whispered, "very much." All these years, and it took imminent death for her to realize that she cared more than she had wanted to. And that, for one person at least, the care had been mutual. "I wish I could do more for you."

"Balderdash. Take care of your man and his daughter. She's yours now too, isn't she? I can hear it in your voice when you speak of her."

"Like I'd given birth to her myself."

A contented murmur, almost without sound, floated past Mrs. Dunwoody's lips. "God's given you your second chance, Fiona Carlton," she said. "Grab it with both hands. And this time, keep your own eyes where they ought to be."

"Mrs. Carlton?" The evening nurse approached in a quiet rustle of skirts. "There's someone here for you, your maid."

"Oh?" Though her heart leapt, Fiona brushed her lips against Mrs. Dunwoody's papery cheek. "I will never forget you," she murmured low in her ear. "Go to sleep now."

" 'To sleep, perchance to dream,' " her raspy voice murmured back, the quote from *Hamlet* drifting wraithlike through the air. "And dreaming, to awaken and know that my sleep was naught but a dream…transporting me across the river Jordan…and I'll see. I'll see…"

Fiona carefully tucked the covers beneath Mrs. Dunwoody's chin. After a last sorrowful look, she hurried across the room after the nurse.

Maisie jumped up from a straight-backed chair when Fiona appeared. "Ma'am, Miz Carlton. You need to return home at once." She was breathing hard, her mobcap was askew, and beneath her shawl she still wore her soiled work apron.

"Lands, Maisie, what on earth—"

"I'm to tell you right up front not to alarm yourself. T'aint nothing bad wrong, or leastways not to his way of thinking. But to order me travel all the way 'cross town, like I was—"

"Maisie." The sharpness brought the housekeeper back under control more effectively than the quiet voice of reason. "Tell me, in one sentence, if you please."

Instead Maisie directed a fierce glare at the curious nurse, yanked the door open, and stalked outside, leaving Fiona with little recourse except to grab her own shawl and hat and follow the girl into the brisk March evening.

"This had better be urgent, to explain your behavior."

Plainly offended, Maisie hung her head. "Not anyone's business but yours," she muttered. "Mr. Sinclair's sent a message, telling me to fetch you since he knew you wouldn't be at home. The note— Well, Miss Sinclair's planning to take the first train out in the morning for Still-waters. And Mr. Sinclair's all in a flapdoodle."

"Leah's going to Stillwaters? In the morning?" Baffled, Fiona hurriedly donned hat and veil, then dragged the shawl about her shoulders. "Maisie, in the note did Jacob say…was Leah—upset?"

"Dunno. I done my duty by Mr. Sinclair. Came and fetched you at once. He's a nice enough gentleman, treats a body kindly. After I got off the streetcar, I ran."

Fiona tried to hide her mounting dread from Maisie as they hurried back down to the corner. Obviously Leah had taken the news poorly, so poorly she felt compelled to flee. *I should have gone with Jacob after all.* He would still have been drawn on a rack between daughter and affianced, but Fiona might have been able to moderate the tugs. Oh, she had been stupid. Stupid and self-centered.

From the moment she knelt at Jacob's feet, she had known Leah would be upset not so much by the prospect of her father marrying, but by the contrast of her own joyless future without Cade. Fiona might have been better able to soothe her more by her presence than her absence; at the very least she could have helped Jacob persuade Leah not to flee like a hysterical young girl.

"Maisie? You'd best commence packing my trunks. If Leah's running away to the mountains, Jacob and I will need to follow."

"Ma'am? Will you be wanting me to accompany you this time? Or will you just want Mr. Sinclair now?"

They reached the corner and stopped, both breathing hard; Fiona finally gathered her wits enough to focus all her attention on Maisie. "There will always be a place for you in our household," she said firmly, once she could speak. "In fact, I'm sure Effie Willowby would embrace you with open arms, as long as you confine yourself to cleaning and leave kitchen duties to her."

"You'll be living at Sinclair Run, then? I never lived nowhere but a city."

What a time for this conversation. Distractedly Fiona glanced down the street, but there was no streetcar in sight. Maisie would worry over the matter like a child with a loose tooth, so there was nothing to be gained by waiting for more auspicious circumstances. Fiona supposed she should be grateful that they were alone.

"Yes," she said. "We'll live at Sinclair Run. Please don't fret.

Remember last fall, all those weeks we were with the MacAllisters, at Tom's Brook? You felt welcomed there, didn't you? And Jacob will welcome you to Sinclair Run as well."

"Well." She tugged down the bib of her apron, then crossed her arms. "He was a gentleman right enough, last fall. Folks thereabouts don't seem to have their noses set quite as high as they do here in Richmond, that's for sure. Long as Miss Leah don't take a notion to move in with you, I reckon I may as well come along. You need looking after, whether you're hitched to a feller or not."

"I wonder how I managed to survive all those years before you arrived," Fiona retorted. "Never mind. Let's table the future for right now, my dear. Listen, I hear the streetcar. Now here's what I need for you to do."

By the time Fiona tracked Jacob down in his hotel, she was exhausted; uncertainty rendered her irritable as a wet cat. She was short with the desk clerk, took offense at the smirking bellboy who went to fetch Jacob, and by the time her fiancé met her in one of the public rooms off the main lobby, she was ready to yank out her hair. But all the ill humor vanished upon her first glimpse of Jacob's lined face and determinedly squared shoulders. She longed to take him in her arms and feel the reciprocal security of his. Mindful of prying eyes, she rushed instead into speech.

"I was visiting at the Alcorn Home for the Blind. Maisie came as soon as she received your note. When you weren't waiting at the house I decided to check here, before going to the school." She hadn't wanted a confrontation with Leah if Jacob was not present.

Using her body as a shield, she reached for his hands. They clung together for several moments.

"How I've needed you, lass. 'Tis a gift, seeing your beautiful face." His grip tightened when she shook her head and frowned. "Don't argue with a man who's spent the last few hours in the midst of a whirlwind. Never in all my born days have I seen my Leah so." He paused, searched her eyes for a second, then slipped his hand beneath her elbow and led her to a nearby chair. "Here now. You're frightened of something. Leah?

Ah. Yes, I see. I should have realized what you'd think, given the nature of my note. I wasn't thinking clearly." He shook his head. "Poor darling. You've been fretting about our own plans, haven't you?"

How he knew her. She had hidden the fear from Maisie; she had halfway concealed it from herself. Yet Jacob understood without a word being spoken. Moved to the point of tears, Fiona all but stammered a reply. "I wasn't sure what to think. I mean, I knew this would be difficult for Leah but I thought—that is, these past months she and I have come to regard each other with a great deal of affection. I should have come with you. I realize that now, Jacob. Obviously Leah's more upset than I anticipated, to be running off to—"

"Hush now, love. It isn't what you think. She's not distraught over our pending marriage. Actually, I…I haven't even told Leah about us."

"I beg your pardon?"

He flushed, eyes crinkling as a sheepish smile deepened the lines in his face. " 'Tis for sure I've created a tempest in a teacup. Forgive me? You see, I wanted to wait to share our news till after supper. First visit with her, like. She looked so forlorn. I persuaded her to come for a walk about the grounds."

"Jacob. I've already snapped at Maisie, and likely the desk clerk will dive under the counter to avoid me. Please just tell me what's happened to Leah, if it isn't our"—she stumbled over the word, still incredulous about the metamorphosis of her status—"our engagement."

Jacob ran a hand around the back of his neck, tugged the lock of hair falling over his forehead, then fiddled with the knot of his tie. "There wasna an opportunity," he finally admitted, the burr thick as thistles. "We were interrupted by the gardener. Fiona, it's not us she's running from. It's Cade she's running *to*. Listen to what I have to tell you, then we'll discuss what best to do."

Twenty minutes later they were still engaged in spirited debate.

"If we follow her to Stillwaters, she might interpret it as interference. She's twenty-six years old, lass. Besides which she's been mothering the entire family since she was four, and these past years she manages her students the same. She's not likely to welcome—"

"And supposing Cade's not there? Or suppose you and Leah are placing the wrong construction on his unannounced appearance? He made no attempt to see her last week, now did he? And no matter how much she's 'mothered' in the past, this is a time when she needs to *be* mothered."

"Didn't you hear what that boy said to the gardener? Cade was *weeping*. Man wouldn't have been there, clearly grieving, if all he wanted was to wipe the dust from off the soles of his feet. He still wants my daughter, Fiona. I feel it, here." He tapped his heart. "I also feel they need to sort it out on their own—"

"Then why the pother over her leaving first thing in the morning?"

"Because I thought she should wait a day or two, think about it. She's always thought things through. 'Tis not like her, to carry on like this, rush headlong when she doesn't know the outcome."

"All the more reason to accompany her," Fiona said, thoroughly exasperated. "We don't even know that Cade's at Stillwaters. Tell me again why Leah seems to think so, when I find it more plausible that he's either gone home to his own family or fled to some isolated spot in the woods even the sunlight can't find."

"I don't know where he is," Leah inserted quietly from behind them, causing Fiona and Jacob to slew around in astonishment. Leah tilted her head, an ironic expression flitting across her face. "But I do know he won't ever return to Miss Esther's School. Why should he? As far as Cade is concerned, he fought one of the most vital battles of his life there—and lost."

The enormous brown eyes, ravaged with the marks of tears and suffering, had aged over the past few weeks. Yet they seemed to Fiona to reflect now more than ever a tensile strength that imbued Leah's nondescript person with an aura of beauty. "I lost too. You helped me to face that, Mrs. Carlton. That's why I have to find Cade. I don't know why he never responded to my letter. But whatever happens when I find him will be determined by mutual understanding—not mutual *mis*understanding. If he has left me forever, then he will have to tell me so to my face."

"My dear," Fiona began, then stopped, glancing at Jacob. He stood there with his hands clasped behind his back and the air of a man about to bolt from the room. Fiona hesitated, equally stymied.

Leah stared from her to Jacob. Abruptly she wrapped her arms around her waist. "I interrupted. I beg your pardon. I should have realized. I'm afraid I rather made a spectacle of myself. I came here to apologize to Papa. I wasn't thinking. Of course he'd send for you."

She backed up a step, looking so uncertain that with an inarticulate protest Fiona hurried to her side, wrapped an arm about her shoulders and tugged her over to Jacob.

"You haven't interrupted anything. Come and sit down. We can talk together, the three of us." Over Leah's head she and Jacob exchanged a wordless communication. "There's a lot for us to talk about, starting with this," she finished. "Jacob?"

With a half-smile tilting his mouth, Jacob leaned to brush noses with his daughter. Then he sat back and stated simply, "Lass, Mrs. Carlton asked me to marry her. I said yes."

Nerves thrumming, Fiona waited for Leah's response, and wondered how she would survive if the girl dissolved into another round of the grief-stricken sobbing that had so discomposed Jacob.

"It's about time," was what Leah said instead. "We've all been waiting for the two of you to come to your senses." She cleared her throat, faint color seeping into the splotched and tear-stained cheeks. "I'm hoping I have done so as well. Perhaps you can tell me how you phrased the question so that my father accepted, Mrs. Carlton. With your permission, I might borrow the tactic as well as the phraseology and use it on Cade, when I find him."

Forty-Seven

*N*ine months had all but obliterated signs of both the accident and the campground, though remnants of wreckage were still scattered about the bottom of the ravine. For the most part the men Benjamin had hired to clean up the site had done a credible job. A pair of raccoons had staked out a den underneath what Cade thought was the remains of part of the coach's undercarriage; he supposed there was a macabre symbolism to be found there, but he was too exhausted to ponder it.

The unusual late winter snowstorm the previous week had vanished in the wake of a southerly wind bringing the promise of spring. Fresh green leaves budded on the hardwoods, and the damp earth exuded new life—feathery ferns, spindly grasses, delicate wildflowers. Cade stood at the base of the ravine, idly scratching his horse's forelock, feeling the warm snuffle of the mare's breath against the back of his head. He'd thought about hiking in on foot, but if the weather took a notion to revert to winter, he was definitely not up to the rigors of another late-season blizzard. It would be too tempting to just lie down and fall asleep, let snow and cold finish him off. No more pain, no more suffering, no more— His hands clenched into fists.

Where had *that* wicked temptation sprung from?

Father God, forgive me. Jesus, O Jesus, hear my cry.

The scents of spring mingled with those of leather and horse and his own sweat. He'd been traveling more than thirty hours without sleep. In the distance he heard the sound of rushing water. The creek would be high, of course, and numbingly cold from the snow. Not at all like last summer. *She'd knelt in the tall grass, then stretched out like a shy fawn and plunged her face in the water.*

Groaning aloud, Cade wrenched his thoughts back to the present. It was late afternoon; he needed to make camp. Nightfall was less than two hours away.

All right, then. Don't think. Just get the job done, one task at a time. He could be as morbid as he liked later.

By the time he'd started a fire, set up his bedroll, and rubbed down, tethered, and fed the mare, he was weaving on his feet. Strange, that. Used to be he could handle up to forty hours with little or no sleep, his only food whatever he gleaned from his surroundings. For an hour or more he sat cross-legged by the fire in a sort of stupor, staring at the flames and pondering how long it had been since he'd enjoyed a good night's rest, eaten a meal that hadn't tasted like chalk dust sticking in his throat.

How long since he'd enjoyed the confidence of a man at peace with himself and the Lord, with his purpose on this earth?

Jesus' agonized cry welled up within Cade until he almost shouted it aloud in the bruised purple dusk. *My God, my God, why hast thou forsaken me?* For months he'd struggled with this unfamiliar sensation of abandonment; even before Leah's rejection he had experienced flashes of life-sucking desolation.

If God was putting him to a Job-like test, Cade was failing it. Miserably.

And he didn't know why. Didn't know what had happened to a faith that once had been as much a part of who he was as the ripe-wheat color of his hair and his green eyes. As certain as the sun rising in the east.

Well, he no longer cared. He was giving up the battle, too dispirited to fight. For this night he'd ensured his survival, but it was still powerfully tempting to take the advice Job's wife laid on her husband: Curse God and die. Cade felt near enough to dead anyway, so he didn't see what difference it made whether he expired from cold or rolled over like a whipped hound and waited for life to finish kicking him to death. God was allowing it, so who was Cade Beringer to deny the Almighty?

He'd been a good boy, and he'd tried to be a good man, honoring his parents and the Lord all his life, except those few rebellious years after Patricia died. His faith had been as much a part of his life as breathing. He hadn't spouted verses to impress people, hadn't shared the love of Jesus to give offense or to create shame or fear. He wasn't a hypocrite.

"Not a hypocrite." Head tipped backward, Cade mumbled the words aloud as he searched the deep blue canopy of a heaven that right now struck him as cold and vast, as indifferent as the sea of human beings that had surrounded him for the past weeks.

He should be wrapping himself in the stillness, restoring his soul. Instead Cade felt as though he were locked inside an airless vault. Tonight, as every night over the past four months, the solitude oppressed instead of refreshed. Even returning to the wilderness he loved failed to provide surcease for the suffering.

Behind him the mare quietly crunched her handful of grain; a pair of whippoorwills called back and forth for a few moments, then gave up. In the background the whispering rush of water echoed an unceasing message: Give up, give up, give up.

Give up—what?

He'd expended himself until futility and failure—and Leah's unfaithfulness—extinguished whatever was left of his soul because, most devastating of all, he'd been forsaken even by the Lord. And it seemed he wasn't to know why. Leah would have laughed.

It was habit more than desire that propelled his arm inside the knapsack to pull out his tattered Bible. How many times over the years had he read by firelight, or occasionally a lantern, then drifted off to sleep in perfect peace and safety? *Why bother now?* the snide voice taunted from somewhere inside his head. *You've been snuffed like a candle from God's consciousness.* He was thirty-four years old, and for almost thirty of those years, he'd lived a life of trust and faith and obedience, and look where it had brought him. Idly Cade flipped through the fragile, crinkly pages, seeing the underscored verses, the notes he'd jotted. *Oh, here was a good one.* "If any man serve me, him will my Father honour."

"I feel mighty honored, Lord." In the spring-moist coolness of the evening the words spattered like buckshot.

At least Jesus grew up knowing from the earliest days of His earthly ministry that He was doomed to rejection, to a bloody and excruciating death. No disillusionments for the Lord, no sir. He already knew human beings were a treacherous, selfish lot. Too bad it had taken good ol' Cade the better part of his own thirty years to come around to that point of view. Stupid of him, thinking that he could change human nature if he was faithful in his service to the Lord.

Jaw clenched, Cade flipped through the pages, his thoughts simmering. There was the scene in Gethsemane, when the Lord asked His closest disciples to watch and pray with Him, and instead they'd fallen asleep. Typical. He wondered what Jesus must have been thinking, knowing what was coming, needing support, and finding it unavailable. Since Jesus was human as well as God's Son, likely He had been... afraid.

Cade slammed the Bible shut, jerking his fingers away as though the cracking leather cover had scorched his fingers. The thought was blasphemous. Jesus, afraid? No, this must be that taunting little voice again, sowing poisonous seeds. The Son of God was sinless, perfect in heart and mind, soul and body. *But Cade Beringer's a worthless wreck of a man, a failure on all counts.*

Heart banging up in his throat, sweat breaking out on his palms and the base of his spine, Cade tried to swallow the bile of the truth that had brought him to his knees: he himself was afraid.

Afraid of the uncertainty of life despite all the Bible promises. Afraid of the future because human greed and indifference obliterated charity and mercy, afraid of the slow but seemingly inevitable death of the wilderness.

He was—*oh, God!* Head bowed, he gave in and let the words sear their message into his being: For the first time in his life he was afraid of being alone. Of a lifetime of loneliness because he had lost everything. Even if he returned to Leah, she would never forgive him after all these months. She didn't love him enough, didn't care enough.

And he couldn't feel God, couldn't hear His voice.

He glared at the book still gripped in his sweat-slicked hands. Abruptly a volcanic rage spewed up, and he surged to his feet, lifted the

Bible to hurl it into the fire. All the promises had been lies. He'd been betrayed, played for a fool all these years. No wonder Leah hadn't come after him. Cade had deceived her as the Lord had deceived him, promising him hope and a future. Abiding love—*ha!* A throttled groan burst forth as he hefted the Bible over his head to hurl it into the flames and—

It stuck to his fingers. The need raged through him in a conflagration, bubbled like molten lava. He stood in front of the fire with every muscle taut, the Bible held high above his head because he wanted…he wanted, yet he simply could not complete the act. Something beyond the moment, beyond his emotions, beyond the fear and hurt and anger that mauled his heart, something deep inside his mind and spirit clamped his fingers around that Bible and hung on.

Like Jesus, hanging in agony on that cross.

Yielding Himself to the will of God so that a man like Cade Beringer could have the freedom to throw the Holy Bible into the fire, yet still be loved. Still be forgiven—if he chose to believe and acted on that faith in spite of how he felt. The way Shadrach, Meshach, and Abednego faced the blazing furnace. The way Job faced his wife and questioning friends.

Like a young woman terrified of the dark braved a sightless cave.

The rage vanished, drowned by the tears that were soaking Cade's beard-roughened face. As though in a dream, he laid the Bible on his bedroll, then began walking toward the creek.

The water ran high, rushing and surging with the power of spring's new life. Mesmerized, Cade stared into the restless flow, hearing as though the water were speaking to him. Jesus telling Peter not to be afraid, to step out of the boat and onto the water…the echoes of other verses urging terrified souls not to be afraid, only to believe. No matter how evil flourished on the earth, no matter how dissolute the human condition, the Lord still reigned supreme. All one had to do was— believe it. Trust God's love for His children, trust that neither tribulation nor distress nor persecutions, principalities, or powers could separate him from the love of God that was found in Jesus.

A single droplet of water splatted against Cade's cheek. It was cold, yet burned like a brand. Paradox, not contradiction. Like Jesus, sinless

Son of God who nevertheless understood every base human emotion because He'd been forsaken by His disciples, betrayed, surrounded by indifferent crowds and evil. And God had to turn away; for that single instant that spanned eternity, God abandoned His Son.

Slowly Cade's fingers rubbed his cheek where the droplet of water now blended with the tears. He would never know for sure if Jesus felt fear in the final hours of His earthly life, but he did know how Jesus responded to betrayal, abandonment, and indifference: "Not my will, but thine... Into thy hands I commend my spirit."

With a hoarse sound Cade dropped to his knees, then stretched out prone on the boggy creek bank and plunged his face and arms into the cold pure water. When he stood back up, streaming and breathless, he laughed aloud.

Forty-Eight

*D*uring off-season, the hotel and resort grounds reminded Jacob of the stories his grandmother used to tell him of enchanted castles in mist-shrouded Scottish glens. Full of secrets, deserted but dignified. Still slumbering beneath the shelter of a forest awakening with the new life of spring. On those few occasions when he'd visited Meredith and her family at Stillwaters during the winter and spring, Jacob liked to wander the grounds at dusk—the gloaming, his grandmother would have said. There was nothing like the smell of wet bark, the resinous tang of a pitch pine. On a day like today, when the softer air of spring caressed the afternoon like Fiona's misty eyes, a man could—

"Granda! I'm a bear! I'm gonna gobble you up!"

Dressed in a natty sailor suit, Sam charged through the trees with his hands spread like claws. Jacob had just enough time to brace himself when Sam, growling surprisingly bearlike growls, launched himself at Jacob's knees.

"No you're not," Jacob pronounced, holding the sturdy little body in the air while the giggling boy tried to wriggle away. "I'm going to skin you for a nice rug in front of your daddy's fireplace!"

They were rolling about the damp earth, gathering dirt and pine needles and dead leaves, when Leah and Fiona strolled up the path.

"I can't tell which of them is the boy and which the grown man," Leah commented.

"The one who will be groaning about his sore back and arthritic knees when he gets up will be the man," Fiona observed.

Like Leah, she was smiling, but Jacob had caught a glimpse of her face while he was tussling with his grandson. Gently but firmly he pinned the squirming lad, promised they would resume the battle after supper if he ate all his vegetables, then told him to go attack his father.

"And mind you stay on the path, my boy."

"I'm a bear. Bears don't stay on the path."

"Would a bear stay on the path if he was chasing a helpless lady?" Fiona asked, kneeling beside the truculent child. "And the lady was going to the kitchen to find out what smells like fresh-baked cookies?"

Sam darted a calculating look up at Jacob, then back at Fiona. He raised his arms and growled. "You have to run. I'm a *mean* bear."

"Oh, dear. I'd better hurry as fast as I can, hadn't I?" She gathered handfuls of her rose-colored wool gown in her hands and set off down the path with enough speed to satisfy an energetic little boy.

Jacob, however, captured Sam's flailing arm and held him in place. "Lad, you may chase Miss Fiona. But you may *not* trip her, or throw your arms around her legs, or cause her to fall."

"I'm a bear. I—"

"I suppose I could take you to your papa myself, and there'd be no cookies since you didn't want to listen."

Sam's lower lip protruded—*just as Meredith's used to,* Jacob thought, biting the inside of his cheek to keep from grinning—but after a second his wee grandson nodded. "Can I go now, Granda?" He chewed on his lower lip, then added, "I'll be a nice bear, for Miss F'ona."

"Give me your word, young man."

The childish blue eyes rounded, and he quit squirming. Even at his tender age, Samuel understood that if he made a promise, he must keep it. "Promise."

He went tearing down the path, and Jacob turned to his youngest daughter, who was staring after Fiona, a troubled frown between her eyes. "Aye, you saw it, too, didn't you? She used to look the same when she first came to Tom's Brook, whenever Daniel Jacob appeared. But she's better, after these past few days here, don't you think? Sam's taken to her the same way Daniel did. She's a lifetime of love stored up, needing to spill out."

Leah nodded slowly. "She's so…incredibly serene. I never realized how, even when life is so full of pain, a person can still survive, still find something to smile about. She's wonderful with children. But there's not a shy or a subtle bone in Sam, and I was worried about the scar."

Jacob finished brushing off dirt and leaves, then gave her a hard hug. "I know. I confess I worried a bit as well. And for what? Wee Sam shows her all his scars, then announces to Meredith that he wants a scar on his face just like Miss Fiona's."

Suddenly Leah turned to bury her face in Jacob's neck. Her arms clutched him with Sam-like vigor. "Everything's worked out for the two of you. Fiona's happy. She glows. And I want… I wish…"

She didn't finish, and after a moment Jacob rubbed between her shoulder blades. "I know, lass," he whispered gruffly. "I know. Be patient. Benjamin's sent out feelers over three states, remember, and Effie's promised to send a telegram straightaway if Cade shows up back home. But think on it." His voice gentled. "From everything you've told me, you need to understand that Cade thinks he's lost you. Finding him might be difficult, especially since you've refused to write his family and inquire of him."

"If he doesn't turn up here by the end of the week, I'll go to North Carolina."

She didn't elaborate, and Jacob was wise enough to press no further, content simply to hold her.

"I asked Fiona when the two of you planned to wed," Leah murmured eventually. "She said probably not until autumn." Abruptly her head popped up and a pair of quizzical brown eyes studied his face. "Then she blushed like a young girl."

Jacob struggled to retain a paternal mien. "Ah, yes. That's right. Autumn. Um…'Twill take time, arranging for the disposal of her town home and most of the contents. Then there's all her visiting. She feels she must make arrangements for other ladies to replace her, and that's sure to take time. Lots of preparation, don't you know."

"Are you sure you're not waiting because you don't know what's going to happen between Cade and me?"

Sighing, Jacob gave her chin a light pinch as they started walking back to the main hotel. "I won't deny we've talked about it. But that's not the reason for waiting. I love her, Leah, not more than I ever loved your mother, but as much, for different reasons. And because I do, I can give her the time she needs."

"Time doesn't always solve problems," Leah muttered. "Seems to me it often creates even larger ones."

"If Cade's hurt is so deep that he needs more time before he can forgive what for him was a mortal wound, what will your response be?"

Two spots of red grew in her cheeks, but her answer was unwavering. "I wouldn't be here now if I hadn't worked out the answer to that weeks ago. If we'd given each other a chance to explain last December, this wretched imbroglio never would have happened. I would have been better able to understand *his* needs—and he, mine. Hindsight is always a provoking teacher, Papa."

She drew in a deep breath. "I suppose now is as good a time as any to tell you. I gave Miss Esther my letter of resignation before I left. I won't be going back. Even though Cade never responded to the letter I sent him, I want him to see that I meant what I said. If he and I can never be reconciled"—her voice wavered for a moment—"I'll find another school. There's always a need for teachers. I'll try to bear life gracefully and not turn my back on living it. Now. Tell me again why you and Fiona are waiting until fall to marry."

"Because," Jacob answered with a slow smile, "there's a time and a season for everything under heaven. Mine and Fiona's, little wren, is autumn." He reached a hand up to tug a silky strand of hair. "Don't go to worrying again. You'll have a mother soon enough. And, God willing, a husband."

He felt a tremor seize her and slid her a sideways glance. Her gaze was fixed upon the distant figures of a regal woman and a small boy, holding hands as they disappeared into the grove of trees that sheltered the back door to the hotel's kitchen.

"Leah."

"Yes, Papa?"

"Don't fear, lass. In her heart, Fiona's been your mother for months now. You aren't going to lose her."

"That's what I thought about Cade."

"I know. Myself as well. 'Tis possible we both took him a bit too much for granted. Now we'll both have to wait and see the truth of it, hmm? It's all a matter of trust—and timing."

Groaning, Leah stopped dead in her tracks. "You can't resist your homilies, can you?" Stretching up, she planted an affectionate kiss on his cheek. "I'm going for a walk. It might be a long one, but I'll stay on the path. And I'll be back in time to help Han Su prepare our supper."

"Never thought I'd meet another soul with skill enough to rival Effie's cooking or yours. And turns out to be not only a man, but a Chinaman."

"He's teaching me how to cook traditional Chinese recipes, did you know? I hope to add them to my cookery curriculum." She paused, shrugged. "If I go back to teaching, that is."

Jacob gave her a final hug, then set her from him. "Go along with you, lass. Life is full of the unexpected. But no matter what happens, the Lord's going to shine His light far enough in front of your feet to keep you from tripping over them."

"I've already done the tripping," Leah said. "Now I'm learning how to keep going, once I manage to pick myself up."

Without looking back, she set off down the trail. Jacob watched until she was swallowed up by the trees before he returned to the main hotel. Leah and Cade must work out their own lives. As for Jacob, he had a bit of planning to do, and a lot of thinking about his idea for Fiona.

Forty-Nine

*S*he was tormenting herself, of course, but Leah refused to let the anguish deflect her from her course. Besides, it wasn't as if she planned to hike the entire distance to the site. Chin lifted, arms swinging, she trod along the hotel's main drive until she reached the faint trail that marked the remains of the old road. Within fifty feet it disappeared into the woods, then zigzagged down a slope until it reached a narrow valley.

Cade. Cade… With every step the past enfolded her, just as the forest did now. She could almost feel the strength of his arms, the swaying motion of their horse. Memories sprouted like the wildflowers coating the ground in confetti colors. Pausing, she knelt by a Spring Beauty peeking through some dead leaves, softly tracing the delicate pink-and-white-striped petals with fingers that trembled. She and Cade would have grown hoarse on this early April day, tossing botanical identifications back and forth in good-natured competition. And he wouldn't care a fig which of them won, because for Cade it wasn't really competition. It was companionship. And love.

Over the past weeks of relentless soul-searching she had come to realize many truths about hers and Cade's relationship, realizations that humbled and appalled her. She had never needed to soften her intellect with him, not even to stifle the thorny struggles over their differing views of God. Not once had Cade ever indicated that her brain intimidated him; he had even seemed to revel in the freedom to discuss anything and everything without restraint. *And I let it slip away.*

She hadn't meant to, but her father was right. She'd taken something rare for granted, something that she had experienced with no other person in her life.

Of course, Cade had seldom missed an opportunity to point out to her that while she might be an intellectual giant, she had never grown much beyond a seedling in spiritual matters.

Leah hated admitting he was right.

More than anything, however, she was ashamed of her intellectual arrogance. Smug in her self-righteousness, she had had to lose everything she cherished before she acknowledged the truth of the gentle accusation Fiona had leveled at her that day in her parlor.

She'd cared more about her needs than Cade's, because she had convinced herself that her service to God was more important than Cade's, her calling more noble. But selfishness, not service, had been her primary motivation. At the Esther Hays School for Young Ladies she enjoyed an exalted position, one she hadn't wanted to lose. She needed the respect of her peers and the adulation of the students, needed to feel confidence in her ability to control her environment.

She had been afraid she would be unable to live up to Cade's idealistic notions of a woman and a wife, so she twisted circumstances in order to place all responsibility on his shoulders.

Too bad her supposed "brilliant intellect" and "bedrock common sense"—Leah kicked a pebble, sending it flying—hadn't helped her reach these conclusions before she destroyed her hopes and Cade's. Right now, she'd trade her mind for poor old Deacon's, if that's what would convince Cade she had learned her lesson. All the way to the marrow of her bones, all the way to her soul.

"I was selfish and a coward," she whispered, then repeated it more loudly, driven by the inexplicable need to confess it here in the woods.

Back at the school, on her knees in her sitting room she had wept her repentance before the Lord. Now she repeated the confession to the absent man she loved. Because of Cade, patches of ancient poplars and massive chestnuts, stately pines and grizzled hemlocks would be spared the bite of a lumberjack's blade. *Lord? I'd appreciate the chance to tell him face to face how wrong I've been.*

She didn't hope, however, for the grief remained too potent. She knew God had forgiven her, but she also knew that she could not completely heal until Cade forgave her as well.

Remorse lodged like a spear in her heart, making it difficult to breathe. For a while she watched a red-cockaded woodpecker work his way up the trunk of a white pine. In the fragrant midmorning air she listened to sounds her ears would never catch in a city, from the woodpecker's rhythmic drilling to the surreptitious scrabble across a lichen-riddled rock a few yards away—a salamander which disappeared in the blink of an eye.

Of course, here in the wilderness there was no girlish laughter, no expectant faces on the cusp of life, no impressionable minds needing guidance and inspiration. Purpose. Discipline. No opportunities to tackle head-on the thorny mechanics of social interaction, no shelves of books through which one could explore faraway lands, exotic peoples.

A sob welled up, then lodged near her breastbone, too massive to be squeezed past her aching vocal cords. The world dissolved in a prism of running colors, but Leah blinked rapidly, sniffed back the emotion, and continued down the uneven trail.

Time passed. The sun rose above the upper canopy of trees, and spread a welcome warmth onto her head. She probably should have brought a parasol, but the contraption seemed nothing but an affectation, and besides, she didn't care a fig if freckles did pop out all over her nose. Garnet had learned to love hers; in fact, largely thanks to Sloan, her middle sister had grown into a beautiful, supremely contented married woman. Like Meredith.

Until she met Jacob, Fiona had been content with her widowed status. And Miss Esther had never remarried, choosing instead to devote her life to her school. Both of them had led fulfilling lives without the bonds of marriage. Until the past summer Leah had thought she was destined for such a path herself.

Perhaps God's ideal for His children *was* the union of male and female, to the benefit of both as well as a stable society. Yet one had only to look around to see that life could never be packaged up neatly and tied with a pretty bow.

There were seldom perfect, simple answers to much of anything.

God? I'm not asking why any longer. But—I need to know how. How to survive, if Cade would not forgive her. How to trust God's overall purpose for her life, when after giving everything up she remained empty-handed and hollow inside.

Somewhere ahead a sound rang out, that of a hoof striking a stone. A horse snorted, or perhaps it was a mule. Somebody else was out exploring the old road. Leah debated whether to slip off into the screen of the woods to avoid conversation or stand her ground. It was probably Hominy. He enjoyed fishing some of the streams during the off-season, when there was more leisure time for them all. Of course, he might also be conducting one of his random circuits of the hotel's boundaries, a weekly ritual ever since Benjamin and Cade discovered J. Preston Clarke's schemes of coercion and lies to illegally develop lands on the hotel's southern border.

Leah stopped dead, the breath ripping from her throat. What if the reason nobody had heard from Cade was because Preston had hired someone, like Lester Turpin and those other bounders, to track him down again? Even from prison it would be possible to orchestrate nefarious plans, and Cade after all had been instrumental in what Clarke would perceive as the ruination of his life. This time Preston wouldn't just use Cade to blackmail Benjamin—he would have Cade killed.

Even as she scolded herself for panicking, she lengthened her stride to almost a run, needing to reach Hominy, needing to hear from him that there were no reports of skullduggery whispering around the mountains.

She plunged around a weed-infested switchback and ducked beneath the dipping branches of a grove of hemlocks, through their needles glimpsing the horse's forelegs. Breathless, she emerged into a bar of sunlight, a dozen feet away from the horse and rider.

It was not Hominy.

All the blood rushed from her head in a roar, and the trees whirled around her; for a stunned moment Leah was terrified that she was about to drop nose-first to the ground.

Not an auspicious manner in which to greet the man you've been longing to find, the man you would follow to the ends of the earth. She tried to take a breath, but her lungs still weren't functioning, and bile swam sickly upward. *Oh, please, God,* she whispered silently. Pleading for strength. The words. The wisdom.

"I..." Nothing else came out. Since she was struggling to keep from making an utter fool of herself, it took awhile to realize that Cade hadn't said anything either.

In fact, she realized as her stupefied gaze wandered from the crown of his shaggy head to the white-knuckled fists bunched around the reins, Cade himself looked near to toppling from the saddle.

"I never expected to see you," he finally said. "Not here, not—like this."

There was a deeper tone in his voice, some indefinable quality of richness she didn't remember—or was she too desperately in love to retain an accurate memory of something she hadn't heard in over four months?

"I..." She blinked when the sour burning rose higher, almost gagging her. Lips pressed tightly together, she tried to count, tried to breathe as Cade had counseled her one long-ago night.

He dismounted but made no move to approach her. He stood holding the reins in his hand, green eyes narrowed against the bright sunlight. "Leah? I'll leave if you want me to. But you look..." He stared down at his boots for a moment, then lifted his head. "If I'd known you were visiting Meredith and Ben, I would have waited for another time," he finished.

He couldn't bear to be around her. The pain of it was too devastating. She couldn't examine it, couldn't think about it, so Leah bent the force of her will on remaining upright and finding words. In a war with words she'd always win, he'd told her once.

"Not here to see them," she got out, and pressed her fist against her middle in an attempt to calm her jerking heart. But Cade had started to frown, and if she'd had the strength Leah would have crawled away in defeat.

He wasn't leaving, but silence was proving to be even more effective to make his point: He so despised her he wanted to neither see nor talk to her.

Well, it didn't matter, because she was struggling not to despise herself. But since he was still here, Leah was going to have her say. God had provided this opportunity, and she might never have another. Cade was riding a horse. If he did run off, she'd never be able to catch him.

"Cade—"

"Leah—"

They spoke at the same time, then both stood like a pair of tree stumps waiting to rot until Cade stiffly inclined his head.

"Go ahead. You need to say something. I'll listen." He spoke with a grave formality so at odds with their once easy familiarity that anger twitched alive, loosening her tongue.

"I'm tracking you down." She squared her shoulders. "Not visiting. I came here to get information from Benjamin about how to find you. There's something I need to say to you, because you *didn't* listen to me, last December."

"I know. I should have—"

"I was wrong, and you were right."

"Never presumed that— *What? What* did you say?"

She twined her hands and took a step closer. "I need to apologize. To…ask you to forgive me."

"Ah." The remaining color leached from his face, leaving the bones in stark prominence, his eyes bleak. "Don't. You don't have to apologize. It's all right, Leah. I—don't worry. I'll be all right." The ghost of a smile was painful to see. "I've learned a new lesson or two about survival, here in the wilderness."

"No, wait. You need to—"

"If it helps, I understand better how hard it was for you to face the darkness when you thought you were all alone." He took a step toward her, then shook himself and instead laid a hand on the horse's neck. "I'll go now. I can see how difficult this is for you as well. Are you…Leah, I never intended to trap you. Make you feel you had to conform to some image of Christian womanhood. I only wanted— Never mind. It doesn't matter." He half turned.

"You said you'd listen. Don't you even think of climbing back on that horse, Cade Beringer." She took two more steps, until they were separated by only a couple of yards.

Words crowded her mind now, thick and fast, boiling up and spilling out. "I know what happened is my fault, not yours. I was selfish and scared. I know I hurt you. I'm not asking you to pretend nothing happened or forget how much I hurt you. When you never replied to my letter, I had to accept that—"

"What letter?" Cade asked hoarsely. "Leah, I never received so much as a sentence from you. That's when I knew it was over between us."

She faltered, her pulse roaring in her ears until she could hear nothing beyond a cotton-wool buzzing. "I wrote you. After the letter you sent me, telling me you'd stay in Richmond." She'd told him that she loved him. That she would follow wherever he needed to go, if he could forgive her. "I asked you to forgive me. You never replied." The buzzing intensified. Her feet—she couldn't feel them. But they must be functioning because now Cade seemed to be looming over her.

Numbly she lifted her gaze. "Cade, if you hate me, I don't know if I can bear it," she whispered. "I know, I do believe that God has forgiven me. But I had to find you, had to face you."

"I forgive you, Leah." His voice was gentle, but remote. "And I'm glad you haven't turned your back on God. That's something, anyway." He seemed to steel himself before adding even more softly, "I did try to turn my back on Him, because I thought He'd abandoned me. I was wrong too." His careful indifference was more wounding than a physical blow. "I couldn't feel His Presence in my life. Sound familiar? I think He wanted me to understand how difficult it was for you, to believe. To…trust."

"Yes. It is." She moistened her rubbery lips. "I'll probably always struggle. But it's worth it. Because I *have* felt God's Presence in my life a time or two over this past year, and I'll do whatever it takes for the chance to experience it again. You taught me how. You gave that to me, along with your love. It's not your fault I didn't know what to do with them both when they were right there in front of me."

"Leah, please don't do this." He lifted his hand, but dropped it again, tension screaming from every taut line of his body. "I don't—"

"I've resigned from Miss Esther's."

Slowly the reins Cade had gathered in his hand slipped back to the pommel. He visibly shuddered; Leah waited in an agony of suspense.

"Why?" he finally asked, the word hoarse.

"Why did you stand outside my rooms last week in the middle of a snowstorm?"

Color surged back up and burned across his cheekbones. "How did you know? Were you *watching*?" He bowed his head, pressing his knuckles against his forehead before he tossed her an accusing look. "So you saw the poor lovestruck suitor, and it made you feel guilty. Well, I've already told you I forgive you, though I have to admit after—"

"I didn't see you, Cade," she interrupted levelly, before he said something both of them would regret. "Nolly and Mr. O'Keefe did. He said to tell you the daffodils and winter iris are blooming nicely now, and he thanks you for your advice."

"Oh." The band of color deepened. "I'm…sorry. I shouldn't have jumped to conclusions like that."

"I would have reacted the same, if positions were reversed." Slowly she held out her hand and tried not to care that her fingers were shaking. "I did, you see, when you never responded to my letter—it never occurred to me that it might have been lost. So can we forgive each other? For everything?"

He was staring at her hand. Slowly, not looking away from it, he brushed the tips of his fingers against hers. The scalding sensation streaked up Leah's arm and punched a startled gasp free. Cade's head lifted. Even more slowly, staring straight into her eyes, he wrapped his fingers around hers until she was engulfed in the burning warmth of his hand.

"Before I let you go," he murmured, "I want to tell you one other thing. I will wonder until the day I die what I could have done differently. Because, Leah Sinclair, I will also love you until the day I die."

A heartbreaking smile curved his mouth when a single tear slipped from the corner of Leah's eye. "At least you haven't forgotten how to weep. No…it's all right. Truly. These past four months have taught me a lesson, one I pray I'll never forget. I don't think I'd survive a second time." His shoulders squared, and he paused before finishing quietly, "I've been afraid, you see. Afraid of failure, afraid of the unknown. Afraid of being…alone. But I've learned that no matter how alone I feel for the moment, or for months at a time, I know, now, that I will never truly be alone. Or lonely. Go back to your students with a peaceful heart, and don't worry about me."

"I can't go back, you noble-minded idiot. I quit, remember?" Leah sniffed, swiping at the tears now steadily dribbling down her face. "I don't understand how you can still love me, because I certainly don't like myself very much. And I"—the sob caught both of them by surprise, but even with a voice quavering out of control she managed to finish her own declaration—"I love you too. I never stopped, not even when I thought you'd ignored my letter, when I was so hurt I wanted to scream and throw things. Instead I wept until I made myself ill."

All of a sudden it was Cade's hands wiping away her tears with fingers as unsteady as her own. "You can tell me what you wrote one day." He cupped her face, his eyes so full of love Leah's tears fell even faster. "For now…" His head descended, and he brushed a tender kiss against her forehead, her damp cheeks, then the corners of her mouth. "I love you," he murmured between kisses. "God as my witness, I love you with all my heart, Leah. If you can bring yourself to forgive *me* for running away like a stiff-necked idiot, I promise"—as in a dream she watched moisture gathering in his vivid green eyes—"to try and listen instead of running in the future."

The future?

"Cade?" Too terrified to believe, hope exploding in her chest like a sunburst, Leah raised her shaking hands to his wrists. "Does that mean…do we still have a future? Together, I mean? With each other?"

"Only as long as we both shall live." Suddenly he wrapped her in a crushing embrace, lifting her completely off her feet and twirling her around. "I love you so much. Thank You, Lord. Thank You…" His voice broke, and he buried his face in the side of her neck.

Leah laid her ear on his chest and listened to the thudding of his heart. An indescribable peace filled her up, spilling into the April afternoon. She didn't know how long they remained thus, nor did she care. She was forgiven. She was loved. For this moment in time, faith ruled over science, love held sway over logic.

And Leah was content.

Four weeks later, Fiona watched while a beaming Jacob gave his youngest daughter into the keeping of Cade Beringer. White cloud tufts drifted across a pure blue sky. Stands of dogwood in full bloom mirrored the clouds, and the rich scents of pine and mountain laurel saturated the dewy air. Instead of organ music, songbirds warbled the processional. Though never losing her smile, Meredith openly wept; Garnet's face reflected a quiet joy. Her hand curled around Sloan's arm as she glanced across at Fiona, and they shared a look that brought a tear to Fiona's eye.

She was accepted here and, if she was reading Garnet's expression rightly, even loved, by all of Jacob's daughters. Of course it hadn't hurt that Fiona had been the one to convince Jacob that in the eyes of God and the law of the land, Leah would be as legally and morally joined to the man she loved here in a flower-strewn meadow as if they had married in the Sinclairs' home church.

"But her sisters were married there. We'll be married there, come October."

"If I asked to be married in Richmond, what would your response be?"

"That so long as you'll say 'I do,' I care not a whit about the where—" Scowling, Jacob conceded the battle. "Oh, aye, all right then. It's just, Leah's never cared for the outdoors overmuch. I don't want her giving in, because she's trying to atone for—"

"Jacob, Leah herself picked the location. She even, from what Meredith assures me is the case, insisted on camping out for her bridal trip. Cade had nothing to do with it. Don't worry over her anymore, my dear. She's going to be fine."

More than fine, Fiona thought now, watching Leah's face as she and Cade exchanged their vows in the very meadow where they had found each other again. Blessed. Blessed by God with love. With trust and renewed faith. A happy lump clogged her throat as she listened to them speak.

They were facing each other now, instead of the minister, and Cade took Leah's hand. "Here, surrounded by the wilderness I love, created by the God I love, I pledge anew my heart, my life, to the woman I love. And I vow before God to love her, to honor her, to protect and provide for her with His help, all the days of our lives." His voice deepened. "No matter where we are led, be it city or town or barren desert, I pledge to honor my love of God, by loving my wife above all else on this earth."

After he slid the ring onto her finger, Fiona watched Leah take a deep breath. For a shimmering moment she gazed at the simple gold ring, then lifted her face to Cade's. "I would like to promise to always be the kind of wife I want to be right now," she began, scarcely above a whisper. "I would like to have the kind of faith that moves mountains into the sea, and a heart that trusts without wanting to understand why. But I have learned that I will never be perfect on this earth. I've also learned that it doesn't matter. Because I have been given the gift of love, first by my family. Then by a very special man. So here and now, in the wilderness I have grown to love, created by a God I have learned to trust, I pledge my heart, and my life, to the man I love. And I vow, before God, to love and honor you, all the days of our lives."

When the minister pronounced Cade and Leah husband and wife, Fiona's hand reached for Jacob's. His fingers, strong but endearingly damp at the moment, tightened around hers. The sideways glance he flicked her way was warm with understanding. *Ah, Jacob, I do love you,* she told him silently, wondering how she would ever find the words or the courage to express it to him with the eloquence he deserved.

And it was there in a mountain meadow, with morning sunshine streaming through the trees, that the solution came to her. It would take time, but then she had the months between May and October. Not nearly enough, but it would have to do. She would be in Richmond for the most part. That would help, but secrecy would be an issue nonetheless. She would have to tell Maisie, of course, and the girls.

But what a wedding gift it would be for the man who had brought her back to life with his love and filled her with all the colors of the rainbow.

Fifty

Two hours later, Hominy knocked on the door of Fiona's suite.

"Miss Leah—I mean, Mrs. Beringer wants to see you before they leave." They grinned at each other. "Sounds strange, doesn't it?"

"It's going to sound equally strange to hear 'Mrs. Sinclair' this autumn and know I'm the one they're addressing."

"What it will sound, is mighty fine."

"Thank you, Hominy. You're a mighty fine fellow yourself. Why hasn't some discerning woman ever grabbed you up?"

A shadow crossed his face, and Fiona wanted to smack herself.

"Reckon the ones I'd have don't cotton to moving around. Mr. Ben and Miz Walker are my family, you see. And the women who'd have me—well, I've come to expect more than I should, for who I am."

"I understand." She turned aside to fetch a shawl, hesitated, then gave in to the urge. "Hominy, you and I, and perhaps Maisie, have had to learn that life is seldom fair, and that polite society—isn't. But I would like you to know that I would be honored if you would consider yourself friend to me, as you are to Benjamin and Meredith. Someday, I'm hoping you'll think of me as family as well." Holding her breath, she lifted her hand. "After Jacob and I are wed, I would be honored if you ever saw fit to pay us a visit at Sinclair Run. With or without the Walkers."

For a long moment the man who refused to call himself anything but a manservant stared down at that hand, before lifting his much larger one to engulf hers. "Thank you, Miz Carlton. I'll…do that, one day."

He left her at the door of the family suite, where Meredith and Garnet were readying Leah for her unusual wedding trip. Fiona watched until Hominy disappeared inside the elevator. Then she took a deep breath and knocked on the door.

"I was beginning to think we'd have to send out a search party." Meredith grabbed her arm, hauling her unceremoniously inside. "What took so long? Leah's been chafing, which means she must be nervous, because Leah never nags."

"Meredith, she's not our mother yet. Try to treat her with a little bit of respect," Garnet called from behind a Chinese silk screen. "No, wait a minute, Leah. She's here now. Finish dressing."

"Mercysake, don't be so prim." Meredith winked at Fiona. "In a way, she's already been my mother-in-law since I married, thanks to her connection with Benjamin's family." Playfully she swatted Fiona's arm. "I still wish you'd told Benjamin years ago when you first came to Still-waters, instead of waiting until last night."

Nobody was more surprised than Fiona when tears spilled from her eyes and a stifled sob broke free. Shirtwaist half-open, the long scarf flapping untied about her neck, Leah flew out from behind the screen and rushed across the room, followed closely by Garnet. Fiona wasn't sure who reached for whom, but the next instant she was surrounded by three weeping girls, everyone holding on to one another as though they would never let go. In between they gasped out half-finished sentences, muddled apologies, and a torrent of uncapped emotion.

"...and I wanted to tell you and Benjamin, but couldn't bear your pity..."

"...don't know how I'll bear it when you and Papa leave..."

"...been alone, so long...afraid to reach out...and now I have all of you..."

"...boys so excited about having a grandmother..."

"...and you were right about everything..."

"...more than anything, to be a mother."

Eventually it was Leah who brought everyone back under control with the watery reminder that this *was* her wedding day, and there would be plenty of opportunities to indulge in excess emotion in the future. In charge once more, she swiftly fastened buttons and wound the scarf around her neck, finishing it off in a tidy four-in-hand knot. "I'd also like to have a moment with—with our mother, alone."

"Whatever for?" Meredith demanded, but Garnet wrapped a gentle arm about her sister's waist and tugged her toward the door.

"Because she's a new bride, and this is her day," she said, smiling at Leah over her shoulder.

"Mercysake, don't tell me they're going to have *that* talk now? Leah's twenty-six. She already knows—"

The door shut firmly behind them, leaving a pool of silence as Fiona and Leah studied each other.

"What is it?" Fiona finally asked quietly. She tugged out her hand-kerchief and offered it to Leah, who rolled her watering eyes and accepted the linen square.

"I just wanted to thank you," she said. "I wouldn't be here, if it weren't for you."

"Oh, I think somehow things would have turned out just the same." Fiona's voice was tranquil. "But if we're expressing gratitude, I might say the same to you. You did save my life, after all."

"I refuse to become any more maudlin than we already have." She inhaled, then blew her breath out in an explosive sigh. "Never mind. I don't know how to say what I want to say without sounding maudlin. Until I met you, I never realized how much I missed, not having a mother. I... From the first time you sat in our parlor, and I saw how difficult it was for you, because of the scar, I've"—she cleared her throat, then shrugged her shoulders—"I've, ah...prayed. That somehow we could be more than mere friends."

"My dear, dear Leah." Spreading her arms, Fiona waited for Leah to step forward, then drew her close. "We are. We are. I'm hoping we can learn from each other how to better express our faith. You see, I pray too. More trustingly, perhaps, because ever since I met your father and you girls, I've come to understand something about myself."

"I know the feeling." After a hard hug, Leah stepped back.

Somehow, sharing didn't come with as much difficulty as Fiona had feared. "After my husband and son perished at sea, I would read the passage in Luke's gospel where the Lord calmed the waves."

Leah nodded.

"I've struggled with that scene ever since. And for the past twenty years or so," she said, "all I've seen are waves and wind—and a Savior asleep, when His disciples were afraid of drowning."

Discomfort was threatening to drown her now, for all she needed to share the truth that had gently dawned in her heart over the past months. "You should go," she muttered, her manner turning brisk. "This can wait for another day."

"No. It can't," Leah said, quietly stepping between Fiona and the door. "You weren't afraid to tell me how wrongheaded I was. Please don't run away now. I think I need to hear what you have to say, as much as you need to share it."

"It's nice," Fiona murmured with a wry smile, "that at least one of Jacob's daughters has a temperament like my own. Very well, my dear. I will try. I will be brief. And you will go to your husband."

"Agreed. If it helps, the more you talk about your faith, I've discovered, the easier it comes. Sort of like teaching."

Or playing the piano... She had her hand halfway to the scar before she caught herself and let her arm drop to her side. "For twenty years I focused on the wind and waves that I thought had destroyed my life. While I never lost my faith in God, I'm afraid I...allowed it to gather dust, I suppose. Then I met your father. You. Your whole family. I do wish I had had the courage before last night to share with Benjamin what his parents meant to me. But you see, until now I was still struggling against the past. Thanks to Irene and Horace Walker, I was able to pursue my dream. But that dream turned into a nightmare that almost destroyed me. And I didn't want to tarnish Benjamin's memories."

Benjamin had told her she'd been foolish. Then he'd hugged her hard enough to crack her ribs. "I wasted so many years," she whispered now, half to herself.

She wandered to the corner of the room where Meredith's gramophone resided in splendor on the polished cherry cabinet Jacob had built. When she recovered control, she turned around, grateful for Leah's perceptiveness. "It was this morning," she managed haltingly, "in your meadow, when that passage in Luke came to me again. The Lord asked His disciples where their faith was. It wasn't supposed to be in their boat, or their swimming ability. And they weren't supposed to focus on the wind and the waves. Neither am I. That's what came to me, Leah."

Like sharing, touch was becoming as vital to Fiona as breathing. She reached out, and when Leah immediately clasped her hand, the cords strangling her ribcage fell away.

"We both misplaced out faith, I daresay," Leah said. "Believe it or not, so did Cade. I think what that makes us, is human."

"Indeed. I'm wondering if it's misplaced faith, more than lack of faith, that gives rise to the isolation and fear. The guilt and self-hatred."

"Careful." Leah laughed a little. "We're starting to sound like my husband and your fiancé. Before you know it, we'll be wanting to lead a prayer meeting."

"Heaven forbid." Oh, the glorious lightness of being part of this family, of being a—Fiona allowed the truth to finish itself in her heart—of being a child of God. "I just hope in the future I'll do a better job of keeping my faith on the One who controls the wind and waves, where it belongs. And that's all the talk I'm capable of for now, my dear."

They exchanged self-conscious hugs, then backed away, smiling at each other.

"Since we are being hopelessly sentimental, are you sure you won't mind, if I—if all of us—call you 'Mother'?" Leah asked. "I mean, it wouldn't feel right calling you 'Mama,' even though I barely remember her."

"Mary Sinclair will always be your mama. I'm content with what I can have, being 'Mother.' And as your mother, I'm going to tell you right now it's time for you to go with your husband, who is no doubt ready to fetch you himself."

"I love you—Mother."

"And I, you." Yes, it was amazing, how easy it had become to say the words aloud.

A knock sounded on the door. "Miz Beringer?" Hominy's voice called. "You still in there? Time to be heading out, ma'am."

"Cade's definitely impatient," Fiona said as she went to open the door. "Tell Mr. Beringer that his mother-in-law is the cause for the delay, but his bride is on her way down."

Grinning, Hominy nodded and left.

Fiona and Leah exchanged a final hug, then Leah fetched her wedding present from Cade, a large tan bag made of heavy duck fabric, filled with camping gear.

"Your new husband selected a very, ah, *unusual* wedding gift," Fiona observed.

"Yes. But for me, it's absolutely perfect."

"Speaking of wedding gifts," Fiona continued before she could change her mind—or another interruption diverted her, "there is one other matter I'd like to discuss on the way downstairs. I'll be sharing this one with your sisters, while you and Cade are on your wedding trip. It's a surprise for your father. My wedding present to him, as it were."

Leah clasped her camper's bag in one hand and thrust her other arm through Fiona's. Heads almost touching, they strolled arm in arm down the corridor.

Fifty-One

*J*acob and Fiona's wedding day dawned a mist-shrouded gray. Thick fog swallowed the mountains, muted the scarlet and gold leaves, and muffled the sound of the Whalens' cows, bawling in the field over the hill.

Jacob stood on the porch, elbows propped on the railing. He scowled at the cloud that had seen fit to settle its damp, lolling carcass over his valley, though nothing could truly dampen his spirits. *Today, Lord. Today You will bless this union, and after all these years there will be a wife at Sinclair Run once more.* Nerves fluttered inside his chest, settled as his gaze dropped to the large cardboard box at his feet. He had only been able to finish the gift for his bride the week before, when the part he had specially ordered back in March finally arrived. Oh, the effort it had taken to reach this day, to have within his grasp both the woman and what he prayed was a tangible manifestation of his love for her.

"What are you doing out here this early? Trying to catch a chill the very morning of your wedding?" Effie unceremoniously picked up the box and marched back across the porch. "Come inside. Sloan and Mr. Walker's man will be here in an hour, and you not even shaved and dressed."

"Call him Hominy. Outside of Fiona, he's the closest remaining tie to family left for Benjamin."

"Hmph. Hominy, then. But he's still Mr. Walker's manservant."

"You won't be so high and mighty, woman, when I bring home my wife."

Effie's snort could have stampeded the Whalens' cows. "Miss Fiona and I reached an understanding months ago," she retorted, giving Jacob one of the looks that always annoyed him. "She and I will manage just fine. We'll manage you just fine as well."

The back of his neck began to burn. "Effie, why are you badgering me about every little thing, and on my wedding day?"

Her face softened all at once. Carefully she laid the box on the hall tree seat. "Because I'm afraid you'll swoon at my feet, for lack of breathing. Don't take on so, Mr. Sinclair. She's right for you, as you're right for her. It's a good match. Seems to me I've even heard a remark or two from you about the Lord bringing it all about?"

"Aye." He gave her a sheepish smile. "Bless you, Effie."

"You're rattled, right enough." Effie's hands went to her hips, not a good sign. "Sakes alive, you're acting like a stripling boy instead of a grown man who's seen three daughters happily wedded. Go along with you now. If you can be back downstairs in half an hour, I'll let you sneak a bite of the snow-cake I've made for the wedding breakfast. Elmira Whitaker will be stopping by in a bit to take it to the MacAllisters' for me, so if you want a piece, you best be about your business."

"You made snow-cake? Using my mother's recipe?"

"I've not known you and your family for a quarter-century for naught. Go on, get yourself prettied up." Her lips twitched in what might have been a smile. "As for the weather, I doubt the Almighty would offend one of His most faithful servants on his wedding day. There'll be sunshine before noon, you mark my words."

The sawdust feeling inside his mouth had abated, and he was aware of the tension sloughing off his shoulders. With a lighter step Jacob picked up the box and started up the stairs. *Aye, Lord. You always know how to keep me where I need to be, and how to get me there.* Halfway to the landing he paused. "Effie!"

She poked her head back through the kitchen door.

"After today, I'd like it very much if you called me 'Jacob.' Folks won't be after talking about us anymore, now will they?"

He left her sputtering and muttering. As Jacob went to prepare himself for the coming nuptials, there was a grin on his face as wide as the sky.

By a little past ten, the grin had vanished, along with any vestige of jocularity. Stiff and silent, Jacob waited in the carriage with Sloan and Benjamin while Hominy pulled the horses to a smooth halt at the church's back door. Above them dawn's gray sky was giving way to mist-washed blue. The fog had lifted from the valley, and sunshine fired the trees surrounding the whitewashed clapboard church with glorious color.

"Need me to carry that in for you?" Sloan asked, gesturing to the box Jacob held on his lap. He'd wrapped it himself, and for the half-hour journey to the church had been blistering himself for not allowing Effie to do the job.

"Nay. I'll keep hold of it."

"You still want to present it to her right after Pastor Keller pronounces you husband and wife?" Benjamin asked, a shade too casually.

"Son, you've asked me that half a dozen times over the past week." Jacob stared down at the pearl gray gloves he was wearing, which matched the tie presently choking him because he'd knotted it too tight. Too bad he hadn't tied the satin ribbon on Fiona's wedding gift the same. "I'm no' in a frame of mind that can lay aside the possibility you're trying to tell me something."

A look of masculine sympathy softened the awareness brimming in Ben's eyes. "Only trying to help a nervous man, Jacob."

He glanced at Sloan, who added, "Wouldn't want you to drop it, break something. Still don't want to tell us what's inside?"

" 'Tis for my wife." Whatever else he might have added was lost when Cade opened the church's back door and waved. All three of Jacob's daughters spilled past him in a swirl of color as bright as the trees. For the next several moments he suffered through a surfeit of mothering, knowing they needed this final moment before they yielded all care of him to another woman. After they shepherded him inside the church to the room where he and his sons-in-law would wait, he set the gift down and held out his arms.

"My lasses." Jacob held each precious face, love overflowing until he thought he'd drown in the flood. "I am so blessed."

One by one they came to him, Meredith first in a pattern as old as her first toddling steps. Her fragrance was rich, filling his nostrils like the ready tears that filled her eyes. She hugged him fiercely. "You will always be our papa," she told him. "But you can let us go now. Mama, too. I bet she's up in heaven, smiling at us all, probably in relief. And it will be wonderful having a mother on earth as well as a father."

Garnet's scent was lighter, like the flowers she loved to draw. Her smile was gentle. "Don't be frightened," she told him. "You've taught us all so much, Papa, about what it means to love, to be loved. God's just returning the favor and answering a lot of prayers."

Leah waited until last and held him a little longer. Her eyes, Jacob realized with a gratitude that left him weak-kneed, were full of a peace he'd almost given up hoping to see. "Believe in the miracle," she whispered, and stole his flagging composure.

⤜✦⤛

It was eleven o'clock. Pastor Keller shook Jacob's hand, told him it was time, and opened the door. Jacob noticed little of the crowd of friends and neighbors filling the pews, heard little of the organ music as he and two of his sons-in-law followed Pastor Keller's portly form into the sanctuary. Dry mouthed, he brushed by a potted palm whose fronds scraped his face, only then realizing that the church was full of greenery. There were splashes of red and gold and orange as well; all the colors of autumn, he realized, a smile finally lighting his face.

"I know it's not traditional, and some of the guests might murmur," Fiona had explained a week earlier, blushing like a girl. "But every time I see the trees blazing away, I remember what you told me."

The autumn of their lives. Might no longer be the spring, he'd said. But neither was it the winter, and the fiery colors of autumn had always been his favorites.

The smile remained intact as one by one his daughters floated down the aisle, radiant in their happiness, carrying sprays of autumn-colored flowers. Jacob's smile deepened.

Then every thought flew from his mind, for his bride had appeared on Benjamin's arm, at the end of the church's center aisle. Her wedding gown was a soft shade of gray. Delicate Irish lace draped her neck and sleeves. Pinned at her throat was her mother's cameo. Bursting with pride and love, Jacob fastened his gaze on her face—her unveiled face.

Above the organ music a low murmur swept the church as she and Benjamin proceeded down the aisle, but Fiona's regal stride never faltered, and the serenely smiling face promised Jacob without a word that she was unashamed and unafraid.

When they stood side by side and repeated their vows, Jacob knew his joy was almost complete. *Almost time,* he thought in a haze of happiness. *Almost time, my dear one.* He couldn't wait for her reaction, when he presented her with his gift. He prayed that she would understand its significance, and—

"At this time of joyful celebration, here in the Lord's house the bride wishes to share something very special with the groom." The pastor nodded to Fiona, then gave Jacob a reassuring smile.

Bewildered, he started in surprise when Fiona clasped both of his hands. "I have pledged my life and my heart to you," she said, the light voice somehow ringing throughout the hushed congregation. "I offer now as well the gift God gave me. In pain and guilt I thought I must renounce it. But your love restored the music to my heart. Now I wish to give some of that back to you."

She lifted his left hand and kissed the ring she had slid into place a moment earlier. Then she released him, turned, and walked to the side of the church, over to a monstrous grand piano. *What is such an instrument doing here in this country church?* It reminded Jacob of the one in the Stillwaters conservatory, and the conclusion slid right past his benumbed mind until in a graceful motion Fiona seated herself on the bench. Her hands rose.

For a blinding instant she gazed across the space straight into Jacob's eyes, then her hands descended to the keys. Sounds filled the room, rippling and flowing and dancing. Heavenly music would sound thus, was his fragment of a thought as, stunned, he took a half-step toward the woman who had vowed never to play the piano again.

"Easy, Jacob." Cade's hand was on his arm, warm and strong. "You wouldn't want to pass out now, would you?"

"Cade…" His throat locked up. "She's— She's playing…she's playing…"

Everyone was looking from him to Fiona, then back, as if nobody could decide which was more fascinating. Jacob steadied his wobbling knees, then laid a hand over Cade's. Neither of them commented on its trembling. "I'm fine, lad. Don't make a fuss. This moment belongs to my wife."

For a second he allowed his gaze to touch on each of his daughters and their husbands. They had known; he could see it plain enough.

But there was something they didn't know. A lump expanded inside his chest, born of pride and humility, awe and amusement. Leah had warned him to expect a miracle. *She hasn't learned about the nature of Your miracles yet, Lord.*

Sometimes, they were delivered with a sense of humor.

The music poured over him, through him, filling his ears with the most joyful noise this side of a choir of angels singing. When the last chord faded into the silence, nobody moved. After a suspended moment, Fiona rose and, with an expression almost of rapture, walked back over to Jacob.

"I love you, Jacob Sinclair," she said, and her voice trembled. "I would like to share my love of music with you. Will you let me?"

The lump inside him burst, spilling forth in a deep booming laugh. Holding her gaze, he lifted her left hand and dropped a kiss on the gold band. "The kiss will have to wait for a few more moments," he murmured for her ears only, which earned him a puzzled frown. Still chuckling, Jacob turned to Pastor Keller.

"I've something for my bride as well," he said. "I'll be back in a moment."

He ignored Meredith's urgent calling of his name, nodded reassurance to Sloan, Benjamin, and Cade, and strode through the side door into the vestry. When he returned seconds later, he was carrying his gift for his bride. The pastor smiled in relief.

Jacob held the box out to Fiona, who looked no doubt every bit as bewildered as Jacob when she had offered her gift to him. "Open it," he said, gently. "Open it up, my loving wife, and see what a wondrous thing the Lord has done to bless this day, and us."

The guests were stirring, aroused beyond politeness by the extraordinary goings on. Leaving their places, Meredith, Garnet, and Leah crowded around, their gazes darting between their father and their new mother. Jacob bit the inside of his cheek to keep from shouting with laughter again.

The ribbon and wrapping paper fell unnoticed to the ground. A pair of hands supported the bottom of the box as Fiona reached inside. She gasped.

"Jacob, it's the most beautiful thing I've ever seen." She searched his face, her eyes brimming. "You made me a heartwood chest."

"Not exactly, my love." He guided her fingers to the turning mechanism. "I thought you needed something a wee bit different. This is a music box. I wanted to give you something that would help you see that there could still be music in your life, even if you never touched a piano."

"Oh." Color pinked her cheeks, and at last the faint uncertainty gave way to a laughter that matched his own. "It will be nice to enjoy them both, won't it?"

"You've no idea of the half of it." Placing his hands on her shoulders, he turned her to face the riveted guests. "Wind it up," he murmured in her ear and squeezed the delicate shoulders once.

Seconds later a tinkling melody tripped lightly throughout the room—the same melody Fiona had just finished playing on the piano. A collective gasp rose. Fiona swiveled free of his hold, turning back around with the music box clutched to her chest. "Jacob. Oh, Jacob...I don't believe this! It's playing the Weber, my favorite piece in all the world. Nobody knew what I've been practicing all these months. I wanted to surprise you, the girls promised not to—how could you know? How—?"

"I'll tell you, one day. For now, let's call it a miracle of God's timing. Not to mention His fine sense of humor." Calmly he relieved her of the music box and handed it to the grinning Benjamin, who in turn offered it to Pastor Keller.

"I think placing it on the altar table would be a fitting conclusion, don't you think, Pastor?"

And so, accompanied by the airy strains of a music box, Jacob Sinclair and Fiona Carlton were pronounced husband and wife. When they recessed down the aisle after their children, there wasn't a dry eye to be found in the sanctuary.

Outside, the noonday sun burned bright in the heavens, setting the Shenandoah Valley ablaze with color. With life. Hand in hand, Jacob and Fiona went forth in love, to embrace them both.

Sara Mitchell

Years ago, a self-confident, intelligent young man invited a shy young woman to go to a football game at the university they attended. After the game, he guided her across the crowded street by gently placing his hand on her back… and the young woman was never the same. Nor was the man.

They spent their honeymoon in the Blue Ridge Mountains and Shenandoah Valley of Virginia, vowing to return one day, to stay for the rest of their lives. Thirty-two years, two daughters, and a baker's dozen novels later, Sara Mitchell still tingles at the touch of that man's hand—and they still plan to move to the Valley.

Thanks to her husband's former career as an air force officer, Mitchell has had an opportunity to live in and visit many diverse locations over the years, from Georgia to Colorado to Great Britain. Those experiences, coupled with her background in history and English, instill an authenticity into the settings of all her books, whether contemporary or historical.

Shenandoah Home and its sequel, *Virginia Autumn,* reflect this life-long love for a place, for the late Victorian era, for storytelling—and for her husband of thirty-two years. "Every book I write includes a love story between a man and a woman, and between God and His fallible children. But while every story is a labor of love, an expression of my faith," Mitchell confesses, "the two Sinclair Legacy books are probably closest to my heart."

At least for now…

At present Mitchell lives in a Virginia suburb of Washington, D.C., where her now civilian husband works as a defense analyst. Mitchell loves to hear from readers, and she can be reached by writing to:

Sara Mitchell
c/o WaterBrook Press
2375 Telstar Drive, Suite 160
Colorado Springs, CO 8092